ADRIFT IN NEW YORK

THE WORLD BEFORE HIM

POPULAR AMERICAN FICTION

⊚⊚

ADRIFT IN NEW YORK

and

THE WORLD BEFORE HIM

Horatio Alger, Jr.

———————

EDITED BY WILLIAM COYLE
Wittenberg University

THE ODYSSEY PRESS · INC · NEW YORK

INTRODUCTION

Estimates of the sales of Horatio Alger's novels range fantastically from 17,000,000 to 300,000,000 copies. The lower figure undoubtedly is nearer the truth, but if it were possible to estimate multiple readers of the same book and readers of his serials in periodicals like *New York Weekly* and *The Golden Argosy*, 300,000,000 readers might not be an exaggeration. Though not the most prolific of American writers, he was unquestionably the most popular. Now, of course, his novels are seldom read except as curiosities. Because they were cheaply manufactured and were often read to pieces, Alger novels are comparatively scarce today. This scarcity and interest in nineteenth-century Americana have created a mild Alger boom, and it seems likely that there are now as many Alger-collectors as Alger-readers.

Though pitifully vulnerable if judged as literature, the Alger novels are significant as expressions of popular culture. He expressed the prevailing ethos of the years between 1870 and 1900 so accurately that his name has passed into the language. When one's eye is alert for it, Alger's name seems to pop up constantly in newspapers and magazines. If a journalist calls a man an Alger hero, describes his career as an Alger success story, or refers to the Alger legend, readers instantly comprehend his meaning. Journalistic references often convey a degree of scorn, but there is nothing scornful about the Horatio Alger Awards, bestowed annually by the American Schools and Colleges Association to honor successful men who have risen from humble circumstances. Recipients of bronze plaques inscribed *Diligence Industry Perseverance* include Bernard Baruch, Harold Stassen, William Zeckendorf, Herbert Hoover, Eddie Rickenbacker, and Dwight D. Eisenhower. The annual ceremony held at the Waldorf Astoria invokes the pieties of an earlier age. According to Norman Vincent Peale, winner of an award in 1952 and later national chairman of the awards committee, "This country needs a new birth of the philosophy and spirit of Horatio Alger, whose books showed that a boy could rise from humble beginnings to outstanding achievement and service."

Alger's name has outlived his books because it has come to represent a national mythology. Even today, when few read his books, millions of Americans pay lip service to his simplistic formulas. To describe Alger's message as the "American Dream" or "Spirit of America" exalts it more than it deserves. It was essentially a primer version of the Protestant Ethic: a young man of good character who works hard and saves his money can—indeed, *will*—achieve power and affluence. This optimistic view of society was most meaningful to the generation that came of age after the Civil War, when an expanding society and a laissez-faire economy made possible the rapid acquisition of wealth. Every town had at least one Alger hero, a poor boy who had risen to control the local bank or factory. Success was a magic word. Revisions of the McGuffey *Eclectic Readers* added selections extolling persistence, punctuality, and similar virtues. The status of Benjamin Franklin as a folk hero was greatly enhanced. Inspirational books exhorting young men to strive for success sold widely. The titles of two of them suggest their content:

> Orison Swett Marden, *Pushing to the Front; or, Success under Difficulties. A Book of Inspiration and Encouragement to All Who Are Struggling for Self-Elevation along the Paths of Knowledge and of Duty.*
>
> A. Craig, comp., *Room at the Top: or, How to Reach Success, Happiness, Fame and Fortune, with Biographical Notices of Successful, Self-Made Men, Who Have Risen from Obscurity to Fame.*

The second was especially practical, since an appendix laid down categorical rules of etiquette, advising a young man how he should conduct himself after reaching the top. The success-mystique reached the public in a variety of forms, but no one expressed it as persuasively and entertainingly as Horatio Alger.

Young readers devoured Alger books for a variety of reasons. He gave them exciting plots filled with last-minute rescues, unmasking of villains, and rewards for heroes. Although his occasional strictures against billiards, tobacco, and liquor seem moralistic today, his novels were much less didactic than most juvenile books of the day. The Alger hero's tongue-tied and clumsy embarrassment in his infrequent encounters with young ladies may have gratified male readers of a certain age. Finally, Alger presented an attractive vision of the passage from adolescence to maturity; after a period of probationary poverty, an Alger hero is accepted as an adult and carries out such missions as investigating a mining operation, locating a missing bookkeeper, or negotiating to buy or sell large stocks of merchandise. However, the essential appeals that made Alger's name a metaphor for a system of values appear to reside in four of his favorite topics: success, individualism, an open class-structure, and the big city.

Success in an Alger novel is always measured in material terms. He was delightfully specific when discussing money, and thousands of boys like Eugene Gant in *Look Homeward, Angel* must have "gloated over the fat money-getting of the Alger books." After the hero of *Bob Burton* has transported a boatload of wheat to St. Louis and rescued a kidnapped child en route, Alger gives us Bob's triumphant bookkeeping:

1400 bushels wheat, at $2.25	$3,150.
Reward	$1,000.
	$4,150.

He was equally precise regarding the budget of a clerk who saved 50¢ a week from his $5.00 salary. Although success in the Alger world is always monetary, he was unintentionally ambivalent concerning its ultimate significance. The image of a Gould, a Harriman, or an Armour might glimmer in the imaginations of his readers, but theirs was not the kind of success Alger portrayed. He ignored the flamboyant millionaires like Jim Fisk and the miserly ones like Hetty Green or Russell Sage; when he needed an example of a successful man, his favorite allusion was the merchant Alexander T. Stewart. As though sensing certain perils in extreme opulence, he usually rewarded a hero rather modestly; a secure position, often in his father-in-law's business, with an income of $10,000 or less a year is typical. An irony of which he must have been unaware is the real nature of the new life achieved by his heroes. Wealthy characters in the novels are either avaricious and inhumane or vapidly sentimental. Throughout a novel, Alger portrayed the world of wealth and fashion as pretentious and cruel or as intolerably dull; then in the last chapter he admitted his hero to this sterile world as though he were opening the gates of paradise.

Regarding the means of attaining success, Alger was also self-contradictory. Superficially, it appears that success is gained by adhering to Franklin's classic triad in *The Way to Wealth*: industry, frugality, and prudence. The gospel of work and thrift, the conviction that idleness and waste are sinful, had deep roots, especially in New England. Alger's heroes express the classic formulas for becoming successful. When Carl Crawford is asked, "You are not rich, I take it?" he confidently replies, "Not yet" (*The Odds Against Him*). Another character announces, "Plenty of poor boys have risen, and why not I" (*Mark Mason's Victory*); another, "I should like to be rich for my mother's sake" (*Herbert Carter's Legacy*); and another, "If hard work will win success, I mean to succeed" (*The Young Adventurer*). Yet a will to win is not the full answer; success comes to the thrifty, industrious Alger hero, but not as a result of his thrift and industry. Hard work and humble thrift are a kind of purification ritual preparing him for the providential moment when he will be enabled to stop a runaway horse, restore a lost child, prevent a theft, or expose a blackmailer. Success comes to him because his heart is pure. As Franklin wrote in a marginal note in his autobiography, one of Alger's favorite books, "Nothing so likely to make a man's fortune as virtue." Steady employment, systematic thrift, courtesy to ladies, kindness to children, and such virtues demonstrate that a young man is worthy of success. The desirable virtues, incidentally, are predominantly secular; Alger's heroes are painfully moral, but they seldom participate in conventional religious observances.

Another of Alger's themes that has deep roots in American culture is individualism, particularly as embodied in the self-made man. Almost every aspect of American experience—Puritanism, the frontier, nineteenth-century activism, Emersonian self-reliance, and political campaign propaganda—had engendered enormous respect for the self-made man. The man who rose to wealth and power through his own efforts gratified the national ego and conscience in several ways: by suggesting a land of unlimited opportunity and faith in the individual will, by providing a rationalization for social inequality since poverty could be linked to laziness or intemperance, and by apppealing to latent anti-intellectualism since the self-made man enjoyed little or no formal education. The individualistic emphasis of the Alger novels is indicated by the fact that slightly more than half of the 106 authentic titles contain the hero's name. Many of the other titles suggest the virtues of self-reliance: *Facing the World, The Odds Against Him, Risen from the Ranks, Shifting for Himself, Strive and Succeed,* and *Struggling Upward.* As Alger put it, "Most of the rich men in New York and other American cities were once poor boys" (*The Young Salesman*). Orison Swett Marden expressed the credo of self-help more ornately: "Among the world's greatest heroes and benefactors are many others [besides James A. Garfield] whose cradles were rocked by want in lowly cottages, and who buffeted the billows of fate without dependence, save upon the mercy of God and their own energies." Despite Alger's emphasis on self-reliancce, his heroes achieve success through the fortuitous assistance of outside agencies, and after becoming successful they surrender much of their independence. Ragged Dick is a untrammeled individualist while blacking boots; as Richard Hunter, Esq., a businessman, he is not only a conformist but something of a self-righteous prig.

Alger gave his readers a satisfying view of the class structure. The upper levels of society are within the grasp of every earnest, ambitious young man; on the other hand, they are scarcely worth the climb. He stressed the mobility of American society; an Alger hero rises both economically and socially. After he has opened a savings account and acquired a new suit and a watch, his manners and his grammar miraculously improve. Alger not only inspired young men to gain the upper rungs of the social ladder, he also comforted those who failed. Sometimes he made a direct appeal to class antagonism, as in *Sink or Swim* after the hero's father has been killed by a train: "It is only the rich who can give themselves up unreservedly to the luxury of grief. The poor must rouse themselves to battle for their bread" or in his description of another hero: "His hands were brown and soiled with labor. It was clear that he was no white-handed young aristocrat" (*Tom Thatcher's Fortune*). Generally, though, he was less extreme and wrote scornfully only of the idle rich, whom he always presented as pretentious parasites. Although he had no talent for satire, he occasionally attempted it as in the foppish and effeminate Percy de Brabazon in *Adrift in New York*, who boasts that he is "weally vewy intimate" with the second cousin of an English lord. Fawning upon aristocrats is condemned, but authentic members of the British nobility are usually described as admirable. To Alger, it seems, the world of wealth and fashion was simultaneously desirable and deplorable, something to be both coveted and condemned. Such a strabismic view of upper-class society occurs in writers of far more literary merit, for example, Henry James and F. Scott Fitzgerald.

For a young reader of the 1880's or 90's, the big city was both more remote and more alluring than it is for today's more sophisticated adolescents. It was the place where fortunes were made and souls were lost, a mixture of El Dorado and Sodom. The country bumpkin craning his neck to gape at tall buildings or making a down payment to purchase Brooklyn Bridge is a familiar figure in American folklore and humor because he was a familiar figure in real life during the years of rapid urban expansion. Alger was one of our first urban novelists, and he wove into each of his New York novels a wealth of practical information that made it a mixture of guidebook and etiquette manual. He located and described landmarks like the Astor House, Central Park, and the Battery. A country boy dreaming of an expedition to the big city could learn that one pays for a restaurant meal at the cashier's desk or that a hotel guest can deposit his valuables in the hotel safe. A young man dining in a fashionable restaurant for the first time might be emboldened to employ the following gambit: "I have a healthy appetite and shall enjoy anything. Please order for me the same as for yourself" (*Jed, the Poorhouse Boy*). Or if invited to a dance, he might venture to reply like Luke Larkin in *Struggling Up-ward*, "You are very kind, and I shall have great pleasure in being present. Shall you have many?" Alger was precise in describing the mores of boarding houses, the tricks of confidence men, the duties of cash boys and telegraph messengers, and the perils of billiard parlors. Here, as elsewhere, his essential message involved a paradox. Reared in the agrarian tradition of idyllic village life, he nevertheless recognized the lure of the metropolis. The farm or small town might have the virtue, but the big city offered the material reward.

Through his crude intuitions and spontaneous inventions, a folk novelist like Alger expresses the dreams, fears, and prejudices of his public. He expresses them because he shares them. Such an affinity between a writer and popular taste is a rare phenomenon that has no relation to literary skill; indeed, subtlety of expression or of insight would militate against such a relationship. Because the popular ethos ordinarily contains contradictory views on the same subject, such a writer cannot be an analyst or a critic; if he self-consciously establishes a particular social or esthetic viewpoint, he loses his rapport with the world of his readers. The contradictions and ambiguities in Alger's novels are not his alone. They existed, and to a degree still exist, in the popular mind. Nevertheless, we live in a non-Algerian society where corporations require that truck drivers be college graduates, executives usually are sons of executives, a reward for returning a lost child must be declared as taxable income, and consumer-extravagance undergirds the economy. As Clifton Fadiman once observed, modern man can say with Hamlet, "There are more things in heaven and earth, Horatio, than are dreamt of in your philosophy."

One of the clichés concerning Alger's novels is that if you read one you have read them all because he used the same plot in each. Actually this judgment is unfair: Alger used *two* basic plots, one rural and one urban. His favorite involves a young country boy, usually the son of a widow, who goes to the city or occasionally to the West or to Australia in order to restore the family's fortunes. His native wit and moral rectitude enable him to cope with the strange and hostile environment, and after enduring appropriate vicissitudes, he is able to return home and pay off the mortgage just ahead of foreclosure. The other basic plot involves a street boy, usually an orphan, who works as a baggage smasher, a bootblack, or a newsboy; sleeps in doorways or packing cases; and spends his money for cigars, fifteen-cent roast beef dinners, and visits to the theatre. A rough diamond, he is slangy and pert, wise in the ways of the city. Since Alger's novels contain little intentional humor, the impudent wisecracks of characters like Ragged Dick were probably transcribed from the talk of actual newsboys that Alger knew at the Newsboys' Lodging House. A slight incident, usually a glimpse of the alluring middle-class world, serves to redeem the hero; he opens a savings account, rents a room, and takes a job in a store or an office.

Either of Alger's basic plots may be combined with the discovery of a surrogate father. After the hero has performed a kindly or a courageous act, a stranger, usually gray-haired and benevolent, reciprocates by outfitting him in new clothes, buying him a watch, and finding him a position in a "counting-room" or engaging him to read aloud. (The gold watch, incidentally, representing both punctuality and material reward, was Alger's favorite symbol of the first step toward success. By an interesting cultural permutation, it has now become a standard gift for retiring employees.) The benefactor usually has relatives who resent the hero and plot against him. If the benefactor is a young man, he often tutors the hero and sometimes engages him as a "companion." Sometimes the hero's actual father plays a posthumous role; mining stock, an invention, or western lands that he left as an apparently worthless legacy prove to be valuable. The novels thus mingle Parsifal or Cinderella with Telemachus. Who can wonder at their appeal?

Although his plots are not all exactly identical, Alger was fond of certain stock characters and situations, which quickly become familiar after one has read several novels. The most common perhaps is the good boy-bad boy conflict, which he probably derived from the didactic Sunday school stories that Mark Twain parodied. The young hero contrasted with a foil was a favorite device of Dickens. Fielding used it in *Tom Jones*. Such a contrast is, in fact, a venerable one that might be traced back to Cain and Abel. The identities of the good and the bad boy are immediately apparent in an Alger story. The hero is introduced with adjectives like *manly, frank, bright,* and *cheerful.* He usually works to support his widowed mother, who earns a pittance by some humble and precarious employment such as braiding straw, making shirts or vests, or (in *The Five Hundred Dollar Check*) sewing covers on baseballs. The good boy's speech may be a trifle stilted, and his trousers invariably are patched, but the reader can follow his adventures with an assurance that his virtue will triumph. The bad boy is just as unmistakable. He is described by adjectives like *haughty, arrogant, imperious,* and *listless.* Like Jonas Webb in *The Errand Boy,* he usually "makes himself very offensive by assuming consequential airs and a lordly bearing." When he is bested by the hero in an essay contest, a skating match, or a class election, he flies into an uncontrollable rage and vows revenge. In the rural novels he is usually the son of the local squire, who pampers him and encourages his persecution of the hero. A reader soon learns to detect the signs that indicate a boy's moral character. Dropping his g's, asking to borrow money, wearing kid gloves, and smoking are all marks of the bad boy. He plays billiards and cards but has no skill in boxing, a sport in which the good boy excels.

Standard episodes also recur. When a country boy loses his job, for example, he often picks berries or catches fish and sells them. Several heroes make excursions to Niagara Falls; at least three of them meet an English nobleman while there. The impending foreclosure of a mortgage is, of course, predictable. When an Alger hero boards a train, he is certain to encounter a glib stranger who tries to sell him a worthless watch or ring, borrow money, or persuade him to change a counterfeit bill. Frequently, on arriving in a city an Alger boy accepts a stranger's invitation to share a room, always for the irresistible reason of saving money. The hero retires early while his roommate visits a saloon or a theatre. Sometimes he prudently hides his money or he awakens in time to detect his companion rifling his valise, but just as often the robber succeeds and the hero must face the big city penniless. In either event he invariably encounters the thief again and exposes him.

For a Unitarian clergyman, trained to place his faith in human benevolence and the brotherhood of man, Alger included a surprising amount of crime in his fiction. The "drop game" designed to swindle strangers by means of a wallet containing fake money, drunkenness, child-beating, shoplifting, forgery, counterfeiting, theft, blackmail, kidnapping, and murder abound in the novels. At least once in every novel, the hero is accused of a crime, usually theft; the false accusation, in fact, was Alger's primary source of suspense. The hero of *Mark Mason's Victory* incurs the enmity of three different criminals, who take turns at trying to implicate him in robberies. Crimes are thwarted or solved and the hero is exonerated by a variety of means. A favorite device is the wallet or cashbox filled with worthless paper; the thief or confidence man gloats over his booty until he examines it when far from the scene. A variation occurs in *Joe's Luck* when the hero and his companions substitute a large rock for a nugget they have found. Alger characters have an incredible memory for currency, which enables them to identify a bill found in the hero's possession and prove that it was not stolen. Likewise, several characters are able to recognize a half-grown boy whom they have not seen since he was kidnapped in infancy. Serial numbers of government bonds, handwriting analysis, and mistaken identity are also favorite means of exonerating an accused hero. A villain in *The Train Boy* disguises himself as a Quaker in order to accuse the hero of theft, but he is foiled when a detective who happens to be nearby notices that he is wearing gaudy rings on his fingers. When an Alger hero is kidnapped and held prisoner, as often happens, he usually effects his escape by persuading a servant or a child to release him. Usually a crime is solved in the simplest possible manner: a minor character overhears a plot or observes a criminal act and then remains silent until the opportune moment for unmasking the villain.

Though not as lurid as most dime novels of the period, Alger's novels are melodramas. The formula for enjoyable melodrama might be stated as *predictable surprise;* both the perils and the escapes are accomplished within a very limited range of means. Reading an Alger novel is like walking a familiar street, encountering both pleasant and unpleasant persons and scenes, not knowing which is coming next, but always comfortably assured of safety and reward at the end of the walk.

The Horatio Algers found in biographies differ as drastically as the good boy and the bad boy of an Alger novel. Two biographers (Herbert R. Mayes and John R. Tebbel) emphasize his neuroticism and describe three love affairs, one of them with a married woman. His other two biographers (Frank Gruber and Ralph D. Gardner) reject or ignore the scandalous episodes and portray an industrious, humanitarian novelist who was a respected and influential citizen of New York. The truth probably lies somewhere between the two versions, but it seems undeniable that Alger was a frustrated and lonely man. In fact, his life —especially the Mayes-Tebbel version—resembles a pathetic parody of his own novels.

Horatio Alger, Jr., was born in Revere, Massachusetts, on January 13, 1832—Friday the thirteenth, appropriately enough. An Alger hero is usually fatherless; if not, his father dies in an early chapter or departs on a sea voyage. Horatio's father, however, was a domineering Unitarian minister, who supervised the boy's every move, force-fed him with knowledge, and insisted that he should become a clergyman. Both Alger's life and his books lend themselves almost too patly to an Oedipal interpretation.

An Alger boy is handsome, physically strong, and adept at games. Horatio, however, was short and pudgy; he suffered from asthma and stuttered badly. His schoolmates made him the butt of practical jokes and nicknamed him Holy Horatio. Instead of being self-taught like his heroes, Horatio was tutored at home until he was ten, attended a public school for a short time, was sent to Gates Academy in Marlborough, Massachusetts, and enrolled at Harvard, where he graduated in 1852. In the novels an Alger hero is sometimes comforted or assisted by a motherly landlady. In Cambridge, however, according to Mayes and Tebbel, Horatio's experience was quite different in the boarding house kept by a widow, Mrs. Frances Curran. He recorded his outrage in his diary: "She stood in the doorway as I passed to my room and had on very little and I might have seen her bare but I did not look. I shall move to where there is greater respect for decency."

After three days in a boarding house kept by a Miss Mullins, Horatio moved into a large house owned by Floyd Thurstone, an elderly recluse. The relationship seems amazingly similar to that he often described in the novels between a young hero and a benevolent father-figure. Thurstone talked with Horatio about his problems and encouraged him to write stories and poems. The house was heavily mortgaged, and Horatio worked hard to win an essay contest so that he could assist his mentor. The forty dollars in prize money did not solve Mr. Thurstone's problems as it would have done in a novel, but it did win his affection and gratitude.

While he was at Harvard, Horatio permitted his father to break up his romance with Patience Stires, apparently the only woman he ever truly loved; but he held out stubbornly against his father's insistence that he should enter the ministry. After his graduation in 1852, he taught school and tutored private pupils and published poems and short stories. He enrolled at Harvard Divinity School in August, 1853, but dropped out in November to return to the precarious professions of teaching and free-lance writing.

Horatio finally completed his theological course in 1860. Just before his graduation, his old friend Floyd Thurstone died and left him a bequest of $2,000. Instead of investing it in a business or at least opening a savings account as an Alger hero would have done, he used the money to make a trip to Europe with two friends. In Paris, according to Mayes, Horatio was seduced more or less forcibly by a cafe entertainer, Elise Monselet. In his diary he registered a classic reaction of a sin-smitten Puritan:"I was a fool to have waited so long. It is not vile as I thought. Without question I will be better off physically, anyhow I have sometimes thought so. She is more passionate than me." Although this entire episode has been denied by two of Alger's biographers, one must grant at least that the grammar of the diary entry sounds authentic. The diary itself, however, from which Mayes supposedly quoted, has never been located. Elise was supplanted by a domineering British art student, Charlotte Evans, from whom Horatio ran away when their ship reached New York.

Perhaps it was remorse for his Parisian escapades that eventually impelled Alger to accept a pastorate. He preached, taught school, and wrote until 1866, when he moved to New York to devote himself to a literary career. He had by this time met William T. Adams (Oliver Optic), who was editing *Student and Schoolmate*. In 1867 Adams accepted for publication in this magazine the story that was to become Alger's eighth published book and to establish him as a popular novelist, *Ragged Dick; or, Street Life in New York.*

Alger's account of a New York street boy gained him the acquaintance of Charles O'Connor, superintendent of the Newsboys' Lodging House, who became his close friend and a minor character in several of his novels. Although he maintained a residence in various boarding houses, Alger spent much of his time at the Lodging. The city was overrun with street arabs—immigrant children, abandoned orphans, and discharged drummer boys. Those who found a refuge at the Lodging apparently accepted Alger with tolerant amusement and sometimes with real affection. He lent them money, counseled them about moral hazards, took them to Barnum's Museum, and thumped the bass drum in their parades.

Although his books were enormously popular, they did not make Alger wealthy. Since he usually sold a story outright to A. K. Loring, Street & Smith, or another publisher, he received few royalties and no return from reissues by other publishing houses. Totally lacking the business acumen of his heroes, he was an easy mark for both genuine and spurious charities and for persons seeking loans or promoting investment schemes.

Alger seems to have been a quiet, somewhat eccentric man, pathetically lonely and ineffectual. The one heroic episode in his life was his campaign against the Italian *padrones,* who bought boys from their parents in Italy, brought them to New York, and sent them out on the streets as musician-beggars. Alger's novel *Phil, the Fiddler* did not suggest a remedy for the evil, since his hero escaped from New York and was adopted by a doctor in a small town, but it did expose the situation. Alger also spoke courageously against the *padrone* system and at least once was beaten up by thugs.

In 1872 or 1873, according to Mayes, Alger decided to settle in Peekskill, New York. A man had recently been murdered in the vicinity, and as a suspicious-looking stranger Alger was arrested. In fact, the victim's widow, Mrs. Edith Hardy, identified him as a man she had seen prowling around the premises before the murder. Within a few

hours the real murderer was apprehended, and the police released
Alger with apologies but still refused to believe that he was the famous author. Mrs. Hardy apologized for her mistake. Unlike one of
his heroes, Alger found no triumph in being vindicated; instead, he
was led into the most humiliating episode of his life. Mrs. Hardy's sister, Mrs. Una Garth, arrived with her husband, and she and Alger
promptly fell in love. Her ardor quickly cooled, and she attempted to
discourage his attentions, but he followed her to Paris. Here he began
writing *Tomorrow,* the serious novel for adults that he had been con-
templating for years. After Una read his opening chapter, she wrote in
her diary "May the Lord spare the man from a knowledge of his own
incapacity!" Desperately and hopelessly in love, Alger became ill and
temporarily lost his reason. The police found him raving in his room
and carried him to a hospital, where he remained until he was well
enough to return to the United States. It should be added that Ralph
D. Gardner's version of this European trip describes a much more in-
nocuous excursion made in the company of his parents, his sister Olive
Augusta Cheney, and her husband.

Another incident denied by Alger's defenders is his adoption of a
young Chinese boy, Wing, in the mid-1870s. Wing's death in a street
accident, according to Mayes, broke Alger's spirit, yet the 1880's were
the most prolific period of his life. At any rate, the death of O'Connor
removed his last intimate friend. He left New York and the Newsboys'
Lodging House and moved to South Natick, Massachusetts, to live
with his sister, Olive. He died in her home on July 18, 1899.

Between 1900 and 1907, sixteen of his novels that had been serialized earlier were published in book form; and Edward Stratemeyer
creator of the Rover Boys, the Bobbsey Twins, and Tom Swift—wrote
eleven more novels that were published under Alger's name.

———————

Despite or perhaps because of the general sameness of Alger's
fiction, selecting two novels as typical is a difficult task. No single
story contains all of the classic Alger ingredients.

The World Before Him seems a representative story of a virtuous
small town boy who makes his own way in the outside world. Frank
Courtney is not compelled to support a widowed mother, but he un-
dergoes the other trials and enjoys the triumphs of this genre. During
Alger's lifetime, the story was serialized by *Golden Days* in 1880 and
again in 1896-7. As a serial it was entitled *Making His Way.* A major
reason for the change of title must have been the fact that the Penn
Company had retitled Alger's *Gerald's Mission* as *Making His Mark*

and published it the year before. *Making His Way* was sometimes used as a subtitle and sometimes as the main title of subsequent reprints. The text used here is that of the first book edition.

As an example of a city novel, one of the "Ragged Dick" or "Tattered Tom" series like *Ben, the Luggage Boy* or *Paul, the Peddler* would have contained more city lore than *Adrift in New York*, but the novels comprising a series often contain overlapping characters and episodes that make them somewhat unsuitable for separate publication. *Adrift in New York* includes an exceptionally rapid reformation of a street boy, one of Alger's most active and admirable heroines, and an abundance of Algeric melodrama. This story, too, was not published in book form until after Alger's death. It was serialized in *Family Story Paper* (1889) and in *Golden Hours* (1901). It appeared next as a two-part supplement of *Comfort Magazine* in May and June, 1902. In 1903 Street & Smith published an abridged version as Number 45 of the *Brave and Bold Weekly*, and in the following year they printed the full story as a paperback in the Medal Library series. It was later issued in several clothbound editions. The text used here is that of *Comfort Magazine*. Several typographical misspellings have been silently emended, capitalization and hyphenation have been made consistent, but Alger's meticulous though eccentric punctuation has not otherwise been altered.

The texts of both novels were kindly supplied by Mr. Ralph D. Gardner of New York City.

WILLIAM COYLE

Wittenberg University

BIBLIOGRAPHY

BIOGRAPHY AND BIBLIOGRAPHY

Dictionary of American Biography. I, 178-179.

This brief account by Ernest Sutherland Bates is readily accessible, but contains numerous errors, including the wrong year of birth.

Edes, Grace Williamson. *Annals of the Harvard Class of 1852.* Cambridge, Massachusetts, 1922.

Enslin, Morton S. "A Checklist of Horatio Alger, Jr.," *Antiquarian Bookman,* XXIV (July 6, 13, 1959), 3-10.

Gardner, Ralph D. *Horatio Alger, or The American Hero Era.* Mendota, Illinois, 1964.

Much research has obviously been devoted to this somewhat worshipful biography; unfortunately, because the author has invented dialogue and dramatized incidents, it is difficult to distinguish between the actual and the imaginary. The bibliography is useful for beginning collectors because it describes first editions and estimates a fair price for each.

Gruber, Frank. *Horatio Alger, Jr.: A Biography and Bibliography.* West Los Angeles, 1961.

The most trustworthy bibliography. A brief biographical sketch rejects or ignores all of the scandalous episodes described by Mayes.

Mayes, Herbert R. *Alger: A Biography Without a Hero.* New York, 1928.

The first and most colorful biography. The bibliography contains many inaccuracies, and subsequent biographers have questioned several of the biographical incidents.

Tebbel, John. *From Rags to Riches: Horatio Alger, Jr., and The American Dream.* New York, 1963.

This biography accepts Alger's three love affairs, his adoption of a Chinese boy, and other incidents described by Mayes and suggests that he was a latent homosexual.

CRITICISM

Some reviews of secondary sources are included in the listing below.

Adams, Franklin P. "Horatio Alger, Jr.," *Esquire*, XXVI (September, 1946), 80; 185-186.

Allen, Frederick Lewis. "Horatio Alger, Jr.," *Saturday Review of Literature*, XVIII (September 17, 1938), 3-4; 16-17.

Benét, William R. "A Monument to Free Enterprise," *Saturday Review*, XXVIII (September 1, 1945), 15-16.

Borland, Hal. "He Made the American Success Story a Success," *New York Times Book Review*, July 19, 1964, p. 16.

Cawletti, John G. "Portrait of the Newsboy as a Young Man," *Wisconsin Magazine of History*, XLV (Winter, 1961-62), 79-83.

Cowley, Malcolm. "The Alger Story," *New Republic*, CXIII (September 10, 1945), 319-320.

"Cynical Youngest Generation," *Nation*, CXXXIV (February 17, 1932), 186.

Downs, Robert B. *Molders of the Modern Mind*. New York, 1961.

Fadiman, Clifton. "Party of One," *Holiday*, XXI (February, 1957), 6-14; 118. (Reprinted, somewhat revised, in *Any Number Can Play*, New York, 1957.)

Falk, Robert. "Notes on the 'Higher Criticism' of Horatio Alger, Jr." *Arizona Quarterly*, XIX (Summer, 1963), 151-167.

Fishwick, Marshall. "The Rise and Fall of Horatio Alger," *Saturday Review*, XXXIX (November 17, 1956), 15-16; 42-43.

"Forgotten Boys' Classic," *Literary Digest*, CXII (January 30, 1932), 20.

Holbrook, Stewart. "'Horatio Alger, Jr., and Ragged Dick," *New York Times Book Review*, July 2, 1944, pp. 9; 12.

——. "Horatio Alger Was No Hero," *American Mercury*, LI (October, 1940), 203-209.

——. *Lost Men of American History*. New York, 1946.

Holland, Norman N. "Hobbling with Horatio; or The Uses of Literature," *Hudson Review*, XII (Winter, 1959-60), 549-557.

"Holy Horatio," *Time*, XLVI (August 13, 1945), 98-102.

"Horatio Alger Books Given Children's Aid Society," *Hobbies*, LXVI April 1, 1961), 110-111.

"Horatio Alger: Inspiration of a Collector," *Hobbies*, LXIV (February, 1960), 108-109.

King, David Ferris. "The Author of the Alger Books for Boys," *New York Times Magazine*, January 10, 1932, p. 21.

Levy, Newman. ' "They Made Me What I Am Today," ' *Atlantic Monthly*, CLXXII (November, 1943), 115-117.

Meehan, Thomas. "Forgettable Centenary: Horatio Alger's," *New York Times Magazine*, June 28, 1964, pp. 22-23; 39.

Nevins, Allan. "Horatio Alger," *Saturday Review of Literature*, IV (May 5, 1928), 840.

Parkhurst, W. "Alger's Vitality," *New Republic*, CXIII (October 1, 1945), 441.

"Phoenix Nest," *Saturday Review of Literature*, XXIX (April 6, 1946), 28.

Pringle, Henry F., and Katharine Pringle. "Rebellious Parson," *Saturday Evening Post*, CCXXIII (February 10, 1951), 30; 156-158.

Raines, Halsey. "Horatio Alger Created 119 Synthetic Heroes," *New York Times Book Review*, April 22, 1928, pp. 2; 22.

Robbins, L. H. "Alger: No Alger Hero," *New York Times Magazine*, July 16, 1939, pp. 11; 17.

Seelye, John. "Who Was Horatio? The Alger Myth and American Scholarship," *American Quarterly*, XVII (Winter, 1965), 749-756.

Stein, Robert. "Clean Living with Elbow Grease," *Saturday Review*, XLVII (March 7, 1964), 35.

Swados, Harvey. "Ragged Dick in the Last Lap," *Nation*, CIC (July 13, 1964), 13-14.

Tebbel, John. "Horatio Alger, Jr., and the American Dream: From Rags to Riches," *Arts and Sciences*, II (Spring, 1963), 17-22.

Time, XI (May 7, 1928), 47-48.

Van Royhl [George A. Phelps]. *Holidays and Philosophical Biographies*. Los Angeles, 1951.

GENERAL BACKGROUND

The listing below is highly selective. Most historical studies of nineteenth-century America discuss the Gilded Age and would be relevant to a study of Alger's career.

Beard, Charles A., and Mary R. Beard. *The Rise of American Civilization*. 2 vols. New York, 1927. Vol. II.

Cawelti, John G. *Apostles of the Self-Made Man*. Chicago, 1965.

Commager, Henry Steele. *The American Mind: An Interpretation of American Thought and Character Since the 1880's*. New Haven, 1950.

Curti, Merle. *The Growth of American Thought*, 3rd edition. New York, 1964.

Fishwick, Marshall. *American Heroes: Myth and Reality*. Washington, D.C., 1954.

Hart, James D. *The Popular Book: A History of America's Literary Taste*. New York, 1950.

Lynn, Kenneth S. *The Dream of Success: A Study of the Modern American Imagination*. Boston, 1955.

Meigs, Cornelia, *et al. A Critical History of Children's Literature*. New York, 1953.

Mott, Frank Luther. *Golden Multitudes: The Story of Best Sellers in the United States*. New York, 1947.

Parrington, Vernon L. *Main Currents in American Thought*, vol. II. *The Romantic Revolution in America*. New York, 1927.

Reynolds, Quentin. *The Fiction Factory; or, From Pulp Row to Quality Street*. New York, 1955.

Rischin, Moses, ed. *The American Gospel of Success: Individualism and Beyond*. Chicago, 1965.

Schlesinger, Arthur M. *The Rise of the City, 1878-1898. A History of American Life*, vol. X. New York, 1933.

Sisk, John P. "Rags to Riches," *Commonweal*, LXVII (January 3, 1958), 352-354.

Stern, Madeleine B. *Imprints on History: Book Publishers and American Frontiers*. Bloomington, Indiana, 1956.

Wecter, Dixon. *The Hero in America: A Chronicle of Hero-Worship*. New York, 1941.

Wyllie, Irvin G. *The Self-Made Man in America: The Myth of Rags to Riches*. New Brunswick, New Jersey, 1954.

CONTENTS

⊚⊚⊚⊚⊚⊚⊚⊚⊚⊚⊚⊚⊚⊚⊚⊚⊚⊚⊚⊚⊚⊚⊚⊚⊚⊚⊚⊚⊚⊚⊚⊚⊚⊚⊚

ADRIFT IN NEW YORK

or

Tom and Florence
Braving the World

⊚⊚⊚⊚⊚⊚⊚⊚⊚⊚⊚⊚⊚⊚⊚⊚⊚⊚⊚⊚⊚⊚⊚⊚⊚⊚⊚⊚⊚⊚⊚⊚⊚⊚⊚

BY HORATIO ALGER, JR.

*Author of "The Ragged Dick" Series,
"The Tattered Tom" Series, "A
Rolling Stone," "Making His
Way," etc. etc.*

Chapter 1

THE MISSING HEIR

"Uncle, you are not looking well to-night."

"I am not well, Florence. I sometimes doubt if I shall ever be any better."

"Surely, uncle, you cannot mean—"

"Yes, my child, I have reason to believe that I am nearing the end."

"I cannot bear to hear you speak so, uncle," said Florence Linden, in irrepressible agitation. "You are not an old man. You are but fifty-four."

"True, Florence, but it is not years only that make a man old. Two great sorrows have embittered my life. First, the death of my dearly loved wife, and next the loss of my boy, Harvey."

"It is long since I have heard you refer to my cousin's loss. I thought you had become reconciled—no, I do not mean that, I thought your regret might be less poignant."

"I have not permitted myself to speak of it, but I have never ceased to think of it day and night."

John Linden paused sadly, then resumed:

"If he had died, I might, as you say, have become reconciled; but he was abducted at the age of four by a revengeful servant whom I had discharged from my employment. Heaven knows whether he is living or dead, but it is impressed upon my mind that he still lives, it may be in misery, it may be as a criminal, while I, his unhappy father, live on in a luxury which I cannot enjoy, with no one to care for me—"

Florence Linden sank impulsively on her knees beside her uncle's chair.

"Don't say that, uncle," she pleaded. "You know that I love you, Uncle John."

"And I, too, uncle."

There was a shade of jealousy in the voice of Curtis Waring as he entered the library through the open door, and, approaching his uncle, pressed his hand.

He was a tall, dark-complexioned man, of perhaps thirty-five, with shifty black eyes and thin lips, shaded by a dark moustache. It was not a face to trust.

Even when he smiled the expression of his face did not soften. Yet

3

he could moderate his voice so as to express tenderness and sympathy.

He was the son of an elder sister of Mr. Linden, while Florence was the daughter of a younger brother.

Both were orphans, and both formed a part of Mr. Linden's household, and owed everything to his bounty.

Curtis was supposed to be in some business downtown; but he received a liberal allowance from his uncle, and often drew upon him for outside assistance.

As he stood with his uncle's hand in his, he was necessarily brought near Florence, who instinctively drew a little away, with a slight shudder indicating repugnance.

Slight as it was, Curtis detected it, and his face darkened.

John Linden looked from one to the other.

"Yes," he said, "I must not forget that I have a nephew and a niece. You are both dear to me, but no one can take the place of the boy I have lost."

"But it is so long ago, uncle," said Curtis. "It must be fourteen years."

"It is fourteen years."

"And the boy is long since dead!"

"No, no!" said John Linden, vehemently. "I do not, I will not, believe it. He still lives, and I live only in the hope of one day clasping him in my arms."

"That is very improbable, uncle," said Curtis, in a tone of annoyance. "There isn't one chance in a hundred that my cousin still lives. The grave has closed over him long since. The sooner you make up your mind to accept the inevitable the better."

The drawn features of the old man showed that the words had a depressing effect upon his mind, but Florence interrupted her cousin with an indignant protest.

"How can you speak so, Curtis?" she exclaimed. "Leave Uncle John the hope that he has so long cherished. I have a presentiment that Harvey still lives."

John Linden's face brightened up.

"You, too, believe it possible, Florence?" he said, eagerly.

"Yes, uncle, I not only believe it possible, but probable. How old would Harvey be if he still lived?"

"Eighteen—nearly a year older than yourself."

"How strange! I always think of him as a little boy."

"And I, too, Florence. He rises before me in his little velvet suit, as he was when I saw him, with his sweet, boyish face, in which his mother's looks were reflected."

"Yet, if still living," interrupted Curtis, harshly, "he is a rough street-boy, perchance serving his time at Blackwell's Island, a hardened young ruffian, whom it would be bitter mortification to recognize as your son."

"That's the sorrowful part of it," said his uncle, in a voice of anguish. "That is what I most dread."

"Then since even if he were living you would not care to recognize him, why not cease to think of him, or else regard him as dead?"

"Curtis Waring, have you no heart?" demanded Florence, indignantly.

"Indeed, Florence, you ought to know," said Curtis, sinking his voice into softly modulated accents.

"I know nothing of it," said Florence, coldly, rising from her recumbent position, and drawing aloof from Curtis.

"You know that the dearest wish of my heart is to find favor in your eyes. Uncle, you know my wish, and approve of it, do you not?"

"Yes, Curtis; you and Florence are equally dear to me, and it is my hope that you may be united. In that case, there will be no division of my fortune. It will be left to you jointly."

"Believe me, sir," said Curtis, with faltering voice, feigning an emotion which he did not feel—"believe me, that I fully appreciate your goodness. I am sure Florence joins with me—"

"Florence can speak for herself," said his cousin, coldly. "My uncle needs no assurances from me. He is always kind, and I am always grateful."

John Linden seemed absorbed in thought.

"I do not doubt your affection," he said; "and I have shown it by making you my joint heirs in the event of your marriage; but it is only fair to say that my property goes to my boy, if he still lives."

"But, sir," protested Curtis, "is not that likely to create unnecessary trouble? It can never be known, and meanwhile—"

"You and Florence will hold the property in trust."

"Have you so specified in your will?" asked Curtis.

"I have made two wills. Both are in yonder secretary. By the first the property is bequeathed to you and Florence. By the second and later, it goes to my lost boy in the event of his recovery. Of course, you and Florence are not forgotten, but the bulk of the property goes to Harvey."

"I sincerely wish the boy might be restored to you," said Curtis; but his tone belied his words. "Believe me, the loss of the property would affect me little, if you could be made happy by realizing your warmest desire; but, uncle, I think it only the part of a friend to point out to you, as I have already done, the baselessness of any such expectation."

"It may be as you say, Curtis," said his uncle, with a sigh. "If I were thoroughly convinced of it, I would destroy the later will, and leave my property absolutely to you and Florence."

"No, uncle," said Florence, impulsively, "make no change; let the will stand."

Curtis, screened from his uncle's view, darted a glance of bitter indignation at Florence.

"Is the girl mad?" he muttered to himself. "Must she forever balk me?"

"Let it be so for the present, then," said Mr. Linden, wearily. "Curtis, will you ring the bell? I am tired, and shall retire to my couch early."

"Let me help you, Uncle John," said Florence, eagerly.

"It is too much for your strength, my child. I am growing more and more helpless."

"I, too, can help," said Curtis.

John Linden, supported on either side by his nephew and niece, left the room and was assisted to his chamber.

Curtis and Florence returned to the library.

"Florence," said her cousin, "my uncle's intentions, as expressed to-night, make it desirable that there should be an understanding between us. Take a seat beside me"—leading her to a sofa—"and let us talk this matter over."

With a gesture of repulsion Florence declined the proffered seat, and remained standing.

"As you please," she answered, coldly.

"Will you be seated?"

"No, our interview will be brief."

"Then I will come to the point. Uncle John wishes to see us united."

"It can never be!" said Florence, decidedly.

Curtis bit his lip in mortification, for her tone was cold and scornful.

Mingled with his mortification was genuine regret, for, as far as he was capable of loving anyone, he loved his fair young cousin.

"You profess to love Uncle John, and yet you would disappoint his cherished hope!" he returned.

"Is it his cherished hope?"

"There is no doubt of it. He has spoken to me more than once on the subject. Feeling that his end is near, he wishes to leave you in charge of a protector."

"I can protect myself," said Florence, proudly.

"You think so. You do not consider the hapless lot of a penniless girl in a cold and selfish world."

"Penniless?" repeated Florence, in an accent of surprise.

"Yes, penniless. Our uncle's bequest to you is conditional upon your acceptance of my hand."

"Has he said this?" asked Florence, sinking into an arm-chair with a helpless look.

"He has told me so more than once," returned Curtis, smoothly. "You don't know how near to his heart this marriage is. I know what you would say: If the property comes to me, I would come to your assistance, but I am expressly prohibited from doing so. I have pleaded with my uncle in your behalf, but in vain."

Florence was too clear-sighted not to penetrate his falsehood.

"If my uncle's heart is hardened against me," she said, "I shall be too wise to turn to you. I am to understand, then, that my choice lies between poverty and a union with you?"

"You have stated it correctly, Florence."

"Then," said Florence, rising, "I will not hesitate. I shrink from poverty, for I have been reared in luxury, but I will sooner live in a hovel—"

"Or a tenement house," interjected Curtis, with a sneer.

"Yes, or a tenement house, than become the wife of one I loathe."

"Girl, you shall bitterly repent that word!" said Curtis, stung to fury.

She did not reply, but, pale and sorrowful, glided from the room to weep bitter tears in the seclusion of her chamber.

Chapter 2

A STRANGE VISITOR

Curtis Waring followed the retreating form of his cousin with a sardonic smile.

"She is in the toils! She cannot escape me!" he muttered. "But"—and here his brow darkened—"it vexes me to see how she repels my advances, as if I were some loathsome thing! If only she would return my love—for I do love her, cold as she is—I should be happy. Can there be a rival? But no! we live so quietly that she has met no one who could win her affections. Why can she not turn to me? Surely I am not so ill-favored, and, though twice her age, I am still a young man. Nay, it is only a young girl's caprice. She shall yet come to my arms, a willing captive."

His thoughts took a turn, as he rose from his seat and walked over to the secretary.

"So it is here that the two wills are deposited!" he said to himself—one making me a rich man, the other a beggar! While the last is in existence I am not safe. The boy may be alive and liable to turn up at any moment. If only he were dead—or the will destroyed—" Here he made a suggestive pause.

He took a bunch of keys from his pocket, and tried one after another, but without success. He was so absorbed in his work that he did not notice the entrance of a dark-browed, broad-shouldered man, dressed in a shabby corduroy suit, till the intruder indulged in a short cough, intended to draw attention.

Starting with guilty consciousness, Curtis turned sharply round, and his glance fell on the intruder.

"Who are you?" he demanded, angrily. "And how dare you enter a gentleman's house unbidden?"

"Are you the gentleman?" asked the intruder, with intentional insolence.

"Yes."

"You own this house?"

"Not at present. It is my uncle's."

"And that secretary—pardon my curiosity—is his?"

"Yes; but what business is it of yours?"

"Not much. Only it makes me laugh to see a gentleman picking a lock. You should leave such business to men like me."

"You are an insolent fellow!" said Curtis, more embarrassed than he liked to confess, for this rough-looking man had become possessed of a dangerous secret. "I am my uncle's confidential agent, and it was on business of his that I wished to open the desk."

"Why not go to him for the key?"

"Because he is sick. But, pshaw! why should I apologize or give any explanations to you? What can you know of him or me?"

"More, perhaps, than you suspect," said the intruder, quietly.

"Then you know, perhaps, that I am my uncle's heir?"

"Don't be too sure of that."

"Look here, fellow," said Curtis, thoroughly provoked, "I don't know who you are nor what you mean, but let me inform you that your presence here is an intrusion, and the sooner you leave the house the better!"

"I will leave it when I get ready."

Curtis started to his feet, and advanced toward his visitor with an air of menace.

"Go at once," he exclaimed, angrily, "or I will kick you out of the door!"

"What's the matter with the window?" returned the stranger, with an insolent leer.

"That's as you prefer; but if you don't leave at once I will eject you."

By way of reply, the rough visitor coolly seated himself in a luxurious easy-chair, and, looking up into the angry face of Waring, said:

"Oh, no, you won't!"

"And why not?" asked Curtis, with a feeling of uneasiness for which he could not account.

"Why not? Because, in that case, I should seek an interview with your uncle, and tell him—"

"What?"

"That his son still lives; and that I can restore him to his—"

The face of Curtis Waring blanched; he staggered as if he had been struck; and he cried out, hoarsely:

"It is a lie!"

"It is the truth, begging your pardon. Do you mind my smoking?" and he coolly produced a common clay pipe, filled and lighted it.

"Who are you?" asked Curtis, scanning the man's features with painful anxiety.

"Have you forgotten Tim Bolton?"

"Are you Tim Bolton?" faltered Curtis.

"Yes; but you don't seem glad to see me?"

"I thought you were—"

"In Australia. So I was, three years since. Then I got homesick, and came back to New York."

"You have been here three years."

"Yes" chuckled Bolton. "You didn't suspect it, did you?"

"Where?" asked Curtis, in a hollow voice.

"I keep a saloon on the Bowery. There's my card. Call round when convenient."

Curtis was about to throw the card into the grate, but on second thought dropped it in his pocket.

"And the boy?" he asked, slowly.

"Is alive and well. He hasn't been starved. Though I dare say you wouldn't have grieved much if he had."

"And he is actually in this city?"

"Just so."

"Does he know anything of—you know what I mean."

"He doesn't know that he is the son of a rich man, and heir to the property which you look upon as yours. That's what you mean, isn't it?"

"Yes. What is he doing? Is he at any work?"

"He helps me some in the saloon, sells papers in the evenings, and makes himself generally useful."

"Has he any education?"

"Well I haven't sent him to boarding-school or college," answered Tim. "He don't know no Greek or Latin or mathematics—phew, that's a hard word! You didn't tell me you wanted him made a scholar of."

"I didn't. I wanted never to see or hear from him again. What made you bring him back to New York?"

"Couldn't keep away, governor. I got homesick, I did. There ain't but one Bowery in the world, and I hankered after that—"

"Didn't I pay you money to keep away, Tim Bolton?"

"I don't deny it, but what's three thousand dollars? Why, the kid's cost me more than that. I've had the care of him for fourteen years, and it's only about two hundred dollars a year."

"You have broken your promise to me!" said Curtis, sternly.

"There's worse things than breaking your promise," retorted Bolton.

Scarely had he spoken than a change came over his face, and he stared open-mouthed behind and beyond Curtis.

Startled himself, Curtis turned, and saw, with a feeling akin to dismay, the tall figure of his uncle standing on the threshold of the left portal, clad in a morning-gown, with his eyes fixed inquiringly upon Bolton and himself.

Chapter 3

AN UNHOLY COMPACT

"Who is that man, Curtis?" asked John Linden, pointing with his thin finger at Tim Bolton, who looked strangely out of place, as, with clay-pipe, he sat in the luxurious library on a sumptuous chair.

"That man?" stammered Curtis, quite at a loss what to say.

"Yes."

"He is a poor man, out of luck, who has applied to me for assistance," answered Curtis, recovering his wits.

"That's it, governor," said Bolton, thinking it necessary to confirm the statement. "I've got five small children at home almost starvin', your honor."

"That is sad. What is your business, my man?"

It was Bolton's turn to be embarrassed.

"My business?" he repeated.

"That is what I said."

"I'm a—blacksmith, but I'm willing to do any honest work."

"That is commendable; but don't you know that it is very ill-bred to smoke a pipe in a gentleman's house?"

"Excuse me, governor!"

And Bolton extinguished his pipe and put it away in a pocket of his corduroy coat.

"I was just telling him the same thing." said Curtis, "Don't trouble yourself any further, uncle. I will inquire into the man's circumstances, and help him if I can."

"Very well, Curtis, I came down because I thought I heard voices."

John Linden slowly returned to his chamber, and left the two alone.

"The governor's gettin' old," said Bolton. "When I was butler here, fifteen years ago, he looked like a young man. He didn't suspect that he had ever seen me before."

"Nor that you had carried away his son, Bolton."

"Who hired me to do it? Who put me up to the job, as far as that goes?"

"Hush! Walls have ears. Let us return to business."

"That suits me."

"Look here, Tim Bolton," said Curtis, drawing up a chair, and lowering his voice to a confidential pitch, "you say you want money?"

"In course I do."

"Well, I don't give money for nothing."

"I know that. What's wanted now?"

"You say the boy is alive?"

"He's very much alive."

"Is there any necessity for his living?" asked Curtis, in a sharp, hissing tone, fixing his eyes searchingly on Bolton, to see how his hint would be taken.

"You mean that you want me to murder him?" said Bolton, quickly.

"Why not? You don't look over scrupulous."

"I am a bad man, I admit it," said Bolton, with a gesture of repugnance, "a thief, a low blackguard, perhaps, but, thank heaven! I am no murderer! And if I was I wouldn't spill a drop of that boy's blood for the fortune that is his by right."

"I didn't give you credit for so much sentiment, Bolton," said Curtis, with a sneer. "You don't look like it, but appearances are deceitful. We'll drop the subject. You can serve me in another way. Can you open this secretary?"

"Yes; that's in my line."

"There is a paper in it that I want. It is my uncle's will. I have a curiosity to read it."

"I understand. Well, I'm agreeable."

"If you find any money or valuables, you are welcome to them. I only want the paper. When will you make the attempt?"

"To-morrow night. When will it be safe?"

"At eleven o'clock. We all retire early in this house. Can you force an entrance?"

"Yes; but it will be better for you to leave the outer door unlocked."

"I have a better plan. Here is my latch-key."

"Good! I may not do the job myself, but I will see that it is done. How shall I know the will?"

"It is in a big envelope, tied with a narrow tape. Probably it is inscribed: 'My will.'"

"Suppose I succeed, when shall I see you?"

"I will come around to your place on the Bowery. Good-night!"

Curtis Waring saw Bolton to the door, and let him out. Returning, he flung himself on a fauteuil.

"I can make that man useful!" he reflected. "There is an element of danger in the boy's presence in New York; but it will go hard if I can't get rid of him! Tim Bolton is unexpectedly squeamish, but there are others to whom I can apply. With gold everything is possible. It's time matters came to a finish. My uncle's health is rapidly failing—the doctor hints that he has heart-disease—and the fortune for which I have been waiting so long will soon be mine, if I work my cards right. I can't afford to make any mistakes now."

Chapter 4

FLORENCE

Florence Linden sat in the library the following evening in an attitude of depression. Her eyelids were swollen, and it was evident she had been weeping. During the day she had had an interview with her uncle, in which he harshly insisted upon her yielding to his wishes, and marrying her cousin, Curtis.

"But, uncle," she objected, "I do not love him."

"Marry him and love will come."

"Never!" she said, vehemently.

"You speak confidently, miss," said Mr. Linden, with irritation.

"Listen, Uncle John. It is not alone that I do not love him. I dislike —I loathe—him."

"Nonsense! that is a young girl's extravagant nonsense."

"No, uncle."

"There can be no reason for such a foolish dislike. What can you have against him?"

"It is impressed upon me, uncle, that Curtis is a bad man. There is something false—treacherous—about him."

"Pooh! child! you are more foolish than I thought. I don't say Curtis is an angel. No man is; at least, I never met any such. But he is no worse than the generality of men. In marrying him you will carry out my cherished wish. Florence, I have not long to live. I shall be glad to see you well established in life before I leave you. As the wife of Curtis you will have a recognized position. You will go on living in this house, and the old home will be maintained."

"But why is it necessary for me to marry at all, Uncle John?"

"You will be sure to marry someone. Should I divide my fortune between you and Curtis, you would become the prey of some unscrupulous fortune-hunter."

"Better that than become the wife of Curtis Waring—"

"I see, you are incorrigible," said her uncle, angrily. "Do you refuse obedience to my wishes?"

"Command me in anything else, Uncle John, and I will obey," pleaded Florence.

"Indeed! You only thwart me in my cherished wish, but are willing to obey me in unimportant matters. You forget the debt you owe me."

"I forget nothing, dear uncle. I do not forget that, when I was a poor little child, helpless and destitute you took me to your arms, and gave me a home, and have cared for me from that time to this as only a parent could."

"You remember that, then?"

"Yes, uncle. I hope you will not consider me wholly ungrateful."

"It only makes matters worse. You own your obligations, yet refuse to make the only return I desire. You refuse to comfort me in the closing days of my life by marrying your cousin."

"Because that so nearly concerns my happiness that no one has a right to ask me to sacrifice all I hold dear."

"I see you are incorrigible," said John Linden, stormily. "Do you know what will be the consequence?"

"I am prepared for all."

"Then listen! If you persist in balking me, I shall leave the entire estate to Curtis."

"Do with your money as you will, uncle. I have no claim to more than I have received."

"You are right there; but that is not all."

Florence fixed upon him a mute look of inquiry.

"I will give you twenty-four hours more to come to your senses. Then, if you persist in your ingratitude and disobedience, you must find another home."

"Oh, uncle, you do not mean that?" exclaimed Florence, deeply moved.

"I do mean it, and I shall not allow your tears to move me. Not another word, for I will not hear it. Take twenty-four hours to think over what I have said."

Florence bowed her head on her hands, and gave herself up to sorrowful thoughts. But she was interrupted by the entrance of the servant, who announced:

"Mr. Percy de Brabazon."

An effeminate-looking young man, foppishly dressed, followed the servant into the room, and made it impossible for Florence to deny herself, as she wished to do.

"I hope I see you well, Miss Florence," he simpered.

"Thank you, Mr. de Brabazon," said Florence, coldly. "I have a slight headache."

"I am awfully sorry, I am, upon my word, Miss Florence. My doctor tells me it is only those whose bwains are vewy active that are troubled with headaches."

"Then, I presume, Mr. de Brabazon," said Florence, with intentional sarcasm, "that you never have a headache."

"Weally, Miss Florence, that is vewy clevah. You will have your joke."

"It was no joke, I assure you, Mr. de Brabazon."

"I—I thought it might be. Didn't I see you at the opewa last evening?"

"Possibly, I was there."

"I often go to the opewa. It's so—so fashionable, don't you know?"

"Then you don't go to hear the music?"

"Oh, of course, but one can't always be listening to the music, don't you know. I had a fwiend with me last evening—an Englishman—a charming fellow, I assure you. He's the second cousin of a lord, and yet—you'll hardly cwedit it—we're weally vewy intimate. He tells me, Miss Florence, that I'm the perfect image of his cousin, Lord Fitz Noodle."

"I am not at all surprised."

"Weally, you are vewy kind, Miss Florence. I thought it a great compliment. I don't know how it is, but evewybody takes me for an Englishman. Strange, isn't it?"

"I am very glad."

"May I ask why, Miss Florence?"

"Because—Well, perhaps I had better not explain. It seems to give you pleasure. You would, probably, prefer to be an Englishman."

"I admit that I have a great admiwation for the English character. It's gweat pity we have no lords in America. Now, if you would only allow me to bring my English fwiend here—"

"I don't care to make any new acquaintances. Even if I did, I prefer my own countrymen. Don't you like America, Mr. de Brabazon?"

"Oh, of courth, if we only had some lords here."

"We have plenty of flunkeys."

"That's awfully clevah, on my word."

"Is it? I am afraid you are too complimentary. You are very good-natured."

"I always feel good-natured in your company, Miss Florence. I—wish I could always be with you."

"Really! Wouldn't that be a trifle monotonous?"

"Not if we were married," said Percy, boldly breaking the ice.

"What do you mean, Mr. de Brabazon?"

"I hope you will excuse me, Miss Florence—Miss Linden, I mean; but I'm awfully in love with you, and have been ever so long—but I never dared to tell you so. I felt so nervous, don't you know. Will you marry me? I'll be awfully obliged if you will."

Mr. de Brabazon rather awkwardly slipped from his chair, and sank on one knee before Florence.

"Please rise, Mr. de Brabazon," said Florence, hurriedly. "It is quite out of the question—what you ask—I assure you."

"Ah! I see how it is," said Percy, clasping his hands sadly. "You love another."

"Not that I am aware of."

"Then I may still hope?"

"I cannot encourage you, Mr. de Brabazon. My heart is free, but it can never be yours."

"Then," said Percy, gloomily, "there is only one thing for me to do."

"What is that?"

"I shall go to the Bwooklyn Bwidge, climb to the parapet, jump into the water, and end my misewable life."

"You had better think twice before adopting such a desperate resolution, Mr. de Brabazon. You will meet others who will be kinder to you than I have been—"

"I can never love another. My heart is broken. Farewell, cruel girl.

When you read the papers to-morrow morning, think of the unhappy Percy de Brabazon!"

Mr. de Brabazon folded his arms gloomily, and stalked out of the room.

"If my position were not so sad, I should be tempted to smile," said Florence. "Mr. de Brabazon will not do this thing. His emotions are as strong as those of a butterfly."

After a brief pause Florence seated herself at the table, and drew toward her writing materials.

"It is I whose heart should be broken!" she murmured; "I, who am driven from the only home I have ever known. What can have turned against me my uncle, usually so kind and considerate? It must be that Curtis has exerted a baleful influence upon him. I cannot leave him without one word of farewell."

She took up a sheet of paper, and wrote rapidly:

"Dear Uncle—You have told me to leave your house, and I obey. I cannot tell you how sad I feel, when I reflect that I have lost your love, and must go forth among strangers—I know not where. I was but a little girl when you gave me a home. I have grown up in an atmosphere of love, and I have felt very grateful to you for all you have done for me. I have tried to conform to your wishes, and I would obey you in all else—but I cannot marry Curtis; I think I would rather die. Let me still live with you as I have done. I do not care for any part of your money—leave it all to him, if you think best—but give me back my place in your heart. You are angry now, but you will some time pity and forgive your poor Florence, who will never cease to bless and pray for you. Good-bye!   FLORENCE."

She was about to sign herself Florence Linden, but reflected that she was no longer entitled to use a name which would seem to carry with it a claim upon her uncle.

The tears fell upon the paper as she was writing, but she heeded them not. It was the saddest hour of her life. Hitherto she had been shielded from all sorrow, and secure in the affection of her uncle; had never dreamed that there would come a time when she would feel obliged to leave all behind her and go out into the world, friendless and penniless, but poorest of all in the loss of that love which she had hitherto enjoyed.

After completing the note, Florence let her head fall upon the table, and sobbed herself to sleep.

An hour and a half passed, the servant looked in, but noticing that her mistress was sleeping, contented herself with lowering the gas, but refrained from waking her.

And so she slept on till the French clock upon the mantel struck eleven.

Five minutes later and the door of the room slowly opened, and a boy entered on tip-toe. He was roughly dressed. His figure was manly and vigorous, and despite his stealthy step and suspicious movements, his face was prepossessing.

He started when he saw Florence.

"What, a sleeping gal!" he said to himself. "Tim told me I'd find the coast clear, but I guess she's sound asleep and won't hear nothing. I don't half like this job, but I've got to do as Tim told me. He says he's my father, so I s'pose it's all right. All the same I shall be nabbed some day, and then the family'll be disgraced. It's a queer life I've led ever since I can remember. Sometimes I feel like leaving Tim and settin' up for myself. I wonder how 'twould seem to be respectable."

The boy approached the secretary, and with some tools he had brought essayed to open it. After a brief delay he succeeded, and lifted the cover. He was about to explore it, according to Tim's directions, when he heard a cry of fear, and turning swiftly saw Florence, her eyes dilated with terror, gazing at him.

"Who are you?" she asked, in alarm, "and what are you doing there?"

Chapter 5

DODGER

The boy sprang to the side of Florence and seized her wrists in his strong, young grasp.

"Don't you alarm the house," he said, "or I'll—"

"What will you do?" gasped Florence, in alarm.

The boy was evidently softened by her beauty, and answered in a tone of hesitation:

"I don't know. I won't harm you if you keep quiet."

"What are you here for?" asked Florence, fixing her eyes on the boy's face; "are you a thief?"

"I don't know—yes, I suppose I am."

"How sad, when you are so young."

"What! miss, do you pity me?"

"Yes, my poor boy; you must be very poor, or you wouldn't bring yourself to steal."

"No. I ain't poor; leastways, I have enough to eat, and I have a place to sleep."

"Then why don't you earn your living by honest means?"

"I can't; I must obey orders."

"Whose orders?"

"Why, the guv'nor's, to be sure."

"Did he tell you to open that secretary?"

"Yes."

"Who is the gov'nor, as you call him?"

"I can't tell; it wouldn't be square."

"He must be a very wicked man."

"Well, he ain't exactly what you call an angel, but I've seen wuss men than the guv'nor."

"Do you mind telling me your own name?"

"No; for I know you won't peach on me. Tom Dodger."

"Dodger?"

"Yes."

"That isn't a surname."

"It's all I've got. That's what I'm always called."

"It is very singular," said Florence, fixing a glance of mingled curiosity and perplexity upon the young visitor.

While the two were earnestly conversing in that subdued light, afforded by the lowered gaslight, Tim Bolton crept in through the door unobserved by either, tip-toed across the room to the secretary, snatched the will and a roll of bills, and escaped, still without attracting attention.

"Oh, I wish I could persuade you to give up this bad life," resumed Florence, earnestly, "and become honest."

"Do you really care what becomes of me, miss?" asked Dodger, slowly.

"I do, indeed."

"That's very kind of you, miss; but I don't understand it. You are a rich young lady, and I'm only a poor boy, livin' in a Bowery dive."

"What's that?"

"Never mind, miss, such as you wouldn't understand. Why, all my life I've lived with thieves and drunkards and bunco men, and—"

"But I'm sure you don't like it. You are fit for something better."

"Do you really think so?" asked Dodger, doubtfully.

"Yes; you have a good face. You were meant to be good and honest, I am sure."

"Would you trust me?" asked the boy, earnestly, fixing his large, dark eyes eloquently on the face of Florence.

"Yes, I would if you would only leave your evil companions and become true to your better nature."

"No one ever spoke to me like that before, miss," said Dodger, his expressive features showing that he was strongly moved. "You think I could be good if I tried hard, and grow up respectable?"

"I am sure you could," said Florence, confidently.

There was something in this boy, young outlaw though he was, that moved her powerfully, and even fascinated her, though she hardly realized it. It was something more than a feeling of compassion for a wayward and misguided youth.

"I could if I was rich like you, and lived in a nice house, and 'sociated with swells. If you had a father like mine—"

"Is he a bad man?"

"Well, he don't belong to the church. He keeps a gin-mill, and has ever since I was a kid."

"Have you always lived with him?"

"Yes; but not in New York."

"Where, then?"

"In Melbourne."

"That's in Australia."

"Yes, miss."

"How long since you came to New York?"

"I guess it's about three years."

"And you have always had this man as a guardian? Poor boy!"

"You've got a different father from me, miss?"

Tears forced themselves to the eyes of Florence, as this remark brought forcibly to her mind the position in which she was placed.

"Alas!" she answered, impulsively, "I am alone in the world."

"What! ain't the old gentleman that lives here your father?"

"He is my uncle; but he is very, very angry with me, and has this very day ordered me to leave the house."

"Why, what a cantankerous old ruffian he is, to be sure!" exclaimed the boy, indignantly.

"Hush! you must not talk against my uncle. He has always been kind to me till now."

"Why, what's up? What's he mad about?"

"He wants me to marry my cousin Curtis—a man I do not even like."

"That's a shame! Is it the dude I saw come out of the house a little while ago?"

"Oh, no; that's a different gentleman. It's Mr. de Brabazon."

"You don't want to marry him, do you?"

"No, no!"

"I'm glad of that. He don't look as if he knew enough to come in when it rained."

"The poor young man is not very brilliant, but I think I would rather marry him than Curtis Waring."

"I've seen him, too. He's got dark hair and a dark complexion, and a wicked look in his eyes."

"You, too, have noticed that?"

"I've seen such as him before. He's a bad man."

"Do you know anything against him?" asked Florence, eagerly.

"Only his looks."

"I am not deceived," murmured Florence. "It's not wholly prejudice. The boy distrusts him, too. So you see, Dodger," she added, aloud, "I am not a rich young lady, as you suppose. I must leave this house, and work for my living. I have no home any more."

"If you have no home," said Dodger, impulsively, "come home with me."

"To the home you have described, my poor boy? How could I do that?"

"No; I will hire a room for you in a quiet street, and you shall be my sister. I will work for you, and give you my money."

"You are kind, and I am glad to think I have found a friend when I need one most. But I could not accept stolen money. It would be as bad as if I, too, were a thief."

"But I am not a thief! That is, I won't be any more."

"And you will give up your plan of robbing my uncle?"

"Yes, I will; though I don't know what my guv'nor will say. He'll half murder me, I expect. He'll be sure to cut up rough."

"Do right, Dodger, whatever happens. Promise me that you never will steal again?"

"There's my hand, miss—I promise. Nobody ever talked to me like you. I never thought much about bein' respectable, and growin' up to be somebody, but if you take an interest in me I'll try hard to do right."

At this moment Mr. Linden, clad in a long morning-gown, and holding a candle in his hand, entered the room and started in astonishment when he saw Florence clasping the hand of one whose appearance led him to stamp as a young rough.

"Shameless girl!" he exclaimed, in stern reproof. "So this is the company you keep when you think I am out of the way!"

Chapter 6

A TEMPEST

The charge was so strange and unexpected that Florence was overwhelmed. She could only murmur:

"Oh, uncle!"

Her young companion was indignant. Already he felt that Florence had consented to accept him as a friend, and he was resolved to stand by her.

"I say, old man," he bristled up, "don't you go to insult her! She's a angel."

"No doubt you think so," rejoined Mr. Linden, in a tone of sarcasm. "Upon my word, miss, I congratulate you on your elevated taste. So this is your reason for not being willing to marry your cousin Curtis?"

"Indeed, uncle, you are mistaken. I never met this boy till to-night."

"Don't try to deceive me. Young man, did you open my secretary?"

"Yes, sir."

"And robbed it into the bargain," continued Linden, going to the secretary and examining it. He did not, however, miss the will, but only the roll of bills. "Give me back the money you have taken from it, you young rascal!'"

"I took nothing, sir."

"It's a lie! The money is gone, and no one else could have taken it."

"I don't allow no one to call me a liar. Just take that back, old man, or I—"

"Indeed, uncle, he took nothing, for he had only just opened the secretary when I woke up and spoke to him."

"You stand by him, of course, shameless girl! I blush to think that you are my niece. I am glad to think that my eyes are opened before it is too late."

The old merchant rung the bell violently and roused the house. Dodger made no attempt to escape, but stood beside Florence in the attitude of a protector. But a short time elapsed before Curtis Waring and the servants entered the room, and gazed with wonder at the tableau presented by the excited old man and the two young people.

"My friends," said John Linden, in a tone of excitement, "I call you to witness that this girl, whom I blush to acknowledge as my niece, has proved herself unworthy of my kindness. In your presence I cut her off, and bid her never again darken my door."

"But what has she done, uncle?" asked Curtis. He was prepared for the presence of Dodger, whom he rightly concluded to be an agent of Tim Bolton, but he could not understand why Florence should be in the library at this late hour. Nor was he able to understand the evidently friendly relations between her and the young visitor.

"What has she done?" repeated John Linden. "She has introduced that young ruffian into the house to rob me. Look at that secretary! He has forced it open, and stolen a large sum of money."

"It is not true, sir," said Dodger, calmly—"about taking the money, I mean. I haven't taken a cent."

"Then why did you open the secretary?"

"I did mean to take money, but she stopped me."

"Oh, she stopped you?" repeated Linden, with withering sarcasm. "Then, perhaps, you will tell me where the money is gone?"

"He hasn't discovered about the will." thought Curtis, congratulating himself.

"If the boy has it, I must manage to give him a chance to escape."

"You can search me if you want to," continued Dodger, proudly. "You won't find no money on me."

"Do you think I am a fool, you young burglar?" exclaimed John Linden, angrily.

"Uncle, let me speak to the boy," said Curtis, soothingly. "I think he will tell me."

"As you like, Curtis; but I am convinced that he is a thief."

Curtis Waring beckoned Dodger into an adjoining room.

"Now, my boy," he said, smoothly, "give me what you took from the secretary, and I will see that you are not arrested."

"But, sir, I didn't take nothing—it's just as I told the old duffer. The girl waked up just as I'd got the secretary open, and I didn't have a chance."

"But the money is gone," said Curtis, in an incredulous tone.

"I don't know nothing about that."

"Come, you'd better examine your pockets. In the hurry of the moment you may have taken it without knowing it."

"No, I couldn't."

"Didn't you take a paper of any kind?" asked Curtis, eagerly. "Sometimes papers are of more value than money."

"No, I didn't take no paper, though Tim told me to."

Curtis quietly ignored the allusion to Tim, for it did not suit his purpose to get Tim into trouble. His unscrupulous agent knew too much that would compromise his principal.

"Are you willing that I should examine you?"

"Yes, I am. Go ahead."

Curtis thrust his hand into the pockets of the boy, who, boy as he was, was as tall as himself, but was not repaid by the discovery of anything. He was very much perplexed.

"Didn't you throw the articles on the floor?" he demanded, suspiciously.

"No, I didn't."

"You didn't give them to the young lady?"

"No; if I had she'd have said so."

"Humph! this is strange. What is your name?"

"Dodger."

"That's a queer name. Have you no other?"

"Not as I know of."

"With whom do you live?"

"With my father. Leastways, he says he's my father."

There was a growing suspicion in the mind of Curtis Waring. He scanned the boy's features with attention. Could this ill-dressed boy—a street boy in appearance—be his long-lost and deeply-wronged cousin?

"Who is it that says he is your father?" he demanded, abruptly.

"Do you want to get him into trouble?"

"No, I don't want to get him into trouble, or you either. Better tell me all, and I will be your friend."

"You're a better sort than I thought at first," said Dodger. "The man I live with is called Tim Bolton."

"I thought so," quickly ejaculated Curtis. He had scarcely got out the words before he was sensible that he had made a mistake.

"What, do you know Tim?" inquired Dodger, in surprise.

"I mean," replied Curtis, lamely, "that I had heard of this man Bolton. He keeps a saloon on the Bowery, doesn't he?"

"Yes."

"I thought you would be living with some such man. Did he come to the house with you to-night?"

"Yes."

"Where is he?"

"He stayed outside."

"Perhaps he is there now."

"Don't you go to having him arrested," said Dodger, suspiciously.

"I will keep my promise. Are you sure you didn't pass out the paper and the money to him? Think, now."

"No, I didn't. I didn't have a chance. When I came into the room yonder I saw the gal asleep, and I thought she wouldn't hear me, but when I'd got the desk open she spoke to me and asked me what I was doin'."

"And you took nothing?"

"No."

"It seems very strange. I cannot understand it. Yet my uncle says the money is gone. Did anyone else enter the room while you were talking with Miss Linden?"

"I didn't see anyone."

"What were you talking about?"

"She said the old man wanted her to marry you, and she didn't want to."

"She told you that?" exclaimed Curtis, in displeasure.

"Yes, she did. She said she'd rather marry the dude that was here early this evenin'."

"Mr. de Brabazon!"

"Yes, that's the name."

"Upon my word, she was very confidential. You are a queer person for her to select as a confidant."

"Maybe so, sir; but she knows I'm her friend."

"You like the young lady, then? Perhaps you would like to marry her yourself?"

"As if she'd taken any notice of a poor boy like me. I told her if her uncle sent her away, I'd take care of her and be a brother to her."

"How would Mr. Tim Bolton—that's his name, isn't it?—like that?"

"I wouldn't take her to where he lives."

"I think, myself, it would hardly be a suitable home for a young lady brought up on Madison Avenue. There is certainly no accounting for tastes. Miss Florence—"

"That's her name, is it?"

"Yes; didn't she tell you?"

"No; but it's a nice name."

"She declines my hand, and accepts your protection. It will certainly be a proud distinction to become Mrs. Dodger."

"Don't you laugh at her!" said Dodger, suspiciously.

"I don't propose to. But I think we may as well return to the library."

"Well," said Mr. Linden, as his nephew returned with Dodger.

"I have examined the boy, and found nothing on his person," said Curtis: "I confess I am puzzled. He appears to have a high admiration for Florence—"

"As I supposed."

"She has even confided to him her dislike for me, and he has offered her his protection."

"Is this so, miss?" demanded Mr. Linden, sternly.

"Yes, uncle," faltered Florence.

"Then you can join the young person you have selected whenever you please. For your sake I will not have him arrested for attempted burglary. He is welcome to what he has taken, since he is likely to marry into the family. You may stay here to-night, and he can call for you in the morning."

John Linden closed the secretary and left the room, leaving Florence sobbing. The servants, too, retired, and Curtis was left alone with her.

"Florence," he said, "accept my hand, and I will reconcile my uncle to you. Say but the word, and—"

"I can never speak it, Curtis! I will take my uncle at his word. Dodger, call for me to-morrow at eight, and I will accept your friendly services in finding me a new home."

"I'll be on hand, miss. Good-night!"

"Be it so, obstinate girl!" said Curtis, angrily. "The time will come when you will bitterly repent your mad decision."

Chapter 7

FLORENCE LEAVES HOME

Florence passed a sleepless night. It had come upon her so suddenly, this expulsion from the home of her childhood, that she could not fully realize it. She could not feel that she was taking her last look at the familiar room, and well-remembered dining-room, where she had sat down for the last time to breakfast. She was alone at the breakfast-table, for the usual breakfast hour was half-past eight, and she had appointed Dodger to call for her at eight.

"Is it true, Miss Florence, that you're going away?" asked Jane, the warm-hearted table-girl, as she waited upon Florence.

"Yes, Jane," answered Florence, sadly.

"It's a shame, so it is! I didn't think your uncle would be so hard-hearted."

"He is disappointed because I won't marry my cousin Curtis."

"I don't blame you for it, miss. I never liked Mr. Waring. He isn't half good enough for you."

"I say nothing about that, Jane; but I will not marry a man I don't love."

"Nor would I, miss. Where are you going, if I may make so bold?"

"I don't know, Jane," said Florence, despondently.

"But you can't walk about the streets."

"A trusty friend is going to call for me at eight o'clock; when he comes admit him."

"It is a—a young gentleman?"

"You wouldn't call him such. He is a boy, a poor boy; but I think he is a true friend. He says he will find me a comfortable room somewhere, where I can settle down and look for work."

"Are you going to work for a living, Miss Florence?" asked Jane, horrified.

"I must, Jane."

"It's a great shame—you, a lady born."

"No, Jane, I do not look upon it in that light. I shall be happier for having my mind and my hands occupied."

"What work will you do?"

"I don't know yet. Dodger will advise me."

"Who, miss?"

"Dodger."

"Who is he?"

"It's the boy I spoke of."

"Shure, he's got a quare name."

"Yes; but names don't count for much. It's the heart I think of, and this boy has a kind heart."

"Have you known him long?"

"I saw him yesterday for the first time."

"Is it the young fellow who was here last night?"

"Yes."

"He isn't fit company for the likes of you, Miss Florence."

"You forget, Jane, that I am no longer a rich young lady. I am poorer even than you. This Dodger is kind, and I feel that I can trust him."

"If you are poor, Miss Florence," said Jane, hesitating, "would you mind borrowing some money of me? I've got ten dollars upstairs in my trunk, and I don't need it at all. It's proud I'll be to lend it to you."

"Thank you, Jane," said Florence, gratefully. "I thought I had but one friend. I find I have two—"

"Then you'll take the money? I'll go right up and get it."

"No, Jane; not at present. I have twenty dollars in my purse, and it will last me till I can earn more."

"But, miss, twenty dollars will soon go," said Jane, disappointed.

"If I find that I need the sum you so kindly offer me, I will let you know, I promise that."

"Thank you, miss."

At this point a bell rang from above.

"It's from Mr. Curtis's room," said Jane.

"Go and see what he wants."

Jane returned in a brief time with a note in her hand.

"Mr. Curtis asked me if you were still here," she explained, "and when I told him you were he asked me to give you this."

Florence took the note, and opening it, read these lines:

> "Florence—Now that you have had time to think over your plan of leaving your old home, I hope you have come to see how foolish it is. Reflect that, if carried out, a life of poverty and squalid wretchedness amid homely and uncongenial surroundings awaits you; while, as my wife, you will live a life of luxury and high social position. There are many young ladies who would be glad to accept the chance which you so recklessly reject. By accepting my hand you will gratify our excellent uncle, and make me the happiest of mortals. You will acquit me of mercenary motives, since you are now penniless, and your disobedience leaves me sole heir to Uncle John. I love you, and it will be my chief object if you will permit it, to make you happy.
>
> "CURTIS WARING."

Florence ran her eyes rapidly over this note, but her heart did not respond and her resolution was not shaken.

"Tell Mr. Waring there is no answer, Jane, if he inquires," she said.

"Was he tryin' to wheedle you into marryin' him?" asked Jane.

"He wished me to change my decision."

"I'm glad you've given him the bounce," said Jane, whose expressions were not always refined. "I wouldn't marry him myself."

Florence smiled. Jane was red-haired and her nose was what is euphemistically called *retroussé*. Even in her own circles she was not regarded as beautiful, and was hardly likely to lead a rich man to overlook her humble station, and sue for her hand.

"Then, Jane, you at least will not blame me for refusing my cousin's hand?"

"That I won't, miss. Do you know, Miss Florence"—and here Jane lowered her voice—"I've a suspicion that Mr. Curtis is married already?"

"What do you mean, Jane?" asked Florence, startled.

"There was a poor young woman called here last month and inquired for Mr. Curtis. She was very sorrowful-like, and poorly dressed. He came up when she was at the door, and he spoke harsh-like, and told her to walk away with him. What they said I couldn't hear, but I've a suspicion that she was married to him, secret-like, for I saw a wedding-ring upon her finger."

"But, Jane, it would be base and infamous for him to ask for my hand when he was already married."

"I can't help it, miss. That's just what he wouldn't mind doin'. Oh, he's a sly deceiver, Mr. Curtis. I'd like to see him foolin' around me."

Jane nodded her head with emphasis, as if to intimate the kind of reception Curtis Waring would get if he attempted to trifle with her virgin affections.

"I hope what you suspect is not true," said Florence, gravely. "I do not like or respect Curtis, but I don't like to think he would be so base as that. If you ever see this young woman again, try to find out where she lives. I should like to make her acquaintance, and be a friend to her if she needs one."

"Shure, Miss Florence, you will be needin' a friend yourself."

"It is true, Jane. I forgot that I am no longer a young lady of fortune, but a penniless girl, obliged to work for a living."

"What would your uncle say if he knew that Mr. Curtis had a wife?"

"We don't know that he has one, and till we do, it would not be honorable to intimate such a thing to Uncle John."

"Shure he wouldn't be so particular. It's all his fault that you're obliged to leave home and go into the streets. Why couldn't he take no for an answer and marry somebody else, if he can find anybody to have him?"

"I wish indeed that he had fixed his affections elsewhere,'" responded Florence, with a sigh.

"Shure he's twice as old as you, Miss Florence, anyway."

"I shouldn't mind that so much, if that was the only objection."

"It'll be a great deal better marryin' a young man."

"I don't care to marry anyone, Jane. I don't think I shall ever marry."

"It's all very well to say that, Miss Florence. Lots of girls say so, but they change their mind. I don't mean to live out always myself."

"Is there any young man you are interested in, Jane?"

"Maybe there is, and maybe there isn't, Miss Florence. If I ever do get married I'll invite you to the wedding."

"And I'll promise to come if I can. But I hear the bell. I think my friend Dodger has come."

"Shall I ask him in, miss?"

"No. Tell him I will be ready to accompany him at once."

She went out into the hall, and when the door was opened the visitor proved to be Dodger. He had improved his appearance so far as his limited means would allow. His hands and face were thoroughly clean; he had bought a new collar and necktie; his shoes were polished, and despite his shabby suit, he looked quite respectable. Getting a full view of him, Florence saw that his face was frank and handsome, his eyes bright, and his teeth like pearls.

"Shure he's a great deal better lookin' than Mr. Curtis," whispered Jane. "Here, Mr. Dodger, take Miss Florence's valise, and mind you takes good care of her."

"I will," answered Dodger, heartily. "Come, Miss Florence, if you don't mind walking over to Fourth Avenue, we'll take the horse cars."

So, under strange guidance, Florence Linden left her luxurious home, knowing not what awaited her. What haven of refuge she might find she knew not. She, like Dodger, was adrift in New York.

Chapter 8

A FRIENDLY COMPACT

Florence, as she stepped on the sidewalk, turned and fixed a last sad look on the house that had been her home for so many years. She had never anticipated such a sundering of home ties, and even now she found it difficult to realize that the moment had come when her life was to be rent in twain, and the sunlight of prosperity was to be darkened and obscured by a gloomy and uncertain future.

She had hastily packed a few indispensable articles in a valise which she carried in her hand.

"Let me take your bag, Miss Florence," said Dodger, reaching out his hand.

"I don't want to trouble you, Dodger."

"It ain't no trouble, Miss Florence. I'm stronger than you, and it looks better for me to carry it."

"You are very kind, Dodger. What should I do without you?"

"There's plenty that would be glad of the chance of helping you," said Dodger, with a glance of admiration at the fair face of his companion.

"I don't know where to find them," said Florence, sadly. "Even my uncle has turned against me."

"He's an old chump!" ejaculated Dodger, in a tone of disgust.

"Hush! I cannot hear a word against him. He has always been kind and considerate till now. It is the evil influence of my cousin Curtis that has turned him against me. When he comes to himself I am sure he will regret his cruelty."

"He would take you back if you would marry your cousin."

"Yes; but that I will never do!" exclaimed Florence, with energy.

"Bully for you!" said Dodger. "Excuse me," he added, apologetically. "I ain't used to talkin' to young ladies, and perhaps that ain't proper for me to say."

"I don't mind, Dodger; your heart is in the right place."

"Thank you, Miss Florence. I'm glad you've got confidence in me. I'll try to deserve it."

"Where are we going?" asked the young lady, whose only thought up to this moment had been to get away from the presence of Curtis and his persecutions.

They had now reached Fourth Avenue, and a horse car was close at hand.

"We're going to get aboard that car," said Dodger, signaling with his free hand. "I'll tell you more when we're inside."

Florence entered the car, and Dodger, following, took a seat at her side.

They presented a noticeable contrast, for Florence was dressed as beseemed her station, while Dodger, in spite of his manly, attractive face, was roughly attired, and looked like a working boy.

When the conductor came along, he drew out a dime and tendered it in payment of the double fare. The money was in the conductor's hand before Florence was fully aware.

"You must not pay for me, Dodger," she said.

"Why not?" asked the boy, "ain't we friends?"

"Yes, but you have no money to spare. Here, let me return the money."

And she offered him a dime from her own purse.

"You can pay next time, Miss Florence. It's all right. Now, I'll tell you where we are goin'. A friend of mine, Mrs. O'Keefe, has a lodgin' house, just off the Bowery. I saw her last night, and she says she's got a good room that she can give you for two dollars a week—I don't know how much you'd be willing to pay, but—"

"I can pay that for a time at least. I have a little money, and I must find some work to do soon. Is this Mrs. O'Keefe a nice lady?"

"She ain't a lady at all," answered Dodger, bluntly. "She keeps a apple-stand near the corner of Bowery and Grand Street; but she's a good respectable woman, and she's good-hearted. She'll be kind to you, and try to make things pleasant; but if you ain't satisfied—"

"It will do—for the present. Kindness is what I need, driven as I am from the home of my childhood. But you, Dodger, where do you live?"

"I'm goin' to take a small room in the same house, Miss Florence."

"I shall be glad to have you near me."

"I am proud to hear you say that. I'm a poor boy, and you're a rich lady, but—"

"Not rich, Dodger. I am as poor as yourself."

"You're a reg'lar lady, anyway. You ain't one of my kind, but I'm going to improve and raise myself. I was readin' the other day of a rich man that was once a poor boy, and sold papers like me. But there's one thing in the way—I ain't got no eddication."

"You can read and write, can't you, Dodger?"

"Yes; I can read pretty well, but I can't write much."

"I will teach you in the evenings, when we are both at leisure."

"Will you?" asked the boy, with a glad smile. "You're very kind—I'd like a teacher like you."

"Then it's a bargain, Dodger," and Florence's face for the first time lost its sad look, as she saw an opportunity of helping one who had befriended her. "But you must promise to study faithfully."

"That I will. If I don't, I'll give you leave to lick me."

"I shan't forget that," said Florence, amused. "I will buy a ruler of good hard wood, and then you must look out. But, tell me, where have you lived hitherto?"

"I don' like to tell you, Miss Florence. I've lived ever since I was a kid with a man named Tim Bolton. He keeps a saloon on the Bowery, near Houston Street. It's a tough place, I tell you. I've got a bed in one corner—it's tucked away in a closet in the day."

"I suppose it is a drinking saloon?"

"Yes that's what it is."

"And kept open very late?"

"Pretty much all night."

"Is this Tim Bolton any relation of yours?"

"He says he's my uncle; but I don't believe it."

"Have you always lived with him?"

"Ever since I was a small kid."

"Have you always lived in New York?"

"No; I was out in Australia. Tim was out in the country part of the time, and part of the time he kept a saloon in Melbourne. There was thieves and burglars used to come into his place. I knew what they were, though they didn't think I did."

"How terrible for a boy to be subjected to such influences."

"But I've made up my mind I won't live with Tim no longer. I can earn my own livin' sellin' papers, or smashin' baggage, and keep away from Tim. I'd have done it before if I'd had a friend like you to care for me."

"We will stand by each other, Dodger. Heaven knows I need a friend, and if I can be a friend to you, and help you, I will."

"We'll get out here. Miss Florence. I told Mrs. O'Keefe I'd call at her stand, and she'll go over and show you your room."

They left the car at the corner of Grand Street, and Dodger led the way to an apple-stand, presided over by a lady of ample proportions, whose broad, Celtic face seemed to indicate alike shrewd good sense and a kindly spirit.

"Mrs. O'Keefe," said Dodger, "this is the young lady I spoke to you about—Miss Florence Linden."

"It's welcome you are, my dear, and I'm very glad to make your acquaintance. You look like a rale leddy, and I don't know how you'll like the room I've got for you."

"I cannot afford to be particular, Mrs. O'Keefe. I have had a—a reverse of circumstances, and I must be content with a humble home."

"Then I'll go over and show it to you. Here, Kitty, come and mind the stand," she called to a girl about thirteen across the street, "and don't let anybody steal the apples. Look out for Jimmy Mahone, he stole a couple of apples right under my nose this mornin', the young spalpeen!"

As they were crossing the street, a boy of fourteen ran up to Dodger.

"Dodger," said he, "you'd better go right over to Tim Bolton's. He's in an awful stew—says he'll skin you alive if you don't come to the s'loon right away."

Chapter 9

THE NEW HOME

"You can tell Tim Bolton," said Dodger, "That I don't intend to come back at all."

"You don't mean it, Dodger?" said Ben Holt, incredulously.

"Yes, I do. I'm going to set up for myself."

"Oh, Dodger," said Florence, "I'm afraid you will get into trouble for my sake!"

"Don't worry about that, Miss Florence. I'm old enough to take care of myself, and I've got tired of livin' with Tim."

"But he may beat you!"

"He'll have to get hold of me first."

They had reached a four-story tenement of shabby brick, which was evidently well filled up by a miscellaneous crowd of tenants: shop girls, mechanics, laborers and widows, living by their daily toil.

Florence had never visited this part of the city, and her heart sank within her as she followed Mrs. O'Keefe through a dirty hallway, up a rickety staircase, to the second floor.

"One more, flight of stairs, my dear," said Mrs. O'Keefe, encouragingly. "I've got four rooms upstairs; one of them is for you, and one for Dodger."

Florence did not reply. She began to understand at what cost she had secured her freedom from a distasteful marriage.

In her Madison Avenue home all the rooms were light, clean and luxuriously furnished. Here—But words were inadequate to describe the contrast.

Mrs. O'Keefe threw open the door of a back room about twelve feet square, furnished in the plainest manner, uncarpeted, except for a strip that was laid, like a rug, beside the bedstead.

There was a washstand, with a mirror, twelve by fifteen inches, placed above it, a pine bureau, a couple of wooden chairs, and a cane-seated rocking chair.

"There, my dear, what do you say to that?" asked Mrs. O'Keefe, complacently. "All nice and comfortable as you would wish to see."

"It is—very nice," said Florence, faintly, sacrificing truth to politeness.

"And who do you think used to live here?" asked the apple-woman.

"I'm sure I don't know."

"The bearded woman in the dime museum," answered Mrs. O'Keefe, nodding her head. "She lived with me three months, and she furnished the room herself. When she went away she was hard up, and I bought the furniture of her cheap. You remember Madame Berger, don't you, Dodger?"

"Oh, yes, I seen her often."

"She got twenty-five dollars a week, and she'd ought to have saved money, but she had a good-for-nothin' husband that drank up all her hard earnin's."

"I hope she didn't drink herself," said Florence, who shuddered at the idea of succeeding a drunken tenant.

"Not a drop. She was a good, sober lady, if she did work in a dime museum. She only left here two weeks ago. It isn't every one I'd be willin' to take in her place, but I see you're a real leddy, let alone that Dodger recommends you. I hope you'll like the room, and I'll do all I can to make things pleasant. You can go into my room any hour, my dear, and do your little cookin' on my stove. I s'pose you'll do your own cookin'?"

"Well, not just at present," faltered Florence. "I am afraid I don't know much about cooking."

"You'll find it a deal cheaper, and it's more quiet and gentale than goin' to the eatin'-houses. I'll help you all I can, and be glad to do it."

"Thank you, Mrs. O'Keefe, you are very kind," said Florence gratefully. "Perhaps just at first you wouldn't object to taking me as a boarder and letting me take my meals with you. I don't think I would like to go to the eating-houses alone."

"To be sure, my dear, if you wish it, and I'll be glad of your company. I'll make the terms satisfactory."

"I have no doubt of that," said Florence, feeling very much relieved.

"If I might be so bold, what kind of work are you going to do?"

"I hardly know. It has come upon me so suddenly. I shall have to do something, for I haven't got much money. What I should like best would be to write—"

"Is it for the papers you mean?"

"Oh, no, I mean for some author or lawyer."

"I don't know much about that," said Mrs. O'Keefe. "In fact I don't mind tellin' you, my dear, that I can't write meself, but I earn a good livin' all the same by my apple-stand. I tell you, my dear." she continued in a confidential tone, "there is a good dale of profit in sellin' apples. It's better than sewin' or writin'. Of course a young leddy like you wouldn't like to go into the business."

Florence shook her head with a smile.

"No, Mrs. O'Keefe," she said. "I am afraid I haven't a business turn, and I should hardly like so public an employment."

"Lor, miss, it's nothin' if you get used to it. There's nothin' dull about my business, unless it rains, and you get used to havin' people look at you."

"It isn't all that are worth looking at like you, Mrs. O'Keefe," said Dodger, slyly.

"Oh, go away wid your fun, Dodger," said the apple woman, good naturedly. "I ain't much to look at, I know."

"I think there's a good deal of you to look at, Mrs. O'Keefe. You must weigh near three hundred."

"I've a good mind to box your ears, Dodger. I only weigh a hundred and ninety-five. But I can't be bothered wid your jokes. Can you sew, Miss Florence?"

"Yes; but I would rather earn my living some other way, if possible."

"Small blame to you for that. I had a girl in Dodger's room last year who used to sew for a livin'. Early and late she worked, poor thing, and she couldn't make but two dollars a week."

"How could she live?" asked Florence, startled, for she knew very little of the starvation wages paid to toiling women.

"She didn't live. She just faded away, and it's my belief the poor thing didn't get enough to eat. Every day or two I'd make an excuse to take her in something from my own table, a plate of meat, or a bit of toast and a cup of tay, makin' belave she didn't get a chance to cook for herself, but she got thinner and thinner, and her poor cheeks got hollow, and she died in the hospital at last."

The warm-hearted apple-woman wiped away a tear with the corner of her apron, as she thought of the poor girl whose sad fate she described.

"You won't die of consumption, Mrs. O'Keefe," said Dodger. "It'll take a good while for you to fade away."

"Hear him now," said the apple-woman, laughing. "He will have his joke, Miss Florence, but he's a good bye for all that, and I'm glad he's goin' to lave Tim Bolton, that ould thafe of the worruld."

"Now, Mrs. O'Keefe, you know you'd marry Tim if he'd only ask you."

"Marry him, is it? I'd lay my broom over his head if he had the impudence to ask me. When Maggie O'Keefe marries ag'in, she won't marry a man wid a red nose."

"Break it gently to him, Mrs. O'Keefe. Tim is just the man to break his heart for love of you."

Mrs. O'Keefe aimed a blow at Dodger, but he proved true to his name, and skillfully evaded it.

"I must be goin'," he said. "I've got to work or I can't pay room rent when the week comes round."

"What are you going to do, Dodger?" asked Florence.

"It isn't time for the evenin' papers yet, so I shall go round to the piers and see if I can't get a job at smashin' baggage."

"But I shouldn't think any one would want to do that," said Florence, puzzled.

"It's what we boys call it. It's just carryin' valises and bundles. Sometimes I show strangers the way to Broadway. Last week an old man paid me a dollar to show him the way to the Cooper Institute. He was a gentleman, he was. I'd like to meet him ag'in. Good-bye, Miss Florence; I'll be back some time this afternoon."

"And I must be goin', too," said Mrs. O'Keefe. "I can't depend on that Kitty; she's a wild slip of a girl, and just as like as not I'll find a dozen apples stole when I get back. I hope you won't feel lonely, my dear."

"I think I will lie down awhile," said Florence. "I have a headache."

She threw herself on the bed, and a feeling of loneliness and desolation came over her.

Her new friends were kind, but they could not make up to her for her uncle's love, so strangely lost, and the home she had left behind.

Chapter 10

THE ARCH CONSPIRATOR

In the house on Madison Avenue, Curtis Waring was left in possession of the field. Through his machinations Florence had been driven from home and disinherited.

He was left sole heir to his uncle's large property, with the prospect of soon succeeding, for, though only fifty-four, John Linden looked at least ten years older, and was as feeble as many men past seventy.

Yet, as Curtis seated himself at the breakfast table an hour after Florence had left the house, he looked far from happy or triumphant.

One thing he had not succeeded in, the conquest of his cousin's heart. Though he loved himself best, he was really in love with Florence, so far as he was capable of being in love with any one.

She was only half his age—scarcely that—but he persuaded himself that the match was in every way suitable.

He liked to fancy her at the head of his table, after the death of his uncle, which he anticipated in a few months at latest.

The more she appeared to dislike him, the more he determined to marry her, even against her will.

She was the only other one likely to inherit John Linden's wealth, and by marrying her he would make sure of it.

Yet she had been willing to leave the home of her youth, to renounce luxury for a life of poverty, rather than to marry him.

When he thought of this his face became set, and its expression stern and determined.

"Florence shall yet be mine," he declared resolutely. "I will yet be master of her fate, and bend her to my will. Foolish girl, how dare she match her puny strength against the resolute will of Curtis Waring?"

Was there any one else whom she loved? he asked himself anxiously. No, he could think of none. On account of his uncle's chronic invalidism, they had neither gone into society, nor entertained visitors, and in the midst of a great city Florence and her uncle had practically led the lives of recluses.

There had been no opportunity to meet young men who might have proved claimants for her hand.

"When did Miss Florence leave the house, Jane?" he inquired, as he seated himself at the table.

"Most an hour since," the girl answered coldly, for she disliked Curtis as much as she loved and admired Florence.

"It is sad, very sad, that she should be so headstrong," said Curtis, with hypocritical sorrow.

"It is sad for her to go away from her own uncle's house," returned Jane.

"And very—very foolish."

"I don't know about that, sir. She had her reasons," said Jane, significantly.

Curtis coughed.

He had no doubt that Florence had talked over the matter with her hand-maiden.

"Did she say where she was going, Jane?" he asked.

"I don't think the poor child knew herself, sir."

"Did she go alone?"

"No sir; the boy that was here last night called for her."

"That ragamuffin!" said Curtis, scornfully. "She certainly shows extraordinary taste for a young lady of family."

"The boy seems a very kind and respectable boy," said Jane, who had been quite won by Dodger's kindness to her young mistress.

"He may be respectable, though I am not so sure of that; but his position in life is very humble. He is probably a bootblack; a singular person to select for the friend of a girl like Florence."

"There's them that stands higher that isn't half so good," retorted Jane, with more zeal than good grammar.

"Did Miss Florence take a cab?"

"No; she just walked."

"But she took some clothing with her?"

"She took a hand-bag—that is all. She will send for her trunk."

"If you find out where she is living, just let me know, Jane."

"I will if she is willing to have me," answered Jane, independently.

"Look here, Jane," said Curtis, angrily, "don't forget that you are not her servant, but my uncle's. It is to him you look for wages, not to Miss Florence."

"I don't need to be told that, sir. I know that well enough."

"Then you know that it is to him that your faithful services are due, not to Florence?"

"I'm faithful to both, Mr. Waring."

"You are aware that my uncle is justly displeased with my cousin?"

"I know he's displeased, but I am sure he has no good reason to be."

Curtis Waring bit his lips. The girl, servant as she was, seemed to be openly defying him. His imperious temper could ill brook this.

"Take care!" he said with a frown. "You seem to be lacking in respect to me. You don't appear to understand my position in this house."

"Oh, yes, I do. I know you have schemed to get my poor young mistress out of the house, and have succeeded."

"I have a great mind to discharge you, girl," said Curtis, with lowering brow.

"I am not your servant, sir. You have nothing to do with me."

"You will see whether I have or not. I will let you remain for a time, as it is your attachment to Miss Florence that has made you forget yourself. You will find that it is for your interest to treat me respectfully."

A feeble step was heard at the door, and John Linden entered the breakfast room. His face was sad, and he heaved a sigh as he glanced mechanically at the head of the table, where Florence usually sat.

Curtis Waring sprung to his feet, and placing himself at his uncle's side, led him to his seat.

"How do you feel this morning, uncle?" he asked, with feigned solicitude.

"Ill, Curtis. I did not sleep well last night."

"I don't wonder, sir. You had much to try you."

"Is—is Florence here?"

"No, sir," answered Jane, promptly. "She left the house an hour ago."

A look of pain appeared on John Linden's pale face.

"Did—did she leave a message for me?" he asked slowly.

"She asked me to bid you good-bye for her," answered Jane, quickly.

"Uncle, don't let yourself be disturbed now with painful thoughts. Eat your breakfast first, and then we will speak of Florence."

John Linden ate a very light breakfast. He seemed to have lost his appetite, and merely toyed with his food.

When he rose from the table, Curtis supported him to the library.

"It is very painful to me—this conduct of Florence's, Curtis," he said as he sank into his arm-chair.

"I understand it fully, uncle," said Curtis. "When I think of it, it makes me very angry with the misguided girl."

"Perhaps I have been too harsh—too stern!"

"You, uncle, too harsh! Why, you are the soul of gentleness. Florence has shown herself very ungrateful."

"Yet, Curtis, I love that girl. Her mother seemed to live again in her. Have I not acted cruelly in requiring her to obey me or leave the house?"

"You have acted only for good. You are seeking her happiness."

"You really think this, Curtis?"

"I am sure of it."

"But how will it all end?" asked Linden, bending an anxious look upon his wily nephew.

"By Florence yielding."

"You are sure of that?"

"Yes. Listen, uncle; Florence is only capricious, like most girls of her age. She foolishly desires to have her own way. It is nothing more serious, I can assure you."

"But she has left the house. That seems to show that she is in earnest."

"She thinks, uncle, that by doing so she can bend you to her wishes. She hasn't the slightest idea of any permanent separation. She is merely experimenting upon your weakness. She expects you will recall her in a week, at the latest. That is all of it."

Like most weak men, it made Mr. Linden angry to have his strength doubted.

"You think that?" he said.

"I have no doubt of it."

"She shall find that I am resolute," he said, irritably. "I will not re-call her."

"Bravo, uncle! Only stick to that, and she will yield unconditionally within a fortnight. A little patience, and you will carry your point. Then all will be smooth sailing."

"I hope so, Curtis. Your words have cheered me. I will be patient. But I hope I shan't have to wait long. Where is the morning paper?"

"I shall have to humor and deceive him," thought Curtis. "I shall have a difficult part to play, but I am sure to succeed at last."

Chapter 11

FLORENCE SECURES EMPLOYMENT

For a few days after being installed in her new home, Florence was like one dazed.

She could not settle her mind to any plan of self-support.

She was too unhappy in her enforced exile from her home, and it saddened her to think that the uncle who had always been so kind was perhaps permanently estranged from her.

Though Mrs. O'Keefe was kind, and Dodger was her faithful friend, she could not accustom herself to her poor surroundings.

She had not supposed luxury so essential to her happiness.

It was worse for her because she had nothing to do but give way to her morbid fancies.

This Mrs. O'Keefe was clear-sighted enough to see.

"I am sorry to see you so down-cast like, my dear young lady," she said.

"How can I help it, Mrs. O'Keefe?" returned Florence.

"Try not to think of your wicked cousin, my dear."

"It isn't of him that I think—it is of my uncle. How could he be so cruel, and turn against me after years of kindness?"

"It's that wicked Curtis that is settin' him against you, take my word for it, Miss Florence. Shure he must be wake-minded to let such a spalpeen set him against a swate young lady like you."

"He is weak in body, not in mind, Mrs. O'Keefe. You are right in thinking that it is Curtis that is the cause of my misfortunes."

"Your uncle will come to his right mind some day, never fear! And now, my dear, shall I give you a bit of advice?"

"Go on, my kind friend. I will promise to consider whatever you say."

"Then you'd better get some kind of work to take up your mind—a bit of sewin' or writin' or anything that comes to hand. I suppose you wouldn't want to mind my apple-stand a couple of hours every day?"

"No," answered Florence. "I don't feel equal to that."

"It would do you no end of good to be out in the open air. It would bring back the roses to your pale cheeks. If you coop yourself up in this dark room, you'll fade away and get thin."

"You are right. I will make an effort and go out. Besides, I must see about work?"

Here Dodger entered the room in his usual breezy way.

In his hand he brandished a morning paper.

"How are you feelin', Florence?" he asked; he had given up saying Miss Florence at her request. "Here's an advertisement that'll maybe suit you."

"Show it to me, Dodger," said Florence, beginning to show some interest.

The boy directed her attention to the following advertisement:

"WANTED.—A governess for a girl of twelve. Must be a good performer on the piano, and able to instruct in French and the usual English branches. Terms must be moderate. Apply to Mrs. Leighton, at 127 W—— Street."

"There, Florence, what do you say to that? That's better than sewin'."

"I don't know, Dodger, whether I am competent."

"You play on the pianner, don't you?"

"Yes."

"Well enough to teach?"

"I think so; but I may not have the gift of teaching."

"Yes, you have. Haven't you been teachin' me every evenin'? You make everything just as clear as mud—no, I don't mean that. You just explain so that I can't help understandin'."

"Then," said Florence, "I suppose I am at liberty to refer to you?"

"Yes; you can tell the lady to call at the office of Dodger, Esq., any mornin' after sunrise, and he'll give her full particulars."

Florence did not immediately decide to apply for the situation, but the more she thought of it the more she felt inclined to do so. The little experience she had had with Dodger satisfied her that she should enjoy teaching better than sewing or writing.

Accordingly, an hour later she put on her street dress and went up-town to the address given in the advertisement.

No. 127 was a handsome, brown-stone house, not unlike the one in which Florence had been accustomed to live. It was a refreshing contrast to the poor tenement in which she lived at present.

"Is Mrs. Leighton at home?" inquired Florence.

"Yes, miss," answered the servant, respectfully. "Whom shall I say?"

"I have come to apply for the situation of governess," answered Florence, feeling rather awkward as she made the statement.

"Ah," said the servant, with a perceptible decline in respect. "Won't you step in?"

"Thank you."

"Well, she do dress fine for a governess," said Nancy to herself. "It's likely she'll put on airs."

The fact was that Florence was dressed according to her past social position—in a costly street attire—but it had never occurred to her that she was too well dressed for a governess.

She took her seat in the drawing-room, and five minutes later there was a rustling heard, and Mrs. Leighton walked into the room.

"Are you the applicant for the position of governess?" she asked, surveying the elegantly-attired young lady seated on the sofa.

"Yes, Mrs. Leighton," answered Florence, easily, for she felt more at home in a house like this than in the tenement.

"Have you taught before?"

"Very little," answered Florence, smiling to herself, as she wondered what Mrs. Leighton would say if she could see Dodger, the only pupil she ever had. "However, I like teaching, and I like children."

"Pardon me, but you don't look like a governess, Miss——"

"Linden," suggested Florence, filling out the sentence. "Do governesses have a peculiar look?"

"I mean as to dress. You are more expensively dressed than the average governess can afford."

"It is only lately that my circumstances have required me to support myself. I should not be able to buy such a dress out of my present earnings."

"I am glad to hear you say that, for I do not propose to give a large salary."

"I do not expect one," said Florence, quietly.

"You consider yourself competent to instruct in music, French and the English branches?"

"Oh, yes."

"Do you speak French?"

"Yes, madam."

"Would you favor me with a specimen of your piano playing?"

There was a piano in the back parlor. Florence removed her gloves, and taking a seat before it, dashed into a spirited selection from Strauss.

Mrs. Leighton listened with surprised approval.

"Certainly you are a fine performer," she said. "What—if I should engage you—would you expect in the way of compensation?"

"How much time would you expect me to give?"

"Three hours daily—from nine to twelve."

"I hardly know what to say. What did you expect to pay?"

"About fifty cents an hour."

Florence knew very well, from the sums that had been paid for her own education, that this was miserably small pay; but it was much more than she could earn by sewing.

"I will teach a month on those terms," she said after a pause.

Mrs. Leighton looked well pleased. She knew that she was making a great bargain.

"Oh, by the way," she said, "can you give references?"

"I can refer to Madame Morrison," naming the head of a celebrated female seminary. "She educated me."

"That will be quite satisfactory," said Mrs. Leighton, graciously. "Can you begin to-morrow?"

"Yes, madam."

"You will then see your pupil. At present she is out."

Florence bowed and withdrew.

She had been afraid Mrs. Leighton would inquire where she lived, and she would hardly have dared to name the humble street which she called home.

She walked toward Fifth Avenue, when, just as she was turning the corner, she met Mr. Percy de Brabazon, swinging a slender cane, and dressed in the extreme of the fashion.

"Miss Linden!" he exclaimed eagerly. "This is—aw—indeed a pleasure. Where are you walking this fine morning? May I—aw—have the pleasure of accompanying you?"

Florence stopped short in deep embarrassment.

Chapter 12

A FRIEND, THOUGH A DUDE

Percy de Brabazon looked sincerely glad to meet Florence, and she herself felt some pleasure in meeting one who reminded her of her former life.

But it was quite impossible that she should allow him to accompany her to her poor home on the east side.

"Thank you, Mr. de Brabazon, but my engagements this morning will hardly permit me to accept your escort," she said.

"I suppose that means that you are going shopping; but I don't mind it, I assure you, and I will carry your bundles," he added, magnanimously.

"That would never do. What! the fashionable Mr. de Brabazon carrying bundles? You would lose your social status."

"I don't mind, Miss Florence, as long as you give me—aw—an approving smile."

"I will give it now, as I bid you good-morning."

"May I—aw—have the pleasure of calling upon you to-morrow evening, Miss Linden?"

"It is evident that you have not heard that I am no longer residing with my uncle."

Mr. de Brabazon looked surprised.

"No, I had not heard. May I ask—aw—where you are wesiding?"

"With friends," answered Florence briefly. "As you are a friend, and will be likely to hear it, I may as well mention that my uncle is displeased with me, and has practically disowned me."

"Then, Miss Florence," said de Brabazon, eagerly, "won't you accept—aw—my heart and hand? My mother will be charmed to receive you, and I—aw—will strive to make you happy."

"I appreciate your devotion, I do, indeed, Mr. de Brabazon," said Florence, earnestly; "but I must decline your offer. I will not marry without love."

"I don't mind that," said Percy, "if you'll agree to take a feller; you'll learn in time to like him a little. I am wich—I know you don't care for that—but I can give you as good a home as your uncle. If you would give me hope—aw—"

"I am afraid I cannot, Mr. de Brabazon, but if you will allow me to look upon you as a friend, I will call upon you if I have need of a friend's services."

"Will you weally?"

"Yes, there is my hand on it. I ought to tell you that I must now earn my own living, and am to give lessons to a young pupil in West ——street, three hours daily."

"You don't mean to say you are actually poor?" said Mr. de Brabazon, horrified.

"Yes, indeed, I am."

"Then, won't you let me lend you some money? I've got more than I need, I have 'pon honor."

"Thank you, I promise to call upon you if I need it."

Mr. de Brabazon looked pleased.

"Would you mind telling where you are going to teach, Miss Florence?"

Florence hesitated, but there was something so sincere and friendly in the young man's manner—dude though he was—that she consented to grant his request.

"I am to teach the daughter of Mr. Robert Leighton."

"Why, Miss Leighton is my cousin," said Percy, in joyous excitement.

"Indeed! Had I known that I would hardly have told you."

"Don't be afwaid! I will be vewy discreet."

"Thank you, and good-morning."

Florence went on her way, cheered and encouraged in spite of herself, by her success in obtaining employment, and by the friendly offers of Mr. de Brabazon.

"It is wrong to get discouraged," she said to herself. "After all, there are warm hearts in the world."

When she entered her humble home, she found Dodger already there. There was an eagerness in his manner, and a light in his eye, that seemed to indicate good news.

"I've been waitin' half an hour to see you, Florence," he said.

"Well, Dodger, what is it?"

"I've got some work for you."

"What is it—sewing on a button, or mending a coat?"

"No, I mean workin' for money. You can play on the pianner, can't you?"

"Yes."

"They want a young lady to play the pianner at a dime museum, for nine dollars a week. It's a bully chance. I just told the manager—

he's a friend of mine—that I had a young lady friend that was a stun-
nin' player, and he wants you to come around and see him."

It was a preposterous idea—so Florence thought—that she should
consent to play at such a place; but she couldn't expect Dodger to
look at the matter in the same light, so she answered pleasantly:

"You are very kind, Dodger, to look out for me, but I shall not need
to accept your friend's offer. I have secured a chance to teach up-
town."

"You have? What'll you get?"

"I am to be employed three hours daily, at fifty cents an hour."

"Geewhillikens! that's good! You'd have to work as much as twelve
hours at the museum for the same pay."

"You see, therefore, that I am provided for—that is, if I suit."

Dodger was a little disappointed. Still, he could not help admitting
that it would be better for Florence to teach three hours, than to work
ten or twelve. As to her having any objection to appearing at a dime
museum, that never occurred to him.

Florence had sent for her trunk, and it was now in her room.

Dodger accompanied an expressman to the house, and luckily saw
Jane, who arranged everything for him.

"How's the old gentleman?" asked Dodger. "Florence wanted me to
ask."

"He's feeble," said Jane, shaking her head.

"Does he miss Florence?"

"That he do."

"Why don't he send for her, then, to come back?" asked Dodger,
bluntly.

"Because Curtis Waring makes him believe she'll come round and
ask forgiveness, if he only holds out. I tell you, Dodger, that Curtis is
a viper."

"So he is," answered Dodger, who was not quite clear in his mind
as to what a viper was. "I'd like to step on his necktie."

"If it wasn't for him, my dear young mistress would be back in the
house within twenty-four hours."

"I don't see how the old gentleman can let him turn Florence out of
the house."

"He's a snake in the grass, Dodger. It may be wicked, but I just
wish something would happen to him. And how is Miss Florence lookin', poor dear?"

"She's lookin' like a daisy."

"Does she worry much?"

"She did at first, but now she's workin' every day, and she looks
more cheerful like."

"Miss Florence workin'! She that was always brought up like a lady?"

"She's teachin' a little girl three hours a day."

"Well, that isn't so bad!" said Jane, relieved. "Teachin' is genteel. I wish I could see her some day. Will you tell her, Dodger, that next Sunday is my day out, and I'll be in Central Park up by the menagerie at three o'clock, if she'll only take the trouble to be up there?"

"I'll tell her, Jane, and I'm sure she'll be there."

A day or two afterward Curtis Waring asked:

"Have you heard from my cousin Florence since she went away?"

"Yes, sir."

"Indeed! Where is she staying?"

"She didn't send me word."

"How, then, did you hear from her?"

"Dodger came with an expressman for her trunk."

Curtis Waring frowned.

"And you let him have it?" he demanded, sternly.

"Of course I did. Why shouldn't I?"

"You should have asked me."

"And what business have you with Miss Florence's trunk, I'd like to know?" said Jane, independently.

"Never mind; you ought to have asked my permission."

"I didn't think you'd want to wear any of Miss Florence's things, Mr. Waring."

"You are silly and impertinent!" said Curtis, biting his lips. "Did that boy tell you anything about her?"

"Only that she wasn't worryin' any for you, Mr. Curtis."

Curtis glared angrily at his cousin's devoted friend, and then, turning on his heel, left the room.

"I'll bring her to terms yet!" he muttered. "No girl of seventeen shall defy me!"

Chapter 13

TIM BOLTON'S SALOON

Not far from Houston Street, on the west side of the Bowery, is an underground saloon, with whose proprietor we are already acquainted.

It was kept by Tim Bolton, whose peculiar tastes and shady characteristics well fitted him for such a business.

It was early evening, and the gas-jets lighted up a characteristic scene.

On the sanded floor were set several tables, around which were seated a motley company, all of them with glasses of beer or whisky before them.

Tim, with a white apron, was moving about behind the bar, ministering to the wants of his patrons. There was a scowl upon his face, for he was not fond of work, and he missed Dodger's assistance.

The boy understood the business of mixing drinks as well as he, and often officiated for hours at a time, thus giving his guardian and reputed father a chance to leave the place and meet outside engagements.

A tall, erect gentleman entered the saloon and walked up to the bar.

"Good-evening, colonel," said Tim.

"Good-evening, sir," said the new-comer, with a stately inclination of the head.

He was really a colonel, having served in the Civil War at the head of a Georgia regiment.

He had all the stately courtesy of a Southern gentleman, though not above the weakness of a frequent indulgence in the strongest fluids dispensed by Tim Bolton.

"What'll you have, colonel?"

"Whisky straight, sir. It's the only drink fit for a gentleman. Will you join me, Mr. Bolton?"

"Of course I will," said Tim, as, pouring out a glass for himself, he handed the bottle to the colonel.

"Your health, sir," said the colonel, bowing.

"Same to you, colonel," responded Tim, with a nod.

"Where is the boy?"

Colonel Martin had always taken considerable notice of Dodger, being naturally fond of boys, and having once had a son of his own, who was killed in a railroad accident when about Dodger's age.

"Danged if I know!" aswered Tim, crossly.

"He hasn't left you, has he?"

"Yes, he's cleared out, the ungrateful young imp! I'd like to lay my hands on the young rascal."

"Was he your son?"

"He was my—stepson," answered Tim, hesitating.

"I see, you married his mother."

"Yes," said Tim, considering the explanation satisfactory, and re-solved to adopt it. "I've always treated him as if he was my own flesh and blood, and I've raised him from a young kid. Now he's gone and left me."

"Can you think of any reason for his leaving you?"

"Not one. I always treated him well. He's been a great expense to me, and now he's got old enough to help me he must clear out. He's the most ungratefullest cub I ever seen."

"I am sorry he has gone—I used to like to have him serve me."

"And now what's the consequence? Here I am tied down to the bar day and night."

"Can't you get some one in his place?"

"Yes, but I'd likely be robbed; I had a bartender once who robbed me of two or three dollars a day."

"But you trusted the boy?"

"Yes, Dodger wouldn't steal—I can say that much for him."

"There's one thing I noticed about the boy," said the colonel, reflectively. "He wouldn't drink. More than once I have asked him to drink with me, but he would always say, 'Thank you, colonel, but I don't like whisky.' I never asked him to take anything else, for whisky's the only drink fit for a gentleman. Do you expect to get the boy back?"

"If I could only get out for a day I'd hunt him up; but I'm tied down here."

"I seed him yesterday, Tim," said a red-nosed man, who had just entered the saloon, in company with a friend of the same general appearance. Both wore silk hats, dented and soiled with stains of dirt, coats long since superannuated, and wore the general look of bar-room loafers.

They seldom had any money, but lay in wait for any liberal strang-er, in the hope of securing a free drink.

"Where did you see him, Hooker?" asked Tim Bolton, with sudden interest.

"Sellin' papers down by the Astor House."

"Think of that, colonel!" said Tim, disgusted. "Becomin' a common newsboy when he might be in a genteel employment! Did you speak to him, Hooker?"

"Yes, I asked him if he had left you."

"What did he say?"

"That he had left you for good—that he was going to grow up respectable!"

"Think of that!" said Tim, with renewed disgust. "Did he say where he lived?"

"No."

"Did he ask after me?"

"No, except he said that you was no relation of his. He said he expected you stole him when he was a kid, and he hoped some time to find his relations."

Tim Bolton's face changed color, and he was evidently disturbed. Could the boy have heard anything, he wondered, for his suspicions were very near the truth?

"It's all nonsense!" he said, roughly. "Next time you see him, Hooker, foller him home, and find out where he lives."

"All right, Tim. It ought to be worth something," he insinuated, with a husky cough.

"That's so. What'll you take?"

"Whisky," answered Hooker, with a look of pleased anticipation.

"You're a gentleman, Tim," he said, as he gulped down the contents of a glass without winking.

Briggs, his dilapidated companion, had been looking on in thirsty envy.

"I'll help Hooker look for Dodger," he said.

"Very well, Briggs."

"Couldn't you stand a glass for me, too, Tim?"

"No," answered Bolton, irritably. "I've been at enough expense for that young rascal already."

But the colonel noticed the pathetic look of disappointment on the face of Briggs, and he was stirred to compassion.

"Drink with me, sir," he said, turning to the overjoyed Briggs.

"Thank you, colonel. You're a gentleman!"

"Two glasses, Tim."

So the colonel drained a second glass, and Briggs, pouring out with trembling fingers as much as he dared, followed suit.

When the last drop was drunk, he breathed a deep sigh of measureless enjoyment.

"If either of you bring that boy in here," said Tim, "I'll stand a couple of glasses for both."

"We're your men, Tim," said Hooker. "Ain't we, Briggs?"

"That's so, Hooker. Shake!"

And the poor victims of drink shook hands energetically. Long since they had sunk their manhood in the intoxicating cup, and henceforth lived only to gratify their unnatural craving for what would sooner or later bring them to a drunkard's grave.

As they left the saloon, the colonel turned to Tim, and said:

"I like whisky, sir; but I'll be hanged if I can respect such men as those."

"They're bums, colonel, that's what they are!"

"How do they live?"

"Don't know. They're in here about every day."

"If it's drink that's brought them where they are, I'm half inclined to give it up; but after all, it isn't necessary to make a beast of yourself. I always drink like a gentleman, sir."

"So you do, colonel."

At this moment a poor woman, in a faded calico dress, with a thin shawl over her shoulders, descended the steps that led into the saloon, and walked up to the bar.

"Has my husband been here to-night?" she asked.

Tim Bolton frowned.

"Who's your husband?" he asked, roughly.

"Wilson."

"No, Bill Wilson hasn't been here to-night. Even if he had you have no business to come after him. I don't want any sniveling women here."

"I couldn't help it, Mr. Bolton," said the woman, putting her apron to her eyes. "If Bill comes in, won't you tell him to come home? The baby's dead, and we haven't a cent in the house!"

Even Tim was moved by this.

"I'll tell him," he said. "Take a drink yourself; you don't look strong. It shan't cost you a cent."

"No," said the woman, "not a drop! It has ruined my happiness, and broken up our home! Not a drop!"

"Here, my good lady," said the colonel, with chivalrous deference, "you have no money. Take this," and he handed the astonished woman a five-dollar bill.

"Heaven bless you, sir!" she exclaimed, fervently.

"Allow me to see you to the street," and the gallant Southern gentleman escorted her up to the sidewalk.

"I'd like to horsewhip that woman's husband. Don't you sell him another drop!" he said, as he returned.

Chapter 14

THE MISSING WILL

An hour after the departure of the colonel there was an unexpected arrival.

A well-dressed gentleman descended the stairs gingerly, looked about him with fastidious disdain, and walked up to the bar.

Tim Bolton was filling an order, and did not immediately observe him.

When at length he turned round he exclaimed in some surprise:

"Mr. Waring!"

"Yes, Bolton, I have found my way here."

"I have been expecting you."

"I came to you for some information."

"Well, ask your questions. I don't know whether I can answer them."

"First, where's my cousin Florence?"

"How should I know? She wasn't likely to place herself under my protection."

"She's with that boy of yours—Dodger, I believe you call him. Where is he?"

"Run away," answered Bolton, briefly.

"Do you mean that you don't know where he is?"

"Yes, I do mean that. I haven't set eyes on him since that night."

"What do you mean by such negligence? Do you remember who he is?"

"Certainly I do."

"Then why do you let him get out of your reach?"

"How could I help it? Here I am tied down to this bar day and night! I'm nearly dead for want of sleep."

"It would be better to close up your place for a week and look for him."

"Couldn't do it. I should lose all my trade. People would say I was closed up."

"And have you done nothing toward his recovery?"

"Yes, I have sent out two men in search of him."

"Have you any idea where he is, or what he is doing?"

"Yes, he has been seen in front of the Astor House, selling papers. I have authorized my agent, if he sees him again, to follow him home, and find out where he lives."

"That is good! Astor House? I may see him myself."

"But why do you want to see him? Do you want to restore him to his rights?"

"Hush!" said Curtis, glancing around him apprehensively. "What we say may be overheard and excite suspicions. One thing may be secured by finding him—the knowledge of Florence's whereabouts."

"What makes you think she and the boy are together?"

"He came for her trunk. I was away from home, or I would not have let it go—"

"It is strange that they two are together, considering their relationship."

"That is what I am afraid they will find out. She may tell him of the mysterious disappearance of her cousin, and he—"

"That reminds me," interrupted Bolton. "He told Hooker—Hooker was the man that saw him in front of the Astor House—that he didn't believe I was his father. He said he thought I must have stolen him when he was a young kid."

"Did he say that?" asked Curtis, in evident alarm.

"Yes, so Hooker says."

"If he has that idea in his head, he may put two and two together and guess that he is the long-lost cousin of Florence. Tim, that boy must be got rid of."

"If you mean what I think you do, Mr. Waring, I'm not with you. I won't consent to harm the boy."

"You said that before. I don't mean anything that will shock your tender heart, Bolton," said Curtis, with a sneer. "I mean carried to a distance—Europe or Australia, for instance. All I want is to keep him out of New York till my uncle is dead. After that I don't care what becomes of him."

"That's better. I've no objection to that. How is the old gentleman?"

"He grieved so much at first over the girl's loss, that I feared he would insist on her being recalled at once. I soothed him by telling him that he had only to remain firm, and she would come round, and yield to his wishes."

"Do you think she will?" asked Tim, doubtfully.

"I intend that she shall!" said Curtis, significantly. "Bolton, I love that girl all the more for her obstinate refusal to wed me. I have made up my mind to marry her with her consent, or without it."

"I thought it was only the estate you were after?"

"I want the estate, and her with it. Mark my words, Bolton, I will have both!"

"You will have the estate, no doubt; Mr. Linden has made his will in your favor, has he not?" and Bolton looked intently in the face of his visitor.

"Hark you, Bolton, there is a mystery I cannot fathom. My uncle made two wills. In the earlier, he left the estate to Florence and myself, if we married, otherwise, to me alone."

"That is satisfactory."

"Yes, but there was another, in which the estate goes to his son, if living. That will has disappeared."

"Is it possible?" asked Bolton, in astonishment. "When was it missed?"

"On the night of the burglary."

"Then you think—"

"That the boy, Dodger, has it. Good heaven! if he only knew that by this will the estate goes to him!" and Waring wiped the perspiration from his brow.

"You are sure that he did not give you the will?" he demanded, eyeing Bolton sharply.

"I have not seen him since the night of the robbery."

"If he has read the will, it may lead to dangerous suspicions."

"He would give it to your cousin, Florence, would he not?"

"Perhaps so. Bolton, you must get the boy back, and take the will from him, if you can."

"I will do my best; but you must remember that Dodger is no longer a small kid. He is a boy of eighteen, strong and well-grown. He wouldn't be easy to manage. Besides, as long as he doesn't know that he has any interest in the will, his holding it won't do any harm. Is the old gentleman likely to live long?"

"I don't know. I sometimes hope—Pshaw! why should I play the hypocrite when speaking to you? Surely it is no sin to wish him better off, since he can't enjoy life!"

"He might if Florence and his son were restored to him."

"What do you mean, Bolton?" asked Curtis, suspiciously.

"What could I mean? It merely occurred to me," said Bolton, innocently. "You say he is quiet, thinkin' the girl will come round?"

"Yes."

"Suppose time passes, and she doesn't? Won't he try to find her? As she is in the city, that won't be hard."

"I shall represent that she has left the city."

"For any particular point?"

"No, that is not necessary."

"And then?"

"If he worries himself into the grave, so much the better for me."

"There is no half way about you, Mr. Waring."

"Why should there be? Listen, Bolton; I have set my all on this cast. I am now thirty-six, and still I am dependent upon my uncle's bounty. I am in debt, and some of my creditors are disposed to trouble me. My uncle is worth—I don't know how much, but I think half a million. What does he get out of it? Food and clothes, but not happiness. If it were mine, all the avenues of enjoyment would be open to me. That estate I must have."

"Suppose you get it, what is there for me?" asked Bolton.

"I will see that you are recompensed if you help me to it."

"Will you put that in writing?"

"Do you take me for a fool? To put it in writing would be to place me in your power! You can trust me."

"Well, perhaps so," said Tim Bolton, slowly.

"At any rate, you will have to. Well, good-night. I will see you again soon. In the meantime, try to find the boy."

Tim Bolton followed him with his eyes, as he left the saloon.

"What would he say," said Bolton to himself, "if he knew that the will he so much wishes to find is in my hands, and that I hold him in my power already?"

Chapter 15

FIRST EXPERIENCES AS A GOVERNESS

"Wish me luck, Dodger!"

"So I do, Florence. Are you goin' to begin teachin' this mornin'?"

"Yes; and I hope to produce a favorable impression. It is very important to me to please Mrs. Leighton and my future pupil."

"I'm sure you'll suit. How nice you look!"

Florence smiled and looked pleased. She had taken pains with her dress and personal appearance, and, being luckily well provided with handsome dresses, had no difficulty in making herself presentable. As she stepped out of the shabby doorway upon the sidewalk no one supposed her to be a tenant, but she was generally thought to be a visitor, perhaps the agent of some charitable association.

"Perhaps all will not judge me as favorably as you do, Dodger," said Florence, with a laugh.

"If you have the headache any day, Florence, I'll take your place."

"You would look rather young for a tutor, Dodger, and I am afraid you would not be dignified. Good-morning! I shall be back to dinner."

"I am glad to find you punctual, Miss Linden," said Mrs. Leighton, graciously, as Florence was ushered into her presence. "This is your future pupil, my daughter Carrie."

Florence smiled and extended her hand.

"I hope we shall like each other," she said.

The little girl eyed her with approval. This beautiful young lady was a pleasant surprise to her, for, never having had a governess, she expected to meet a stiff, elderly lady, of stern aspect. She readily gave her hand to Florence, and looked relieved.

"Carrie," said Mrs. Leighton, "you may show Miss Linden the way to the schoolroom."

"All right, mamma," and the little girl led the way up-stairs to a back room on the third floor.

"So this is to be our school-room, is it, Carrie?" said Florence. "It is a very pleasant room."

"Yes; but I should have preferred the front chamber. Mamma thought that I might be looking into the street too much. Here there is only a backyard, and nothing to look at."

"Your mamma seems very judicious," said Florence, smiling. "Are you fond of study?"

"Well, I ain't exactly fond, but I will do my best."

"That is all that can be expected."

"Do you know, Miss Linden, you don't look at all like what I expected."

"Am I to be glad or sorry for that?"

"I thought you would be an old maid, stiff and starched, like May Robinson's governess."

"I am not married, Carrie, so perhaps you may regard me as an old maid."

"You'll never be an old maid," said Carrie, confidently. "You are too young and pretty."

"Thank you, Carrie," said Florence, with a little blush. "You say that, I hope, because you are going to like me."

"I like you already," said the little girl, impulsively. "I've a cousin that will like you, too."

"A young girl?"

"No; of course not. He is a young man. His name is Percy de Bra-bazon. It is a funny name, isn't it? You see, his father was a French-man."

Florence was glad that she already knew from Percy's own mouth of the relationship, as it saved her from showing a degree of surprise that might have betrayed her acquaintance with the young man.

"What makes you think your cousin would like me, Carrie?"

"Because he always likes pretty girls. He is a masher."

"That's slang, Carrie. I am sure your mamma wouldn't approve your using such a word."

"Don't tell her. It just slipped out. But about Percy—he wants very much to be married."

Florence was not surprised to hear this, for she had the best reason for knowing it to be true.

"Is he a handsome young man?" she asked, demurely.

"He's funny looking. He's awful good-natured, but he isn't the sort of young man I would like," concluded Carrie, with amusing positive-ness.

"I hope you don't let your mind run on such things. You are quite too young."

"Oh, I don't think much about it. But Percy is a dude. He spends a sight for clothes. He always looks as if he had just come out of a bandbox."

"Is he in any business?"

"No; he has an independent fortune, so mamma says. He was in Europe last year."

"I think, Carrie, we must give up talking and attend to business. I should have checked you before, but I thought a little conversation would help us to get acquainted. Now show me your books and I will assign your lessons."

"Don't give me too long lessons, please, Miss Linden."

"I will take care not to task you beyond your strength. I don't want my pupil to grow sick on my hands."

"I hope you won't be too strict. When May Robinson makes two mis-takes her governess makes her learn her lessons over again."

"I will promise not to be too strict. Now let me see your books."

The rest of the forenoon was devoted to study.

Florence was not only an excellent scholar, but she had the art of imparting knowledge, and, what is very important, she was able in a few luminous words to explain difficulties and make clear what seemed to her pupil obscure.

So the time slipped quickly and pleasantly away, and it was noon before either she or her pupil realized it.

"It can't be twelve," said Carrie, surprised.

"Yes, it is. We must defer further study till to-morrow."

"Why, it is a great deal pleasanter than going to school, Miss Linden. I dreaded studying at home, but now I like it."

"I hope you will continue to, Carrie. I can say that the time has passed away very pleasantly for me."

As Florence prepared to resume her street-dress, Carrie said:

"Oh, I forgot! Mamma asked me to invite you to stay to lunch with me. I take lunch as soon as school is out, at twelve o'clock, so I won't detain you long."

"Thank you, Carrie; I will stay with pleasure."

"I am glad of that, for I don't like to sit down to the table alone. Mamma is never here at this time. She goes out shopping or making calls, so poor I have to sit down to the table alone. It will be ever so much pleasanter to have you with me."

Florence was by no means sorry to accept the invitation.

The meals she got at home were by no means luxurious, and the manner of serving them was by no means what she enjoyed.

Mrs. O'Keefe, though a good friend and kind-hearted woman, was not a model housekeeper, and Florence had been made fastidious by her early training. Lunch was, of course, a plain meal, but what was furnished was of the best quality, and her table service was such as might be expected in a luxurious home.

Just as Florence was rising from the table, Mrs. Leighton entered the room in street dress.

"I am glad you remained to lunch, Miss Linden," she said. "You will be company for my little girl, who is very sociable. Carrie, I hope you were a good girl and gave Miss Linden no trouble."

"Ask Miss Linden, mamma," said Carrie, confidently.

"Indeed, she did very well," said Florence. "I foresee that we shall get along admirably."

"I am glad to hear that. She is apt to be indolent."

"I won't be with Miss Linden, mamma. She makes the studies so interesting."

After Florence left the house, Carrie pronounced an eulogium upon her which led Mrs. Leighton to congratulate herself upon having secured a governess who had produced so favorable an impression on her little girl.

"Was you kept after school, Florence?" asked Dodger, as she entered her humble home. "I am afraid you'll find your dinner cold."

"Never mind, Dodger. I am to take dinner—or lunch, rather—at the house where I am teaching; so hereafter Mrs. O'Keefe need not wait for me."

"And how do you like your place?"

"It is everything that is pleasant. You wished me good luck,

Dodger, and your wish has been granted."

"I was lucky, too, Florence. I've made a dollar and a quarter this mornin'."

"Not by selling papers, surely?"

"Not all. A gentleman gave me fifty cents for takin' his valise to the Long Branch boat."

"It seems we are both getting rich," said Florence, smiling.

Chapter 16

DODGER BECOMES AMBITIOUS

"Ah, there, Dodger!"

Dodger, who had been busily and successfully selling evening papers in front of the Astor House, turned quickly as he heard his name called.

His glance rested on two men, dressed in soiled white hats and shabby suits, who were apparently holding each other up, having both been imbibing.

He at once recognized Hooker and Briggs, for he had waited upon them too many times in Tim's saloon not to recognize them.

"Well," he said, cautiously, "what do you want?"

"Tim has sent us for you!" answered the two, in unison.

"What does he want of me?"

"He wants you to come home. He says he can't get along without you."

"He will have to get along without me," said the boy, independently. "Tell him I'm not goin' back!"

"You're wrong, Dodger," said Hooker, shaking his head, solemnly. "Ain't he your father?"

"No, he ain't."

"He says he is," continued Hooker, looking puzzled.

"That don't make it so."

"He ought to know," put in Briggs.

"Yes; he ought to know!" chimed in Hooker.

"No doubt he does, but he can't make me believe he's any relation of mine."

"Just go and argy the point with him," said Hooker coaxingly.

"It wouldn't do no good."

"Maybe it would. Just go back with us, that's a good boy."

"What makes you so anxious about it?" asked Dodger, suspiciously.

"Well," said Hooker, coughing, "we're Tim's friends, don't you know."

"What's he goin' to give you if I go back with you?" asked the boy, shrewdly.

"A glass of whisky!" replied Hooker and Briggs, in unison.

"Is that all?"

"Maybe he'd make it two."

"I won't go back with you," said Dodger, after a moment's thought; "but I don't want you to lose anything by me. Here's a dime apiece, and you can go and get a drink somewhere else."

"You're a trump, Dodger," said Hooker, eagerly, holding out his hand.

"I always liked you, Dodger," said Briggs, with a similar motion.

"Now, don't let Tim know you've seen me," said the newsboy, warningly.

"We won't."

And the interesting pair ambled off in the direction of the Bowery.

"So Tim's sent them fellers after me?" soliloquized Dodger. "I guess I'll have to change my office, or maybe Tim himself will be droppin' down on me some mornin'. It'll be harder to get rid of him than of them chumps."

So it happened that he used to take down his morning papers to the piers on the North River, and take his chance of selling them to passengers from Boston and other ports arriving by the Fall River boats, and others from different points.

The advantage of this was that he often got a chance to serve as guide to strangers visiting the city for the first time, or as porter, to carry their valises or other luggage.

Being a bright, wide-awake boy, with a pleasant face and manner, he found his service considerably in demand; and on counting up his money at the end of the first week, he found, much to his encouragement, that he had received on an average about a dollar and twenty-five cents per day.

"That's better than sellin' papers alone," thought he. "Besides, Tim isn't likely to come across me here. I wonder I didn't think of settin' up for myself before!"

In the evening he spent an hour, and sometimes more, pursuing his studies, under the direction of Florence. At first his attention was given chiefly to improving his reading and spelling, for Dodger was far from fluent in the first, while his style of spelling many words was strikingly original.

"Ain't I stupid, Florence?" he asked one day, after spelling a word of three syllables with such ingenious incorrectness as to convulse his young teacher with merriment.

"Not at all, Dodger. You are making excellent progress; but sometimes you are so droll that I can't help laughing."

"I don't mind that if you think I am really gettin' on."

"Undoubtedly you are!"

"I make a great many mistakes," said Dodger, dubiously.

"Yes, you do; but you must remember that you have taken lessons only a short time. Don't you think you can read a good deal more easily than you did?"

"Yes; I don't trip up half so often as I did. I'm afraid you'll get tired of teachin' me."

"No fear of that, Dodger. As long as I see that you are improving, I shall feel encouraged to go on."

"I wish I knew as much as your other scholar."

"You will in time if you go on. You mustn't get discouraged."

"I won't!" said Dodger, stoutly. "If a little gal like her can learn, I'd ought to be ashamed if I don't—a big boy of eighteen."

"It isn't the size of the boy that counts, Dodger."

"I know that, but I ain't goin' to give in and let a little gal get ahead of me!"

"Keep to that determination, Dodger, and you will succeed in time, never fear."

On the whole, Florence enjoyed both her pupils. She had the faculty of teaching and she became very much interested in both.

As for Dodger, she thought, rough diamond as he was, that she saw in him the making of a manly man, and she felt that it was a privilege to assist in the development of his intellectual nature.

Again, he had picked up a good deal of slang from the nature of his associates, and she set to work to improve his language, and teach him refinement.

It was necessarily a slow process, but she began to find after a time that a gradual change was coming over him.

"I want you to grow up a gentleman, Dodger," she said to him one day.

"I'm too rough for that, Florence. I'm only an ignorant street-boy."

"You are not going to be an ignorant street-boy all your life. I don't see why you should not grow up a polished gentleman."

"I shall never be like that Brabazon young man," said he.

"No, Dodger; I don't think you will," said Florence, laughing. "I don't want you to become effeminate nor a dude. I think I should like you less then than I do now."

"Do you like me, Florence?" asked Dodger, brightening up.

"To be sure I do. I hope you don't doubt it."

"Why, it don't seem natural like. You're a fashionable young lady—"

"Not very fashionable, Dodger, just at present."

"Well, a high-toned young lady—one of the tip-tops, and I am a rough Bowery boy."

"You were once, but you are getting over that rapidly. Did you ever hear of Andy Johnson?"

"Who was he?"

"He became President of the United States. Well, at the age of twenty-one he could neither read nor write."

"At twenty-one?" repeated Dodger. "Why, I'm only eighteen, and I do know something of readin' and writin'."

"To be sure! Well, Andy Johnson was taught to read and write by his wife. He kept on improving himself till, in course of time, he became a United States Senator, Vice-President, and afterward, President. Now, I don't expect you to equal him, but I see no reason why you should not become a well-educated man if you are content to work, and keep on working."

"I will keep on, Florence," said Dodger, earnestly. "If I ever find my relations I don't want them to be ashamed of me."

It was not the first time he had referred to his uncertain origin.

"Won't Tim Bolton tell you anything about your family?"

"No; I've asked him more'n once. He always says he's my father, and that makes me mad."

"It is strange," said Florence, thoughtfully. "I had a young cousin stolen many years ago."

"Was it the son of an old gentleman you lived with on Madison Avenue?"

"Yes; it was the son of Uncle John. It quite broke him down. After my cousin's loss he felt that he had nothing to live for."

"I wish I was your cousin, Florence," said Dodger, thoughtfully.

"Well, then, I will adopt you as my cousin, or brother, whichever you prefer!"

"I would rather be your cousin."

"Then cousin let it be! Now we are bound to each other by strong and near ties."

"But when your uncle takes you back you'll forget all about poor Dodger."

"No, I won't, Dodger. There's my hand on it. Whatever comes, we are friends forever."

"Then I'll try not to disgrace you, Florence. I'll learn as fast as I can, and see if I don't grow up to be a gentleman."

Chapter 17

A MYSTERIOUS ADVENTURE

Several weeks passed without changing in any way the position or employment of Dodger or Florence.

They had settled down to their respective forms of labor, and were able not only to pay their modest expenses, but to save up something for a rainy day.

Florence had but one source of regret.

She enjoyed her work, and did not now lament the luxurious home which she had lost.

But she did feel sore at heart that her uncle made no sign of regret for their separation.

From him she received no message of forgiveness or reconciliation.

"He has forgotten me!" she said to herself, bitterly. "He has cast me utterly out of his heart. I do not care for his money, but I do not like to think that my kind uncle—for he was always kind till the last trouble—has steeled his heart against me forever."

But she learned through a chance meeting with Jane, that this was not so.

"Mr. Linden is getting very nervous and low-spirited," said the girl, "and sits hour after hour in the library looking into the fire, a-fotchin' deep sighs every few minutes. Once I saw him with your photograph— the one you had taken last spring—in his hands, and he looked sad-like when he laid it down."

"My dear uncle! Then he does think of me sometimes?"

"It's my belief he'd send for you if Curtis would let him."

"Surely Curtis cannot exercise any restraint upon him?"

"He has frequent talks with the old gentleman. I don't know what he says, but it's sure to be something wicked. I expect he does all he can to set him against you. Oh, he's a cunning villain, he is, even if he is your cousin, Miss Florence."

"And do you think my uncle is unhappy, Jane?" said Florence, thoughtfully.

"That I do, miss."

"He never was very bright or cheerful, you know."

"But he never was like this. And I do think he's gettin' more and more feeble."

"Do you think I ought to call upon him, and risk his sending me away?"

"It might be worth tryin', Miss Florence."

The result of this conversation was that Florence did make up her mind the very next afternoon to seek her old home. She had just reached the front steps, and was about to ascend them, when the door opened and Curtis appeared.

He started at the sight of his cousin.

"Florence!" he said. "Tell me why you came here?"

"I am anxious about my uncle." she said. "Tell me, Curtis, how he is."

"You know he's never in vigorous health," said Curtis, evasively.

"But is he as well as usual?"

"He is about the same as ever. One thing would do more for him than anything else."

"What's that?"

"Your agreement to marry me"—and he fixed his eyes upon her face eagerly.

Florence shook her head.

"I should be glad to help my uncle," she said, "but I cannot agree to marry you."

"Why not?" he demanded, roughly.

"Because I do not love you, and never shall," she responded, firmly.

"In other words, you refuse to do the only thing that will restore our uncle to health and happiness?"

"It is too much to ask." Then, fixing her eyes upon him keenly: "Why should uncle insist upon this marriage? Is it not because you have influenced him in the matter?"

"No," answered Curtis, falsely. "He has some secret reason, which he will not disclose to me, for desiring it."

Florence had learned to distrust the words of her wily cousin.

"May I not see him?" she asked. "Perhaps he will tell me."

"No; I cannot permit it."

"You cannot permit it? Are you, then, our uncle's guardian?"

"No, and yes. I do not seek to control him, but I wish to save him from serious agitation. Should he see you, and find that you are still rebellious, the shock might kill him."

"I have reason to doubt your words." said Florence, coldly. "I think you are resolved to keep us apart."

"Listen, and I will tell you a secret; Uncle John has heart disease, so the doctor assures me. Any unwonted agitation might kill him instantly. I am sure you would not like to expose him to such a risk."

He spoke with apparent sincerity, but Florence did not feel certain that his words were truthful.

"Very well," she said. "Then I will give up seeing him."

"It is best, unless you are ready to accede to his wishes—and mine."

She did not answer, but walked slowly away.

"It would never do to have them meet!" muttered Curtis. "The old gentleman would ask her to come back on any terms, and then all my scheming would be upset. That was a happy invention of mine, about heart disease," he continued, with a low laugh. "Though she only half believed it, she will not dare to run the risk of giving him a shock."

It was about this time that the quiet tenor of Dodger's life was interrupted by a startling event.

He still continued to visit the piers, and one afternoon about six o'clock, he stood on the pier awaiting the arrival of the day boat from Albany, with a small supply of evening papers under his arm.

He had sold all but half a dozen when the boat touched the pier. He stood watching the various passengers as they left the boat and turned their steps in different directions, when someone touched him on the shoulder.

Looking up he saw standing at his side a man of slender figure, with gray hair and whiskers.

"Boy," he said, "I am a stranger in the city. Can I ask your assistance?"

"Yes, sir; certainly," answered Dodger, briskly.

"Do you know where the nearest station of the elevated road is?"

"Yes, sir."

"I want to go up-town, but I know very little about the city. Will you accompany me as guide? I will pay you well."

"All right, sir," answered Dodger.

It was just the job he was seeking.

"We shall have to walk a few blocks, unless you want to take a carriage."

"It isn't necessary. I am strong, in spite of my gray hair."

And indeed he appeared to be.

Dodger noticed that he walked with the elastic step of a young man, while his face certainly showed no trace of wrinkles.

"I live in the West," said the stranger, as they walked along. "I have not been here for ten years."

"Then you have never ridden on the elevated road?" said Dodger.

"N-no," answered the stranger, with curious hesitation.

Yet when they reached the station he went up the staircase and purchased his ticket with the air of a man who was thoroughly accustomed to doing it.

"I suppose you won't want me any longer," said Dodger, preparing to resign the valise he was carrying, and which, by the way, was remarkably light considering the size.

"Yes, I shall need you," said the other, hurriedly. "There may be some distance to walk after we get up-town."

"All right, sir."

Dodger was glad that further service was required, for this would of course increase the compensation which he would feel entitled to ask.

They entered one of the cars and sat down side by side.

The old gentleman drew a paper from his pocket and began to read, while Dodger, left to his own devices, sat quiet and looked about him.

He was rather surprised that the old gentleman, who, according to his own representation, was riding upon the elevated road for the first time, seemed to feel no curiosity on the subject, but conducted himself in all respects like an experienced traveler.

"He's a queer customer!" thought Dodger. "However, it's all one to me, as long as he pays me well for the job."

They got out at 125th Street, and struck down toward the river, Dodger carrying the valise.

"I wonder where we're goin'?" he asked himself.

At length they reached a wooden house of three stories, standing by itself, and here the stranger stopped.

He rang the bell, and the door was opened by a hump-backed negro, who looked curiously at Dodger.

"Is the room ready, Julius?" asked the old man.

"Yes, sir."

"Boy, take the valise up-stairs, and I will follow you."

Up two flights of stairs walked Dodger followed by the old man and the negro.

The latter opened the door of a back room, and Dodger, obedient to directions, took the valise inside and deposited it on a chair.

He had hardly done so when the door closed behind him, and he heard the slipping of a bolt.

"What does all this mean?" Dodger asked himself, in amazement.

Chapter 18

IN A TRAP

"Hold on, there! Open that door!" exclaimed Dodger, when he found himself imprisoned in the back chamber.

There was no answer.

"I say, let me out!" continued our hero, beginning to kick at the panels.

This time there was an answer.

"Stop that kicking, boy! I will come back in fifteen minutes and explain all."

"Well," thought Dodger, "this is about the strangest thing that ever happened to me. However, I can wait fifteen minutes."

He sat down on a cane chair—there were two in the room—and looked about him.

He was in an ordinary bedroom, furnished in the usual manner. There was nothing at all singular in its appearance.

On a book-shelf were a few books, and some old numbers of magazines. There was one window looking into a backyard, but as the room was small it was sufficient to light the apartment.

Dodger looked about in a cursory manner, not feeling any particular interest in his surroundings, for he had but fifteen minutes to wait, but he thought it rather queer that it should be thought necessary to lock him in.

He waited impatiently for the time to pass.

Seventeen minutes had passed when he heard the bolt drawn. Fixing his eyes eagerly on the door he saw it open, and two persons entered.

One was the hump-backed negro, carrying on a waiter a plate of buttered bread, and a cup of tea; the other person was—not the old man, but, to Dodger's great amazement, a person well remembered, though he had only seen him once—Curtis Waring.

"Set down the waiter on the table, Julius," said Waring.

Dodger looked on in stupefaction. He was getting more and more bewildered.

"Now you can go!" said Curtis, in a tone of authority.

The negro bowed, and after he had disposed of the waiter, withdrew.

"Do you know me, boy?" asked Curtis, turning now and addressing Dodger.

"Yes; you are Mr. Waring."

"You remember where you last saw me?"

"Yes, sir. At your uncle's house on Madison Avenue."

"Quite right."

"How did you come here? Where is the old man whose valise I brought from the Albany boat?"

Curtis smiled, and drew from his pocket a gray wig and whiskers.

"You understand now, don't you?"

"Yes, sir; I understand that I have been got here by a trick."

"Yes," answered Curtis, coolly. "I have deemed it wise to use a little stratagem. But you must be hungry. Sit down and eat your supper while I am talking to you."

Dodger was hungry, for it was past his usual supper-time, and he saw no reason why he should not accept the invitation.

Accordingly, he drew his chair up to the table and began to eat. Curtis seated himself on the other chair.

"I have a few questions to ask you, and that is why I arranged this interview. We are quite by ourselves," he added, significantly.

"Very well, sir; go ahead."

"Where is my cousin Florence? I am right, I take it, in assuming that you know where she is."

"Yes, sir; I know," answered Dodger, slowly.

"Very well, tell me."

"I don't think she wants you to know."

Curtis frowned.

"It is necessary I should know!" he said, emphatically.

"I will ask her if I may tell you."

"I can't wait for that. You must tell me at once."

"I can't do that."

"You are mistaken; you can do it."

"Then I won't!" said Dodger, looking his companion full in the face.

Curtis Waring darted a wicked look at him, and seemed ready to attack the boy who was audacious enough to thwart him, but he restrained himself and said:

"Let that pass for the present. I have another question to ask. Where is the document you took from my uncle's desk on the night of the burglary?"

And he emphasized the last word.

Dodger looked surprised.

"I took no paper," he said.

"Do you deny that you opened the desk?"

"No."

"When I came to examine the contents in the presence of my uncle, it was found that a document—his will—had disappeared, and with it a considerable sum of money."

And he looked sharply at Dodger.

"I don't know anything about it, sir. I took nothing."

"You can hardly make me believe that. Why did you open the desk if you did not propose to take anything?"

"I did intend to take something. I was under orders to do so, for I wouldn't have done it of my own free will; but the moment I got the desk open I heard a cry, and looking round, I saw Miss Florence looking at me."

"And then?"

"I was startled, and ran to her side."

"And then you went back and completed the robbery?"

"No, I didn't. She talked to me so that I felt ashamed of it. I never stole before, and I wouldn't have tried to do it then, if—if someone hadn't told me to."

"I know whom you mean—Tim Bolton."

"Yes; Tim Bolton, since you know."

"What did he tell you to take?"

"The will and the money."

"Exactly. Now we are coming to it. You took them, and gave them to him?"

"No, I didn't. I haven't seen him since that night."

Curtis Waring regarded the boy thoughtfully. His story was straightforward, and it agreed with the story told by Tim himself. But, on the other hand, he denied taking the missing articles, and yet they had disappeared.

Curtis decided that both he and Tim had lied, and that this story had been concocted between them.

Probably Bolton had the will and the money (the latter he did not care for), and this thought made him uneasy, for he knew that Tim Bolton was an unscrupulous man, and quite capable of injuring him, if he saw the way clear to do so.

"My young friend," he said, "your story is not even plausible. The articles are missing, and there was no one but yourself and Florence who were in a position to take them. Do you wish me to think that my cousin Florence robbed the desk?"

"No, sir; I don't. Florence wouldn't do such a thing," said Dodger, warmly.

"Florence. Is that the way you speak of a young lady?"

"She tells me to call her Florence. I used to call her Miss Florence, but she didn't care for it."

"It seems you two have become very intimate," said Curtis, with a sneer.

"Florence is a good friend to me. I never had so good a friend before."

"All that is very affecting; however, it isn't to the point. Do you know," he continued, in a sterner tone, "that I could have you arrested for entering and breaking open my uncle's desk with burglarious intent?"

"I suppose you could," said Dodger; "but Florence would testify that I took nothing."

"Am I to understand, then, that you refuse to give me any information as to the will and the money?"

"No, sir; I don't refuse. I would tell you if I knew."

Curtis regarded the boy in some perplexity.

He had every appearance of telling the truth.

Dodger had one of those honest, truthful countenances which lend confirmation to any words spoken. If the boy told the truth, what could have become of the will—and the money? As to the former, it might be possible that his uncle had destroyed it, but the disappearance of the money presented an independent difficulty.

"The will is all I care for," he said, at length. "The thief is welcome to the money, though there was a considerable sum."

"I would find the will for you if I could," said Dodger, earnestly.

"You are positive you didn't give it to Tim Bolton?"

"Positive, sir. I haven't seen Tim since that night."

"You may be speaking the truth, or you may not. I will talk with you again to-morrow," and Curtis rose from his chair.

"You don't mean to keep me here?" said Dodger, in alarm.

"I shall be obliged to do so."

"I won't stay!" exclaimed Dodger, in excitement, and he ran to the door, meaning to get out; but Curtis drew a pistol from his pocket and aimed it at the boy.

"Understand me, boy," he said, "I am in earnest, and I am not to be trifled with."

Dodger drew back, and Curtis opened the door and went out, bolting it after him.

Chapter 19

AN ATTEMPT TO ESCAPE

While Dodger had no discomfort to complain of, it occurred to him that Florence would be alarmed by his long absence, for now it seemed certain that he would have to remain overnight.

If only he could escape he would take care not to fall into such a trap again.

He went to the window and looked out, but the distance to the ground was so great, for the room was on the third floor, that he did not dare to imperil his life by attempting a descent.

If there had been a rope at hand he would not have felt afraid to make the attempt.

He examined the bed to see if it rested upon cords, but there were slats instead.

As has already been said, there were no houses nearby.

That part of the city had not been much settled, and it was as solitary as it is in the outskirts of a country village.

If he could only reveal his position to some person outside, so as to insure interference, he might yet obtain his freedom.

With this thought he tore a blank leaf from one of the books in the room, and hastily penciled the following lines:

"I am kept a prisoner in this house. I was induced to come here by a trick. Please get someone to join you, and come and demand my release."

Some weeks before Dodger could not have written so creditable a note, but he had greatly improved since he had been under the influence and instruction of Florence.

Dodger now posted himself at the window and waited anxiously for someone to pass, so that he might attract his attention and throw down the paper.

He had to wait for fifteen minutes. Then he saw approaching a young man, not far from twenty-one, who looked like a young mechanic, returning from his daily work.

Now was Dodger's opportunity. He put his head out of the window and called out:

"Hello, there!"

The young man looked and saw him at the window.

"What do you want?" he asked.

"Catch this paper, and read what there is on it."

He threw down the leaf, which, after fluttering in the gentle evening breeze, found its way to the ground and was picked up.

After reading it, the young man looked up and said:

"I'll go round to the door and inquire."

He was as good as his word. He went to the outer door and rang the bell.

Julius came to the door.

"What's wanted, boss?" he said.

"You've got a boy locked up in a room."

"Who told you, boss?"

"He threw down a paper to me, telling me he was kept a prisoner."

"What did he say?" asked Julius.

The young man read the note aloud.

"What have you to say to that, you black imp?" he demanded, sternly.

The ready wit of Julius served him in this emergency.

"Dat boy is crazy as a loon, boss!'" he answered, readily. "We have to keep him shut up for fear he'll kill some of us."

"You don't say!" ejaculated the young mechanic. "He don't look like it."

"No, he don't; dat's a fact, boss. Fact is, dat boy is the artfullest lunytick you ever seed. He tried to kill his mother last week."

"Is that true?"

"Dat's so, boss. And all de while he looks as innocent as a baby. If I was to let him out he'd kill somebody, sure."

"I never would have believed it," said the young man.

"If you want to take the risk, boss, you might go up, and see him. I b'lieve he's got a carvin'-knife about him, but I don't dare to go up and get it away. It would be as much as this nigger's life is worth."

"No," answered the young man, hastily. "I don't want to see him. I never did like crazy folks. I'm sorry I gave you the trouble to come to the door."

"Oh, no trouble, boss."

"I guess I've fixed dat boy!" chuckled Julius. "Ho, ho! he can't get ahead of old Julius! Crazy as a loon, ho, ho!"

Dodger waited anxiously for the young man to get through his interview. He hoped that he would force his way up to the third floor, draw the bolt, and release him from his imprisonment.

He kept watch at the window, and when the young man reappeared, he looked at him eagerly.

"Did you ask them to let me out?" he shouted.

The other looked up at him with an odd expression of suspicion and repulsion.

"You're better off where you are," he said.

"But they have locked me up here."

"And reason enough, too!"

"What makes you say that?"

"Because you're crazy as a loon."

"Did the black man say that?" inquired Dodger, indignantly.

"Yes, he did—said you tried to kill your mother, and had a carving-knife hidden in the room."

"It's a lie—an outrageous lie!" exclaimed Dodger, his eyes flashing.

"Don't go into one of your tantrums," said the man, rather alarmed; "it won't do any good."

"But I want you to understand that I am no more crazy than you are!"

"Sho? I know better. Where's your carving-knife?"

"I haven't got any; I never had any. That negro has been telling you lies. Just go to the door again, and insist on seeing me."

"I wouldn't das't to. You'd stab me."

"Listen to me!" said Dodger, getting out of patience. "I'm not crazy. I'm a newsboy and baggage-smasher. An old man got me to bring his valise here, and then locked me up. Won't you go round to the station-house and send a policeman here?"

"I'll see about it," said the young man, who did not believe a word that Dodger had said to him.

"He won't do it!" said Dodger to himself, in a tone of discouragement. "That miserable nigger has made him believe I am a lunatic. I'll have him up anyway."

Forthwith he began to pound and kick so forcibly that Julius came up-stairs on a run, half inclined to believe that Dodger had really become insane.

"What do you want, boy?" he inquired from outside the door.

"I want you to unbolt the door and let me out."

"I couldn't do it nohow," said Julius. "It would be as much as my place is worth."

"I will give you a dollar—five dollars—if you will only let me out. The man who brought me here is a bad man, who is trying to cheat his cousin—a young lady—out of a fortune."

"Don't know nothin' 'bout that," said Julius.

"He has no right to keep me here."

"Don't know nothin' 'bout that, either. I'm actin' accordin' to orders."

"Look here," said Dodger, bethinking himself of what had just happened. "Did you tell that young man who called here just now that I was crazy?"

Julius burst into a loud guffaw.

"I expect I did," he laughed. "Said you'd got a long carvin'-knife hid in de room."

"What made you lie so?" demanded Dodger, sternly.

"Couldn't get rid of him no other way. Oh, how scared he looked when I told him you tried to kill your mother."

And the negro burst into another hearty laugh which exasperated Dodger exceedingly.

"How long is Mr. Waring going to keep me here? Did he tell you?" Dodger asked, after a pause.

"No; he didn't say."

"When is he coming here again?"

"Said he'd come to-morrow, most likely."

"Will you bring me a light?"

"Couldn't do it. You'd set the house on fire."

It seemed useless to prolong the conversation.

Dodger threw himself on the bed at an early hour, but he did not undress, thinking there might possibly be a chance to escape during the night.

But the morning came and found him still a prisoner, but not in the solitary dwelling.

Chapter 20

A MIDNIGHT RIDE

Curtis Waring had entrapped Dodger for a double purpose.

It was not merely that he thought it possible the boy had the will, or knew where it was.

He had begun to think of the boy's presence in New York as dangerous to his plans.

John Linden might at any time learn that the son, for whose disappearance he had grieved so bitterly, was still living in the person of this street-boy. Then there would be an end of his hopes of inheriting the estate.

Only a few months more and the danger would be over, for he felt convinced that his uncle's tenure of life would be brief. The one essential thing, then, seemed to be to get Dodger out of the city.

The first step had already been taken; what the next was will soon appear.

Scarcely had Dodger failed in his attempt to obtain outside assistance when an unaccountable drowsiness overcame him, considerably to his surprise.

"I don't know what's come to me," he said to himself. "It can't be more than seven or eight o'clock, and yet I feel so sleepy I can hardly keep my eyes open. I haven't worked any harder than usual today, and I can't understand it."

Dodger had reason to be surprised, for he didn't usually retire till eleven o'clock.

In a city like New York, where many of the streets are tolerably well filled even at midnight, people get in the way of sitting up much later than in the country, and Dodger was no exception to this rule.

Yet here he was ready to drop off to sleep before eight o'clock. To him it was a mystery, for he did not know that the cup of tea which he had drunk at supper had been drugged by direction of Curtis Waring, with an ulterior purpose, which will soon appear.

"I may as well lie down, as there is nothing else to do," thought Dodger. "There isn't much fun sitting in the dark. If I can sleep, so much the better."

Five minutes had scarcely passed after his head struck the pillow, when our hero was fast asleep.

At eleven o'clock a hack stopped in front of the house, and Curtis Waring descended from it.

"Stay here," said he to the driver. "There will be another passenger. If you are detained I will make it right when I come to pay you."

"All right sir," said the hackman. "I don't care how long it is if I am paid for my time."

Curtis opened the door with a pass-key, and found Julius dozing in a chair in the hall.

"Wake up, you sleepy-head," he said. "Has anything happened since I left here?"

"Yes, sir; de boy tried to get away."

"Did he? I don't see how he could do that. You kept the door bolted, didn't you?"

"Yes, sir; but he throwed a piece of paper out'n de window, sayin' he was kep' a prisoner here. A young man picked it up, and came to de house to ax about it."

Curtis looked alarmed.

"What did you say?" he inquired apprehensively.

"Told him de boy was crazy as a loon—dat he tried to kill his mother las' week, and had a carvin'-knife hid in his room."

"Good, Julius! I didn't give you credit for such a fertile imagination."

"What's dat, massa?" asked Julius, looking puzzled.

"I didn't know you were such a skillful liar."

"Yah! yah!" laughed Julius, quite comprehending this compliment. "I reckon I can twis' de trufe pretty well, Massa Curtis!"

"You have done well, Julius," said Curtis, approvingly. "Here's a dollar!"

The negro was quite effusive in his gratitude.

"What did the young man say?"

"He looked scared. I tol' him he could go up and see de boy if he wasn't afeared of the carvin'-knife, but he said he guessed he wouldn't—he didn't like crazy folks."

Curtis laughed heartily.

"So it all ended as it should. Did the boy make any more trouble?"

"Yes; he pounded and kicked till I had to go up and see what was de matter. I didn't give him no satisfaction, and I guess he went to bed."

"He ought to be in a deep sleep by this time. I will go up and see. Go up with me, Julius, for I may have to ask you to help me bring him down."

Though Julius was naturally a coward, he felt quite brave when he had company, and he at once went up-stairs with Curtis Waring.

Curtis drew the bolt, and, entering the chamber, his glance fell upon Dodger, fast asleep on the bed.

"I am glad the boy did not undress," he said. "It will save me a great deal of trouble. Now, Julius, you can take his feet and I will lift his head, and we will take him down-stairs."

"S'pos'n he wakes up, Massa Curtis?"

"He won't wake up. I took care the sleeping potion should be strong enough to produce profound slumber for eighteen hours."

"Seems as if he was dead," said Julius nervously.

"Tush, you fool! He's no more dead than you or I."

The hackman looked curious when the two men appeared with their sleeping burden, and Curtis felt that some explanation was required.

"The boy has a very painful disease," he said, "and the doctor gave him a sleeping-draught. He is going abroad for his health, and, under the circumstances, I think it best not to wake him up. Drive slowly and carefully to Pier No.—, as I don't want the boy aroused if it can be helped."

"All right, sir."

"Julius, you may lock the door and come with me. I shall need your help to get him on board the ship."

"All right, Massa Curtis."

"And mind you don't go to sleep in the carriage, you black rascal!" added Curtis, as he saw that the negro found it hard to keep his eyes open.

"All right, massa, I'll keep awake. How am I to get home?"

"I will instruct the hackman to take you home."

"Yah, yah; I'll be ridin' like a gemleman!"

The journey was successfully accomplished, but it took an hour, for, according to directions, the hackman did not force his pace, but drove slowly, till he reached the North River pier indicated.

At the pier was a large, stanch vessel—the Columbia—bound for San Francisco, round Cape Horn.

All was dark, but the second officer was pacing the deck.

Curtis Waring hailed him.

"What time do you get off?"

"Early to-morrow morning."

"So the captain told me. I have brought you a passenger."

"The captain told me about him."

"Is his stateroom ready?"

"Yes, sir. You are rather late."

"True; and the boy is asleep, as you will see. He is going to make the voyage for his health, and, as he has been suffering some pain, I thought I would not wake him up. Who will direct me to his stateroom?"

The mate summoned the steward, and Dodger, still unconscious, was brought on board and quietly transferred to the bunk that had been prepared for him.

It was a critical moment for poor Dodger, but he was quite unconscious of it.

"What is the boy's name?" asked the mate.

"Arthur Grant. The captain has it on his list. Is he on board?"

"Yes; but he is asleep."

"I do not need to see him. I have transacted all necessary business with him—and paid the passage money. Julius, bring the valise."

Julius did so.

"This contains the boy's clothing. Take it to the stateroom, Julius."

"All right, Massa Curtis."

"What is your usual time between New York and San Francisco?" asked Curtis, addressing the mate.

"From four to six months. Four months is very short, six months very long. We ought to get there in five months, or perhaps a little sooner, with average weather."

"Very well. I believe there is no more to be said. Good-night!"

"Good-night, sir."

So he is well out of the way for five months!" soliloquized Curtis. "In five months much may happen. Before that time I hope to be in possession of my uncle's property. Then I can snap my fingers at fate."

Chapter 21

A SEASICK PASSENGER

The good ship Columbia had got fifty miles under way before Dodger opened his eyes.

He looked about him languidly at first, but this feeling was succeeded by the wildest amazement, as his eyes took in his unusual surroundings.

He had gone to sleep on a bed—he found himself on awakening in a ship's bunk.

He half rose in his berth, but the motion of the vessel and a slight feeling of dizziness compelled him to resume a recumbent position.

"I must be dreaming," thought Dodger. "It's very queer. I am dreaming I am at sea. I suppose that explains it."

He listened and heard the swish of the waters as they beat against the sides of the vessel.

He noted the pitching of the ship, and there was an unsteady feeling in his head, such as those which have gone to sea will readily recall.

Dodger became more and more bewildered.

"If it's a dream, it's the most real dream I ever had," he said to himself.

"This seems like a ship's cabin," he continued, looking about him. "I think if I got up I should be seasick. I wonder if people ever get seasick in dreams."

There was another pitch, and Dodger instinctively clung to the edge of his berth, to save himself from being thrown out.

"Let me see," he said, trying to collect his scattered recollection. "I went to sleep in a house up-town—a house to which Curtis Waring lured me, and then made me a prisoner. The house was somewhere near One Hundred and Thirty-fifth Street. Now it seems as if I was on board a ship. How could I get here? I wish somebody would come in that I could ask."

As no one came in, Dodger got out of the berth, and tried to stand on the cabin floor.

But before he knew it he was staggering like one intoxicated, and his head began to feel bad, partly, no doubt, on account of the sleeping potion which he had unconsciously taken.

At this moment the steward entered the cabin.

"Hello, young man! Have you got up yet?" he asked.

"Where am I?" asked Dodger, looking at him with a dazed expression.

"Where are you? You're on the good ship Columbia, to be sure."

"Are we out to sea?"

"Of course you are."

"How far from land?"

"Well, about fifty miles, more or less, I should judge."

"How long have I been here?"

"It seems to me you have a poor memory. You came on board late last evening."

"I suppose Curtis Waring brought me," said Dodger, beginning to get his bearings.

"There was a gentleman came with you—so the mate told me. I don't know his name."

"Where is the ship bound?"

"To San Francisco, round Cape Horn. I supposed you knew that."

"I never heard of the ship Columbia before, and I never had any idea of making a sea voyage."

The steward looked surprised.

"I suppose your guardian arranged about that. Didn't he tell you?"

"I have no guardian."

"Well, you'll have to ask Captain Barnes about that. I know nothing, except that you are a passenger, and that your fare has been paid."

"My fare paid to San Francisco?" asked Dodger, more and more at sea, both mentally and physically.

"Yes; we don't take any dead-heads on the Columbia."

"Can you tell me what time it is?"

"About twelve o'clock. Do you feel hungry?"

"N-not very," returned Dodger, as a ghastly expression came over his face, and he tumbled back into his berth, looking very pale.

The steward smiled.

"I see how it is," he said; "you are getting initiated."

"What's that?"" muttered Dodger, feebly.

"You're going to be seasick. You'll hardly be able to appear at the dinner table."

"It makes me sick to think of eating," said Dodger, feebly.

As he sank back in his berth, all thoughts of his unexpected position gave way to an overpowering feeling of seasickness.

He had never been tried in this way before, and he found the sensation far from agreeable.

"If only the vessel would stop pitching," he groaned. "Oh, how happy I should be if I were on dry land."

But the vessel wouldn't stop—even for a minute.

The motion, on the other hand, seemed to increase, as was natural, for they were getting further and further from land and were exposed to the more violent winds that swept the open ocean.

There is something about seasickness that swallows up and draws away all minor cares and anxieties, and Dodger was too much affected to consider how or why it was that he so unexpectedly found himself a passenger to California.

"Lie flat on your back," said the steward. "You will feel better if you do."

"How long is it going to last?" groaned Dodger.

"Oh, you'll feel better to-morrow. I'll bring you some porridge presently. You can get that down, and it is better to have something on your stomach."

He was right. The next day Dodger felt considerably better, and ventured to go upon deck. He looked about him in surprise.

There had been a storm, and the waves were white with foam.

As far as the eye could see there was a tumult and an uproar.

The ship was tossed about like a cockleshell. But the sailors went about their work unruffled. It was no new sight for them.

Though his head did not feel exactly right, the strong wind entered Dodger's lungs, and he felt exhilarated. His eyes brightened, and he began to share in the excitement of the scene.

Pacing the deck was a stout, bronzed seaman, whose dress made it clear even to the inexperienced eyes of Dodger that he was the captain.

"Good morning, Master Grant," he said pleasantly. "Are you getting your sea legs on?"

The name was unfamiliar to Dodger, but he could see that the remark was addressed to him.

"Yes, sir," he answered.

"Ever been to sea before?"

"No, sir."

"You'll get used to it. Bless me, you'll stand it like an old sailor before we get to 'Frisco."

"Is it a long voyage, captain?" asked Dodger.

"Five months, probably. We may get there a little sooner. It depends on the winds and weather."

"Five months," said Dodger to himself, in a tone of dismay. The captain laughed.

"It'll be a grand experience for a lad like you, Arthur!" said the captain, encouragingly.

Arthur! So his name was Arthur! He had just been called Master Grant, so Arthur Grant was his name on board ship.

Dodger was rather glad to have a name provided, for he had only been known as Dodger heretofore, and this name would excite surprise. He had recently felt the need of a name, and didn't see why this wouldn't answer his purpose as well as any other.

"I must write it down so as not to forget it," he resolved. "It would seem queer if I forgot my own name."

"I shouldn't enjoy it much if I were going to be seasick all the time," he answered.

"Oh, a strong, healthy boy like you will soon be all right. You don't look like an invalid."

"I never was sick in my life."

"But your guardian told me he was sending you on a sea voyage for your health."

"Did Mr. Waring say that?"

"Yes; didn't you know the object of your sea trip?" asked Captain Barnes in surprise.

"No."

"There may be some tendency to disease in your system—some hereditary tendency," said the captain, after a pause. "Were your parents healthy?"

"They—died young," answered Dodger, hesitatingly.

"That accounts for your guardian's anxiety. However, you look strong enough, in all conscience; and if you're not healthy, you will be before the voyage ends."

"I don't know what I am to do for clothes," said Dodger, as a new source of perplexity presented itself. "I can't get along with one shirt and collar for five months."

"You will find plenty of clothes in your valise. Hasn't it been given you?"

"No, sir."

"You may ask the steward for it. You didn't think your guardian would send you on a five months' voyage without a change of clothing, did you?"

And the captain laughed heartily.

"I don't know Mr. Waring very well," said Dodger, awkwardly.

As he went down stairs to inquire about the valise, this question haunted him:

"Why did Curtis Waring send him on a sea-voyage?"

Chapter 22

THE OTHER PASSENGER

Dodger sought the steward, and asked for his valise.

"Isn't it in your stateroom?" asked that functionary.

"I haven't seen it."

"I remember now. It was put with the luggage of the other passenger. I will show it to you."

He took Dodger to a part of the ship where freight was stored, and pointed to a sizeable valise, with a card attached to it on which was inscribed the name:

"Arthur Grant."

"This must be yours," he said.

"Yes; I suppose so," answered Dodger, glad to have found out the new name which had been given him, otherwise he would have supposed the valise belonged to some other person.

He took the valise to his stateroom, and finding a key tied to the handle, he opened it at once.

It proved to contain a very fair supply of underclothing, socks, handkerchiefs, etc., with a tooth-brush, a hair-brush and comb, and a sponge. Never in his life had Dodger been so well supplied with clothing before. There were four white shirts, two tennis shirts, half a dozen handkerchiefs and the same number of socks, with three changes of underclothing.

"I begin to feel like a gentleman," said Dodger to himself, complacently.

That was not all. At the bottom of the valise was an envelope, sealed, on which was inscribed the name:

"Dodger."

"That is for me, at any rate," thought our hero. "I suppose it is from Curtis Waring."

He opened the envelope, and found inclosed twenty-five dollars in bills, with a few lines written on a half sheet of paper. These Dodger read, with interest and curiosity. They were as follows:

"DODGER.—The money inclosed is for you. When you reach California you will find it of use. I have sent you out there because you will find in a new country a better chance to rise than in the city of New York. I advise you to stay there and grow up with the country. In New York you were under the influence of a bad man, from whom it is best that you should be permanently separated. I know something of the early history of Tim Bolton. He was detected in a crime, and fled to escape the consequences. You are not his son, but his nephew. Your mother was his sister, but quite superior to himself. Your right name is Arthur Grant, and it will be well for you to assume it hereafter. I have entered you in the list of passengers under that name.

"I thought you had taken the will from my uncle's desk, but I am inclined to think you had nothing to do with it. If you know where it is, or whether Bolton has it, I expect you to notify me in return for the money I have expended in your behalf. In that case you can write to me, No.—Madison Avenue

"CURTIS WARING."

Dodger read this letter over twice, and it puzzled him.

"He seems from the letter to take an interest in me," he soliloquized. "At any rate, he has given me money and clothes, and paid my passage to California. What for, I wonder? I don't believe it is to get me away from the bad influence of Tim. There must be some other reason."

There was another part of the letter with which Dodger did not agree.

Curtis asserted positively that he was the nephew of Tim Bolton, while he was positive that there was no relationship between them.

In that case, Curtis must have been an early acquaintance of Tim's. At any rate, he seemed to know about his past life.

Dodger now comprehended his present situation fully. He was a passenger on the ship Columbia, and there was no chance of leaving it. He had ascertained on inquiry that the vessel would not put in anywhere, but would make the long voyage direct. It would be over four months, at any rate, before he could communicate with Florence, and in the meantime, she and Mrs. O'Keefe, whom he recognized as a good friend, would conclude that he was dead.

It was very provoking to think that he could not even telegraph, as that would relieve all anxiety, and he felt sure that Florence was enough his friend to feel anxious about him.

He had just closed up his valise, when a young man of dark complexion, and of an attractive, intellectual expression, entered the cabin.

He nodded pleasantly to Dodger, and said:

"I suppose this is Arthur Grant?"

"Yes, sir," answered Dodger, for he had decided to adopt the name.

"We ought to become close friends, for we are, I believe, the only passengers."

"Then you are a passenger, too?" said Dodger, deciding, after a brief scrutiny, that he should like his new acquaintance.

"Yes. My name is Randolph Leslie. I have been, for the last five years, a reporter on leading New York daily papers, and worked so closely that my health has become somewhat affected. My doctor recommended a sea voyage, and I have arranged for a pretty long one."

"What papers have you worked for?"

"Oh, all the leading ones—Tribune, World, Herald and Sun—sometimes one, and sometimes another. Your reason for taking this trip can hardly be the same as mine. You don't look as if your health required you to travel."

"No," answered Dodger, smiling; "but I understand that the gentleman who engaged my passage said I was going to sea for my health."

"If I were as robust as you, I shouldn't give much thought to my health. Do you intend to remain in California?"

"I don't know what I do intend," replied Dodger. "I didn't know I was going to California at all till I woke up in my stateroom."

The young man looked surprised.

"Didn't you know the destination of the vessel when you came on board?" he asked.

"I was brought aboard in my sleep."

"This is curious. It looks to me as if you had a story to tell."

"Of course, I don't want to be curious, but if there is any way in which I can help you, by advice, or in any other way, I am quite ready to do so."

Dodger paused, but only briefly. This young man looked friendly, and might help him to penetrate the mystery which at present baffled him.

At any rate, his experience qualified him to give friendly advice, and of this Dodger felt that he stood in need.

"I ought to tell you, to begin with," he said, "that I am a poor boy, and made my living as best I could, by carrying baggage, selling papers, etc."

"I don't think any the worse of you for that. Did you live at the lodging-houses?"

"No; until lately I lived with a man who keeps a saloon on the Bowery, and tended bar for him."

"What was his name? As a reporter I know the Bowery pretty well."

"Tim Bolton."

"Tim Bolton? I know his place well. I think I must have seen you there. Your face looked to me familiar as soon as I set eyes on you."

"Very likely. A good many people came into Tim's. I couldn't pretend to remember them all."

"Was Tim a relative of yours?"

"I don't believe he was. I always thought that he got hold of me when I was a kid. I don't remember the time when I wasn't with him."

"I suppose you have always lived in New York?"

"No; I lived for several years in Australia. Tim was in the same business there. I came on with him a year or more since."

"Do you think you ever lived in New York before?"

"Yes; Tim has told me that I was born in New York."

"I understand that you have left Tim now?"

"Yes."

"Why, may I ask?"

"Because I didn't like the business he was in. But I liked it better than the one he wanted me to go into."

"What was that?"

"Burglary."

The young reporter started in surprise.

"Well," he said, "this is a new tack for Tim. However, I never looked upon him as a man who would shrink from any violation of the laws, except murder. I don't think he would do that."

"No; Tim isn't quite so bad. He isn't the worst man alive, though he is a rather hard customer. It was his wanting me to enter a house on Madison Avenue and open a desk that led to me going on this trip."

"Tell me about it, if you don't mind."

Thus invited, Dodger told his story to Randolph Leslie, keeping nothing back.

He finished by showing him the letter he had found in the valise.

Chapter 23

THROUGH THE GOLDEN GATE

"Well, this is certainly a remarkable letter," said the reporter, as he handed it back to Dodger. "I am at a loss to understand the interest which this man appears to feel in you."

"I look upon him as my enemy," said Dodger. "But an enemy doesn't spend so much money upon another as he has."

"Unless he has an object in it," amended Leslie, shrewdly. "Do you know of any connection this man has with you?"

"No; I never heard of him till I entered his house," and Dodger flushed as he thought that his entrance into the mansion on Madison Avenue had been as a burglar.

"I seems to me that he knows more about you than you do about him. It also seems to me that he is anxious to get you out of New York, the further away the better."

"But what harm could I do him in New York?" asked Dodger, puzzled.

"That is a question which I cannot answer. You say he was instrumental in getting his cousin Florence out of the house?"

"Yes; he wanted to marry her."

"And she would not consent?"

"No; I think she hates him."

"How old is she?"

"Seventeen."

"And he?"

"He looks about thirty-five."

"The difference in years isn't great enough to constitute an obstacle, provided she loved him. I am thirty years old."

"I am sure Forence would prefer you to Curtis Waring."

"Don't flatter me. I am vain enough already. The time may come when I may ask your good offices with Miss Linden. What I was about to ask was: Is Miss Linden also entitled to a share in her uncle's estate?"

"She is just as nearly related to him as Mr. Waring."

"Then I can understand his wishing to get rid of her. I don't know why he should want to send you to a distance. I suppose there can't be any relationship?"

"Is it likely that I—a poor street boy—should be related to a rich man like Mr. Linden?"

"It don't seem likely, I admit," said Leslie, musingly. "Well, I suppose," he continued, after a pause, "there is no use in speculating about the matter now. The important point is, what are we to do with ourselves during the four or five months we must spend on shipboard?"

"I don't know what I can do," said Dodger. "I can't sell papers, and I can't smash baggage."

"And there appears to be no need of your doing either, as you are provided with board and lodging till we reach shore."

"That seems strange to me, for I've always had to hustle for a living."

"I was about to make a proposal to you. But first let me ask you about your education. I suppose you are not an accomplished scholar?"

"I'm about as ignorant as they make 'em," answered Dodger, drolly. "Tim was afraid to send me to college, for fear I'd get to know too much for my business."

"Tending bar doesn't require an acquaintance with Latin and Greek. Would you like to know more?"

"I wish I did. Forence was teaching me nights when I was in New York. Now I've got to give up all that."

"Not necessarily. Listen to me, Arthur. Before I came to New York to go into journalism, I taught school for two years; and I believe I may say that I was tolerably successful. Suppose I take you as a scholar?"

"I should like it very much, Mr. Leslie, but I'm afraid I haven't got money enough to pay you."

"That is true. You will need all the money you have when you land in California. Twenty-five dollars won't go far—still you have all the money that is necessary, for I do not intend to charge you anything."

"You are very kind to me, Mr. Leslie, considerin' you don't know me," said Dodger, gratefully.

"On the contrary, I think I know you very well. But about the kindness—my motives are somewhat mixed. I should like to do you a service, but I should also like to find an employment for myself that will make the days less monotonous. I have a collection of books in my trunk, enough for our needs, and if you will agree we will commence our studies to-morrow."

"I should like it very much. I'd like to show Florence, when I see her, that I have improved. Till I saw her I didn't care much, but when I talk with her I feel awfully ignorant."

"In four months a great deal can be accomplished. I don't know how quick you are to learn. After we have had one or two lessons I can judge better."

Two days later Mr. Leslie pronounced his opinion, and a favorable one.

"You have not exaggerated your ignorance," he said to Dodger. "You have a great deal to learn, but on the other hand you are quick, have a retentive memory, and are very anxious to learn. I shall make something of you."

"I learn faster with you than with Florence," said Dodger.

"Probably she would succeed better with girls, but I hold that a male teacher is better for boys. How long are you willing to study every day?"

"As long as you think best."

"Then we will say from two to three hours. I think you have talent for arithmetic. I don't expect to make you fit for a bookkeeper, but I hope to make you equal to most office boys by the time we reach San Francisco. What do you intend to do in California?"

"I don't know. I should like to go back to New York, but I shall not have money enough."

"No; twenty-five dollars would go but little way toward the passage. Evidently Mr. Waring did not intend to have you return, or he would have provided you with more."

"That is just why I should like to go back. I am afraid he will do some harm to Florence."

"And you would like to be on hand to protect her?"

Randolph Leslie smiled.

"You seem to take a good deal of interest in Florence, if I may make as free with her name as you do."

"Yes; I do, Mr. Leslie."

"If you were only a little older I might suspect the nature of that interest."

"I am older than she is."

"In years, yes. But a young lady of seventeen, brought up as she has been, is older by years than a boy of eighteen. I don't think you need apprehend any harm to Miss Linden, except that Mr. Waring may cheat her out of her rightful share of the inheritance. Is her uncle in good health?"

"No, sir; he is a very feeble man."

"Is he an old man?"

"Not so very old. I don't believe he is over sixty."

Really, Mr. Linden was but fifty-four, but, being a confirmed invalid, he looked older.

"Should you say that he was likely to live very long?"

"No," answered Dodger. "He looks as if you could knock him over with a feather. Besides, I've heard Florence say that she was afraid her uncle could not live long."

"Probably Curtis Waring is counting upon this. If he can keep Florence and her uncle apart for a few months, Mr. Linden will die, and he will inherit the whole estate. What is this will he speaks of in the letter you showed me?"

"I don't know, sir."

"Whatever the provisions are, it is evident that he thinks it important to get it into his possession. If favorable to him, he will keep it carefully. If unfavorable, I think a man like him would not hesitate to suppress it."

"No doubt you are right, sir. I don't know much about wills," said Dodger.

"No; I suppose not. You never made any, I suppose," remarked the reporter, with a smile.

"I never had nothing to leave," said Dodger.

"Anything would be a better expression. As your tutor I feel it incumbent upon me to correct your grammar."

"I wish you would, Mr. Leslie. What do you mean to do when you get to San Francisco?"

"I shall seek employment on one of the San Francisco daily papers. Six months or a year so spent will restore my health, and enable me to live without drawing upon my moderate savings."

"I expect I shall have to work, too, to get money to take me back to New York."

And now we must ask the reader to imagine four months and one week passed.

There had been favorable weather on the whole, and the voyage was unusually short.

Dodger and the reporter stood on deck, and with eager interest watched the passage through the Golden Gate. A little later and the queen city of the Pacific came in sight, crowning the hill on which a part of the city is built, with the vast Palace Hotel a conspicuous object in the foreground.

Chapter 24

FLORENCE IN SUSPENSE

We must now return to New York, to Dodger's old home.

When he did not return at the usual hour neither Florence nor Mrs. O'Keefe was particularly disturbed.

It was thought that he had gone on some errand of unusual length, and would return an hour or two late.

Eight o'clock came, the hour at which the boy was accustomed to repair to Florence's room to study, and still he didn't make his appearance.

"Dodger's late this evening, Mrs. O'Keefe," said Florence, going up to the room of her landlady.

"Shure he is. It's likely he's gone to Brooklyn or up to Harlem, wid a bundle. He'll be comin' in soon."

"I hope he will be well paid for the errand, since it keeps him so long."

"I hope so, too, Florence, for he's a good boy, is Dodger. Did I tell you how he served the rapscallion that tried to stale my apples the other day?"

"No; I should like to hear it."

"A big, black-bearded man came along, and asked me for an apple.

" 'You can have one for two pennies,' says I.

" 'But I haven't got them,' says he.

" 'Then you must go widout it,' says I.

" 'We'll see about that,' says he.

"And what do you think?—the fellow picked out one of my biggest apples, and was walkin' away! That made me mad.

" 'Come back, you thafe of the world!' says I.

" 'Silence, you old hag!' says he.

" 'Actilly he called me an old hag! I wanted to go after him, but there was two hoodlums hangin' round, and I knew they'd carry off some of my apples, when, just as I was at my wits' end, Dodger came round the corner.

" 'Dodger,' I screamed, 'go after that man! He's taken one of my apples, widout lave or license!'

"Upon that, Dodger, brave as a lion, walked up to the man, and says he:

" 'Give back that apple, or pay for it!'

" 'What's that to you, you impudent young rascal?' says the man, raisin' the apple to his mouth. But he didn't get a chance to bite it, for Dodger, with a flip of his hand, knocked it on the sidewalk, and I picked it up. Wasn't the man mad just?

" 'I'll smash you, boy,' he growled.

" 'I'm a baggage-smasher myself,' says Dodger, 'and I can smash as well as you.'

"Wid that the man up with his fist and struck at Dodger, but he dodged the blow, and gave him one for himself wid his right. Just then up came a cop.

" 'What's all this?' says he.

" 'That man tried to run off wid one of my apples,' says I.

" 'Come along,' says the cop. 'You're wanted at the station-house.'

" 'It's a lie,' says the man. 'I paid the woman for the apple, and that young rascal knocked it out of my hand.'

" 'I know the boy,' says the cop, 'and he ain't one of that kind. I'll let you go if you buy five apples from the lady, and pay for 'em.'

"The man made up an ugly face, but he didn't want to be locked up, and so he paid me a dime for five apples."

"Dodger is very brave," said Florence. "Sometimes I think he is too daring. He is liable to get into trouble."

"If he does he'll get himself out of it, never you fear. Dodger can take care of himself."

Nine o'clock came, and Florence became alarmed. She had not been aware how much she depended upon the company of her faithful friend, humble as his station was.

Again she went into Mrs. O'Keefe's room. The apple-woman had been out to buy some groceries and had just returned.

"I am getting anxious about Dodger," said Florence. "It is nine o'clock."

"And what's nine o'clock to a boy like him! Shure he's used to bein' out at all hours of the night."

"I shall feel relieved when he comes home. What should I do without him?"

"Shure I'd miss him myself—but it isn't the first time he has been out late."

"Perhaps that terrible Tim Bolton has got hold of him," suggested Florence.

"Tim isn't so bad, Florence. He isn't fit company for the likes of you, but there's worse men nor Tim."

"Didn't he send out Dodger to commit a burglary?"

"And if he hadn't you'd never made Dodger's acquaintance."

"That's true; but it doesn't make burglary any more excusable. Don't you really think Tim Bolton has got hold of him?"

"If he has, he won't keep him long, I'll make oath of that. He might keep him over night, but Dodger would come back in the morning."

Florence was somewhat cheered by Mrs. O'Keefe's refusal to believe that Dodger was in any serious trouble, but she could not wholly free herself from uneasiness. When eleven o'clock came she went to bed very unwillingly, and got very little rest during the night. Morning came, and still Dodger did not show up. As we know, he was fairly started on his long voyage, though he had not yet recovered consciousness.

Florence took a very light breakfast, and at the usual time went to Mrs. Leighton's to meet her pupil. When the study hours were over, she did not remain to lunch, but hurried back, stopping at Mrs. O'Keefe's apple-stand just as that lady was preparing to go home to prepare dinner.

"Have you seen anything of Dodger, Mrs. O'Keefe?" asked Florence, breathlessly.

"No, I haven't, Florence. I've had my eye out watchin' for him, but he hasn't showed up."

"Isn't there anything we can do?" asked Florence, anxiously.

"Well, we might go round and see Tim—and find out whether he's got hold of him."

"Let us go at once."

"Shure I didn't know you cared so much for the boy," said Mrs. O'Keefe, with a shrewd look at Florence's anxious face.

"Why shouldn't I care for him? He is my only friend."

"Is he now? And what's the matter wid Bridget O'Keefe?" asked the apple-woman.

"Excuse me, Mrs. O'Keefe. I know very well you are my friend, and a kind friend, too. I shouldn't have forgotten you."

"It's all right, Florence. You're flustrated like, and that's why you forget me."

"I have so few friends that I can't spare one," continued Florence.

"That's so. Come along wid me, and we'll see what Tim has to tell us."

A short walk brought the two strangely assorted companions to the entrance of Tim Bolton's saloon.

"I'm afraid to go in, Mrs. O'Keefe," said Florence.

"Come along wid me, my dear, I won't let anything harm you. You ain't used to such a place, but I've been here more than once to fill the growler. Be careful as you go down the steps, Florence."

Tim Bolton was standing behind the bar, and as he heard steps he looked carelessly toward the entrance, but when he saw Florence, his indifference vanished. He came from behind the bar, and advanced to meet her.

"Miss Linden," he said.

Florence shrank back and clung to her companion's arm.

"Is there anything I can do for you? I am a rough man, but I'm not so bad as you may think."

"That's what I told her, Tim," said Mrs. O'Keefe. "I told Florence there was worse men than you."

"Thank you, Mrs. O'Keefe. Can I offer you a glass of whisky?"

The apple-woman was about to accept, but she felt an alarmed tug at her arm, and saw that Florence would be placed in an embarrassing position if she accepted. So, by an exercise of self-denial—for Mrs. O'Keefe was by no means insensible to the attractions of whisky, though she never drank to excess—she said:

"Thank you kindly, Mr. Bolton. I won't take any just now; but I'll remind you of your offer another day."

"Have it your own way, Mrs. O'Keefe. And now, what can I do for you and Miss Linden?"

"Oh, Mr. Bolton," broke in Florence, unable to bear the suspense longer, "where is Dodger?"

Chapter 25

FINDING A CLEW

Tim Bolton looked at Florence in undisguised astonishment.

"Dodger!" he repeated. "How should I know? I supposed that you had lured him away from me."

"He didn't like the business you were in. He preferred to make his living in some other way."

"Then why do you ask me where he is?"

"Because he did not come home last night. Shure he rooms at my house," put in Mrs. O'Keefe, "and he hasn't showed up since—"

"And you thought I might have got hold of him?" said Bolton, inquiringly.

"Then you are mistaken. I haven't seen the boy for weeks."

Tim Bolton spoke so straightforwardly that there was no chance to doubt his word.

"When he was living with you, Mr. Bolton," continued Florence, "did he ever stay away like this?"

"No," answered Bolton, "Dodger was always very regular about comin' home."

"Then something must have happened to him," said Florence, anxiously.

"He might have got run in," suggested the apple-woman. "Some of them cops is mighty officious."

"Dodger would never do anything to deserve arrest," Florence said, quickly.

"Thrue for you, Florence, but some innersent parties are nabbed. I know of one young man who was standin' on a strate corner waitin' for the cars, when a cop came up and arristed him for disorderly conduct."

"But that is shameful!" said Florence, indignantly.

"Thrue for you, my dear. We might go round to police headquarters and inquire if the boy's been run in."

"What do you think, Mr. Bolton?" asked Florence.

Tim Bolton seemed busy thinking. Finally he brought down his hand forcibly on the bar, and said:

"I begin to see through it."

Florence did not speak, but she fixed an eager look of inquiry on the face of the saloon-keeper.

"I believe Curtis Waring is at the bottom of this," he said.

"My cousin!" exclaimed Florence, in astonishment.

"Yes, your cousin, Miss Linden."

"But what can he have against poor Dodger? Is it because the boy has taken my part and is a friend to me?"

"He wouldn't like him any better on account of that; but he has another and a more powerful reason."

"Would you mind telling me what it is? I cannot conceive what it can be?"

"At present," answered Bolton, cautiously, "I prefer not to say anything on the subject. I will only say that the boy's disappearance interferes with my plans, and I will see if I can't find out what has become of him."

"If you only will, Mr. Bolton, I shall be so grateful. I am afraid I have misjudged you. I thought you were an enemy of Dodger's."

"Then you were mistaken. I have had the boy with me since he was a kid, and though I've been rough with him at times, maybe, I like him, and I may some time have a chance to show him that old Tim Bolton is one of his best friends."

"I will believe it now, Mr. Bolton," said Florence, impulsively, holding out her hand to the burly saloon-keeper.

He was surprised, but it was evident that he was pleased, also, and he took the little hand respectfully in his own ample palm, and pressed it in a friendly manner.

"There's one thing more I want you to believe, Miss Linden," he said, "and that is, that I am your friend, also."

"Thank you, Mr. Bolton. And now let us all work together to find Dodger."

"You can count on me, Miss Linden. If you'll tell me where you live, I'll send or bring you any news I may hear."

"I live with Mrs. O'Keefe, my good friend here."

"I haven't my kyard with me, Tim," said the apple-woman, "but I'll give you my strate and number. You know my place of business?"

"Yes."

"If you come to me there, I'll let Florence know whatever you tell me. She is not always at home."

The two went away, relieved in mind, for, helpless and bewildered as they were, they felt that Tim Bolton would make a valuable ally.

When they had gone, Tim turned to Hooker and Briggs, who were lounging at a table, waiting for some generous customer to invite them to the bar.

"Boys," said Tim, "has either of you seen anything of Dodger lately?"

"No," answered the two in unison.

"Have you heard anything of him?"

"I heard that he was baggage-smashin' down by the steamboat landings." said Hooker.

"Go down there, both of you, and see if you can see or hear anything of him."

"All right, Tim."

And the two left the saloon and took a westerly route toward the North River piers.

Three hours later they returned.

"Have you heard anything?" asked Bolton. "Did you see Dodger?"

"No; we didn't see him."

"But you heard something?"

"Yes; we found a boy, a friend of his, that said the last he saw of Dodger was last evenin'."

"Where did he see him?"

"Near the pier of the Albany boats."

"What was he doin'?"

"Carryin' a valise for a man."

"What kind of a man? How did he look?"

"He had gray hair and gray whiskers."

Tim was puzzled by the description.

If, as he suspected, Curtis were concerned in the abduction, this man could not have been he.

"The man was a passenger by the Albany boat, I suppose?"

"No; that was what looked queer. Before the Albany boat came in the man was layin' round with his valise, and the boy thought he was goin' off somewhere. But when the boat came in he just mixed in with the passengers, and came up to the entrance of the pier. Two boys asked to carry his valise, but he shook his head till Dodger came round, and he engaged him right off."

Tim Bolton nodded knowingly.

"It was a plan," he said. "The man wanted to get hold of Dodger. What puzzles me is, that you said he was an old man."

"His hair and beard were gray."

"And Curtis has no beard, and his hair is black."

"But the boy said he didn't look like an old man, except the hair. He walked off like a young man."

Tim Bolton's face lighted up with sudden intelligence.

"I'll bet a hat it was Curtis in disguise," he soliloquized.

"That's all we could find out, Mr. Bolton," said Briggs, with another longing look at the bar.

"It is enough! You have earned your whisky. Walk up, gentlemen!"

Hooker and Briggs needed no second invitation.

"Will either of you take a note for me to Mrs. O'Keefe? For another drink, of course."

"I will, Tim," said Hooker, eagerly.

"No; take me, Mr. Bolton," entreated Briggs.

"You can both go," said Tim, generously. "Wait a minute, and I'll have it ready for you."

He found a half sheet of note-paper, and scribbled on it this message:

> "Mrs. O'Keefe—Tell Miss Linden that I have a clew. I am almost surtin her cozen has got away with Dodger. He won't hurt him, but he will get him out of the city. Wen I heer more I will right.
>
> "T. BOLTON."

Chapter 26

BOLTON MAKES A DISCOVERY

"I see it all," Bolton said to himself, thoughtfully, "Curtis Waring is afraid of the boy—and of me. He's circumvented me neatly, and the game is his—so far my little plan is dished. I must find out for certain whether he's had anything to do with gettin' Dodger out of the way, and then, Tim Bolton, you must set your wits to work to spoil his little game."

Bolton succeeded in securing the services of a young man who had experience at tending bar, and about eight o'clock, after donning his best attire, he hailed a Fourth Avenue surface car and got aboard.

Getting out at the proper street, he made his way to Madison Avenue, and ascended the steps of John Linden's residence.

The door was opened by Jane, who eyed the visitor with no friendly glance.

"What do you want?" she asked, in a hostile tone.

"Is Mr. Waring at home?"

"I don't know."

"Is Miss Florence at home?"

"Do you know her?" she asked.

"Yes; I am a friend of hers."

Jane evidently thought that Florence must have made some queer friends.

"Have you seen her lately?" she asked, eagerly.

"I saw her to-day."

"Is she well?"

"Yes; she is well, but she is in trouble."

"Is she—Does she need any money?"

"No; it isn't that. The boy Dodger has disappeared, and she is afraid something has happened to him."

"Oh, I am so sorry! He was a good friend to Miss Florence."

"I see you know him. I am trying to help him and her."

"But you asked for Mr. Waring?" said Jane, suspiciously.

"So I did. Shall I tell you why?"

"I wish you would."

"I think he has had something to do with gettin' Dodger out of the way, and I'm goin' to try to find out."

"He won't tell you."

"You don't understand. I shall make him think I am on his side. Was he at home last night?"

"He went away at dinner-time, and he didn't come home till after twelve, I ought to know, for he'd forgot his latch-key, and I had to get up and let him in. I won't do it again. I'll let him stay out first."

"I see; he was with Dodger, no doubt. Did you say he was in?"

"No, sir; but he will be in directly. Won't you step into the library?"

"Shall I meet the old gentleman there?" asked Bolton, in a tone of hesitation.

"No. He goes up to his chamber directly after dinner."

"How is he?"

"I think he's failing."

"I hope there is no immediate danger," said Bolton, anxiously.

"No; but he's worrying about Miss Florence. It's my belief that if she was at home, he'd live a good while."

"Doesn't he ask for her?"

"Mr. Curtis tells him she'll come round soon if he'll only be firm. I don't see, for my part, why Mr. Linden wants her to marry such a disagreeable man. There's plenty better husbands she could get. Come in, sir, and I'll tell him as soon as he comes in. Shall you see Miss Florence soon?"

"I think so."

"Then tell her not to give up. Things will come right some time."

"I'll tell her."

Bolton was ushered into the library, where, amid the fashionable furniture, he looked quite out of place. He did not feel so, however, for he drew a cigar out of his pocket and, lighting it nonchalantly, leaned back in a luxurious arm-chair and began to smoke.

"Curtis Waring is well fixed—that's a fact!" he soliloquized. "I suppose he is the master here, for the old man isn't likely to interfere. Still he will like it better when his uncle is out of the way."

He had to wait but fifteen minutes in solitude, for at the end of that time Curtis Waring appeared.

He paused on the threshold, and frowned when he saw who it was that awaited him.

"Jane told me that a gentleman was waiting to see me," he said.

"Well, she was right."

"And you, I suppose, are the gentleman?" said Curtis, in a sneering tone.

"Yes; I am the gentleman," remarked Bolton, coolly.

"I am not in the habit of receiving visits from gentlemen of your class. However, I suppose you have an object in calling."

"It shall go hard with me if I don't pay you for your sneers some day," thought Bolton; but he remained outwardly unruffled.

"Well," he answered, "I can't say that I have any particular business to see you about. I saw your cousin recently."

"Florence?" asked Curtis, eagerly.

"Yes."

"What did she say? Did you speak with her?"

"Yes. She doesn't seem any more willin' to marry you."

Curtis Waring frowned.

"She is a foolish girl," he said. "She doesn't know her own mind."

"She looks to me like a gal that knows her own mind particularly well."

"Pshaw! what can you know about it?"

"Then you really expect to marry her some time, Mr. Waring?"

"Certainly I do."

"And to inherit your uncle's fortune?"

"Of course. Why not?"

"I was thinkin' of the boy."

"The boy is dead—"

"What?" exclaimed Bolton, jumping to his feet in irresistible excitement.

"Don't be a fool. Wait till I finish my sentence. He is dead so far as his prospects are concerned. Who is there that can identify him with the lost child of John Linden?"

"I can."

"Yes; if anyone would believe you. However, it is for your interest to keep silent."

"That is just what I want to know. I suppose you can make it for my interest."

"Yes, and I will—after I get the property. I don't believe in counting my chickens before they are hatched."

"Of course you know that the boy has left me?"

"Yes," answered Curtis, indifferently. "He is with my cousin, I believe."

"Yes; and through her I can learn where he is, and get hold of him if I desire."

A cynical smile played over the face of Curtis Waring.

"Do you propose to get him back?" he asked, shrugging his shoulders.

"I am right," thought Bolton, shrewdly. "From his manner it is easy to see that Curtis is quite at ease as regards Dodger. He knows where he is!"

"You asked me what business I came about, Mr. Waring," he said, after a pause.

"Yes."

"Of course I am devoted to your interest, but is it quite fair to make me wait till you come into your fortune before allowing me anything?"

"I think so."

"You don't seem to consider that I can bring the boy here and make him known to your uncle as the son he lost so long ago?"

"You are quite sure you can bring the boy here?" asked Curtis.

"Why not? I have only to go to Florence and ask her to send the boy to me."

"You are quite at liberty to do so, if you like, Tim Bolton," said Curtis, with a mocking smile. "I am glad, at any rate, that you have shown me what is in your mind. You are very sharp, but you are not quite so sharp as I am."

"I don't understand you."

"Then I will be more explicit. It's out of your power to make use of the boy against me, because—"

"Well?"

"Because he is not in the city."

"Where is he, then?"

"Where you are not likely to find him."

"If you have killed him—" Bolton began, but Curtis interrupted him.

"The boy is safe—I will tell you that much," he said; "but for reasons which you can guess, I think it better that he should be out of New York. When the proper time comes, and all is safe, he may come back, but not in time to help you in your cunning plans, Mr. Tim Bolton."

"Then I suppose," said Bolton, assuming an air of mortification and discomfiture, "it is no use for me to remain here any longer."

"You are quite right. I wish you a pleasant journey home. Give my love to Florence when you see her."

"That man is a fiend!" soliloquized Bolton, as he walked back leisurely to his place of business. "Let me get hold of Dodger, and I will foil him yet!"

Chapter 27

DODGER STRIKES LUCK

When Dodger landed in San Francisco, in spite of the fact that he had made the journey against his will, he felt a natural exhilaration and pleasure in the new and striking circumstances and scenes in which he found himself placed.

It was in the year 1877, and the city was by no means what it is now. Yet it probably contained not far from two hundred thousand people, lively, earnest, enterprising. All seemed busy and hopeful, and Dodger caught the contagion.

As he walked with the reporter to a modest hotel, where the rates were a dollar and a half a day, not far from Montgomery Street, Randolph Leslie asked:

"How do you like San Francisco thus far, Arthur?"

It will be remembered that Dodger, feeling that the name by which he had hitherto been known was hardly likely to recommend him, adopted the one given him by Curtis Waring.

"I think I shall like it ever so much," answered Dodger. "Everybody seems to be wide-awake."

"Do you think you will like it better than New York?"

"I think a poor boy will have more chance of making a living here. In New York I was too well known. If I got a place anywhere someone would recognize me as Tim Bolton's boy—accustomed to tend bar —or some gentleman would remember that he had bought papers of me. Now nobody knows me, and I can start fair."

"There is a great deal in what you say," returned Leslie. "What do you think of trying to do?"

"First of all I will write a letter to Florence, and tell her I am all right. How long does it take a letter to go from here to New York?"

"About seven days."

"And it took us over four months to come! That seems wonderful."

"Yes; there is a great difference between coming by sea round Cape Horn, and speeding across the country on an express train."

"If I could only know how Florence is getting along." Dodger said, anxiously. "I suppose she thinks I am dead."

"You forget the letter you gave to the vessel we spoke off the coast of Brazil."

"Yes; but do you think it went straight?"

"The chances are in favor of it. However, your idea is a good one. Write, by all means, and then we will discuss future plans."

"What are your plans, Mr. Leslie?"

"I shall try to secure a reporter's berth on one of the daily papers— the Call or Chronicle. I will wait for a few days, however, as I have a few hundred dollars by me, and can afford to take a little time to look around."

"I wish I were as well provided; but I have less than twenty-five dollars."

"Don't worry about that, Arthur," said Randolph, laying his hand affectionately on the boy's shoulder. "I shall not allow you to want."

"Thank you, Mr. Leslie," said Dodger, gratefully. "It's something new to me to have a friend like you. But I don't want to be any expense to you. I am large enough and strong enough to earn my own living."

"True; and I feel sure you will have a chance in this enterprising city."

They bought copies of the day's papers, and Dodger looked eagerly over the advertising columns.

At length he saw an advertisement that read as follows:

"WANTED—A young man of 18 or 20, to assist in the office of a local express. Inquire at No. — —— St."

"Do you think I would answer for such a place?" he asked.

"I don't see why not. At any rate, 'nothing venture, nothing gain.' You may as well go round and inquire. And, by the way, as your suit is rather shabby, let me lend you one of mine. We are of nearly the same size."

"Thank you, Mr. Leslie."

"Fine feathers make fine birds, you know, and a neat dress always increases the chances of an applicant for employment, though, when it is carried too far, it is apt to excite suspicion. I remember a friend of mine advertised for a bookkeeper. Among the applicants was a young man wearing a sixty-dollar suit, a ruffled shirt, a handsome gold watch, and a diamond pin. He was a man of taste, and he was strongly impressed with the young man's elegant appearance. So, largely upon the strength of these, he engaged him, and in less than six months discovered that he had been swindled to the extent of eight hundred dollars by his aesthetic bookkeeper."

"Then I will leave my diamond pin at home," said Dodger, smiling.

"Suppose they ask me for recommendations?"

"I will go with you and indorse you. I happen to know one or two prominent gentlemen in San Francisco—among them the president of a bank—and I presume my indorsement will be sufficient."

Dodger went back to the hotel, put on a suit of Mr. Leslie's, got his boots blacked, and then, in company with the young reporter, went to the express office.

"I am afraid someone will have been engaged already," said the reporter; "but if not, your chances will be good."

They entered a good-sized office on a prominent street, and Dodger inquired for Mr. Tucker.

A small man of about forty, keen-eyed and alert, eyed him attentively.

"I am Mr. Tucker," he said.

"I saw your advertisement for an assistant, Mr. Tucker," said Dodger, modestly; "have you filled the place?"

"Let me see," said Tucker, reflectively, "you are the ninth young man who has applied—but the place is still open."

"Then I am afraid you won't want me, as you have rejected so many."

"I don't know. How long have you been in the city?"

"I only just arrived."

"Where from?"

"From New York."

"Have you any idea of going to the mines when you get money enough?"

"I think I would prefer to remain in the city."

"Good! How is your education?"

"I have never been to college," answered Dodger, with a smile.

"Good! I don't care for your college men. I am a practical man myself."

"I am a poor scholar, but Mr. Leslie tells me I write a fair hand."

"Let me see a specimen of your writing."

Now Dodger had taken special pains on the voyage to improve his penmanship, with excellent results.

So it happened that the specimen which he furnished had the good fortune to please Mr. Tucker.

"Good!" he said. "You will a part of the time be taking orders. Your handwriting is plain, and will do. Never mind about Latin and Greek. You won't need it. Chinese would be more serviceable to you here. When can you go to work?"

"To-morrow morning. To-day, if necessary," answered Dodger, promptly.

Mr. Tucker seemed pleased with this answer.

"To-morrow morning let it be, then! Hours are from eight in the morning till six at night."

"Very well, sir."

"Your wages will be fifteen dollars a week. How will that suit you?"

Dodger wanted to indulge in a loud whoop of exaltation, for fifteen dollars was beyond his wildest hopes; but he was too politic to express his delight. So he contented himself with saying:

"I shall be quite satisfied with that."

"Oh, by the way, I suppose I ought to have some reference," said Mr. Tucker, "though as a general thing I judge a good deal by outward appearance."

"I can refer to my friend, Mr. Leslie, here."

"And who will indorse him?" asked the expressman, shrewdly.

"I see, Mr. Tucker, you are a thorough man of business. I can refer you to Mr.——, president of the—— Bank in this city."

"That is sufficient, sir. I am sure you would not refer me to him unless you felt satisfied that he would speak favorably of you. I won't, therefore, take the trouble to inquire. Where are you staying?"

"At the Pacific Hotel; but we shall take a private apartment within a day or two."

As they passed out of the office, Randolph Leslie said:

"You've done splendidly, Arthur."

"Haven't I? I feel like a millionaire."

"As you are to go to work to-morrow, we may as well take up a room at once. It will be cheaper."

In a short time they had engaged a neat suite of rooms, two in number, not far from the Palace Hotel, at twenty dollars per month.

The next day Leslie procured a position on the San Francisco Chronicle, at twenty-five dollars per week.

Chapter 28

FLORENCE RECEIVES A LETTER

The discovery, through Tim Bolton, that Curtis Waring had a hand in the disappearance of Dodger, partially relieved the anxiety of Florence—but only partially.

He might be detained in captivity, but even that was far better than an accident to life or limb.

She knew that he would try to get word to her at the earliest opportunity, in order to relieve her fears.

But week after week passed, and no tidings came.

At length, at the end of ten weeks, a note came to her, written on a rough sheet of paper, the envelope marked by a foreign stamp.

It ran thus:

"Dear Florence—I am sure you have worried over my disappearance. Perhaps you thought I was dead, but I was never better in my life. I am on the ship Columbia, bound for San Francisco, around Cape Horn; and just now, so one of the officers tells me, we are off the coast of Brazil.

"There is a ship coming North, and we are going to hail her and give her letters to carry home, so I hope these few lines will reach you all right. I suppose I am in for it, and must keep on to San Francisco. But I haven't told you yet how I came here.

"It was through a trick of your cousin, Curtis Waring. I haven't time to tell you about it; but I was drugged and brought aboard in my sleep; when I woke up I was forty miles at sea.

"Don't worry about me, for I have a good friend on board, Mr. Randolph Leslie, who has been a reporter on one of the New York daily papers. He advises me to get something to do in San Francisco, and work till I have earned money enough to get home. He says I can do better there, where I am not known, and can get higher pay. He is giving me lessons every day, and he says I am learning fast.

"The ship is almost here, and I must stop. Take good care of yourself, and remember me to Mrs. O'Keefe, and I will write you again as soon as I get to San Francisco.

DODGER.

"P. S.—Don't let on to Curtis that you have heard from me,
or he might try to play me some trick in San Francisco."

Florence's face was radiant when she had read this letter.

Dodger was alive, well, and in good spirits. The letter arrived during the afternoon, and she put on her street-dress at once and went
over to the apple-stand, and read the letter to Mrs. O'Keefe.

"Well, well!" ejaculated the apple-woman. "So it's that ould thafe of
the world, Curtis Waring, that has got hold of poor Dodger, just as
Tim told us? It seems mighty quare to me that he should want to stale
poor Dodger. If it was you now I could understand it."

"It seems strange to me, Mrs. O'Keefe," said Florence, thoughtfully.
"I thought it might be because Dodger was my friend, but that
doesn't seem to be sufficient explanation. Don't you think we ought to
show this letter to Mr. Bolton?"

"I was goin' to suggest that same. If you'll give it to me, Florence,
I'll get Mattie to tend my stand, and slip round wid it to Tim's right
off."

"I will go with you, Mrs. O'Keefe."

Mattie, who was playing round the corner, was summoned.

"Now, Mattie, just mind the stand, and don't be runnin' away, or
them boys will get away wid my whole mornin's profits. Do you hear?"

"Yes, mum."

"And don't you be eatin' all the while you are here. Here's one
apple you can have," and the apple-woman carefully picked out one
that she considered unsalable.

"That's specked, Mrs. O'Keefe," objected Mattie.

"And what if it is? Can't you bite out the specks? The rest of the
apple is good. You're gettin' mighty particular."

Mattie bit a piece out of the sound part of the apple, and, when
Mrs. O'Keefe was at a safe distance, gave the rest to a lame bootblack, and picked out one of the best apples for her own eating.

"Bridget O'Keefe is awful mane wid her apples!" soliloquized Mattie, "but I'm too smart for her. Tryin' to pass off one of her old
specked apples on me! If I don't take three good ones, I'm a sinner!"

Arrived at the front of the saloon, Mrs. O'Keefe penetrated the interior, and met Tim near the door.

"Have you come in for some whisky, old lady?" asked Tim, in a
jesting tone.

"I'll take that by and by. Florence is outside, and we've got some
news for you."

"Won't she come in?"

"No; she don't like to be seen in a place like this. She's got a letter from Dodger."

"You don't mean it!" ejaculated Tim, with sudden interest. "Where is he?"

"Come out and see."

"Good-afternoon, Miss Linden," said Tim, gallantly. "So you've news from Dodger?"

"Yes; here is the letter."

Bolton read it through attentively.

"Curtis is smart," he said, as he handed it back. "He couldn't have thought of a better plan for getting rid of the boy. It will take several months for him to reach 'Frisco, and after that he can't get back, for he won't have any money."

"Dodger says he will try to save money enough to pay his way back."

"It will take him a good while."

"It doesn't take long to come back by cars, does it?"

"No; but it costs a great deal of money. Why, it may take Dodger a year to earn enough to pay his way back on the railroad."

"A year!" exclaimed Florence, in genuine dismay—"a year, in addition to the time it takes to go out there! Where will we all be at the end of that time?"

"Not in jail, I hope," answered Bolton, jocularly. "I am afraid your uncle will no longer be in the land of the living."

A shadow came over Florence's face.

"Poor Uncle John!" she said, sadly. "It is terrible to think he may die thinking hardly of me."

"Leavin' his whole fortune to Curtis," continued Tim.

"That is the least thing that troubles me," said Florence.

"A woman's a queer thing," said Tim, shrugging his shoulders. "Here's a fortune of maybe half a million, and half of it rightfully yours, and you don't give it a thought."

"Not compared with the loss of my uncle's affections."

"Money's a good deal more practical than affection."

"Perhaps so, from your standpoint, Mr. Bolton," said Florence, with dignity.

"No offence, miss. When you've lived as long as I, you'll look at things different. Well, I'm glad to hear from the lad. If Curtis had done him any harm, I'd have got even with him if it sent me to jail."

A quiet, determined look replaced Tim Bolton's usual expression of easy good humor. He could not have said anything that would have ingratiated him more with Florence.

"Thank you, Mr. Bolton," she said, earnestly. "I shall always count upon your help. I believe you are a true friend of Dodger—"

"And of yours, too, miss—"

"I believe it," she said, with a smile that quite captivated Tim.

"If it would be any satisfaction to you, Miss Florence," he continued, "I'll give Curtis Waring a lickin'. He deserves it for persecutin' you and gettin' you turned out of your uncle's house."

"Thank you, Mr. Bolton; it wouldn't be any satisfaction to me to see Curtis injured in any way."

"You're too good a Christian, you are, Miss Florence."

"I wish I deserved your praise, but I can hardly lay claim to it. Now, Mr. Bolton, tell me what can I do to help Dodger?"

"I don't see that you can do anything now, as it will be most three months before he reaches 'Frisco. You might write to him toward the time he gets there."

"I will."

"Direct to the post-office. I think he'll have sense enough to ask for letters."

"I wish I could send him some money, I am afraid he will land penniless."

"If he lands in good health you can trust him for makin' a livin'. A New York boy, brought up as he was, isn't goin' to starve where there are papers to sell and errands to run. Why, he'll light on his feet in 'Frisco, take my word for it."

Florence felt a good deal encouraged by Tim's words of assurance, and she went home with her heart perceptibly lightened.

But she was soon to have trials of her own, which for the time being would make her forgetful of Dodger.

Chapter 29

MRS. LEIGHTON'S PARTY

"Miss Linden," said Mrs. Leighton, one day in the fourth month of Dodger's absence, "Carrie has perhaps told you that I give a party next Thursday evening."

"She told me," answered the governess.

"I expected Professor Bouvier to furnish dancing music—in fact, I had engaged him—but I have just received a note stating that he is unwell, and I am left unprovided. It is very inconsiderate on his part," added the lady, in a tone of annoyance.

Florence did not reply. She took rather a different view of the professor's letter, and did not care to offend Mrs. Leighton.

"Under the circumstances," continued the lady, "it has occurred to me that, as you are really quite a nice performer, you might fill his place. I shall be willing to allow you a dollar for the evening. What do you say?"

Florence felt embarrassed. She shrank from appearing in society in her present separation from her family, yet could think of no good excuse. Noticing her hesitation, Mrs. Leighton added, patronizingly:

"On second thought, I will pay you a dollar and a half" (Professor Bouvier was to have charged ten dollars), "and you will be kind enough to come in your best attire. You seem to be well provided with dresses."

"Yes, madam, there will be no difficulty on that score."

"Nor on any other, I hope. As governess in my family, I think I have a right to command your services."

"I will come," said Florence, meekly. She felt that it would not do to refuse after this.

As she entered the handsomely decorated rooms on the night of the party, she looked around her nervously, fearing to see someone whom she had known in earlier days. She noticed one only—Percy de Brabazon, whose face lighted up when he saw her, for he had been expecting to meet her.

She managed to convey a caution by a quiet movement, as it would not be wise for Mrs. Leighton to know of their previous acquaintance. But Percy was determined to get an opportunity to speak to her.

"Who is that young lady, Aunt Mary?" he asked. "The one standing near the piano."

"That is Carrie's governess," answered Mrs. Leighton, carelessly.

"She seems quite a lady-like person."

"Yes. I understand she has seen better days. She is to play for us in the absence of Professor Bouvier."

"Will you introduce me, aunt?"

"Why?" asked Mrs. Leighton, with a searching look.

"I should like to inquire about Carrie's progress in her studies," said the cunning Percy.

"Oh, certainly," answered the aunt quite deceived by his words.

"Miss Linden," she said, "let me introduce my nephew, Mr. de Brabazon. He wishes to inquire about Carrie's progress in her studies."

And the lady sailed off to another part of the room.

"I can assure you, Mr. de Brabazon," said Florence, "that my young charge is making excellent progress."

"I can easily believe it, under your instruction," said Percy.

"I am very glad you take such an interest in your cousin," added Florence, with a smile. "It does you great credit."

"It's only an excuse, you know, to get a chance to talk with you, Miss Linden. May I say Miss Florence?"

"No," answered Florence decidedly. "It won't do. You must be very formal."

"Then tell me how you like teaching?"

"Very well, indeed."

"It must be an awful bore, I think."

"I don't think so. Carrie is a warm-hearted, affectionate girl. Besides, she is very bright, and gives me very little trouble."

"Don't you think you could take another pupil, Miss Linden?"

"A young girl?"

"No, a young man. In fact, myself."

"What could I teach you, Mr. de Brabazon?"

"Lots of things. I am not very sound in—in spelling and grammar."

"What a pity," answered Florence, with mock seriousness. "I am afraid your aunt would hardly consent to have a boy of your size in the school-room."

"Then perhaps you could give me some private lessons in the afternoon?"

"That would not be possible."

Just then Mrs. Leighton came up.

"Well," she said, "what does Miss Linden say of Carrie?"

"She has quite satisfied my mind about her," answered Percy, with excusable duplicity. "I think her methods are excellent. I was telling her that I might be able to procure her another pupil."

"I have no objection as long as it does not interfere with Carrie's hours. Miss Linden, there is a call for music. Will you go to the piano and play a Strauss waltz?"

Florence inclined her head obediently.

"Let me escort you to the piano, Miss Linden," said Percy.

"Thank you," answered Florence, in a formal tone.

For an hour Florence was engaged in playing waltzes, gallops, and lanciers music. Then a lady who was proud of her daughter's proficiency volunteered her services to relieve Florence.

"Now you can dance yourself," said Percy, in a low tone. "Will you give me a waltz?"

"Not at once. Wait till the second dance."

Percy de Brabazon was prompt in presenting himself as soon as permitted, and he led Florence out for a dance.

Both were excellent dancers, and attracted general attention.

Florence really enjoyed dancing, and forgot for a time that she was only a guest on sufferance, as she moved with rhythmic grace about the handsome rooms.

Percy was disposed to prolong the dance, but Florence was cautious.

"I think I will rest now, Mr. de Brabazon," she said.

"You will favor me again later in the evening?" he pleaded.

"I hardly think it will be wise."

But when, half an hour later, he asked her again, Florence could not find it in her heart to say no. It would have been wise if she had done so. A pair of jealous eyes were fixed upon her. Miss Emily Carter had for a considerable time tried to fascinate Mr. de Brabazon, whose wealth made him a very desirable match, and she viewed his decided penchant for Florence with alarm and indignation.

"To be thrown in the shade by a governess is really too humiliating!" she murmured to herself in vexation. "If it were a girl in my own station, I should not care so much," and she eyed Florence with marked hostility.

"Mamma," she said, "do you see how Mr. de Brabazon is carrying on with Mrs. Leighton's governess? Really, I think it very discreditable."

Mrs. Carter looked through her gold eyeglasses at the couple.

"Is the girl really a governess?" she asked. "She is very well dressed."

"I don't know where she got her dress, but she is really a governess."

"She seems very bold."

"So she does."

Poor Florence. She was far from deserving their unkindly remarks.

"I suppose she is trying to ensnare young de Brabazon," said Emily spitefully. "People of her class are very artful. Don't you think it would be well to call Mrs. Leighton's attention? Percy de Brabazon is her nephew, you know."

"True. The suggestion is a good one, Emily."

Mrs. Carter was quite as desirous as her daughter of bringing about an alliance with Percy, and she readily agreed to second her plans.

"She looked about for Mrs. Leighton, and took a seat at her side.

"Your nephew seems quite attentive to your governess," she commenced.

"Indeed! In what way?"

"He has danced with her three or four times, I believe."

"It looks rather marked."

"So it does," said Mrs. Leighton. "He is quite inconsiderate."

"Oh, well, it is of no great consequence. She is quite stylish for a governess, and doubtless your nephew is taken with her."

"That will not suit my views at all," said Mrs. Leighton, coldly. "I shall speak to her to-morrow."

"Pray don't. It really is a matter of small consequence—quite natural, in fact."

"Leave the matter with me. You have done quite right in mentioning it."

At twelve o'clock the next day, when Florence had just completed her lessons with Carrie, Mrs. Leighton entered the room.

"Please remain a moment, Miss Linden," she said. "I have a few words to say to you."

Mrs. Leighton's tone was cold and unfriendly, and Florence felt that something unpleasant was coming.

Chapter 30

FLORENCE IS FOLLOWED HOME

"I am listening, madam," said Florence, inclining her head.

"I wish to speak to you about last evening, Miss Linden."

"I hope my playing was satisfactory, Mrs. Leighton. I did my best."

"I have no fault to find with your music. It came up to my expectations."

"I am glad of that, madam."

"I referred, rather, to your behavior, Miss Linden."

"I don't understand you, Mrs. Leighton," Florence responded, in unaffected surprise. "Please explain."

"You danced several times with my nephew, Mr. Percy de Brabazon."

"Twice, madam."

"I understood it was oftener. However, that is immaterial. You hardly seemed conscious of your position."

"What was my position, Mrs. Leighton?" asked Florence, quietly, looking her employer full in the face.

"Well—ahem!" answered Mrs. Leighton, a little ill at ease, "you were a hired musician."

"Well?"

"And you acted as if you were an invited guest."

"I am sorry you did not give me instructions as to my conduct," said the governess, coldly. "I should not have danced if I had been aware that it was prohibited."

"I am sorry, Miss Linden, that you persist in misunderstanding me. Mr. de Brabazon being in a different social position from yourself, it looked hardly proper that he should have devoted himself to you more than to any other lady."

"Did he? I was not aware of it. Don't you think, under the circumstances, that he is the one whom you should take to task? I didn't invite his attentions."

"You seemed glad to receive them."

"I was. He is undoubtedly a gentleman."

"Certainly he is. He is my nephew."

"It was not my part to instruct him as to what was proper, surely."

"You are very plausible. Miss Linden, I think it right to tell you that your conduct was commented upon by one of my lady guests as unbecoming. However, I will remember, in extenuation, that you are unaccustomed to society, and doubtless erred ignorantly."

Florence bowed, but forebore to make any remark.

"Do you wish to speak further to me, Mrs. Leighton?" she asked.

"No, I think not."

"Then I will bid you good-morning."

When the governess had left the house, Mrs. Leighton asked herself whether in her encounter with her governess the victory rested with her, and she was forced to acknowledge that it was at least a matter of doubt.

"Miss Linden is a faithful teacher, but she does not appear to appreciate the difference that exists between her and my guests. I think, however, that upon reflection, she will see that I am right in my strictures upon her conduct."

Florence left the house indignant and mortified. It was something new to her to be regarded as a social inferior, and she felt sure that there were many in Mrs. Leighton's position who would have seen no harm in her behavior on the previous evening.

Four days afterward, when Florence entered the Madison Avenue car to ride down-town, she had scarcely reached her seat when an eager voice addressed her:

"Miss Linden, how fortunate I am in meeting you!"

Florence looked up and saw Mr. de Brabazon sitting nearly opposite her.

Though she felt an esteem for him, she was sorry to see him, for, with Mrs. Leighton's rebuke fresh in her mind, it could only be a source of embarrassment, and, if discovered, subject her in all probability to a fresh reprimand.

"You are kind to say so, Mr. de Brabazon," she replied.

"Not at all. I hoped I might meet you again soon. What a pleasant time we had at the party."

"I thought so at the time, but the next day I changed my mind."

"Why, may I ask?"

"Because your aunt, Mrs. Leighton, took me to task for dancing with you twice."

"Was she so absurd?" ejaculated Percy, in surprise.

"It is not necessarily absurd. She said our social positions were so different that it was unbecoming for me to receive attention from you."

"Rubbish!" exclaimed Percy, warmly.

"I am afraid I ought not to listen to such strictures upon the words of my employer."

"I wish you didn't have to teach."

"I can't join you in that wish. I enjoy my work."

"But you ought to be relieved from the necessity."

"We must accept things as we find them," said Florence, gravely.

"There is a way out of it," said Percy, quickly. "You understand me, do you not?"

"I think I do, Mr. de Brabazon, and I am grateful to you, but I am afraid it can never be."

Percy remained silent.

"How far are you going?" asked Florence, uneasily, for she did not care to have her companion learn where she lived.

"I intend to get out at Fourteenth Street."

"Then I must bid you good-afternoon, for we are already at Fifteenth Street."

"If I can be of any service to you, I will ride farther."

"Thank you," said Florence, hastily, "but it is quite unnecessary."

"Then, good-morning!"

And Percy descended from the car.

In another part of the car sat a young lady, who listened with sensations far from pleasant to the conversation that had taken place between Florence and Mr. de Brabazon.

It was Emily Carter, whose jealousy had been excited on the evening of the party. She dropped her veil, fearing to be recognized by Mr. de Brabazon, with whom she was well acquainted. She, too, had intended getting off at Fourteenth Street, but decided to remain longer in the car.

"I will find out where that girl lives," she resolved. "Her conduct with Percy de Brabazon is positively disgraceful. She is evidently doing her best to captivate him. I feel that it is due to Mrs. Leighton, who would be shocked at the thought of her nephew's making a low alliance, to find out all I can, and put her on her guard."

She kept her seat, still keeping her veil down, for it was possible that Florence might recognize her; and the car moved steadily onward till it turned into the Bowery.

"Where on earth is she leading me?" Miss Carter asked herself. "I have never been in this neighborhood before. However, it won't do to give up, when I am, perhaps, on the verge of some important discoveries."

Still the car sped on. Not far from Grand Street Florence left the car, followed, though she was unconscious of it, by her aristocratic fellow-passenger.

Florence stopped a moment to speak to Mrs. O'Keefe at her apple-stand.

"So you're through wid your work, Florence. Are you goin' home?"

"Yes, Mrs. O'Keefe."

"Then I'll go wid you, for I've got a nasty headache, and I'll lie down for an hour."

They crossed the street, not noticing the veiled young lady, who followed within earshot, and listened to their conversation. At length they reached the tenement-house—Florence's humble home—and went in.

"I've learned more than I bargained for," said Emily Carter, in malicious exultation. "I am well repaid for coming to this horrid part of the city. I wonder if Mr. de Brabazon knows where his charmer lives? I will see that Mrs. Leighton knows, at any rate."

Chapter 31

FLORENCE IS DISCHARGED

Mrs. Leighton sat in her boudoir with a stern face and tightly compressed lips. Miss Carter had called the previous afternoon and informed her of the astounding discoveries she had made respecting the governess.

She rang the bell.

"Janet," she said, "when the governess comes you may bring her up to me here."

"Yes, ma'am."

"She's going to catch it—I wonder what for?" thought Janet, as she noted the grim visage of her employer.

So when Florence entered the house she was told that Mrs. Leighton wished to see her at once.

"I wonder what's the matter now?" she asked herself. "Has she heard of my meeting her nephew in the car?"

When she entered the room she saw at once that something was wrong.

"You wished to see me, Mrs. Leighton?" she said.

"Yes," answered Mrs. Leighton, grimly. "Will you be seated?"

Florence sat down a few feet from her employer and waited for an explanation.

She certainly was not prepared for Mrs. Leighton's first words:

"Miss Linden, where do you live?"

Florence started, and her face flushed.

"I live in the lower part of the city," she answered, with hesitation.

"That is not sufficiently definite."

"I live at No. 27 —— Street."

"I think that is east of the Bowery."

"You are right, madam."

"You lodge with an apple-woman, do you not?"

"I do," answered Florence, calmly.

"In a tenement-house?"

"Yes, madam."

"And you actually come from such a squalid home to instruct my daughter!" exlaimed Mrs. Leighton, indignantly. "It is a wonder you have not brought some terrible disease into the house."

"There has been no case of disease in the humble dwelling in which I make my home. I should be as sorry to expose your daughter to any danger of that kind as you would be to have me."

"It is a merciful dispensation of Providence, for which I ought to be truly thankful. But the idea of receiving in my house an inmate of a tenement-house! I am truly shocked. Is this apple-woman your mother?"

"I assure you that she is not," answered Florence, with a smile which she could not repress.

"Or your aunt?"

"She is in no way related to me. She is an humble friend."

"Miss Linden, your tastes must be low, to select such a home and such a friend."

"The state of my purse had something to do with the selection, and the kindness shown me by Mrs. O'Keefe, when I needed a friend, will explain my location further."

"That is not all. You met in the Madison Avenue car yesterday my nephew, Mr. Percy de Brabazon."

"It is coming," thought Florence. "Who could have seen us?" Then aloud:

"Yes, madam."

"Was it by appointment?"

"Do you mean to insult me, Mrs. Leighton?" demanded Florence, rising and looking at the lady with flashing eyes.

"I never insult anybody," replied Mrs. Leighton, coldly. "Pray, resume your seat."

Florence did so.

"Then I may assume that it was accidental. You talked together with the freedom of old friends?"

"You are correctly informed."

"You seem to make acquaintances very readily, Miss Linden. It seems singular, to say the least, that after meeting my nephew for a single evening, you should become such intimate friends."

"You will be less surprised, Mrs. Leighton, when I say that Mr. de Brabazon and I are old friends. We have met frequently."

"Where, in heaven's name?" ejaculated Mrs. Leighton.

"At my residence."

"Good heavens!" exclaimed the scandalized lady. "Does my nephew Percy visit at the home of this apple-woman?"

"No, madam. He does not know where I live."

"Then will you explain your previous statement?"

"I am at present suffering reversed circumstances. It is but a short time since I was very differently situated."

"I won't inquire into your change of circumstances. I feel compelled to perform an unpleasant duty."

Florence did not feel called upon to make any reply, but waited for Mrs. Leighton to finish speaking.

"I shall be obliged to dispense with your services as my daughter's governess. It is quite out of the question for me to employ a person who lives in a tenement-house."

Florence bowed acquiescence, but she felt very sad. She had become attached to her young charge, and it cost her a pang to part from her.

Besides, how was she to supply the income of which this would deprive her?

"I bow to your decision, madam," she said, with proud humility.

"You will find here the sum that I owe you, with payment for an extra week in lieu of notice."

"Thank you. May I bid Carrie good-by?"

"It is better not to do so, I think. The more quietly we dissolve our unfortunate connection the better!"

Florence's heart swelled, and the tears came to her eyes, but she could not press her request.

She was destined, however, to obtain the privilege which Mrs. Leighton denied her. Carrie, who had become impatient, came downstairs and burst into the room.

"What keeps you so long, Miss Linden?" she said. "Is mamma keeping you?"

Florence was silent, leaving the explanations to Mrs. Leighton.

"Miss Linden has resigned her position as your governess, Carrie."

"Miss Linden going away! I won't have her go! What makes you go, Miss Linden?"

"Your mamma thinks it best," answered Florence, with moistened eyes.

"Well, I don't!" exclaimed Carrie stamping her foot, angrily. "I won't have any other governess but you."

"Carrie, you are behaving very unbecomingly," said her mother.

"Will you tell me, mamma, why you are sending Miss Linden away?"

"I will tell you some other time."

"But I want to know now."

"I am very much displeased with you, Carrie."

"And I am very much displeased with you, mamma."

I do not pretend to defend Carrie, whose conduct was hardly respectful enough to her mother; but with all her faults she had a warm heart, while her mother had always been cold and selfish.

"I am getting tired of this," said Mrs. Leighton. "Miss Linden, as you are here to-day, you may give Carrie the usual lessons. As I shall be out when you get through, I will bid you good-by now."

"Good-by, Mrs. Leighton."

Carrie and Florence went to the school-room for the last time.

Florence gave her young pupil a partial explanation of the cause which had led to her discharge.

"What do I care if you live in a poor house, Miss Linden?" said Carrie, impetuously. "I will make mamma take you back!"

Florence smiled; but she knew that there would be no return for her.

When she reached her humble home she had a severe headache and lay down. Mrs. O'Keefe came in later to see her.

"And what's the matter with you, Florence?" she asked.

"I have a bad headache, Mrs. O'Keefe."

"You work too hard, Florence, wid your teachin'. That is what gives you the headache."

"Then I shan't have it again, for I have got through with my teaching."

"What's that you say?"

"I am discharged."

"And what's it all about?"

Florence explained matters. Mrs. O'Keefe became indignant.

"She's a mean trollop, that Mrs. Leighton!" she exclaimed, "and I'd like to tell her so to her face. Where does she live?"

"It will do no good to interfere, my good friend. She is not willing to receive a governess from a tenement-house."

"Shure you used to live in as grand a house as herself."

"But I don't now."

"Don't mind it too much, mavourneen. You'll soon be gettin' another scholar. Go to sleep now, and you'll sleep the headache away."

Florence finally succeeded in following the advice of her humble friend.

She resolved to leave till the morrow the cares of the morrow.

She had twelve dollars, and before that was spent she hoped to be in a position to earn some more.

Chapter 32

AN EXCITING ADVENTURE

Dodger soon became accustomed to his duties at Tucker's express office, in his new San Francisco home. He found Mr. Tucker an exacting, but not an unreasonable, man. He watched his new assistant closely for the first few days, and was quietly taking his measure.

At the end of the first week he paid the salary agreed upon—fifteen dollars.

"You have been with me a week, Arthur," he said.

"Yes, sir."

"And I have been making up my mind about you."

"Yes, sir," said Dodger, looking up inquiringly. "I hope you are satisfied with me?"

"Yes, I think I may say that I am. You don't seem to be afraid of work."

"I have always been accustomed to work."

"That is well. I was once induced to take the son of a rich man in the place you now occupy. He had never done a stroke of work, having always been at school. He didn't take kindly to work, and seemed afraid that he would be called upon to do more than he had bargained for. One evening I was particularly busy, and asked him to remain an hour overtime.

"'It will be very inconvenient, Mr. Tucker,' said the young man, 'as I have an engagement with a friend.'

"He left me to do all the extra work, and—I suppose you know what happened the next Saturday evening?"

"I can guess," returned Dodger, with a smile.

"I told him that I thought the duties were too heavy for his constitution, and he had better seek an easier place. Let me see—I kept you an hour and a half overtime last Wednesday."

"Yes, sir."

"You made no objection, but worked on just as if you liked it."

"Yes, sir; I am always willing to stay when you need me."

"Good! I shan't forget it."

Dodger felt proud of his success, and put away the fifteen dollars with a feeling of satisfaction. He had never saved half that sum in the same time before.

"Curtis Waring did me a favor when he sent me out here," he reflected; "but as he didn't mean it, I have no occasion to feel grateful."

Dodger found that he could live for eight dollars a week, and he began to lay by seven dollars a week with the view of securing funds sufficient to take him back to New York.

He was in no hurry to leave San Francisco, but he felt that Florence might need a friend. But he found that he was making progress slowly.

At that time the price of a first-class ticket to New York was one hundred and twenty-eight dollars, besides the expense of sleeping-berths amounting then, as now, to twenty-two dollars extra. So it looked as if Dodger would be compelled to wait at least six months before he should be in a position to set out on the return journey.

About this time Dodger received a letter from Florence, in which she spoke of her discharge by Mrs. Leighton.

"I shall try to obtain another position as teacher," she said, concealing her anxiety. "I am sure, in a large city, I can find something to do."

But Dodger knew better than she the difficulties that beset the path of an applicant for work, and he could not help feeling anxious for Florence.

"If I were only in New York," he said to himself, "I would see that Florence didn't suffer. I will write her to let me know if she is in need, and I will send her some money."

About this time he met with an adventure which deserves to be noted.

It was about seven o'clock one evening that he found himself in Mission Street.

At a street corner his attention was drawn to a woman poorly dressed, who held by the hand a child of three.

Her clothing was shabby, and her attitude was one of despondency. It was clear that she was ill and in trouble.

Dodger possessed quick sympathies, and his own experience made him quick to understand and feel for the troubles of others.

Though the woman made no appeal, he felt instinctively that she needed help.

"I beg your pardon," he said; with as much deference as if he were addressing one favored by fortune, "but you seem to be in need of help?"

"God knows, I am!" said the woman sadly.

"Perhaps I can be of service to you. Will you tell me how?"

"Neither I nor my child has tasted food since yesterday."

"Well, that can be easily remedied," said Dodger, cheerfully. "There is a restaurant close by. I was about to eat supper. Will you come in with me?"

"I am ashamed to impose upon the kindness of a stranger," murmured the woman.

"Don't mention it. I shall be very glad of company," said Dodger, heartily.

"But you are a poor boy. You may be ill able to afford the expense."

"I am not a millionaire," said Dodger, "and I don't see any immediate prospect of my building a palace on Nob Hill—where live some of San Francisco's wealthiest citizens—but I am very well supplied with money."

"Then I will accept your kind invitation."

It was a small restaurant, but neat in its appointments, and, as in most San Francisco restaurants, the prices were remarkably moderate.

At an expense of twenty-five cents each, the three obtained a satisfactory meal.

The woman and child both seemed to enjoy it, and Dodger was glad to see that the former became more cheerful as time went on.

There was something in the child's face that looked familiar to Dodger. It was a resemblance to some one that he had seen, but he could not for the life of him decide who it was.

"How can I ever thank you for your kindness?" said the lady, as she arose from the table. "You don't know what it is to be famished—"

"Don't I?" asked Dodger. "I have been hungry more than once, without money enough to buy a meal."

"You don't look it," she said.

"No, for now I have a good place and am earning a good salary."

"Are you a native of San Francisco?"

"No, madam. I can't tell you where I was born, for I know little or nothing of my family. I have only been here a short time. I came from New York."

"So did I," said the woman, with a sigh. "I wish I were back there again."

"How came you to be here? Don't answer if you prefer not to," Dodger added, hastily.

"I have no objection. My husband deserted me, and left me to shift for myself and support my child."

"How have you done it?"

"By taking in sewing. But that is a hard way of earning money. There are too many poor women who are ready to work for starvation wages, and so we all suffer."

"I know that," answered Dodger. "Do you live near here?"

The woman mentioned a street near by.

"I have one poor back room on the third floor," she explained; "but I should be glad if I were sure to stay there."

"Is there any danger of your being ejected?"

"I am owing for two weeks' rent, and this is the middle of the third week. Unless I can pay up at the end of this week I shall be forced to go out into the streets with my poor child."

"How much rent do you pay?"

"A dollar a week."

"Then three dollars will relieve you for the present?"

"Yes; but it might as well be three hundred," said the woman, bitterly.

"Not quite; I can supply you with three dollars, but three hundred would be rather beyond my means."

"You are too kind, too generous! I ought not to accept such a liberal gift."

"Mamma, I am tired. Take me up in your arms," said the child.

"Poor child! He has been on his feet all day," sighed the mother.

She tried to lift the child, but her own strength had been undermined by privation, and she was clearly unable to do so.

"Let me take him!" said Dodger. "Here, little one, jump up!"

He raised the child easily, and despite the mother's protest, carried him in his arms.

"I will see you home, madam," he said.

"I fear the child will be too heavy for you."

"I hope not. Why, I could carry a child twice as heavy."

They reached the room at last—a poor one, but a welcome repose from the streets.

"Don't you ever expect to see your husband again?" asked Dodger. "Can't you compel him to support you?"

"I don't know where he is," answered the woman, despondently.

"If you will tell me his name, I may come across him some day."

"His name," said the woman, "is Curtis Waring." Dodger stared at her, overwhelmed with surprise.

Chapter 33

AN IMPORTANT DISCOVERY

"Curtis Waring!" ejaculated Dodger, his face showing intense surprise. "Is that the name of your husband?"

"Yes. Is it possible that you know him?" asked the woman, struck by Dodger's tone.

"I know a man by that name. I will describe him, and you can tell me whether it is he. He is rather tall, dark hair, sallow complexion, black eyes, and a long, thin nose."

"It is like him in every particular. Oh, tell me where he is to be found?"

"He lives in New York. He is the nephew of a rich man, and is expecting to inherit his wealth. Through his influence a cousin of his, a young lady, has been driven from home."

"Was he afraid she would deprive him of the estate?"

"That was partly the reason. But it was partly to revenge himself on her because she would not agree to marry him."

"But how could he marry her?" exclaimed the unfortunate woman, "when he is already married to me?"

"Neither she nor any one of his family or friends knew that he was already married. I don't think it would trouble him much."

"But it must be stopped!" she exclaimed wildly. "He is my husband. I shall not give him up to any one else."

"So far as Florence is concerned—she is the cousin—she has no wish to deprive you of him. But is it possible that you are attached to a man who has treated you so meanly?" asked Dodger, in surprise.

"There was a time when he treated me well, when he appeared to love me," was the murmured reply. "I cannot forget that he is the father of my child."

Dodger did not understand the nature of women or the mysteries of the female heart, and he evidently thought this poor woman very foolish to cling with such pertinacity to a man like Curtis Waring.

"Do you mind telling me how you came to marry him?" he asked.

"It was over four years ago that I met him in this city," was the reply. "I am a San Francisco girl. I had never been out of California. I was considered pretty then," she added, with a remnant of pride, "faded as I am to-day."

Looking closely in her face, Dodger was ready to believe this.

Grief and privation had changed her appearance, but it had not altogether effaced the bloom and beauty of youth.

"At any rate, he seemed to think so. He was living at the Palace Hotel, and I made his acquaintance at a small social gathering at the house of my uncle. I am an orphan, and was perhaps the more ready to marry on that account."

"Did Mr. Waring represent himself as wealthy?"

"He said he had expectations from a wealthy relative, but did not mention where he lived."

"He told the truth, then."

"We married, securing apartments on Kearney Street. We lived together till my child was born, and for three months afterward. Then Mr. Waring claimed to be called away from San Francisco on business. He said he might be absent six weeks. He left me a hundred dollars, and urged me to be careful of it, as he was short of money, and needed considerable for the expenses of the journey. He left me, and I have never seen or heard from him since."

"Did he tell you where he was going, Mrs. Waring?"

"No; he said he would be obliged to visit several places—among others, Colorado, where he claimed to have some mining property. He told me that he hoped to bring back considerable money."

"Did you think he meant to stay away altogether?"

"I don't know what to think. Well, I lived on patiently, for I had perfect confidence in my husband. I made the money last me ten weeks instead of six, but then I found myself penniless."

"Did you receive any letters in that time?"

"No, and it was that that worried me. When at last the money gave out, I began to pawn my things—more than once I was tempted to pawn my wedding-ring, but I would not bring my mind to do that. I did not like to think ill of my husband, and was forced, as the only alternative, to conclude that he had met with some accident, perhaps had died. I have not felt certain that this was not so till you told me this evening that you know him."

"I can hardly say that I know him well, yet I know him a good deal better than I wish I did. But for him I would not now be in San Francisco."

"How is that? Please explain."

Dodger told her briefly the story of his abduction.

"But what motive could he have in getting you out of New York? I cannot understand."

"I don't understand myself, except that I am the friend of Florence."

"His cousin?"

"Yes."

"But why should she be compelled to leave her uncle's home?"

"Because Curtis Waring made him set his heart upon the match. She had her choice, to marry Curtis or to leave the house, and forfeit all chance of the estate. She chose to leave the house."

"She ought to know that he has no right to marry," said the poor woman, who, not understanding the dislike of Florence for the man whom she herself loved, feared that she might yet be induced to marry him.

"She ought to know, and her uncle ought to know," said Dodger. "Mrs. Waring, I can't see my way clear yet. If I were in New York I would know just what to do. Will you agree to stand by me, and help me?"

"Yes, I will," answered the woman, earnestly.

"I will see you again to-morrow evening. Here is some money to help you along for the present. Good-night."

Dodger, as he walked away, pondered over the remarkable discovery he had made.

It was likely to prove of the utmost importance to Florence.

Her uncle's displeasure was wholly based upon her refusal to marry Curtis Waring, but if it should be proved to him that Curtis was already a married man, there would seem no bar to reconciliation.

Moreover, and this was particularly satisfactory, it would bring Curtis himself into disfavor.

Florence would be reinstated in her rightful place in her uncle's family, and once more be recognized as heiress to at least a portion of his large fortune.

This last consideration might not weigh so much with Florence, but Dodger was more practical, and he wished to restore her to the social position which she had lost through the knavery of her cousin.

But in San Francisco—at a distance of over three thousand miles—Dodger felt at a loss how to act.

Even if Mr. Linden was informed that his nephew had a wife living in San Francisco, the statement would no doubt be denied by Curtis, who would brand the woman as an impudent adventuress.

"The absent are always in the wrong," says a French proverb.

At all events, they are very much at a disadvantage, and therefore it seemed imperatively necessary, not only that Dodger, but that Curtis Waring's wife, should go to New York to confront the unprincipled man whose schemes had brought sorrow to so many.

It was easy to decide what plan was best, but how to carry it out presented a difficulty which seemed insurmountable.

The expenses of a journey to New York for Dodger, Mrs. Waring and her child would not vary far from five hundred dollars, and where to obtain this money was a problem.

Randolph Leslie probably had that sum, but Dodger could not in conscience ask him to lend it, being unable to furnish adequate security, or to insure repayment.

"If I could only find a nugget," thought Dodger, knitting his brows, "everything would be easy."

But nuggets are rare enough in the gold fields, and still rarer in city streets.

He who trusts wholly to luck, trusts to a will-o'-the-wisp, and is about as sure of success as one who owns a castle in Spain.

The time might come when Dodger, by his own efforts, could accumulate the needed sum, but it would require a year at least, and in that time Mr. Linden would probably be dead.

Absorbed and disturbed by these reflections, Dodger walked slowly through the darkened streets till he heard a stifled cry, and looking up, beheld a sight that startled him.

On the sidewalk lay the prostrate figure of a man. Over him, bludgeon in hand, bent a ruffian, whose purpose was only too clearly evident.

Chapter 34

JUST IN TIME

Dodger, who was a strong, stout boy, gathered himself up and dashed against the ruffian with such impetuosity that he fell over his intended victim, and his bludgeon fell from his hand.

It was the work of an instant to lift it, and raise it in a menacing position.

The discomfited villain broke into a volley of oaths, and proceeded to pick himself up.

He was a brutal-looking fellow, but was no larger than Dodger, who was as tall as the majority of men.

"Give me that stick," he exclaimed, furiously.

"Come and take it," returned Dodger, undaunted.

The fellow took him at his word, and made a rush at our hero, but a vigorous blow from the bludgeon made him cautious about repeating the attack.

"Curse you!" he cried, between his teeth. "I'd like to chaw you up."

"I have no doubt you would," answered Dodger; "but I don't think you will. Were you going to rob this man?"

"None of your business!"

"I shall make it my business. You'd better go, or you may be locked up."

"Give me that stick, then."

"You'll have to do without it."

He made another rush, and Dodger struck him such a blow on his arm that he winced with pain.

"Now I shall summon the police, and you can do as you please about going."

Dodger struck the stick sharply on the sidewalk three times, and the ruffian, apprehensive of arrest, ran round the corner just in time to rush into the arms of a policeman.

"What has this man been doing?" asked the city guardian, turning to Dodger.

"He was about to rob this man."

"Is the man hurt?"

"Where am I?" asked the prostrate man, in a bewildered tone.

"I will take care of him, if you will take charge of that fellow."

"Can you get up, sir?" asked Dodger, bending over the fallen man.

The latter answered by struggling to his feet and looking about him in a confused way.

"Where am I?" he asked. "What has happened?"

"You were attacked by a ruffian. I found you on the sidewalk, with him bending over you with this club in his hand."

"He must have followed me. I was imprudent enough to show a well-filled pocket-book in a saloon where I stopped to take a drink. No doubt he planned to relieve me of it."

"You have had a narrow escape, sir."

"I have no doubt of it. I presume the fellow was ready to take my life, if he found it necessary."

"I will leave you now, sir; if you think you can manage."

"No, stay with me. I feel rather upset."

"Where are you staying, sir?"

"At the Palace Hotel. Of course you know where that is?"

"Certainly. Will you take my arm?"

"Thank you."

Little was said till they found themselves in the sumptuous hotel, which hardly has an equal in America.

"Come up to my room, young man; I want to speak to you."

It was still early in the evening, and Dodger's time was his own.

He had no hesitation, therefore, in accepting the stranger's invitation.

On the third floor the stranger produced a key and opened the door of a large, handsomely-furnished room.

"If you have a match, please light the gas."

Dodger proceeded to do so, and now, for the first time, obtained a good view of the man he had rescued. He was a man of about the average height, probably not far from fifty, dressed in a neat business suit, and looked like a substantial merchant.

"Please be seated."

Dodger sat down in an easy-chair conveniently near him.

"Young man," said the stranger, impressively, "you have done me a great favor."

Dodger felt that this was true, and did not disclaim it.

"I am very glad I came up just as I did," he said.

"How large a sum of money do you think I had about me?" asked his companion.

"Five hundred dollars?"

"Five hundred dollars! Why, that would be a mere trifle."

"It wouldn't be a trifle to me, sir," said Dodger.

"Are you poor?" asked the man, earnestly.

"I have a good situation that pays me fifteen dollars a week, so I ought not to consider myself poor."

"Suppose you had a considerable sum of money given you, what would you do with it?"

"If I had five hundred dollars, I should be able to defeat the schemes of a villain, and restore a young lady to her rights."

"That seems interesting. Tell me the circumstances."

Dodger told the story as briefly as he could. He was encouraged to find that the stranger listened to him with attention.

"Do you know," he said, reflectively, "you have done for me what I once did for another—a rich man. The case was very similar. I was a poor boy at the time. Do you know what he gave me?"

"What was it, sir?"

"A dollar! What do you think of that for generosity?"

"Well, sir, it wasn't exactly liberal. Did you accept it?"

"No. I told him that I didn't wish to inconvenience him. But I asked you how much money you supposed I had. I will tell you. In a wallet I have eleven thousand dollars in bank-notes and securities."

"That is a fortune," said Dodger, dazzled at the mention of such a sum.

"If I had lost it, I have plenty more, but the most serious peril was to my life. Through your opportune assistance I have escaped without loss. I fully appreciate the magnitude of the service you have done me. As an evidence of it, please accept these bills."

He drew from the roll two bills and handed them to Dodger.

The boy, glancing at them mechanically, started in amazement. Each bill was for five hundred dollars.

"You have given me a thousand dollars!" he gasped.

"I am aware of it. I consider my life worth that, at least. James Swinton never fails to pay his debts."

"But, sir, a thousand dollars—"

"It's no more than you deserve. When I tell my wife, on my return to Chicago, about this affair, she will blame me for not giving you more."

"You seem to belong to a liberal family, sir."

"I detest meanness, and would rather err on the side of liberality. Now, if aggreeable to you, I will order a bottle of champagne, and solace ourselves for this little incident."

"Thank you, Mr. Swinton, but I have made up my mind not to drink anything stronger than water. I have tended bar in New York, and what I have seen has given me a dislike for liquor of any kind."

"You are a sensible young man. You are right, and I won't urge you. There is my card, and if you ever come to Chicago, call upon me."

"I will, sir."

When Dodger left the Palace Hotel, he felt that he was a favorite of fortune.

It is not always that the money we need is so quickly supplied.

He resolved to return to New York as soon as he could manage it, and take with him the wife and child of Curtis Waring.

This would cost him about five hundred dollars, and he would have the same amount left.

Mr. Tucker was reluctant to part with Dodger.

"You are the best assistant I ever had," he said. "I will pay you twenty dollars a week, if that will induce you to stay."

"I would stay if it were not very important for me to return to New York, Mr. Tucker. I do not expect to get a place in New York as good."

"If you come back to San Francisco at any time, I will make a place for you."

"Thank you, sir."

Mrs. Waring was overjoyed when Dodger called upon her and offered to take her back to New York.

"I shall see Curtis again," she said. "How can I ever thank you?"

But Dodger, though unwilling to disturb her dreams of happiness, thought it exceedingly doubtful if her husband would be equally glad to see her.

Chapter 35

THE DARKEST DAY

When Florence left the employ of Mrs. Leighton she had a few dollars as a reserve fund. As this would not last long, she at once made an effort to obtain employment.

She desired another position as governess, and made application in answer to an advertisement.

Her ladylike manner evidently impressed the lady to whom she applied.

"I suppose you have taught before?" she said.

"Yes, madam."

"In whose family?"

"I taught the daughter of Mrs. Leighton, of West — Street."

"I have heard of the lady. Of course you are at liberty to refer to her?"

"Yes, madam," but there was a hesitation in her tone that excited suspicion.

"Very well; I will call upon her and make inquiries. If you will call to-morrow morning, I can give you a decisive answer."

Florence fervently hoped that this might prove favorable; but was apprehensive, and with good reason, it appeared.

When she presented herself the next day, Mrs. Cole said:

"I am afraid, Miss Linden, you will not suit me."

"May I ask why?" Florence inquired, schooling herself to calmness.

"I called on Mrs. Leighton," was the answer. "She speaks well of you as a teacher, but—she told me some things which make it seem inexpedient to engage you."

"What did she say of me?"

"That, perhaps, you had better not inquire."

"I prefer to know the worst."

"She said you encouraged the attentions of her nephew, forgetting the difference in social position, and also that your connections were not of a sort to recommend you. I admit, Miss Linden, that you are very ladylike in appearance, but I can hardly be expected to admit into my house, in the important position of governess to my child, the daughter or niece of an apple-woman."

"Did Mrs. Leighton say that I was related to an apple-woman?"

"Yes, Miss Linden. I own I was surprised."

"It is not true, Mrs. Cole."

"You live in the house of such a person, do you not?"

"Yes, she is an humble friend of mine, and has been kind to me."

"You cannot be very fastidious. However, that is your own affair. I am sorry to disappoint you, Miss Linden, but it will be quite impossible for me to employ you."

"Then I will bid you good-morning, Mrs. Cole," said Florence, sore at heart.

"Good-morning. You will, I think, understand my position. If you applied for a position in one of the public schools, I don't think that your residence would be an objection."

Florence left the house, sad and despondent. She saw that Mrs. Leighton, by her unfriendly representations, would prevent her from getting any opportunity to teach. She must seek some more humble employment.

"Well, Florence, did you get a place?" asked Mrs. O'Keefe, as she passed that lady's stand.

"No, Mrs. O'Keefe," answered Florence, wearily.

"And why not? Did the woman think you didn't know enough?"

"She objected to me because I was not living in a fashionable quarter—at least that was one of her objections."

"I'm sure you've got a nate, clane home, and it looks as nate as wax all the time."

"It isn't exactly stylish," said Florence, with a faint smile.

"You are, at any rate. What does the woman want, I'd like to know?"

"She doesn't want me. It seems Mrs. Leighton did not speak very highly of me."

"The trollop! I'd like to give her a box on the ear, drat her impudence!" said the irate apple-woman. "And what will you be doin' now?"

"Do you think I can get some sewing to do, Mrs. O'Keefe?"

"Yes, Miss Florence—I'll get you some vests to make; but it's hard work and poor pay."

"I must take what I can get," sighed Florence. "I cannot choose."

"If you'd only tend an apple-stand, Miss Florence! There's Mrs. Brady wants to sell out on account of the rheumatics, and I've got a trifle in the savings bank—enough to buy it. You'd make a dollar a day, easy."

"It isn't to be thought of, Mrs. O'Keefe. If you will kindly see about getting me some sewing I will see how I can get along."

The result was that Mrs. O'Keefe brought Florence in the course of the day half a dozen vests, for which she was to be paid the munificent sum of twenty-five cents each.

Florence had very little idea of what she was undertaking.

She was an expert needlewoman, and proved adequate to the work, but with her utmost industry she could only make one vest in a day, and that would barely pay her rent.

True, she had some money laid aside on which she could draw, but that would soon be expended, and then what was to become of her?

"Shure, I won't let you starve, Florence," said the warm-hearted apple-woman.

"But, Mrs. O'Keefe, I can't consent to live on you."

"And why not? I'm well and strong, and I'm makin' more money than I nade."

"I couldn't think of it, though I thank you for your kindness."

"Shure, you might write a letter to your uncle."

"He would expect me, in that case, to consent to a marriage with Curtis. You wouldn't advise me to do that?"

"No; he's a mane blackguard, and I'd say it to his face."

Weeks rolled by, and Florence began to show the effects of hard work and confinement.

She grew pale and thin, and her face was habitually sad.

She had husbanded her savings as a governess as closely as she could, but in spite of all of her economy it dwindled till she had none left.

Henceforth she must depend on twenty-five cents a day, and this seemed well-nigh impossible.

In this emergency the pawnbroker occurred to her.

She had a variety of nice dresses, and she had also a handsome ring given her by her uncle on her last birthday.

This she felt sure must have cost fifty dollars. It was a trial to part with it, but there seemed to be no alternative.

"If my uncle has withdrawn his affection from me," she said to herself, "why should I scruple to pawn the ring? It is the symbol of a love that no longer exists."

So she entered the pawnbroker's—the first that attracted her attention—and held out the ring.

"How much will you lend me on this?" she asked, half frightened at finding herself in such a place.

The pawnbroker examined it carefully. His practiced eye at once detected its value, but it was not professional to admit this.

"Rings is a drug in the market, young lady," he said. "I've got more than I know what to do with. I'll give you—four dollars."

"Four dollars!" repeated Florence, in dismay. "Why, it must have cost fifty. It was bought in Tiffany's."

"You are mistaken, my dear. Did you buy it yourself there?"

"No, my uncle gave it to me."

"He may have said he paid fifty dollars for it," said the pawnbroker, wagging his head, "but we know better."

"But what will you give?" asked Florence, desperately.

"I'll give you five dollars, and not a penny more," said the broker, surveying her distressed face shrewdly. "You can take it or not."

What could Florence do?

She must have money, and feared that no other pawnbroker would give her more.

"Make out the ticket, then," she said, with a sigh.

This was done, and she left the place, half timid, half ashamed, and wholly discouraged.

But the darkest hour is sometimes nearest the dawn. A great and overwhelming surprise awaited her. She had scarcely left the shop when a glad voice cried:

"I have found you at last, Florence!"

She looked up and saw—Dodger.

But not the old Dodger. She saw a nicely-dressed young gentleman, larger than the friend she had parted with six months before, with a brighter, more intelligent, and manly look.

"Dodger!" she faltered.

"Yes, it is Dodger."

"Where did you come from?"

"From San Francisco. But what have you been doing in there?"

And Dodger pointed in the direction of the pawnbroker's shop.

"I pawned my ring."

"Then I shall get it back at once. How much did you get on it?"

"Five dollars."

"Give me the ticket, and go in with me."

The pawnbroker was very reluctant to part with the ring, which he made sure would not be reclaimed; but there was no help for it.

As they emerged into the street, Dodger said:

"I've come back to restore you to your rights, and give Curtis Waring the most disagreeable surprise he ever had. Come home, and I'll tell you all about it. I've struck luck, Florence, and you're going to share it."

Chapter 36

MRS. O'KEEFE IN A NEW ROLE

No time was lost in seeing Bolton and arranging a plan of campaign.

Curtis Waring, nearing the accomplishment of his plans, was far from anticipating impending disaster.

His uncle's health had become so poor, and his strength had been so far undermined, that it was thought desirable to employ a sick-nurse. An advertisement was inserted in a morning paper, which luckily attracted the attention of Bolton.

"You must go, Mrs. O'Keefe," he said to the apple-woman. "It is important that we have some one in the house—some friend of Florence and the boy—to watch what is going on."

"Bridget O'Keefe is no fool. Leave her to manage."

The result was that among a large number of applicants Mrs. O'Keefe was selected by Curtis as Mr. Linden's nurse, as she expressed herself willing to work for four dollars a week, while the lowest outside demand was seven.

We will now enter the house, in which the last scenes of our story are to take place.

Mr. Linden, weak and emaciated, was sitting in an easy-chair in his library.

"How do you feel this morning, uncle?" asked Curtis, entering the room.

"I am very weak, Curtis. I don't think I shall ever be any better."

"I have engaged a nurse, uncle, as you desired, and I expect her this morning."

"That is well, Curtis. I do not wish to confine you to my bedside."

"The nurse is below," said Jane, the servant, entering.

"Send her up."

Mrs. O'Keefe entered in the sober attire of a nurse. She dropped a curtsey.

"Are you the nurse I engaged?" asked Curtis.

"Yes, sir."

"Your name, please."

"Mrs. Barnes, sir."

"Have you experience as a nurse?"

"Plenty, sir."

"Uncle, this is Mrs. Barnes, your new nurse. I hope you will find her satisfactory."

"She looks like a good woman," said Mr. Linden, feebly. "I think she will suit me."

"Indade, sir, I'll try."

"Uncle," said Curtis, "I have to go down-town. I have some business to attend to. I leave you in the care of Mrs. Barnes."

"Shure, I'll take care of him, sir."

"Is there anything I can do for you, Mr. Linden?" asked the new nurse, in a tone of sympathy.

"Can you minister to a mind diseased?"

"I'll take the best care of you, Mr. Linden, but it isn't as if you had a wife or daughter."

"Ah, that is a sore thought! I have no wife or daughter; but I have a niece."

"And where is she, sir?"

"I don't know. I drove her from me by my unkindness. I repent bitterly, but it's now too late."

"And why don't you send for her to come home?"

"I would gladly do so, but I don't know where she is. Curtis has tried to find her, but in vain. He says she is in Chicago."

"And what should take her to Chicago?"

"He says she is there as a governess in a family."

"By the brow of St. Patrick!" thought Mrs. O'Keefe, "if that Curtis isn't a natural-born liar. I'm sure she'd come back if you'd send for her, sir."

"Do you think so?" asked Linden, eagerly.

"I'm sure of it."

"But I don't know where to send."

"I know of a party that would be sure to find her."

"Who is it?"

"It's a young man. They call him the Dodger. If any one can find Miss Florence, he can."

"You know my niece's name?"

"I have heard it somewhere. From Mr. Waring, I think."

"And you think this young man would agree to go to Chicago and find her?"

"Yes, sir, I make bold to say he will."

"Tell him to go at once. He will need money. In yonder desk you will find a picture of my niece and a roll of bills. Give them to him and send him at once."

"Yes, sir, I will. But if you'll take my advice, you won't say anything to Mr. Curtis. He might think it foolish."

"True! If your friend succeeds, we'll give Curtis a surprise."

"And a mighty disagreeable one, I'll be bound," soliloquized Mrs. O'Keefe.

"I think, Mrs. Barnes, I will retire to my chamber, if you will assist me."

She assisted Mr. Linden to his room, and then returned to the library.

"Mrs. Barnes, there's a young man inquiring for you," said Jane, entering.

"Send him in, Jane."

The visitor was Dodger, now neatly dressed.

"How are things going, Mrs. O'Keefe?" he asked.

"Splendid, Dodger. Here's some money for you."

"What for?"

"You're to go Chicago and bring back Florence."

"But she isn't there."

"Nivir mind. You're to pretend to go."

"But that won't take money."

"Give it to Florence, then. It's hers by rights. Won't we give Curtis a surprise? Where's his wife?"

"I have found a comfortable boarding-house for her. When had we better carry out this programme? She's very anxious to see her husband."

"The more fool she. Kape her at home and out of his sight, or there's no knowin' what he'll do. And, Dodger, dear, kape an eye on the apple-stand. I mistrust Mrs. Burke that's runnin' it."

"I will. Does the old gentleman seem to be very sick?"

"He's wake as a rat. Curtis would kill him soon if we didn't interfere. But we'll soon circumvent him, the snake in the grass! Miss Florence will soon come to her own, and Curtis Waring will be out in the cold."

"The most I have against him is that he tried to marry Florence when he had a wife already."

"He's as bad as they make 'em, Dodger. It won't be my fault if Mr. Linden's eyes are not opened to his wickedness."

Chapter 37

THE DIPLOMACY OF MRS. O'KEEFE

Mrs. O'Keefe was a warm-hearted woman, and the sad, drawn face of Mr. Linden appealed to her pity.

"Why should I let the poor man suffer when I can relieve him?" she asked herself.

So the next morning, after Curtis had, according to his custom, gone down-town, being in the invalid's sick-chamber, she began to act in a mysterious manner. She tip-toed to the door, closed it, and approached Mr. Linden's bedside with the air of one about to unfold a strange story.

"Whist, now," she said, with her finger on her lips.

"What is the matter?" asked the invalid, rather alarmed.

"Can you bear a surprise, sir?"

"Have you any bad news for me?"

"No; it's good news, but you must promise not to tell Curtis."

"Is it about Florence? Your messenger can hardly have reached Chicago."

"He isn't going there, sir."

"But you promised that he should," said Mr. Linden, disturbed.

"I'll tell you why, sir. Florence is not in Chicago."

"I—don't understand. You said she was there."

"Begging your pardon, sir, it was Curtis that said so, though he knew she was in New York."

"But what motive could he have had for thus misrepresenting matters?"

"He doesn't want you to take her back."

"I can't believe you, Mrs. Barnes. He loves her, and wants to marry her."

"He couldn't marry her if she consented to take him."

"Why not? Mrs. Barnes, you confuse me."

"I won't deceive you as he has done. There's rason in plinty. He's married already."

"Is this true?" demanded Mr. Linden in excitement.

"It's true enough; more by token, to-morrow, whin he's out, his wife will come here and tell you so herself."

"But who are you who seem to know so much about my family?"

"I'm a friend of the pore girl you've driven from the house, because she would not marry a rascally spalpeen that's been schemin' to get your property into his hands."

"You are a friend of Florence. Where is she?"

"She's in my house, and has been there ever since she left her home."

"Is she—well?"

"As well as she can be whin she's been workin' her fingers to the bone wid sewin' to keep from starvin'."

"My God! what have I done?"

"You've let Curtis Waring wind you round his little finger—that's what you've done, Mr. Linden."

"How can I see Florence?"

"How soon can you bear it?"

"The sooner the better."

"Then it'll be to-morrow, I'm thinkin', that is if you won't tell Curtis."

"No, no; I promise."

"I'll manage everything, sir. Don't worry now."

Mr. Linden's face lost its anxious look—so that when, later in the day, Curtis looked into the room he was surprised.

"My uncle looks better," he said.

"Yes, sir," answered the nurse. "I've soothed him like."

"Indeed! You seem to be a very accomplished nurse."

"Faith, that I am, sir, though it isn't I that should say it."

"May I ask how you soothed him?" inquired Curtis anxiously.

"I told him that Miss Florence would soon be home."

"I do not think it right to hold out hopes that may prove ill-founded."

"I know what I am about, Mr. Curtis."

"I dare say you understand your business, Mrs. Barnes, but if my uncle should be disappointed, I am afraid the consequences will be lamentable."

"Do you think he'll live long, sir?"

Curtis shrugged his shoulders.

"It is very hard to tell. My uncle is a very feeble man."

"And if he dies, I suppose the property goes to you?"

"I suppose so."

"But where does Florence come in?"

"It seems to me, Mrs. Barnes, that you take a good deal of interest in our family affairs," said Curtis, suspiciously.

"That's true, sir. Why shouldn't I take an interest in a nice gentleman like you?"

Curtis smiled.

"I am doing my best to find Florence. Then our marriage will take place, and it matters little to whom the property is left."

"But I thought Miss Florence didn't care to marry you?"

"It was only because she thinks cousins ought not to marry. It's a foolish fancy, and she'll get over it."

"Thrue for you, sir. My first husband was my cousin, and we always agreed, barrin' an occasional fight—"

"I don't think Florence and I will ever fight, Mrs. Barnes."

"What surprises me, Mr. Curtis, is that a nice-lookin' gentleman like you hasn't been married before."

Curtis eyed her keenly, but her face told him nothing.

"I never saw one I wanted to marry till my cousin grew up," he said.

"I belave in marryin', meself. I was first married at sivinteen."

"How long ago was that, Mrs. Barnes?"

"It's long ago, Mr. Curtis. I'm an old woman now. I was thirty-five last birthday."

Curtis came near laughing outright, for he suspected—what was true—that the nurse would never see her fiftieth birthday again.

"Then you are just my age," he said.

"If I make him laugh he won't suspect nothing," soliloquized the wily nurse. "That's a pretty big lie, even for me."

"Shure I look older, Mr. Curtis," she said aloud. "What wid the worry of losin' two fond husbands, I look much older than you."

"Oh, you are very well preserved, Mrs. Barnes."

Curtis went into his uncle's chamber.

"How are you feeling, uncle?" he asked.

"I think I am better," answered Mr. Linden, coldly, for he had not forgotten Mrs. Barnes's revelations.

"That is right. Only make an effort, and you will soon be strong again."

"I think I may. I may live ten years to annoy you."

"I fervently hope so," said Curtis, but there was a false ring in his voice that his uncle detected. "How do you like the new nurse?"

"She is helping me wonderfully. You made a good selection."

"I will see that she is soon discharged," Curtis inwardly resolved. "If her being here is going to prolong my uncle's life, and keep me still waiting for the estate, I must clear the house of her."

"You must not allow her to buoy you up with unfounded hopes, uncle. She has been telling you that Florence will soon return."

"Yes; she seems convinced of it."

"Of course she knows nothing of it. She may return, but I doubt whether she is in Chicago now. I think the family she was with has gone to Europe."

"Where did you hear that, Curtis?" asked Mr. Linden, with unwonted sharpness.

"I have sources of information which at present I do not care to impart. Rest assured that I am doing all I can to get her back."

"You still want to marry her, Curtis?"

"I do, most certainly."

"I shall not insist upon it. I should not have done so before."

"Have you changed your mind, uncle?"

"Yes; I have made a mistake, and I have decided to correct it."

"What has come over him?" Curtis asked himself. "Some influence hostile to me has been brought to bear. It must be that nurse. I will quietly dismiss her to-morrow, paying her a week's wages, in lieu of warning. She's evidently a meddler."

Chapter 38

THE CLOSING SCENE

The next day Tim Bolton, dressed in a jaunty style, walked up the steps of the Linden mansion.

"Is Mr. Waring at home?" he asked.

"No, sir; he has gone down-town."

"I'll step in and wait for him. Please show me to the library."

Jane, who had been taken into confidence by the nurse, showed him at once into the room mentioned.

Half an hour later Curtis entered.

"How long have you been here, Bolton?"

"But a short time. You sent for me."

"I did."

"On business?"

"Well, yes."

"Is there anything new?"

"Yes, my uncle is failing fast."

"Is he likely to die soon?"

"I shouldn't be surprised if he died within a week."

"I suspect Curtis means to help him! Well, what has that to do with me?" he asked. "You will step into the property, of course?"

"There's a little difficulty in the way which I can overcome with your help."

"What is it?"

"I can't get him to give up the foolish notion that the boy he lost is still alive."

"It happens to be true."

"Yes; but he must not know it. Before he dies I want him to make a new will, revoking all others, leaving all the property to me."

"Will he do it?"

"I don't know. As long as he thinks the boy is living, I don't believe he will. You see what a drawback that is."

"I see. What can I do to improve the situation?"

"I want you to sign a paper confessing that you abducted the boy—"

"At your instigation."

"That must not be mentioned. You will go on to say that a year or two later—the time is not material—he died of typhoid fever. You can say that you did not dare to reveal this before, but do so now, impelled by remorse."

"Have you got it written out? I can't remember all them words."

"Yes; here it is."

"All right," said Bolton, taking the paper and tucking it into an inside pocket, "I'll copy it out in my own handwriting. How much are you going to give me for doing this?"

"A thousand dollars."

"Cash?"

"I can't do that. I have met with losses at the gaming-table, and I don't dare ask money from my uncle at this time. He thinks I am thoroughly steady."

"At how much do you value the estate?"

"At four hundred thousand dollars. I wormed it out of my uncle's lawyer the other day."

"And you expect me to help you to that amount for only a thousand dollars?"

"A thousand dollars is a good deal of money."

"And so is four hundred thousand. After all, your uncle may not die."

"He is sure to."

"You seem very confident."

"And with good reason. Leave that to me. I promise you, on my honor, to pay you two thousand dollars when I get the estate."

"But what is going to happen to poor Dodger, the rightful heir?"

"Well, let it be three hundred dollars a year."

"Where is he now?"

"I don't mind telling you, as it can do no harm. He is in California."

"Whew! That was smart. How did you get him there?"

"I drugged him, and had him sent on board a ship bound for San Francisco, round Cape Horn. The fact is, I was getting a little suspicious of you, and I wanted to put you beyond the reach of temptation."

"You are a clever rascal, Curtis. After all, suppose the prize should slip through your fingers?"

"It won't. I have taken every precaution."

"When do you want this document?"

"Bring it back to me this afternoon, copied and signed. That is all you have to do; I will attend to the rest."

While this conversation was going on there were unseen listeners.

Behind a portiere Mrs. Barnes, the nurse, and John Linden, heard every word that was said.

"And what do you think now, sir?" whispered Mrs. O'Keefe (to give her real name).

"It is terrible. I would not have believed Curtis capable of such a crime. But is it really true, Mrs. Barnes? Is my lost boy alive?"

"To be sure he is."

"Have you seen him?"

"I know him as well as I know you, sir, and better, too."

"Is he—tell me, is he a good boy? Curtis told me that he might be a criminal."

"He might be, but he isn't. He's as dacent and honest a boy as iver trod shoe leather. You'll be proud of him, sir."

"But he's in California."

"He was; but he's got back. You shall see him to-day, and Florence, too, sir. Hark! I hear the door-bell. They're here now. I think you had better go in and confront Curtis."

"I feel weak, Mrs. Barnes. Let me lean on you."

"You can do that, and welcome, sir."

The nurse pushed aside the portiere, and the two entered the library—Mrs. Barnes rotund and smiling, Mr. Linden gaunt and spectral, looking like one risen from the grave.

Curtis eyed the pair with a startled look.

"Mrs. Barnes," he said, angrily, "what do you mean by taking my uncle from his bed and bringing him down here? It is as much as his life is worth. You seem unfit for your duties as nurse. You will leave the house to-morrow, and I will engage a substitute."

"I shall lave whin I git ready, Mr. Curtis Waring," said the nurse, her arms akimbo. "Maybe somebody else will lave the house. Me and Mr. Linden have been behind the curtain for twenty minutes, and he has heard every word you said."

Curtis turned livid, and his heart sank.

"It's true, Curtis," said John Linden's hollow voice. "I have heard all. It was you who abducted my boy, and have made my life a lonely one all these years. Oh, man! man! how could you have the heart to do it?"

Curtis stared at him with parched lips, unable to speak.

"Not content with this, you drove from the house my dear niece, Florence. You made me act cruelly toward her. I fear she will not forgive me."

But just then the door opened, and Florence, rushing into the room, sank at her uncle's feet.

"Oh, uncle," she said, "will you take me back?"

"Yes, Florence, never again to leave me. And who is this?" he asked, fixing his eyes on Dodger, who stood shyly in the doorway.

"I'll tell you, sir," said Tim Bolton. "That is your own son, whom I stole away from you when he was a kid, being hired to do it by Curtis Waring."

"It's a lie," said Curtis, hoarsely.

"Come to me, my boy," said Linden, with a glad light in his eyes.

"At last Heaven has heard my prayers," he ejaculated. "We will never be separated. I was ready to die, but now I hope to live for many years. I feel that I have a new lease of life."

With a baffled growl Curtis Waring darted a furious look at the three.

"That boy is an impostor," he said. "They are deceiving you."

"He is my son. I see his mother's look in his face. As for you, Curtis Waring, my eyes are open at last to your villainy. You deserve nothing at my hands; but I will make some provision for you."

There was another surprise.

Curtis Waring's deserted wife, brought from California by Dodger, entered the room, leading by the hand a young child.

"Oh, Curtis," she said, reproachfully. "How could you leave me? I have come to you, my husband, with our little child."

"Begone! woman!" said Curtis, furiously. "I will never receive nor recognize you!"

"Oh, sir," she said, turning to Linden, "what shall I do?"

"Curtis Waring," said Linden, sternly, "unless you receive this woman and treat her properly, you shall receive nothing from me."

"And if I do?"

"You will receive an income of two thousand dollars a year, payable quarterly. Mrs. Waring, you will remain here with your child till your husband provides another home for you."

Curtis slunk out of the room, but he was too wise to refuse his uncle's offer.

He and his wife are living in Chicago, and he treats her fairly well, fearing that, otherwise, he will lose his income.

Mr. Linden looks ten years younger than he did at the opening of the story.

Florence and Dodger (now known as Harvey Linden) live with him.

Dodger, under a competent private tutor, is making up the deficiencies in his education.

It is early days yet to speak of marriage, but it is possible that Florence may marry a cousin, after all.

Tim Bolton has turned over a new leaf, given up his saloon, and is carrying on a country hotel within fifty miles of New York.

He has five thousand dollars in the bank, presented by Dodger, with his father's sanction, and is considered quite a reputable citizen.

As for Mrs. O'Keefe, she still keeps the apple-stand, being unwilling to give it up; but she, too, has a handsome sum in the bank, and calls often upon her two children, as she calls them.

In the midst of their prosperity Florence and Dodger will never forget the time when they were adrift in New York.

⦿⦿⦿⦿⦿⦿⦿⦿⦿⦿⦿⦿⦿⦿⦿⦿⦿⦿⦿⦿⦿⦿⦿⦿⦿⦿⦿⦿⦿⦿⦿⦿⦿⦿⦿⦿

THE WORLD BEFORE HIM

⦿⦿⦿⦿⦿⦿⦿⦿⦿⦿⦿⦿⦿⦿⦿⦿⦿⦿⦿⦿⦿⦿⦿⦿⦿⦿⦿⦿⦿⦿⦿⦿⦿⦿⦿⦿

BY HORATIO ALGER, JR.

Author of "The Odds Against Him,"
"Making His Mark," etc.

Chapter 1

TWO SCHOOL FRIENDS

Two boys were walking in the campus of the Bridgeville Academy. They were apparently of about the same age—somewhere from fifteen to sixteen—but there was a considerable difference in their attire.

Herbert Grant was neatly but coarsely dressed, and his shoes were of cowhide, but his face indicated a frank, sincere nature, and was expressive of intelligence.

His companion was dressed in a suit of good cloth, his linen was of the finest, his shoes were of calfskin, and he had the indefinable air of a boy who had been reared in luxury.

He had not the broad, open face of his friend—for the two boys were close friends—but his features were finely chiseled, indicating a share of pride, and a bold, self-reliant nature.

He was, however, an attractive boy, and in spite of his pride possessed a warm, affectionate heart and sterling qualities, likely to endear him to those who could read and understand him.

His name was Frank Courtney, and he is the hero of my story.

"Have you written your Latin exercises, Frank" asked Herbert.

"Yes; I finished them an hour ago."

"I was going to ask you to write them with me. It is pleasanter to study in company."

"Provided you have the right sort of company," rejoined Frank.

"Am I the right sort of company?" inquired Herbert, with a smile.

"You hardly need to ask that, Herbert. Are we not always together? If I did not like your company, I should not seek it so persistently. I don't care to boast, but I have plenty of offers of companionship which I don't care to accept. There is Bob Stickney, for instance, who is always inviting me to his room; but you know what he is—a lazy fellow, who cares more to have a good time than to study. Then there is James Cameron, a conceited, empty-headed fellow, who is very disagreeable to me."

"You don't mention your stepbrother, Mark Manning."

"For two reasons—he doesn't care for my company, and of all the boys I dislike him the most."

"I don't like him myself. But why do you dislike him so much?"

"Because he is a sneak—a crafty, deceitful fellow, always scheming for his own interest. He hates me, but he doesn't dare to show it. His father is my mother's husband, but the property is hers, and will be mine. He thinks he may some day be dependent on me, and he conceals his dislike in order to stand the better chance by and by. I only hope that it may be long before my dear mother is called away!"

"How did she happen to marry again, Frank?"

"I can hardly tell. It was a great grief to me. Mr. Manning was a penniless lawyer, who ingratiated himself with mother, and urged her till she consented to marry him. He is very soft-spoken, and very plausible, and he managed to make mother—who has been an invalid for years—think that it would be the best thing for her to delegate her cares to him, and provide me with a second father."

There was a scornful bitterness in Frank's tone as he pronounced the last words.

"Well," he continued, "he had managed to extract a promise from mother, before I knew or suspected his design. It was three years ago, and I was not quite thirteen; but I can well remember how badly I felt when mother told me of the engagement. I remonstrated strongly, till I saw that she was becoming nervous and agitated, and I desisted because I did not want to pain her. I tried hard to treat Mr. Manning civilly, but I have no doubt I seemed cold and sulky. At any rate, the marriage took place, and Mr. Manning and Mark came to the Cedars to live. You know that is the name of our place."

"Yes. It must have been very disagreeable for you."

"I can hardly tell you how much so."

"How has your stepfather treated you?"

"I am bound to say, Herbert, that I have nothing to complain of. He has not attempted to control or tyrannize over me. He has always been polite, and has tried to be fatherly. If anything, I should say that he has been too deferential and too soft-spoken. I have not had any of my privileges curtailed, or been deprived of anything to which I was accustomed."

"I am surprised at that. That is not the general reputation of stepfathers."

"That is true, Herbert; but I am convinced that Mr. Manning is not acting himself. He has an object in disguising his real nature. He is my secret enemy—I am sure of that—and some time or other he will show himself in his true colors. That will not probably affect me while my dear mother lives. The property is hers, and he would lose his hold upon her and the management of the estate if he should ill-treat me. I heartily hope that mother will live till I am a man. I shall then feel better able to defeat my stepfather's schemes."

"Your mother is likely to live, is she not, Frank?"

"She is a consumptive, Herbert," said Frank, gravely. "It is in her family. Still, there may be no immediate danger. Her oldest sister, my Aunt Maria, lived for twenty years after her lungs had become affected, and this gives me hope that mother may linger as long."

"Mr. Manning is kind to her, I hope?"

Frank's eyes flashed.

"He would not dare be anything else!" he answered, quickly. "This is all that reconciles me to the marriage," he went on, more calmly. "My stepfather is certainly attentive and kind to my mother. His soft manner seems to me sometimes rather sickening and unmanly. Still, mother's nature is gentle, and if it suits her, I have nothing to say."

"Your stepbrother, Mark Manning, enjoys the same advantages as yourself, does he not?" asked Herbert.

"Yes."

"Then his father's marriage proved a good thing for him."

"That is true. When he first came to the house he was poorly dressed, and had evidently been used to living in a poor way. He was at once provided with a complete outfit as good as my own, and from that time as much has been spent on him as on me. Don't think that I am mean enough to grudge him any part of the money expended upon him. If he were like you, I could like him, and enjoy his society; but he is just such another as his father."

"That reminds me, Frank, to ask you a question. How is it that you, who are rich, and the heir of a large fortune, have become the friend of a poor boy like me? I am the son of a poor carpenter, who has hard work to provide a decent living for his family, yet you take more notice of me than of any other boy in the academy."

"Take notice isn't the right way to express yourself, Herbert. That would imply inferiority on your part."

"Most people would consider me inferior, Frank."

"Just because I am richer than you? I am not so foolish. If I were to lose all my money, would you like me any less?"

"Not a bit, Frank."

"Then you see money has nothing to do with it. I go with you, Herbert, because I like you. You don't want me to flatter you, and so I won't explain why I like you. I should like nothing better than to have you with me for the next few years."

"That can't be," said Herbert, sighing. "You will go to college, but there is no chance of that for me."

"I have been thinking of that, Herbert," said Frank, earnestly, "but I didn't like to tell you what I proposed until I knew whether I could carry it out. I am going to ask my mother to pay your expenses through college. You could room with me, and I would promise to be extra economical, if necessary, in order to make the additional expense less."

Herbert was surprised and moved by this generous proposal. He put his arm affectionately round the neck of his friend, and said, impulsively:

"Dear Frank, how kind you are! But it would be altogether too much for you to give or me to accept."

"No, it wouldn't, Herbert. Do you think I would value the money in comparison with the pleasure I should have in your society, and the satisfaction of feeling that I was helping you on in the world? When you became a great lawyer or statesman, I should take credit to myself for having given you the chance to become distinguished."

"I might disappoint you, Frank. You would be more likely to become distinguished than I."

"There would be no rivalry between us, but we would try to improve our advantages."

"It may never come to pass, Frank, but I will not forget your kind intentions. I should like nothing better than to go to college, now that I am so nearly prepared. Some people think father foolish not to have taken me from the academy sooner, but he says a good education will always help me. Even without going to college, I know enough to teach a common school, and when I am old enough I shall probably become a teacher."

"Provided I cannot arrange better for you."

Here Herbert's attention was drawn to a boy, who was approaching with a yellow envelope in his hand.

"Frank," he said, suddenly, "there's Mark Manning. He looks as if he had something to say to you. He has either a letter or a telegram in his hand."

Chapter 2

THE TELEGRAM

Frank's heart gave a great bound at the suggestion of a telegram. A telegram could mean but one thing—that his mother had become suddenly worse.

He hurried to meet his stepbrother.

"Is that a telegram, Mark?" he asked, anxiously.

"Yes."

"Is it anything about mother? Tell me quick!"

"Read it for yourself."

Frank drew the telegram from the envelope, and read it hastily:

"My wife is very sick. I wish you and Frank to come home at once."

"When does the next train start, Herbert?" asked Frank, pale with apprehension.

"In an hour."

"I shall go by that train."

"I don't think I can get ready so soon," said Mark, deliberately.

"Then you can come by yourself," replied Frank, impetuously. "I beg your pardon, Mark," he added. "I cannot expect you to feel as I do. It is not your mother."

"It is my stepmother," said Mark.

"That is quite different. But I must not linger here. I will go at once to Doctor Brush, and tell him of my summons home. Good-bye, Herbert, till we meet again."

"I will go with you to the depot, Frank," said his friend, sympathizingly. "Don't wait for me. Go ahead, and make your preparations for the journey. I will be at your room in a quarter of an hour."

"You won't go by the next train, Mark?" questioned Herbert.

"No. I don't care to rush about as Frank is doing."

"You would if it were your own mother who was ill."

"I am not sure. It wouldn't do any good, would it?"

"You would naturally feel anxious," said Herbert.

"Oh, yes, I suppose so!" answered Mark, indifferently.

Mark Manning was slender and dark, with a soft voice and rather effeminate ways. He didn't care for the rough sports in which most boys delight; never played baseball or took part in athletic exercises, but liked to walk about, sprucely dressed, and had even been seen on the campus on a Saturday afternoon with his hands encased in kid gloves.

For this, however, he was so ridiculed and laughed at that he had to draw the gloves off and place them in his pocket.

It is needless to say that he was not a favorite among his school-fellows.

At a large school, manliness commands respect and favor, and an effeminate boy, unless excused by ill-health, is ridiculed or despised.

For this, however, Mark cared little. He, as well as Frank, was liberally supplied with spending money, and was content to follow his own course, whether it suited his school-fellows or not.

The Cedars, the handsome residence of Frank's family, was situated twenty miles from Bridgeville, the seat of the classical academy at which the stepbrothers were being educated.

It was the custom of both to go home on Saturday morning, and return by an early train on Monday.

It was now the middle of the week, and, therefore, nearly three days had passed since Frank had seen his mother. Then, though weak, she had not seemed more so than usual, and he had come away from home feeling no particular anxiety.

It was evident that his mother's disease had taken a sudden and un-favorable turn.

As Frank and Herbert walked together to the railway station, the latter said:

"It seems to me, Frank, that the telegram should have been sent to you, rather than to Mark Manning. You are the one who is most interested in the contents."

"I thought of that, Herbert, but I was too much affected by the contents to speak of it. I am not surprised, however. It is like Mr. Manning. It jarred upon me to have him speak of mother as his wife. She is so, but I never could reconcile myself to the fact."

"Do you remember your father—your own father, Frank?"

"You need not have said, 'your own father.' I don't recognize Mr. Manning as a father, at all. Yes, I remember him. I was eight years old when he died. He was a fine-looking man, always kind—a man to be loved and respected. There was not a particle of similarity between him and Mr. Manning. He was strong and manly."

"How did it happen that he died so young?"

"He was the victim of a railway accident. He had gone to New York on business, and was expected back on a certain day. The train on which he was a passenger collided with a freight train, and my poor father was among the passengers who were killed. The news was almost too much for my mother, although she had not yet become an invalid. It brought on a fit of sickness lasting for three months. She has never been altogether well since."

"After all, Frank, the gifts of Fortune, or rather Providence, are not so unequally distributed as at first appears. You are rich, but father-less. I am poor enough, but my father and mother are both spared me."

"I would gladly accept poverty if my father could be restored to life, and my mother be spared to me for twenty years to come."

"I am sure you would, Frank," said Herbert. "Money is valuable, but there are some things far more so."

They had reached the station by this time, and it was nearly the time for the train to start. Frank bought his ticket, and the two friends shook hands and bade each other good-bye.

In an hour Frank was walking up the long avenue leading to the front door of the mansion.

The door was opened by his stepfather.

"How is mother?" asked Frank, anxiously.

"I am grieved to say that she is very sick," said Mr. Manning, in a soft voice. "She had a severe hemorrhage this morning, which has weakened her very much."

"Is she in—in danger?" faltered Frank.

"I fear she is."

"I suppose I can see her?"

"Yes; but it will be better not to make her talk much."

"I will be careful, sir."

Frank waited no longer, but hurried to his mother's room. As he entered, and his glance fell on the bed and its occupant, he was shocked by the pale and ghastly appearance of the mother whom he so dearly loved. The thought came to him instantly:

"She cannot live."

He found it difficult to repress a rising sob, but he did so for his mother's sake. He thought that it might affect her injuriously if he should display emotion.

His mother smiled faintly as he approached the bed.

"Mother," said Frank, kneeling by the bedside, "are you very ill?"

"Yes, Frank," she answered, almost in a whisper. "I think I am going to leave you."

"Oh, don't say that, mother!" burst forth in anguish from Frank's lips. "Try to live for my sake."

"I should like to live, my dear son," she faintly answered; "but if it is God's will that I should die, I must be reconciled. I leave you in his care."

Here Mr. Manning entered the room.

"You will be kind to my boy?" said the dying mother.

"Can you doubt it, my dear?" replied her husband, in the soft tones which Frank so much disliked. "I will care for him as if he were my own."

"Thank you. Then I shall die easy."

"Don't speak any more, mother. It will tire you, and perhaps bring on another hemorrhage."

"Frank is right, dearest. You had better not exert yourself any more at present."

"Didn't Mark come with you?" asked Mr. Manning of Frank.

"No, sir."

"I am surprised that he should not have done so. I sent for him as well as you."

"I believe he is coming by the next train," said Frank. "He thought he could not get ready in time for my train."

"He should not have left you to come alone at such a time."

"I didn't wish him to inconvenience himself, Mr. Manning. If it had been his mother, it would have been different."

Mr. Manning did not reply. He understood very well that there was no love lost between Mark and his stepson.

Chapter 3

FRANK'S BEREAVEMENT

Early in the evening Mark made his appearance. Supper had been over for an hour, and everything was cold. In a house where there is sickness, the regular course of things is necessarily interrupted, and, because he could not have his wants attended to immediately, Mark saw fit to grumble and scold the servants. He was not a favorite with them, and they did not choose to be bullied.

Deborah, who had been in the house for ten years, and so assumed the independence of an old servant, sharply reprimanded the spoiled boy.

"You ought to be ashamed, Mr. Mark," she said, "of making such a fuss when my poor mistress lies up-stairs at the point of death."

"Do you know to whom you are speaking?" demanded Mark, imperiously, for he could, when speaking with those whom he regarded as inferiors, exchange his soft tones for a voice of authority.

"I ought to know by this time," answered Deborah, contemptuously. "There is no other in the house like you, I am glad to say."

"You are very impertinent. You forget that you are nothing but a servant."

"A servant has the right to be decently treated, Mr. Mark."

"If you don't look out," said Mark, in a blustering tone, "I will report you to my father, and have you put out of the house."

Deborah was naturally incensed at this rude speech, but she was spared the trouble of replying. Frank entered the room at this moment in time to hear Mark's last words.

"What is this about being put out of the house?" he asked, looking from Mark to Deborah, in a tone of unconscious authority, which displeased his stepbrother.

"That is my business," replied Mark, shortly.

"Mr. Mark has threatened to have me put out of the house because he has to wait for his supper," said Deborah.

"It wasn't for that. It was because you were impertinent. All the same, I think it is shameful that I can't get anything to eat."

"I regret, Mark," said Frank, with cool sarcasm, "that you should be inconvenienced about your meals. Perhaps you will excuse it, as my poor mother is so sick that she requires extra attention from the servants. Deborah, if possible, don't let Mark wait much longer. It seems to be very important that he should have his supper."

"He shall have it," assured Deborah, rather enjoying the way in which Mark was put down—"that is, if he don't get me put out of the house."

"You had better not make any such threats in future, Mark," said Frank, significantly.

"Who's to hinder?" snapped Mark.

"I am," answered Frank, pointedly.

"You are nothing but a boy like me," retorted Mark.

"My mother is mistress here, and I represent her."

"Things may change soon," muttered Mark; but Frank had left the room, and did not hear him.

Mark did not trouble himself even to inquire for his stepmother, but went out to the stable and lounged about until bedtime. He seemed very much bored, and so expressed himself.

"It's a nuisance having sickness in the house," said he to the coachman.

"Especially if you happen to be sick yourself," responded the coachman, dryly.

"It's a nuisance, anyway. A fellow can't do anything, and the house is turned upside down."

He spoke in an aggrieved tone, as if Mrs. Manning were very inconsiderate to fall sick and occasion annoyance to him.

Mark was not a favorite with the coachman, who was devoted to Frank. Like Deborah, he had been in the family before Mr. Manning gained a footing there, and was disposed to regard him and his son as interlopers, though he treated them with formal respect.

"I don't think you will be troubled long, Mr. Mark," said he, gravely.

"You mean that my stepmother will die?" inquired Mark, interested, but not appearing very much grieved.

"My poor mistress is in her last sickness, Mr. Mark."

"Oh, well, we must all die some time!" said Mark, lightly.

"He hasn't any more heart than a grindstone," said the coachman to himself, as Mark went back to the house. "I do hope Mrs. Manning will tie up the property so that this boy and his father can't make ducks and drakes of it. It'll be bad times for us when we lose our good mistress. Mr. Manning's a sneak, and the boy's a little worse, if anything. Frank's a fine, manly boy, and worth a dozen of him."

Frank wished to sit up all night with his mother, but, as she had a professional nurse, it was thought best that he should obtain his regular rest, the nurse promising to call the family if any change should be apparent in her patient's condition.

About half-past four in the morning there was a summons.

"Mrs. Manning is worse," said the nurse. "I don't think she can last long."

Mr. Manning and Frank hastened to her room. Mark protested that he was too tired to get up, and, in spite of his father's remonstrance, remained in bed. Frank was too absorbed in his own sorrow to notice or care for Mark's absence.

If he had thought about it at all, he would have considered it a relief that his stepbrother should be away. His mother was lying in a stupor, but recovered for a few minutes before death.

One last glance of love—though she could no longer speak—assured Frank that she knew him and loved him to the last.

The memory of that look often came back to him in the years that followed, and he would not have parted with it for anything that earth could give.

Just as the clock struck five, his mother breathed her last. The boy gazed upon the inanimate form, but he was dazed, and could not realize that his mother had left him, never to return.

"She is gone," said Mr. Manning, softly.

"Dead!" ejaculated Frank.

"Yes, her sufferings are over. Let us hope she is better off. My boy, I think you had better return to your bed. You can do nothing for your mother now."

"I would rather stay here," said Frank, sadly. "I can at least look at her, and soon I shall lose even that comfort."

The thought was too much for the poor boy, and he burst into tears.

"Do as you please, Frank," assented Mr. Manning. "I feel for you, and I share in your grief. I will go and tell Mark of our sad loss."

He made his way to Mark's room and entered. He touched Mark, who was in a doze, and he started up.

"What's the matter?" he asked, crossly.

"Your poor mother is dead, Mark."

"Well, there was no need to wake me for that," said the boy, irritably. "I can't help it, can I?"

"I think, my son, you might speak with more feeling. Death is a solemn thing."

"There's nobody here but me," reminded Mark, sneering.

"I don't catch your meaning," said his father, showing some annoyance, for it is not pleasant to be seen through.

"Why should you care so much?" continued Mark. "I suppose you will be well provided for. Do you know how she has left the property? How much of it goes to Frank?"

"I can't say," said Mr. Manning. "I never asked my wife."

"Do you mean to say, father, that you don't know how the property is left?" asked Mark, with a sharp glance at his father.

"I may have my conjectures," admitted Mr. Manning. "I don't think my dear wife would leave me without some evidences of her affection. Probably the bulk of the estate goes to your brother, and something to me. Doubtless we shall continue to live here, as I shall naturally be your brother's guardian."

"Don't call him my brother," growled Mark.

"Why not? True, he is only your stepbrother; but you have lived under the same roof, and been to school together, and this ought to strengthen the tie between you."

"I don't like Frank," said Mark. "He puts on altogether too many airs."

"I had not observed that," replied his father.

"Well, I have. Only this evening he saw fit to speak impudently to me."

"Indeed! I am really amazed to hear it," said Mr. Manning.

"Oh, he thinks he is the master of the house, or will be, and he presumes on that."

"He is unwise," said Mr. Manning. "Even if the whole property descends to him, which I can hardly believe possible, I, as his guardian, will have the right to control him."

"I hope you'll do it, father. At any rate, don't let him boss over me, for I won't stand it."

"I don't think he will boss over you," answered his father, in a slow, measured voice, betraying, however, neither anger nor excitement. "Of course, I should not permit that."

Mark regarded his father fixedly.

"I guess the old man knows what's in the will," he said to himself. "He knows how to feather his own nest. I hope he's feathered mine, too."

Mr. Manning passed from his son's room and went softly up-stairs, looking thoughtful.

Any one who could read that impassive face would have read trouble in store for Frank.

Chapter 4

MRS. MANNING'S WILL

During the preparations for the funeral, Frank was left pretty much to himself.

He regarded the future with apathy. As a matter of course, his stepfather would be his guardian, but he didn't apprehend any troublesome interference with his liberty.

Mr. Manning's manner was so soft and to him had been so deferential, that he did not understand the man. It didn't occur to him that it was assumed for a purpose.

That manner was not yet laid aside. His stepfather offered to comfort him, but Frank listened in silence. Nothing that Mr. Manning could say had the power to lighten his load of grief. So far as words could console him, the sympathy of Deborah and the coachman, both old servants, whom his mother trusted, had more effect, for he knew that it was sincere, and that they were really attached to his mother.

Of Mr. Manning he felt a profound distrust, which no words of his stepfather could possibly remove.

As to Mark, he was not old enough to put on the mask, and went about the house studying his own comfort, and looking out for his own selfish interests.

"I shall be glad when the funeral is over," he said, impatiently. "The whole house seems to be upset. I can't get even a good meal."

Deborah, to whom this was addressed, responded, indignantly:

"You haven't any more feeling than a stone, Mr. Mark, so you haven't, or you wouldn't talk so while that dear lady, who has always been so kind to you, lies dead upstairs."

"I can't help it, can I?" said the boy, sullenly.

"No; but you can behave decently for the short time we shall have her with us."

"I'm not going to be lectured by a servant," said Mark, insolently.

"Servants have some rights," said Deborah, independently. "Why can't you imitate Mr. Frank? He isn't half so hard to please as you, though he is the owner of the property."

"Is he, though?" sneered Mark.

"To-be-sure he is!"

"He won't be the master of the house, though—I can tell you that!"

"Who will be?"

"My father."

"Who told you that?" asked Deborah, keenly.

"There was no need of anybody telling me it. Of course my father will be Frank's guardian, and he'll make him stand round, you may depend on that."

Deborah looked significantly at the coachman, suspecting that Mark had had some hint from his father.

"We can tell better after the will is read," she replied, coldly.

As Mark left the room, she said to the coachman:

"I am afraid trouble is in store for Mr. Frank. I can't help thinking Mr. Manning is up to some trick."

"Shouldn't wonder at all," agreed Richard Green. "It would be just like him. But Mr. Frank isn't the one to be cheated without making a fuss about it."

"Little he thinks about the property now, poor boy," said Deborah. "That boy's heart was wrapped up in his mother, and she was always thinking of him. Why should she be taken, and such a miserable creature as her husband be left?"

"It isn't always the good that live longest," said Richard, sententiously. "To my mind, it seems to be pretty much the other way. I expect Mark will give us a good deal of trouble."

"Like father, like son," quoted Deborah.

"The boy's a good deal worse than his father. Mr. Manning likes to have things his own way, but he's soft-spoken, while Mark is rough and impudent."

"I hope he will go off to school, and stay there. We can do better without him than with him," said Deborah.

Meanwhile, Mr. Manning was looking from an upper window down the fine avenue, and his eye ranged from left to right over the ample estate with a glance of self-complacent triumph.

"All mine at last!" he said to himself, exultingly. "What I have been working for has come to pass. Three years ago I was well-nigh penniless, and now I am a rich man. I shall leave Mark the master of a great fortune. I have played my cards well. No one will suspect anything wrong. My wife and I have lived in harmony. There will be little wonder that she has left all to me. There would be, perhaps, but for the manner in which I have taken care he shall be mentioned in the will—I mean, of course, in the will I have made for her."

He paused, and, touching a spring in the wall, a small door flew open, revealing a shallow recess.

In this recess was a folded paper, tied with a red ribbon.

Mr. Manning opened it, and his eyes glanced rapidly down the page.

"This is the true will," he said to himself. "I wish I could summon courage to burn it. It would be best out of the way. That, if found out, would make me amenable to the law, and I must run no risk. In this secret recess it will never be found. I will replace it and the document which I have had prepared will take its place, and no one will be the wiser."

On the day after the funeral, the family solicitor and a few intimate friends, who had been invited by Mr. Manning, assembled in the drawing-room of the mansion to hear the will read.

Mr. Manning himself notified Frank of the gathering and its object.

He found our hero lying on the bed in his chamber, sad and depressed.

"I don't like to intrude upon your grief, my dear boy," said his stepfather, gently, "but it is necessary. The last will of your dear mother and my beloved wife is about to be read, and your presence is necessary."

"Couldn't it be put off?" asked Frank, tremulously. "It seems too soon to think of such things."

"Pardon me, my dear Frank, but it is quite needful that there should be an immediate knowledge of the contents of the will, in order that the right person may look after the business interests of the estate. I assure you that it is the invariable custom to read the will immediately after the funeral."

"If that is the custom, and it is necessary, I have nothing to say. When is the will to be read?"

"At three o'clock, and it is now two."

"Very well, sir; I will come down in time."

"Of course there can't be much doubt as to the contents of the will," pursued Mr. Manning. "You are doubtless the heir, and as you are a minor, I am probably your guardian. Should such be the case, I hope that the relations between us may be altogether friendly."

"I hope so," said Frank, gravely.

At three o'clock the members of the family, with a few outside friends, gathered in the drawing-room. The family solicitor, Mr. Ferret, held in his hand what purported to be the last will of Mrs. Manning.

The widowed husband had directed the lawyer to the bureau of the deceased lady as likely to contain her will. It was found without trouble in the topmost drawer.

Deborah and the coachman had speculated as to whether they would be invited to attend at the reading of the will.

Their doubts were set at rest by an invitation from Mr. Manning himself.

"You were so long in the service of my dear wife," he said, "that it is fitting that you should be present at the reading of her will, in which it is quite probable that you may be personally interested."

"He is uncommonly polite, I am sure," thought Deborah, disposed for the moment to think more favorably of the man whom she had never been able to like.

"My friends," said the lawyer, after a preliminary cough, "you are assembled to listen to the will of Mrs. Manning, just deceased. The document which I hold in my hand I believe to be such an instrument. I will now open it for the first time."

He untied the ribbon, and began reading the will.

It commenced with the usual formula, and proceeded to a few bequests of trifling amount.

Deborah and Richard Green were each left two hundred dollars, "as a slight acknowledgment of their faithful service."

One or two friends of the family were remembered, but to an inconsiderable extent. Then came the important clause:

"All the rest and residue of the property of which I may die possessed I leave to my beloved husband, James Manning, whose devoted affection has made happy the last years of my life. Having implicit confidence in his good judgment and kindness of heart, I request him to make proper provision for my dear son Frank, whose happiness I earnestly desire. I hope that he will consent to be guided by the wisdom and experience of his stepfather, who, I am sure, will study his interests and counsel him wisely. In my sorrow at parting with my dear son, it is an unspeakable comfort to me to feel that he will have such a guardian and protector."

Frank listened with amazement, which was shared by all present.

Practically, he was disinherited, and left wholly dependent upon his stepfather.

Chapter 5

DISINHERITED

The contents of the will created general astonishment. There was not one in the room who didn't know the devotion of Mrs. Manning to her son Frank, yet while speaking of him affectionately, she had treated him, as they considered, most cruelly. Why should she have left such a dangerous power in her husband's hands?

And how was Mr. Manning affected?

He summoned to his face an expression of bewilderment and surprise, and, feeling that all eyes were fixed upon him, he turned toward the lawyer.

"Mr. Ferret," he said, "I need hardly say that this will surprises me very much, as I see that it does the friends who are present. Are you sure that there is no codicil?"

"I have been unable to discover any, Mr. Manning," said the lawyer, gravely, as he scanned the face of the widower keenly.

Mr. Manning applied his handkerchief to his eyes, and seemed overcome by emotion.

"I knew my dear wife's confidence in me," he said, in a tearful voice, "but I was not prepared for such a striking manifestation of it."

"Nor I," said Mr. Ferret, drily.

"Knowing her strong attachment to Frank," pursued Mr. Manning, "I feel the full extent and significance of that confidence when she leaves him so unreservedly to my care and guidance. I hope that I may be found worthy of the trust."

"I hope so, sir," said Mr. Ferret, who, sharp lawyer as he was, doubted whether all was right, and was willing that Mr. Manning should be made aware of his feeling. "It is certainly a very remarkable proviso, considering the affection which your wife entertained for her son."

"Precisely, Mr. Ferret. It shows how much confidence the dear departed felt in me."

"So far as I can see, the boy is left wholly dependent upon you."

"He shall not regret it!" said Mr. Manning, fervently. "I consecrate my life to this sacred trust."

"You acquiesce in the arrangement, then, Mr. Manning?"

"I cannot do otherwise, can I?"

"There is nothing to prevent your settling the property, or any part of it, on the natural heir, Mr. Manning. You must pardon me for saying that it would have been wiser had your wife so stipulated by will."

"I cannot consent to reverse, or in any way annul, the last wishes of my dear wife," said Mr. Manning, hastily. "It was her arrangement solely, and I hold it sacred. She has put upon me a serious responsibility, from which I shrink, indeed, but which I cannot decline. I will do all in my power to carry out the wishes of my late wife."

Mr. Ferret shrugged his shoulders.

"I am not surprised at your decision, sir," he said, coldly. "Few men would resist the temptation. My duty is discharged with the reading of the will, and I will bid you good-afternoon!"

"My dear sir," said Mr. Manning, fervently, "permit me to thank you for the service you have rendered! Permit me also to express my high appreciation of your professional character and attainments, and to say that I hope you will allow me to call them into requisition should I hereafter have need to do so!"

Mr. Ferret acknowledged this compliment coldly enough.

He merely bowed.

With a general bow to the company, in which suavity and deference were combined, Mr. Manning left the room, followed by Mark.

He was a crafty man. He knew that the strange will would be discussed, and he thought it best that the discussion should come at once, that it might be the sooner dismissed.

Deborah, faithful old servant, was in a blaze of indignation.

She went up quickly to Frank, and said:

"It's a shame, Mr. Frank, so it is!"

"If my mother made that will, it is all right," replied Frank, loyally.

"But she didn't, Mr. Frank! I know she would never do such a thing. She loved you too dearly, and she would not cheat you out of your rightful inheritance."

"No more she would, Mr. Frank," said the coachman, chiming in.

"I don't know what to think," said Frank. "It has surprised me very much."

"Surprised you!" exclaimed Deborah. "You may well say that. You might have knocked me down with a feather when I heard that the property was left to that man. Depend upon it, he knows all about it."

"You mean Mr. Manning?"

"To-be-sure, I mean him! Oh, he's managed artfully! I say that for him. He's got it all into his own hands, and you haven't a cent."

"If it was my mother's will I wouldn't complain of that, Deborah. It was hers to do with as she liked, and I know, at any rate, that she loved me."

"There's one thing surprises me," said Richard Green. "If so be as the will isn't genuine, how does it happen that you and I come in for a legacy, Deborah?"

"It's meant for a blind," answered Deborah. "Oh, he's the artfullest man!"

"You may be right, Deborah. I must say the will sounded all right."

"Maybe it was copied from the mistress' will."

This conversation took place in one corner of the room.

It ceased as Mr. Ferret advanced toward the disinherited boy.

"Frank," said he, in a tone of sympathy, "I am very sorry for the provisions of the will."

"So am I, sir," replied the boy. "It isn't pleasant to be dependent on Mr. Manning."

"Particularly when the whole estate should be yours."

"I wouldn't have minded if half had been left to him, provided I had been entirely independent of him."

"I appreciate your feelings, Frank. I knew your father, and I am proud to say that he was my friend. I knew your mother well, and I esteemed her highly. I hope you will let me regard myself as your friend also."

"Thank you, Mr. Ferret! I am likely to need a friend. I shall remember your kind proposal. Now, I want to ask you one question."

"Ask, and I shall answer."

"Did my mother consult with you about making this will?"

"No, Frank."

"Did she ever say anything that would lead you to think she would leave the property according to the provisions of this will?"

"Not a word."

"Was there another will?"

"Yes. I wrote her will at her direction more than a year ago. This will is dated only three months ago, and, of course, takes precedence of it, even if the other is in existence."

"Can you tell me what were the provisions of the other will?"

"A legacy of ten thousand dollars was left to Mr. Manning, and the rest of the estate to you, except the small legacies, which were all larger than in the will I have read. For instance, Deborah and Richard Green were each put down for five hundred dollars."

"So they suffer as well as I?"

"Yes."

"Have you any idea, Mr. Ferret, of the value of the estate which falls into Mr. Manning's hands?"

"I have some idea, because I have talked with your mother on the subject. This estate is worth fifty thousand dollars at least, and there are fully fifty thousand dollars in money and bonds. The legacies do not altogether exceed one thousand dollars, and therefore it may be said that your stepfather has fallen heir to one hundred thousand dollars."

"I suppose there is nothing I can do, Mr. Ferret?"

"Not unless you can show that this will which I have read is not a genuine document. That would be difficult."

"Did you notice my mother's signature?"

"Yes. I am not an expert, but I cannot detect any difference greater than maybe existed between two signatures of the same person."

"Then I suppose there is nothing to be done at present. I expect to have a hard time with Mr. Manning."

"How has he treated you in the past, Frank?" asked the lawyer.

"I have had nothing to complain of; but then he was not master of the estate. Now it is different, and I think his treatment of me will be different."

"You may be right. You remember what I said, Frank?"

"That I could regard you as a friend? I won't forget it, Mr. Ferret."

One by one the company left the house, and Frank was alone.

Left alone and unsustained by sympathy, he felt more bitterly than before the totally unexpected change in his circumstances.

Up to the last hour he had regarded himself as the heir of the estate. Now he was only a dependent of a man whom he heartily disliked.

Could it be that this misfortune had come to him through the agency of his mother?

"I will not believe it!" he exclaimed, energetically.

He felt that he would be the better for a breath of fresh air. He sauntered slowly down the avenue, when a sight greeted him which kindled his indignation.

His stepbrother, Mark Manning, was riding, a little distance in advance, upon his horse—a horse which, two years before, his mother had given him.

Frank's eyes flashed, and he hurried forward to overtake him.

Chapter 6

AJAX

_____

A few words by way of explanation will be in place.

Among those who heard the will read was Mark Manning. Though he felt little interest in his stepmother, he was very much interested in learning the disposition of her property.

Had it fallen to Frank, he would have been very much annoyed, as this would have made a great gulf between them. As the heir of a large property, Frank would be of infinitely more consequence than a penniless boy like himself, or be likely to think himself so, and this the jealous spirit of Mark Manning could ill brook.

His gratified amazement may be conjectured when he heard the will read, and found that Frank himself was the penniless boy, while he was the son and heir of the possessor of the estate.

A boy with a conscience might have felt some compunction at the grievous wrong which his stepbrother had suffered, but Mark was not the kind of boy to be troubled by such considerations. He felt a thrill of exultation which he did not even attempt to conceal.

Had Frank looked at his stepbrother, he would have seen the expression of triumph in his eyes, but our hero was too much occupied with his own sad reflections to look about the room.

"The old man has feathered his nest well," thought Mark. "Oh, he's sly as a fox, father is. You don't catch him napping. Master Frank will find his wings pretty well clipped. He can't fly very high now. He will have to look to father and me for support. I never felt so happy in my life."

Had Mr. Manning been a good, conscientious man, Mark would not have felt half so proud of him as at that moment. Young as he was, the boy idolized success, however attained, and felt that it was well to get rich, however questionable the means.

"He does it well," thought Mark, when his father, at the close of the reading, expressed his surprise at the disposition of the property. "Oh, he's a sly old fox!" he chuckled, inwardly. "He's a great man, father is."

When Mr. Manning left the room, Mark followed him.

He was impatient to congratulate him upon his success.

Mr. Manning made his way up-stairs to the room where he spent much of his time. He was about to close the door when Mark came up.

"Is it you, Mark?" he asked, in a low tone.

"Yes, father. May I come in?"

"Certainly. I have been very much surprised by the will, Mark."

"There's nobody here but me, father," replied Mark, with a meaning grin.

"I don't understand you, my son."

"I mean that you have been very smart, father. I congratulate you."

"I am, of course, glad of your good opinion, Mark," said the arch dissembler, who was not willing to lift the mask, even in the presence of his own son; "but really I am afraid I don't deserve your compliment, if you mean that I knew anything about the disposition of the property."

"Have it as you please, father. I suppose it is best to know nothing about it. How did you manage it?"

"Mark!" reproved his father, sharply, "let me warn you to cease speaking in this manner. It is not safe. Let it be supposed that I exercised undue influence over the mind of your stepmother, and an attempt would be made by Frank to upset the will. If his lawyer could make a jury believe that the charge was well founded, the attempt would be successful, and I need not say that your position, as well as mine, would be very materially altered."

Mark was sensibly impressed by this view of the case. The prospect of having the property snatched away, however remote, alarmed him, and he understood that he must be prudent.

"You are right, father," he said. "It's nothing to me how the property came to you, but I'm glad you've got it. How much are you going to give me?"

"Ahem! you will share in the advantage of it," responded his father.

"Won't you give me ten thousand dollars down?"

"If I did, I should feel obliged to do the same for Frank."

"I don't see why."

"We don't wish to make talk, and as it is a great deal will be said about the will. Be patient, my son. When I am gone, you will be well provided for."

"But you may live a long time, and I should like to feel safe."

Mr. Manning was not thin-skinned nor sensitive, but the cold-blooded selfishness of his son did stir him a little.

"You must have confidence in me, Mark," he said, rather coldly. "You are my only son. You are all I have to live for. You need not be afraid that you will suffer neglect."

"Are we going back to school—Frank and I?" asked Mark.

"I don't know; that will be decided in due time. Don't you want to go?"

"Well, I don't mind finishing the term, but now you have a fortune it is not necessary that I should study so hard. I shall have enough to live upon."

"I suppose the same may be said of your stepbrother."

"He isn't your son, and will have to take what you choose to give him. Of course I am your son and heir."

Mr. Manning coughed.

"You seem to forget, Mark," he reminded, "that the property came from Frank's mother."

"She gave it to you, didn't she?"

"Yes, but—"

"Then it is yours now. It makes no difference whom it used to belong to."

Mr. Manning smiled.

"Mark will know how to take care of himself," he thought. "He is very shrewd."

Just then Mark's thoughts were turned in a different direction.

Looking from the window, he saw Frank's horse grazing near the stable.

This horse had been given to Frank as a birthday gift only a few months previous. He was a handsome animal, and Frank was very proud of him. He had become an excellent horseman, and when at home was often seen galloping over the country roads.

Mark could ride, but not so well. He had no horse of his own, and more than once had envied Frank his possession of his spirited steed. But his father had objected to buying him one.

"You must remember, Mark," he said, "that I have very little money of my own. Mrs. Manning is abundantly able to buy a horse for Frank, but you are not her son. You'll have to wait."

With this arrangement, Mark was, as may be supposed, far from satisfied. He had no resource, however, but to accept his father's advice.

Now, however, as his glance fell upon the horse, he felt that the time had come for a change. It would never do for Frank to have a horse, while he, Mr. Manning's heir, was without one.

"Now you can give me a horse, father," he said.

"There are horses enough in the stable, Mark. It costs a good deal of money to keep so many. I feel more like selling a horse than buying another. I have a good income, but no money to throw away."

"Then is Frank to have a horse and I none at all?" demanded Mark.

"Frank has no horse," replied Mr. Manning, coolly.

"Isn't Ajax his horse?"

"He calls him so, but he has no legal title to him. The will, in leaving the property to me, makes no exception in the case of the horse. I shall have to feed him, and he is therefore mine."

"Then give him to me, father," said Mark, eagerly.

"I can't do that. There would be the same objection to your owning him."

"I can ride him, though, can't I?"

"If I decide to keep him. One horse is enough for you and Frank."

"Frank will be mad!" said Mark, in a tone of satisfaction. "He never would let me ride Ajax—that is, not often."

"It is not for him to say now," assured Mr. Manning.

"I mean to have my share of riding, now," declared Mark. "I will go out this very afternoon!"

"Hadn't you better wait till to-morrow, Mark?"

"No time like the present, father. I'll have a fine gallop."

Before his father could object, he was out of the house and at the stable, where Richard Green had resumed his duties.

"Richard," said Mark, in a tone of authority, "saddle Ajax; I am going to ride."

"Does Mr. Frank say you can ride him?" questioned the coachman.

"It is no business of Frank's," answered Mark, haughtily.

"Isn't it his horse?"

"No, it isn't. It belongs to my father."

"It was given to Mr. Frank on his birthday."

"Nothing was said about it in the will. Father says I may ride it whenever I please."

This was not exactly what Mr. Manning had said, but Mark was not a stickler for the truth.

"Mr. Frank will make a fuss," warned Richard.

"Let him!" said Mark. "He can settle matters with my father. I want Ajax saddled right off."

"I will obey orders, Mr. Mark, but I don't think it is right."

"That doesn't matter. My father is master here, and if he says I can ride Ajax, I will."

"There'll be trouble, I know," said the coachman, as he saw Mark ride out of the yard.

Chapter 7

MARK'S DISCOMFITURE

Frank's indignation was roused when he saw Mark on his horse, and he hurried forward till he was near enough to be heard by his stepbrother.

"What are you doing on that horse, Mark Manning?" he asked, sternly.

Mark had always been a little afraid of Frank, who, as he had reason to know, excelled him in physical strength. Now, backed by the knowledge that Frank was less favorably situated than himself as regards property, he felt an increase of courage, and disposed to be defiant.

"I am riding," he rejoined, shortly.

"And what business have you to be riding my horse without permission?" demanded Frank, with flashing eyes.

"He is not your horse," retorted Mark.

"What do you mean by that?" said Frank, beginning to suspect that there was something underneath which he did not understand.

"I suppose you heard the will, didn't you?"

"Well?"

"Was anything said in the will about Ajax going to you?"

"Oh, that's it, is it?" returned Frank, his lip curling. "Did you take out my horse with your father's knowledge?"

"What has that to do with it?"

"Did you ask him if you might use it?"

"Suppose I did!"

"Does he say Ajax doesn't belong to me?"

"Yes, he does. I hope you are satisfied now."

"So, not content with robbing me of the estate, he must even take my birthday gift," said Frank, bitterly.

"You'd better not say that he robbed you of the estate," growled Mark, concluding that Frank was inclined to yield.

"You'd better get off that horse!" said Frank, angrily.

Mark hesitated, but inclination, and the thought that his father would back him, decided him to hold out.

"Good-bye!" said he, with mock politeness, raising his hat. "I'm off!"

"Ajax!" called Frank, quickly.

Frank had perfect control over his horse. As a rider, he was at once fearless and kind, and the animal was attached to him.

No sooner did he hear Frank's voice than he turned at once, and, in spite of Mark's pulling at the rein, advanced to Frank and rubbed his nose against his hand.

"Good fellow!" said Frank, stroking him.

Mark was humiliated by his inability to control the animal, and colored with anger and vexation.

"Let go that horse, Frank Courtney!" he ordered.

"It strikes me that you had better get off," replied Frank, coolly.

"You will repent this!" exclaimed Mark, furiously.

"Let me advise you hereafter not to interfere with my property," said Frank.

Mark twitched the reins angrily, and, raising his whip, struck the horse. It was an unfortunate experiment.

Ajax disliked Mark as much as he liked his master, and, on feeling the lash, reared and plunged, while his rider turned pale and clung to his seat in an ecstasy of terror.

The truth must be told that Mark possessed very little physical courage, and found his position very uncomfortable.

"Stop making the horse plunge!" he cried, almost breathless.

Frank smiled. It was not in human nature not to enjoy the discomfiture of his rival.

"You brought it on yourself," he said. "Why did you strike him?"

By this time Ajax had become quiet, and Mark made haste to slide off his back.

"I'll tell my father how you spoiled my ride!" he said, fiercely.

"Do so, if you like," replied Frank, contemptuously. "If you allude to the conduct of the horse, it is your own fault."

"He was acting well enough till you came up."

"You'd better not attempt to ride him again. Then you will have no reason to complain."

"If I don't ride him, you shan't!" retorted Mark.

"Who's going to prevent me?"

"My father will prevent you."

Frank had not intended to ride. He was in no mood to do so while his loss was so recent, but he was provoked by the words and behavior of Mark, and his answer was to leap on the back of Ajax and turn his head down the avenue, before his stepbrother had divined his intention.

Mark saw the tables so completely turned upon him that he screamed:

"Come back here, if you know what is best for yourself!"

"You must be crazy!" answered Frank, and deigned no further notice of his stepbrother's anger.

"I'll be even with him for this—see if I don't!" muttered Mark, as he slowly took his way back to the house.

On the way he met the coachman.

The latter stopped short, and asked him, in surprise:

"What have you done with Ajax, Mr. Mark?"

"What have I done with him?" repeated Mark. "I'd like to shoot him."

"Why, what's the matter?"

"If you must know, Frank set him to rearing and plunging so that it was not safe to ride him."

"And you got off."

"Yes."

"Why didn't you bring him back?"

"Because I didn't choose to."

"Did Mr. Frank get on his back?"

"Yes."

"Oh, I understand!" said the coachman, with a significant smile, that angered and mortified Mark.

"Perhaps you don't understand as much as you suppose!" he snapped. "I don't think he'll ride the horse again very soon."

"I thought there'd be trouble," soliloquized the coachman, as he went back to the stable, "and that Mr. Frank wouldn't come off second best. This is only the beginning. That boy Mark means to kick up a fuss, and I mistrust he and his father together will make the house pretty uncomfortable. All the same, I am glad Mr. Frank got back his horse."

Mark could not wait for his anger to cool. He straightway sought his father, and proceeded to prefer complaints against Frank, taking care to make his case as strong as possible without very strict adherence to the truth.

"You say that Frank tried to make the horse throw you?" inquired the father.

"To be sure he did. He was very angry because I presumed to use him."

"Did you tell him that you had my permission, Mark?"

"Yes, I did; but it made no difference. He hasn't the slightest respect for you."

Mr. Manning's voice was not quite so soft as usual as he said:

"He had better have a care. I do not propose to indulge him as his mother did. Of one thing he may rest assured—that I intend to be master in this house and on this estate."

"Good for you, father! I thought you wouldn't knuckle down to a mere boy like him," said Mark, artfully trying to fan the flames of his father's resentment.

Mr. Manning smiled, but the smile was not a pleasant one.

"Probably Frank does not understand me," he said. "During his mother's life I forbore to assert myself or my authority out of regard for her feelings. I saw much in Frank's conduct and manners that I could not approve, but I put a restraint upon myself for the sake of my dear wife. I believe I made her happy, and at this hour I feel repaid for all my sacrifices."

He was about to relapse into a sentimental mood, but Mark did not sympathize with it. He chose to construe his father's words in a way not intended.

"Yes, father, you are well repaid. You are a rich man now."

"That was not exactly what I intended to convey, Mark," said his father, coughing in an embarrassed way.

"Well, it doesn't matter. You can do as you please now, and I hope you'll make Frank keep his place."

"You may be assured that I will," said his father, compressing his thin lips. "When Frank comes in, will you send him to me, if you see him?"

"I will make it my business to see him," said Mark, in a tone of satisfaction. "Just give it to him red-hot, father!"

"Mark, I am shocked at your expression. It is not refined."

Mark shrugged his shoulders and left his father's presence, not particularly mortified by the rebuke. In fact, hard as it is to say it, he had rather a contempt for his father, though he believed in his sharpness and his ability.

But Mark saw through him. He understood very well that his parent was an arch-dissembler and a hypocrite, and for such a man even he could not feel respect.

He lay in wait till Frank returned from his ride, and greeted him thus:

"My father wants to see you right off."

"Where is your father?"

"In his room."

"I will go up to him," answered Frank, gravely. "I, too, wish to see him!"

Chapter 8

AN UNSATISFACTORY INTERVIEW

Frank entered the room in which his stepfather sat. His air was manly and his bearing that of a boy who respects himself, but there was none of the swagger which some boys think it necessary to exhibit when they wish to assert their rights.

Mr. Manning, in a flowered dressing-gown, sat at a table, with a sheet of paper before him and a lead-pencil in his hand. Short as had been the interval since his accession to the property, he was figuring up the probable income he would derive from the estate.

He looked up as Frank entered the room, and surveyed him with cold and sarcastic eyes. His soft tones were dropped.

"Mr. Manning," began Frank, "I wish to ask you a question."

"And I wish to ask you a question," replied his stepfather. "Odd coincidence, isn't it?" he added, with a sneer.

"Very well, sir," said Frank in no wise daunted by his manner. "As you are the older, I will first listen to what you have to say."

"You are very considerate, I am sure," said Mr. Manning, with an unpleasant smile. "Let me ask you, in a word, to explain your outrageous treatment of Mark."

"What does he say I have done?"

"It is hardly necessary to answer that question, since you know very well what you have done."

"I know very well what I have done, but I don't know what he may choose to say I have done."

"Do you mean to charge him with untruth?"

"Not until I know whether he has made a misstatement."

"He says that you caused Ajax to rear and plunge, and so compelled him to dismount."

"Did he mention that he struck the horse, and that this was the cause of its rearing and plunging?"

"No."

"Then he omitted a very important part of the truth."

"Did you do nothing to incite the horse to his bad behavior?"

"No, sir. I called the horse by name, and he responded."

"Humph! I begin to understand. Would Mark have had any difficulty with the horse had you not been present?"

"Perhaps not."

"So I thought," replied Mr. Manning, triumphantly.

"Please wait till I have finished, sir," said Frank, calmly. "In that case, Mark would probably not have struck the horse. That caused him to rear."

"By your own confession, your presence occasioned all the difficulty," said Mr. Manning, perversely. "Did you not order him to get off the horse?"

"Yes, sir."

"After he had told you that he had taken it from the stable by my permission?"

"Yes, sir."

"Then you defied my authority," said Mr. Manning, sternly. "What excuse have you for this?"

"You seem to have forgotten, Mr. Manning, that the horse was a birthday present to me."

"That meant only that you were to have the chief use of it. Was the horse left to you in the will?"

"There was very little reference to me in the will," said Frank, bitterly.

"So you would complain of your poor mother, would you?" said his stepfather, in a tone of virtuous indignation.

"I cannot believe that my mother made that will."

Mr. Manning colored. He scented danger. Should Frank drop such hints elsewhere, he might make trouble, and lead to a legal investigation, which Mr. Manning had every reason to dread.

"This is very foolish," he said, more mildly. "No doubt you are disappointed, but probably your mother has provided wisely. You will want for nothing, and you will be prepared for the responsibilities of manhood under my auspices."

Mr. Manning's face assumed a look of self-complacence as he uttered these last words.

"I have no blame to cast upon my dear mother," said Frank. "If she made that will, she acted under a great mistake."

"What mistake, sir?"

"She failed to understand you."

"Do you mean to imply that I shall be false to my trust?"

"Not at present, sir. I don't wish to judge of you too hastily. Now, may I ask my question?"

"You have not answered mine. But let that pass. Ask your question."

"Is Mark to share with me the use of Ajax?"

"Yes."

"Though he is my horse?"

"You are mistaken. He is my horse."

"Yours!"

"Certainly. He comes to me with the rest of the property."

"And I have absolutely nothing?"

"What does it matter? You and Mark will have the use of Ajax, while I pay for his feed. My ownership will bring me no advantage."

"I have nothing further to say, sir," said Frank, as he turned to go down-stairs.

"But I have," said Mr. Manning.

"Very well, sir."

"I demand that you treat my son Mark with suitable respect, and forbear to infringe upon his rights."

Frank looked up, and answered, with spirit:

"I shall treat Mark as well as he treats me, sir. Is that satisfactory?"

"I apprehend," said Mr. Manning, "that you may make some mistakes upon that point."

"I will try not to do so, sir."

Frank left the room, and this time was not called back.

His stepfather looked after him, but his face expressed neither friendliness nor satisfaction.

"That boy requires taming," he said to himself. "He is going to make trouble. I must consider what I will do with him."

As Mr. Manning reviewed Frank's words, there was one thing which especially disturbed him—the doubt expressed by his stepson as to his mother's having actually made the will.

He saw that it would not do for him to go too far in his persecution of Frank, as it might drive the latter to consult a lawyer in regard to the validity of the will by which he had been disinherited.

When Frank left his stepfather's presence, he went out to the stable. There he found Richard Green, the coachman, who had general charge of the horses.

"Well, Mr. Frank," said Richard, smiling, "did you have a pleasant ride?"

"No, Richard; I had too much on my mind to enjoy it."

"Mr. Mark came back in a bad temper," chuckled the coachman.

"I suppose I interrupted his ride," said Frank.

"Served him right. What business has he to take out your horse?"

"Mr. Manning has just told me that it is not my horse."

"Whose is it, then, I'd like to know?"

"He says it is his, and that it was left to him with the property."

"There's no end to that man's impudence!" ejaculated Richard. "Didn't your mother give it to you for your birthday?"

"That appears to count for nothing, Richard. Mr. Manning says that Mark shall have the same use of it that I have."

"Are you going to submit to it, Mr. Frank?"

"I don't know yet what I shall do. I am likely to see a good deal of trouble. If my mother really made that will—which I can't believe—she little suspected how unhappy she was going to make me."

"She was too good to suspect the badness of others, Mr. Frank. She thought old Manning was really all that he pretended to be, and that he would be as kind to you as she was herself. When she was alive, he was always as soft as—as silk."

"His manner has changed now," said Frank, gravely. "Excuse me, Richard, for finding fault with you, but don't call him old Manning."

"Why not, Mr. Frank?"

"I have no liking for Mr. Manning—in fact, I dislike him—but he was the husband of my mother, and I prefer to speak of him respectfully."

"I dare say you are right, Mr. Frank, but, all the same, he don't deserve it. Is Mr. Mark to ride Ajax, then?"

"If he asks for it, you are to saddle Ajax for him. I don't want you to get into any trouble with Mr. Manning on my account, Richard."

"I don't care for that, Mr. Frank. I can get another place, and I don't much care to serve Mr. Manning."

"I would rather you would stay if you can, Richard. I don't want to see a new face in the stable."

"I don't think he means to keep me long, Mr. Frank. Deborah and I will have to go, I expect, and he'll get some servants of his own here."

"Has he hinted anything of this, Richard?" asked Frank, quickly.

"No; but he will soon, you may depend on it. I won't lose sight of you, though. I've known you since you were four years old, and I won't desert you, if I can do any good—nor Deborah, either."

"I have two friends, then, at any rate," said Frank to himself. "That is something."

Chapter 9

A SCHOOL FRIEND

Early Monday morning it had been the custom for Frank and Mark to take the train for Bridgeville, to enter upon a new week at the academy.

Frank felt that it would be better for him to go back without any further vacation, as occupation would serve to keep him from brooding over his loss.

"Are you ready, Mark?" he asked, as he rose from the breakfast-table.

"Ready for what?"

"To go back to school, of course."

"I am not going back this morning," answered Mark.

"Why not?" asked Frank, in some surprise.

"I am going to stay at home to help father," said Mark, with a glance at Mr. Manning.

"If I can be of any service to you, sir, I will stay, too," said Frank, politely.

"Thank you, but Mark will do all I require," replied his stepfather.

"Very well, sir."

Frank appeared at the academy with a grave face and subdued manner, suggestive of the great loss he had sustained. From his school-fellows, with whom he was a favorite, he received many words of sympathy—from none more earnest or sincere than from Herbert Grant.

"I know how you feel, Frank," he said, pressing the hand of his friend. "If I could comfort you I would, but I don't know how to do it."

"I find comfort in your sympathy," said Frank. "I look upon you as my warmest friend here."

"I am glad of that, Frank."

To Herbert alone Frank spoke of his mother and her devoted affection; but even to him he did not like to mention the will and his disinheritance. He did not so much lament the loss of the property as that he had lost it by the direction of his mother, or rather because it would generally be supposed so.

For himself, he doubted the genuineness of the will, but he felt that it was useless to speak of it, as he was unprepared with any proofs.

So it happened that when, on Wednesday afternoon, Mark Manning made his appearance, Frank's change of position, as respected the property, was neither known nor suspected by his school-fellows. It was soon known, however, and of course, through Mark.

The boys immediately noticed a change in Mark. He assumed an air of consequence, and actually strutted across the campus. Instead of being polite and attentive to Frank, he passed him with a careless nod, such as a superior might bestow on an inferior.

"What has come over Mark?" asked Herbert of Frank, as the two were walking together from recitation.

"How do you mean?"

"He holds his head higher than he used to do. He looks as if he had been elected to some important office."

"You will soon learn, Herbert," said Frank. "Make a pretext to join him, and let the news come from him."

Herbert looked puzzled.

"Do you wish me to do this?" he asked.

"Yes, I have a reason for it."

"Very well. I am always ready to oblige you, Frank, but I hope Mark won't think I have suddenly formed a liking for his society."

"If he does, you can soon undeceive him."

"That is true."

Herbert left the side of his friend, and sauntered toward Mark.

As Herbert was known as Frank's especial friend, Mark was at first surprised, but quickly decided that his improved position had been communicated by Frank, and that Herbert was influenced by it. That is to say, he judged Herbert to be as mean and mercenary as himself.

Herbert's position was too humble to entitle him to much notice from Mark, but the latter was pleased with the prospect of detaching from Frank his favorite friend.

"You came back rather late, Mark," said Herbert.

"Yes," answered Mark, with an air of importance. "I remained at home a short time, to help my father in his accounts. You know the property is large, and there is a good deal to do."

"I should think that was Frank's place, to help about the accounts."

"Why?"

"The property is his, of course!"

"Did he tell you that?" asked Mark, sharply.

"He has not said a word about the property."

"No, I suppose not," said Mark, with a sneering laugh.

"Has anything happened? Didn't his mother leave as much as was expected?" went on Herbert, quite in the dark.

"Yes, she left a large estate, but she didn't leave it to him."

"To whom, then?"

"To my father!" replied Mark, with conscious pride. "Frank has nothing. He is entirely dependent upon father."

"Did his mother leave him nothing, then?" asked Herbert, in pained surprise.

"Nothing at all," assured Mark, complacently.

"That is very strange and unjust."

"I don't look upon it in that light," said Mark, nettled. "My father knows what is best for him. He will provide for him just as his mother did before."

"But when Frank is of age, doesn't he come into possession of the estate then?"

"No, of course not. Didn't I tell you it beongs to father? Frank is a poor boy—as poor as you," said Mark, in a tone of evident satisfaction.

"Or you," added Herbert, pointedly.

"You are mistaken," said Mark, quickly. "I am father's heir."

"Suppose your father dies—how will the property go?"

"I suppose something will be left to Frank, unless my father leaves me the property, with directions to provide for him."

"Would you think that right and just?" demanded Herbert, indignantly.

"Of course I would. My stepmother knew what she was about when she made her will. I see you are surprised. You won't be quite so thick with Frank now, I expect."

"Why shouldn't I be?"

"Because he is just as poor as you are. He never can help you."

"Mark Manning, I believe you are about the meanest boy I ever encountered, and you judge me by yourself!"

"Do you mean to insult me? Mind what you say!" blustered Mark, unpleasantly surprised at this outburst from a boy whom he expected would now transfer his allegiance from Frank to himself.

"I mean that you and your father have robbed Frank of his inheritance, and glory in it, and you think that I am mean enough to desert him because he is no longer rich. It makes no difference to me whether he is rich or poor. I think I like him all the better because he has been so badly treated. As for you, I despise you, and shall continue to, even if you get the whole of Frank's money."

"You forget that you are talking to a gentleman, you low-born mechanic!" said Mark, angrily.

"You a gentleman!" replied Herbert, contemptuously. "Then I never want to be one!"

He walked away, leaving Mark very much incensed.

"When I am a rich man, he may repent having insulted me," muttered Mark.

Herbert went back to Frank.

"Well, did he tell you?" asked Frank, quietly.

"Yes; and he actually appeared to think I would be ready to desert you because you were poor, and follow him about."

"I am not afraid of that, Herbert."

"I don't think Mark will have that idea any more. I gave him a piece of my mind, and left him very angry. But what does it all mean, Frank?"

"I know no more than you do, Herbert. I cannot understand it."

"What could have induced your mother to make such a will?"

"I cannot believe my mother ever made such a will; but, if she did, I am very sure that she was overpersuaded by my stepfather, who is one of the most plausible of men."

"What shall you do about it?"

"What can I do? I am only a boy. I have no proof, you know."

"How are you likely to be treated?"

"I have had a little foretaste of that."

And Frank related the incident about Ajax.

"It looks very bad for you, Frank," admitted Herbert, in a tone of sympathy.

"I don't so much care for the loss of the property, Herbert," said Frank, "but I am afraid I shall have all sorts of annoyances to endure from Mark and his father. But I won't anticipate trouble. I will do my duty, and trust that things will turn out better than I fear."

The next afternoon a letter was placed in Frank's hands. It was in a brown envelope, and directed in a cramped and evidently unpracticed hand, with which Frank was not familiar.

On opening it, a glance at the signature showed that it was from Richard Green, the coachman. It commenced:

"DEAR MR. FRANK: This comes hoping you are well. I have no good news to tell. Mr. Manning has sold your horse, Ajax, and he is to be taken away to-night. I thought you ought to know it, and that is why I take my pen in hand to write."

There was more, but this is all that was important.

Frank's face flushed with anger. He immediately went in search of Mark, who, he felt assured, knew of the sale.

Chapter 10

A NEW PLAN

Mark was in his room, where Frank found him trying on a new necktie. Though decidedly plain, Mark fancied himself very good-looking, and spent no little time on personal adornment. In particular, he had a weakness for new neckties, in which he indulged himself freely.

When the boys came to the academy, the principal proposed that they should room together; but both objected, and Mark had a room to himself—no one caring to room with him.

"Take a seat, Frank," said Mark, condescendingly. "Is there anything I can do for you?"

"Yes," answered Frank. "I hear that your father has sold Ajax, or is intending to do so. Will you tell me if it is true?"

"I believe it is," replied Mark, indifferently.

"And what right has he to sell my horse?" demanded Frank, indignantly.

"You'd better ask him," said Mark, with provoking coolness.

"It is an outrage," declared Frank.

"As to that," said his stepbrother, "you can't expect father to be at the expense of feeding your horse."

"With my money?"

"The money is legally his. Besides, it is a vicious brute. I haven't forgotten how he treated me the other day."

"It was all your fault. Why did you lash him?"

"Horses were meant to be whipped," said Mark. "If they were not, what do we have whips for?"

"At any rate, Ajax gave you a lesson on the subject," rejoined Frank, significantly. "Do you know to whom your father has sold Ajax?"

"To Colonel Vincent, I believe."

"I am glad, at any rate, that he will have a good master."

"How did you learn about his being sold?" inquired Mark, in considerable curiosity.

Frank reflected that a true answer might get the coachman into trouble, and replied, guardedly:

"I prefer not to tell you."

"I don't need to be told," said Mark. "I am sure it was either Deborah or Richard Green who wrote you. Wasn't it?"

"You are at liberty to guess."

"You can't keep it from me. I will soon find out."

"Just as you please. I may have heard from your father, for aught you know."

"I know you didn't, for he cautioned me not to tell you."

"Indeed!" said Frank. "Did he give any reason for concealing it? It seems to me that, as Ajax was bought for me, I ought to be the first to be informed."

"Father said you would make a fuss, and it was just as well you should not know till the horse was gone. I will let him know that he has spies in the house."

"You are mean enough to do so, Mark Manning, I know very well. It will be better for you not to meddle with matters that don't concern you."

"You'd better not insult me," threatened Mark, angrily, "or it will be the worse for you."

Frank laughed.

"I am not easily frightened," he said. "I am prepared for the consequences of my actions."

Frank felt that there would be no advantage in prolonging the interview, or carrying on further a war of words.

He sought out his friend Herbert, and communicated to him this last infraction of his rights.

"It is too bad, Frank!" said his sympathizing friend.

"Yes, it is," said Frank, gravely; "but I fear it is only the beginning of annoyances. I don't believe I can ever live in any place with Mr. Manning or Mark."

"Will it be necessary?"

"I presume so. I have no money, as you know. All has gone to him. Herbert, I tell you frankly, I envy you and your position."

"Though my father is a poor man?"

"Yes; for, at least, you have a peaceful home, and a father and mother who love you. I have a stepfather, who will do all he can to make me miserable."

"Would you be willing to work for your own support, Frank?"

"Yes; far rather than remain a dependent on Mr. Manning."

"Suppose you should go away," suggested Herbert.

Frank shook his head.

"I wouldn't do that except in case of extreme necessity. I know that if my mother knows what goes on here, it would grieve her for me to take such a step."

"Suppose your stepfather should consent to your leaving home?"

"Then I would do so gladly. I am willing to work, and I think I could make a living in some way."

"Why not ask him?"

Frank's face brightened.

"Thank you for the hint, Herbert," he said. "I will think of it, and I may act upon it."

Frank was naturally self-reliant and energetic. He was not disposed to shrink from the duties of life, but was ready to go forth to meet them. The idea which Herbert had suggested commended itself to him the more he thought of it.

In spite, therefore, of the news which he had received about Ajax, he resumed his cheerfulness, much to the surprise of Mark, whose natural suspicion led him to conjecture that Frank had some plan in view to circumvent his father.

"If he has, he'd better give it up," reflected Mark. "The old man's as sly as a fox. A mere boy like Frank can't get the better of him."

At the close of the week, both the boys went home. They were on board the same train and the same car, but did not sit together. When they reached the house, Mr. Manning was not at home.

Frank went out to the stable at once to see Richard Green, the coachman.

He found him, indeed, but he also found another man, a stranger, who appeared to be employed in the stable.

"Who is this, Richard?" asked Frank.

"My successor," responded the coachman.

"Are you going to leave?"

"Come out with me, Mr. Frank, and I will tell you. I've had notice to leave," he said, "and so has Deborah. It came last evening. Mr. Manning got a letter from Bridgeville—I know that, because I brought it home from the post-office—which appeared to make him angry. He called Deborah and me and told us that he should not need our services any longer."

"Did he give you any reason?"

"Yes; he said that he could have our places filled for a good deal less money, and he has no doubt we could do as well elsewhere."

"He has filled your place pretty soon."

"He has indeed. This man came this morning. I think Mr. Manning had sent for him already. I told you the other day we should soon be discharged."

"I know it; but I can tell you what has hastened it."

"What then?"

"Mark wrote his father that I had learned about the sale of Ajax, and that the information came from you or Deborah."

"I think it likely, Mr. Frank, for Mr. Manning seemed mighty cool. I hope you won't take it too much to heart that Ajax is sold."

"I am not sure but I am glad of it."

The coachman looked at him in surprise.

"I thought you would be very angry," he said.

"So I was at first, but he has been sold to a man who will treat him well, and I shall be glad to think of that when I'm away from home."

"You don't mean to run away, Mr. Frank?"

"No, but I mean to get my stepfather's permission to go, if I can."

"Where do you mean to go, may I ask?"

"Somewhere where I can earn my living, without depending upon anybody. You know very well, Richard, how miserable I should be to stay here in dependence upon Mr. Manning."

"But to think that you, to whom the property rightfully belongs, should go away and work for a living, while that man and his son occupy your place. I can't bear to think of it."

"I have done a good deal of thinking within a few days, and I don't shrink from the prospect. I think I should rather enjoy being actively employed."

"But you were to go to college, Mr. Frank."

"I know it, Richard, but I am not sure whether it would be for the best. My tastes are for an active business life, and I don't care for a profession."

"Do you think your stepfather will give you a start?"

"In the way of money?"

"Yes."

"I don't know. If he won't, I have still fifty dollars in the savings bank, which I have saved from my pocket-money. I will take that."

"Mr. Frank, will you promise not to be offended at what I'm going to say?"

"I don't think you would say anything that ought to offend me, Richard."

"Then I want you to take the money that comes to me by the will— Mr. Manning is to pay it to me on Monday. I don't need it, and you may."

Frank shook his head.

"You are very kind, Richard, but I will get along with fifty dollars, unless Mr. Manning supplies me with more. If I really need money at any time, I will think of your offer."

"That's something, at any rate," said Richard, partly reconciled. "You won't forget it now, Mr. Frank?"

"No, Richard, I promise you."

Frank left the stable and went thoughtfully into the house.

Chapter 11

THE NEW OWNER OF AJAX

Frank and Mark took supper alone, Mr. Manning having left word that he would not return till later in the evening.

After supper, Frank decided to go over to call upon Colonel Vincent, the new owner of Ajax. His estate was distant about three-quarters of a mile from the Cedars.

As Frank started, Mark asked, rather uneasily:

"Where are you going, Frank?"

"To see Ajax," answered our hero.

"Do you mean to make any fuss about him? I wouldn't advise you to."

"Thank you for your advice."

"I wonder what he is going to do?" thought Mark. "Of course he can't do anything now."

He did not venture to propose to accompany Frank, knowing that his company would not be acceptable.

"Is Colonel Vincent at home?" inquired Frank, at the door of a handsome house.

"Yes, Mr. Courtney," replied the colored servant, pleasantly, for Frank was a favorite among all classes in the neighborhood. "Come right in, sir. De colonel am on de back piazza."

Frank followed the servant through the hall which intersected the house, and stepped out on the back piazza.

A stout, elderly gentleman was taking his ease in a large rustic rocking-chair.

"Good-evening, Colonel Vincent," our hero said.

"Good-evening, Frank, my boy," returned the colonel, heartily. "Glad to see you. Haven't you gone back to school?"

"Yes, sir; but I came home to spend Sunday. It doesn't seem much like home now," he added, as his lip quivered.

"You have suffered a great loss, my dear boy," said the colonel, feelingly.

"The greatest, sir. My mother was all I had."

"I suppose Mr. Manning will keep up the establishment?"

"I suppose so, sir; but it is no longer home to me."

"Don't take it too hard, Frank. I was sorry about the will."

"So was I; because it makes me dependent on a man whom I dislike."

"Don't be too prejudiced, Frank. I never took any fancy to your stepfather myself; but then we don't need to like everybody we associate with."

"I hear you have bought my horse, Colonel Vincent," said Frank, desiring to change the subject.

"Was Ajax your horse?"

"Yes. It was given me as a birthday present by my mother."

"I had some such idea, and expressly asked Mr. Manning whether the horse was not yours."

"What did he answer?"

"That it was only nominally yours, and that he thought it best to sell it, as both you and Mark were absent at school, and had no time to use it."

"I am not surprised at anything Mr. Manning may say," said Frank.

"It's too bad! I'll tell you what I will do, Frank. I haven't paid for the horse yet. I will return it to Mr. Manning, and tell him that I bought it under a misapprehension of the ownership. I don't think he will make any trouble."

"I would rather have you keep it, Colonel Vincent."

"You would!" exclaimed the colonel, in surprise.

"Yes. If you should return Ajax, Mr. Manning would sell him to some one else, and you, I know, will treat him well."

"But you will lose the use of him. No, you won't, though. Come over to my stable when you like, and, if he is not in use, you can take him out."

"Thank you, sir! You are very kind. While I am in the neighborhood, I won't forget your generous offer. But I mean to go away."

"You mean to go away! Where?"

"Out into the world. Anywhere, where I can find work and make a living."

"But surely this is not necessary. Your stepfather will provide for you without your working."

"I have no reason to doubt it, Colonel Vincent; but I shall be happier in the world outside."

"Of course you will let Mr. Manning know of your intention to leave home?"

"I shall ask his permission to go at the end of my school term. That comes in a couple of weeks."

"Where will you go?"

"A cousin of my father lives at Newark, New Jersey. I think I shall go to him first, and ask his advice about getting a place either there or in New York."

"You will need some money to start with. Do you think Mr. Manning will give you any?"

"I don't know, sir! That won't prevent my going. I have fifty dollars in a savings bank, saved up from my allowance, and that will be all I shall need."

"If you have any difficulty on that score, Frank, remember that I was your father's friend, and mean to be yours. Apply to me at any time when you are in a strait."

"I will, sir, and thank you heartily."

"That was a strange will, Frank. I don't want to put any ideas into your head to disturb you, but had your mother ever led you to suspect that she intended to leave you dependent on your stepfather?"

"Never, sir!"

"Don't you think she would have done so, had she had such a plan in view?"

"I do," said Frank, quickly.

The colonel's eye met his, and each knew what the other suspected.

"There is nothing for me to do at present," continued Frank. "If Mr. Manning does not interfere with my plans, I shall not trouble him."

"I will hint as much when I see him. It may clear the way for you."

"I wish you would, sir."

"Come and see me again, Frank," said the colonel, as Frank rose to go.

"I certainly will, sir."

"Your father's son will always be welcome at my house. When did you say your school term closes?"

"In a fortnight."

"I will see your stepfather within a few days. By-the-way, Frank, wouldn't you like a gallop on Ajax to-night?"

"Yes, sir; I should enjoy it."

"Come out to the stable with me, then."

Ajax whinnied with delight when he saw his old, or rather his young master, and evinced satisfaction when Frank stroked him caressingly.

"Sam," said Colonel Vincent, "Frank is to ride Ajax whenever he pleases. Saddle him for his use whenever he asks you."

"That I will, sir," replied Sam. "Often and often I've seen Mr. Frank on his back. Doesn't he ride well, though?"

"Don't flatter me, Sam," said Frank, laughing.

Five minutes later he was on the back of his favorite horse, galloping down the road.

"I hope I shall meet Mark," thought Frank. "I would like to give him something to tell his father about."

Considering the manner in which Mark had treated his stepbrother, Frank may be excused for the wish to puzzle him a little.

Finding himself lonely, Mark decided to take a walk not long after Frank's departure. He was sauntering along the road, when he heard the sound of hoofs, and, to his surprise, saw his stepbrother mounted on Ajax.

His first thought was that Frank had gone to Colonel Vincent's stable and brought away Ajax without permission, in defiance of Mrs. Manning's will. He resolved to take him to task for it immediately. Frank purposely slackened the speed of his horse in order to give Mark the chance he sought.

"Why are you riding Ajax?" asked Mark.

"It is a pleasant evening," answered Frank, "and I thought I should enjoy it."

"Where did you get him?"

"From Colonel Vincent's stable, where he never ought to have been taken," replied Frank, with spirit.

"You seem to think you can do anything you like, Frank Courtney," said Mark, provoked, certain now that his suspicions were well-founded.

"Is there any particular reason why I should not ride Ajax?" demanded Frank.

"You have made yourself liable to arrest for horse-stealing," said Mark. "It would serve you right if Colonel Vincent should have you arrested and tried."

"I don't think he will gratify your kind wishes, Mark."

"Just wait and see what my father has to say to you."

"I have only done what I had a perfect right to do; but I can't stop to dispute with you. I must finish my ride. Hey, Ajax!"

As he spoke, the horse broke into a gallop, and Mark was left looking after him in a disturbed frame of mind.

"I'll tell my father as soon as he gets home," he decided; and he kept his word.

In consequence, Frank, by that time returned, was summoned into Mr. Manning's presence.

"What is this I hear?" he began. "Did you ride Ajax this evening?"

"Yes, sir."

"Where did you find him?"

"In Colonel Vincent's stable."

"This is a high-handed proceeding, Frank Courtney. Have you any excuse to offer?"

"None is needed, sir. Colonel Vincent has given me permission to ride him whenever I please."

"It appears to me, Mark," said Mr. Manning, sharply, "that you have been very foolish."

"How should I know?" replied Mark, mortified by the collapse of his sensation. "Frank didn't tell me he had leave to use the horse."

And he left the room, looking very sheepish.

Chapter 12

MARK YIELDS TO TEMPTATION

There are some boys, as well as men, who cannot stand prosperity.

It appeared that Mark Manning was one of these.

While his stepmother was living and his father's prospects—and consequently his own—were uncertain, he had been circumspect in his behavior and indulged in nothing that could be considered seriously wrong.

When his father came into possession of a large fortune, and his pocket-money was doubled, Mark began to throw off some of the restraint which, from motives of prudence, he had put upon himself.

About the middle of the next week, as Frank was taking a walk after school hours, he was considerably surprised to see Mark come out of a well-known billiard room, frequented by men and boys of idle habits.

The students of the Bridgeville Academy were strictly forbidden this or any other such resort, and I am sure that my boy-readers will agree with me that this rule was a very proper one.

Mark Manning appeared to be excited. His face was flushed, and his breathing rapid. With him was James Carson, one of the poorest scholars and most unprincipled boys in the academy. It was rather surprising that he had managed for so long to retain his position in the institution, but he was crafty and took good care not to be caught.

To go back a little, it was chiefly owing to James Carson's influence that Mark had entered the rooms.

When he learned that Mark's worldly prospects had improved, and that he had a large supply of pocket-money, he determined to cultivate his acquaintance—though privately he thought Mark a disagreeable boy—with the intention of obtaining for himself a portion of Mark's surplus means.

At the first of the term he had made similar advances to Frank, but they were coldly received, so much so that he did not think it worth while to persevere in courting the latter's intimacy.

He succeeded better with Mark, his crafty nature teaching him how to approach him.

"Mark," he said, with a great show of cordiality, "I am delighted to hear of your good fortune. I always liked you, and I think you deserve to be rich."

"Thank you!" said Mark, much gratified, for he liked flattery. "I am sure I am very much obliged to you."

"Oh, not at all! I only say what I think. Shall I tell you why I am particularly glad?"

"Yes, if you like," replied Mark, in some curiosity.

"Because I like you better than that young muff, your stepbrother. I hope you won't be offended at my plain speaking," he added, artfully.

"Certainly not!" assured Mark, almost as well pleased with abuse of Frank as with praise of himself. "To tell you the truth, I don't like Frank myself. He is my stepbrother, to be sure, but he always makes himself disagreeable to me."

"Then you are not offended with me?"

"Of course not! How can I expect you to like Frank, when I don't myself?"

James Carson was perfectly aware of the feeling between the stepbrothers, and his assumed ignorance was so transparent that Mark, had he not been blinded by his self-conceit, might easily have seen through it.

"I suppose," continued the crafty flatterer, "you will see a little life now that you are your own master and have plenty of money."

"I don't know exactly what you mean, James. There isn't much life to be seen in Bridgeville."

"That is true; but still there is some. Suppose, now"—by this time they were in front of a long low building which contained a billiard and pool-table—"suppose now we go in and have a game of billiards."

"It's against the rules, isn't it?" asked Mark.

"What do you care for the rules?" said James contemptuously.

"If the old man hears of it, we shall get into hot water."

By the "old man" Mark meant the Rev. Dr. Brush, the venerable and respected principal of the Bridgeville Academy, but such boys as he have very little respect for the constituted authorities.

"Why need he know it? We will slip in when no one is looking. Did you ever play a game of billiards?"

"I never played more than half a dozen games in my life."

"You ought to know how to play. It is a splendid game. Come in."

Mark did not make very strong opposition, and the two boys, first looking cautiously in different directions, entered the building.

While Mark was looking around the room, James Carson addressed himself to a man who seemed to be in attendance.

"John, give me the balls. We are going to play a game of billiards."

"All right, sir."

"I'll discount you, Mark," said James, "to give you a fair chance. It is about the same thing as giving you half the game. Or, if you like, I will give you seventeen points to start with, and then you will only have seventeen to make, while I am making thirty-four."

"I like that better."

"Very well. Now shall we play with the understanding that which-ever one loses is to pay for the use of the balls? Now let us string for the lead."

There is no need of describing the game in detail. Mark was only a novice, while James could really make three or four points to his one. He restrained himself, however, so that he only beat Mark by two points.

"You did splendidly, Mark," he said. "Considering how little you have played, you did remarkably well. Why, you made a run of three."

"Yes, I did pretty well," said Mark, flattered by his companion's praises.

"I had hard work to beat you, I can tell you that. As it was, you came within two points of beating. Don't you like the game?"

"Very much."

"I thought you would. Shall we have another game?"

"I don't mind," answered Mark.

He knew that he ought to be in his room writing a composition to be delivered the next day, but such obligations sat easily upon Mark, and he did not hesitate long.

That time James allowed him to score sixteen, so that Mark was only beaten by one point.

"You see, you are improving," said James. "I played a better game that time than before, and still you came within one of beating me."

"I think I shall become a good player in time," said Mark, complacently.

"Yes, and in a very short time. Now," went on James, "'shall we have another."

"I don't know about that. You beat me both of the other games."

"That's true; but you play better now than you did at first."

"That may be so."

"I expect to lose this game, but that will only increase the interest of the game."

So Mark was persuaded, and the game was played.

James Carson managed to let Mark beat him by five shots, and the latter was correspondingly elated.

"You beat me, after all," grumbled James, pretending to be much disappointed, "and by five points. I'll tell you what I'll do—I'll give you the same odds, and we will play just one more game. I suppose it's foolish, but I'll risk it."

"Done!" said Mark, eagerly.

His cupidity was excited, and he felt sure of winning this, as he had the previous games. But James had no idea of playing off now, and he played a better game, as he was well able to do. The result was that Mark was beaten by three points.

He looked quite crestfallen.

"I had better shows than you," said James. "I couldn't do it once in five times. Will you play again?"

Mark agreed to it with some hesitation, and he was again beaten.

"You had luck against you. Another day you will succeed better. Have you played enough?"

"Yes," said Mark, annoyed.

He had four games to pay for, which amounted to two dollars, and this made rather an expensive afternoon.

Mark was flushed and excited as he left the billiard-room just as Frank came up, as described in the first part of the chapter. On the whole, he was sorry to meet his stepbrother just at this time.

Frank stopped, and his attention was drawn to Mark's flushed face.

Chapter 13

MARK GETS INTO TROUBLE

Mark nodded slightly, and was about to pass without a word, when Frank said, quietly:

"I am sorry to see you coming out of such a place, Mark."

"What is it to you, anyway?" replied Mark rudely.

"Not much, perhaps, but I don't like to see my acquaintances coming out of a resort like this."

"It won't hurt you."

"No, it won't hurt me, but if the principal should hear of it, it would not be pleasant for you. You know students are strictly forbidden to enter there."

"I suppose you mean to tell on me?"

"You are mistaken. I am not a tale-bearer."

"Then there is no need to say any more about it. Come along, James!"

Frank's interference was well meant, but, as we shall see, it did harm rather than good.

As Mark turned away he had half decided not to enter it again. He was two dollars out of pocket, and this did not suit him at all.

In fact, Mark was rather a mean boy, and it was with considerable reluctance that he had handed over to his companion the two dollars with which to pay for the games.

Moreover, he was mortified at losing the two games of billiards when so great odds had been given him.

James Carson was no scholar, but he was sharp enough to perceive the state of Mark's feelings, and he also saw how he was affected by Frank's remonstrance.

He decided to take advantage of this, and strengthen his hold on Mark.

"Well, Mark," he said, "I suppose you'll give up playing billiards now."

"Why should I?"

"Because your stepbrother doesn't approve of it. You won't dare to go into the rooms after he has forbidden you," he continued, with a sneer.

"What do you mean, James? Do you suppose I care that" (snapping his fingers) "for what Frank says, or even thinks, either?"

"I didn't but you might stand in fear of him."

"Do you mean to insult me?" demanded Mark, hotly.

"Insult you! My dear friend, what can you be thinking of? Why, I like you ten times as much as that muff, Frank Courtney."

"Then what did you mean by what you said?" asked Mark, more calmly.

"I will tell you. I got an idea, from what Frank said once, that he was in charge of you—well, not exactly that, but that he looked after you."

This was a wicked falsehood, as Frank had never intimated any such thing. In fact, he had generally kept quite aloof from Mark.

Mark, however, fell into the trap, and never thought of doubting what his companion said.

"If Frank said that, I've a great mind to whip him," declared Mark, angrily.

"Oh, I wouldn't notice him, if I were you!" advised James. "For my part, I didn't believe what he said. I felt sure that a fine, spirited boy like you wouldn't submit to his dictation."

"I should say not—the impudent fellow!"

"When he spoke to you just now," went on James, "one would really have thought he was your uncle, or guardian, and that you were a little boy."

"I'll show him what I think of him and his advice. I hadn't thought of playing again to-morrow, but now I will."

"Bravo! I like your spirit!" said James, admiringly. "It is just the way to treat him. Shall I come round with you about the same hour as to-day?"

"Yes, I wish you would."

When the two boys parted company, James Carson smiled to himself.

"What an idiot Mark is!" he thought. "He thinks he is his own master, but I am going to twist him round my little finger. He's a sweet youth, but he's got money, and I mean to have some of it. Why, he tells me his father allows him eight dollars a week for spending-money. If I manage well, I can get more than half away from him."

The next day James called for Mark as agreed upon, and again the two boys went to the billiard room. The performance of the day before was repeated.

James Carson, while flattering Mark's poor play, managed to beat in every game but one.

"I am very unlucky," grumbled Mark, in a tone of dissatisfaction.

"So you were, Mark," admitted his sympathizing friend. "You made some capital shots, though, and if I hadn't been so lucky, you would have come out the victor in every game."

"But I didn't."

"No, you didn't; but you can't have such poor luck all the time."

"I guess I'd better give up billiards. In two days I have spent five dollars. It doesn't pay."

"No doubt Frank will be gratified when he hears you have given up playing. He will think it is because you are afraid of him."

James had touched the right chord, and poor Mark was once more in his toils.

"It's lucky for me that Frank spoke to him," thought James. "It makes it much easier for me to manage him."

One thing, however, James had not taken into account. There were others besides Frank who were liable to interfere with his management, and who had the authority to make their interference effectual.

On the day succeeding, as James and Mark were in the campus, Herbert Grant approached them.

Now Herbert, as we have said, was the janitor of the academy. He also was employed by the principal to summon students who had incurred censure to his study, where they received a suitable reprimand from Doctor Brush.

It was not a pleasant duty, but some one must do it, and Herbert always discharged it in a gentlemanly manner, which could not, or ought not, to offend the school-fellows who were unlucky enough to receive a summons.

"Boys," said he, "I am sorry to be the bearer of unpleasant news, but Doctor Brush would like to see you in his study."

"Both of us?" asked James.

"Yes."

"Are there any others summoned?"

"No."

Mark and his companion looked at each other with perturbed glances. No one cared to visit the principal on such an errand. Corporal punishment was never resorted to in the Bridgeville Academy, but the doctor's dignified rebuke was dreaded more than blows would have been from some men.

"What do you think it is, James?" asked Mark, uneasily.

"I think it's the billiards," answered James, in a low voice.

"But how could he have found it out? No one saw us go in or come out."

The billiard rooms was at some distance from the academy building, and for that reason the two boys had felt more secure in visiting it.

"I'll tell you how it came out," said James, quickly.

"How?"

"You remember Frank saw us coming out day before yesterday."

"He said he wouldn't tell."

"I know he said so, but it was too good an opportunity for him to gratify his spite against you. You may depend upon it, Mark, that we are indebted for this little favor to your kind stepbrother."

It was not very difficult for Mark to believe anything against Frank, and he instantly adopted his companion's idea.

"The mean sneak!" he said. "I'll come up with him! I'll tell my father not to give him any money for the next month. I'll—I'll get him to apprentice Frank to a shoemaker! Perhaps then he won't put on so many airs."

"Good for you! I admire your pluck!" approved James, slapping Mark on the back. "You are true grit, you are! Just teach the fellow a lesson."

"See if I don't!"

Mark nodded his head resolutely, and went into the presence of Doctor Brush, thirsting for vengeance against his stepbrother, who, he felt persuaded, had informed against him.

If Frank had known his suspicions he would have been very much surprised. As it happened, however, he did not even know that his stepbrother had been summoned to the doctor's study. Had he met Herbert, the latter would have told him; but after receiving his list, it so chanced that he and his friend did not meet.

The fact was, that a young man employed as tutor in mathematics in the academy, while taking an afternoon walk, had seen Mark and James Carson leaving the billiard-room, and, as in duty bound, had reported the same to the principal.

Mr. Triangle, however, had not been observed by either of the two boys, and therefore they were led off on a false scent.

"What do you think the old man will say?" questioned Mark, anxiously, as they ascended the stairs to the principal's study.

"He'll give us a raking down, I suppose," replied James. "He will come down heavy on us."

"I wish I were out of it."

"Oh, it's not worth minding! We haven't committed any great crime, have we? What's the harm in a game of billiards?"

"Not much, perhaps; but breaking school rules is certainly punishable."

The boys knocked at the door, and the full, deep voice of Doctor Brush was heard to say, "Come in!"

Chapter 14

SUSPENDED

Doctor Brush was seated in a large armchair at a table covered with papers. He was an elderly man of dignified presence, not a petty tyrant such as is sometimes found in a similar position, but a man who commanded respect without an effort.

Mark Manning and James Carson entered his presence a little nervously.

"Young gentlemen," said the doctor, gravely, "I am informed that you have violated one of the rules of the academy by frequenting a billiard-room."

"Who told you, sir?" asked Mark.

"That is not to the purpose," answered the principal, gravely.

"But I should like to know who informed on me," persisted Mark.

"Whoever did so acted as your true friend, Manning; but there is no occasion for you to know who it is. Is it true?"

Mark would have been glad to deny the charge, and would not have felt any scruples about doing so, if it would have done any good. But it was clear, even to him, that he would not be believed, and that denial would only make his position worse. So he made a virtue of necessity, and replied:

"I have been in once or twice, sir."

"Exactly how many times have you been there?"

"Three times."

"What did you do there?"

"We played billiards."

"Carson, you accompanied Manning, did you not?" said Doctor Brush, turning to Mark's companion.

"Yes, sir."

"And I suppose you also played billiards?"

"Well, yes, sir, I believe I did."

"You were aware, were you not, that it was against the regulations of the school?"

"I suppose it must have slipped my mind," said James, trying to look as innocent as possible.

Doctor Brush frowned, for he saw clearly that this was but a subterfuge.

"If this were true," he continued, "it would be no excuse. As students, it is your duty to make yourselves acquainted with the rules that govern the institution. In point of fact, I cannot believe that either of you is ignorant of the rule forbidding students to frequent places where such games are played. It is hardly necessary for me to defend the propriety of this rule. Extravagance is a fruitful source of vice and crime, and I cannot allow the youth under my charge to form habits of indulgence which may blast all their prospects, and lead to the most ruinous consequences."

"We didn't play much," said Mark.

"I shall not inquire how much you played. In playing a single game, you violated the rule of the school, and I cannot pass over it."

"What is he going to do with us, I wonder?" thought Mark.

He was not required to wonder long.

"As this is your first offense, so far as I know," proceeded the principal, "I will not be severe. You are both suspended from the institution for the remainder of the term, and are required to leave Bridgeville by the early train to-morrow morning for your respective homes. I shall write to your parents, explaining the cause of your suspension."

But a week remained of the term, and the punishment was mild, but both boys were mortified and left the study crestfallen.

Mark was the first to recover his spirits.

"It is not so bad, James," he said. "Tomorrow will be Saturday, and I should go home, anyway. I don't mind staying at home next week."

"What will your father say?"

"Oh, I'll make it all right with him! I don't mind much what he says. I guess he got into scrapes himself when he was a boy."

"My father isn't so easily managed. Just as likely as not, he'll cut off my allowance for a month; and that'll be no joke!"

"My father won't do that," said Mark. "If he did, I would raise a fuss."

"Would that do any good?"

"I guess it would!"

"Mark, you are a true friend of mine, aren't you?" asked James.

"Yes," assured Mark, but not very warmly.

"Of course, I know you are, and you will do me a favor, won't you?"

"What is it?" asked Mark, cautiously.

"Lend me five dollars till the beginning of next term."

"I haven't got the money, James. You know how much I have spent in the last two or three days. I've hardly got money enough to take me home."

"Can't you borrow it of Frank for me?"

"Ask him yourself. I am not going to ask a favor of the boy who reported me."

"You'll have money when you get home, won't you?"

"I presume so."

"Then just send me a five-dollar bill in a letter. The old man will cut off my allowance during vacation, and it will do me no end of good."

If he had known Mark a little better, he would have spared himself the trouble of asking a loan.

"You must excuse me," said Mark, coldly. "I am saving my money for a particular purpose, and can't spare five dollars."

"I would pay you back at the beginning of the term."

"No, I can't do it," said Mark, looking annoyed. "Stay! There is Frank, just across the campus. I am going over to charge him with betraying us."

Frank, who was quite ignorant of Mark's trouble, was surprised when the latter approached him with a frown and exclaimed, harshly:

"You won't make anything by what you have done, Frank Courtney!"

"Will you be kind enough to tell me what I have done?" asked Frank, calmly.

"You've been to Doctor Brush and told him about our playing billiards."

"You are entirely mistaken, Mark. I did not suppose he knew."

"It must have been you. He told us some one had informed him, and you were the only one who knew. It's a mean trick, isn't it, Carson?"

"Awfully mean!"

"I have already told you that the information did not come from me. It may be the best thing for you that it has been found out, for it was doing you no good to frequent such places."

"I don't want to hear any of your preaching, Frank Courtney. I can manage my own affairs without any advice from you."

"I don't care to intrude any advice," replied Frank. "I have not much reason to feel interested in you."

"You'd better look out how you treat me, though," said Mark, insolently. "I know very well you dislike me, but it won't be safe for you to show it while you are a dependent on my father."

"I don't propose to be a dependent on him long," said Frank, quickly. "The truth of it is, you and your father are dependent upon property which of right belongs to me. The time may come when I shall be able to show this."

"What does he mean?" thought Mark, in alarm. "Will he contest the will?"

It was perhaps an evidence of Mark's shrewdness that he had some doubts about the validity of the will under which his father inherited.

It was possible that his stepmother might have made the will through the influence of her husband; but devoted as she was to Frank, and generally a clear-sighted woman in matters of business, it did not seem very probable.

"There's been some trickery," Mark told himself, "and my father knows what it is. However, that's his affair, not mine, and I am glad that he has got the property. I shall fare better, at any rate, and if there's any fuss made, they can't say anything against me."

It was important that Frank should be prevented from doing anything that might lead to an investigation which might develop facts better left in secret.

Mark did not reply to Frank's last words, but walked away with James Carson.

The latter, however, soon made an excuse for leaving Mark, from whom he had no more to hope, and went back to find Frank.

Our hero regarded him with some surprise, and waited for him to speak.

With an assumption of frankness, Carson said:

"I want to tell you, Frank, that I don't believe with Mark that you informed against us."

"You do no more than justice," responded Frank.

"Of course you know that Mark is prejudiced against you."

"Yes."

"And that makes him ready to suspect you of anything. Doctor Brush has suspended us for the remainder of the term."

"I am sorry to hear it."

"Oh, it won't matter much! It's only a week, you know. But there is one little inconvenience to me. I have spent so much money lately that I have hardly funds enough to carry me home."

Frank didn't like James Carson, but he was of a generous and helpful disposition.

"Can I be of any service to you?" he asked.

"If you could lend me five dollars till the beginning of next term, it would be a great help."

Frank drew a five-dollar bill from his pocketbook, and handed it to James.

"Thank you," said the latter, joyfully. "I'll be sure to return it."

"I didn't think it would be so easy," he chuckled, as he walked away. "With the ten dollars in my purse, part of it saved from my allowance and this money, I am in funds. Mark's a mean fellow. I wish I could have made something out of him."

Chapter 15

MR. MANNING'S NEW PLAN

Mark so represented his school difficulty to his father that he incurred but slight censure.

Indeed, Mr. Manning was so absorbed in plans for getting the greatest enjoyment out of the estate of which he had obtained possession by doubtful means that he didn't care to be disturbed about such a trifle as his son's suspension.

He felt more disposed to blame Frank, whom Mark charged with betraying him.

"What does Frank say about it?" asked Mr. Manning.

"Of course he denies it," replied Mark, "but it can't be any one else."

"He is acting very unwisely," said Mr. Manning, compressing his thin lips.

"So I told him, but he said he didn't mean to be a dependent on you long."

"How is he going to avoid it?"

"I don't know."

"I have had some intimation from Colonel Vincent, who appears to be in his confidence. He wants to leave us."

"To go away?"

"Yes."

"But you won't let him?"

"I have been thinking about that, Mark, and I may give my permission. The fact is, he stands in the way of some plans I have formed. I am thinking of traveling."

"Not without me?"

"No; you shall go with me, but I don't care to take Frank."

"You might leave him at school."

"I might, but how do I know that he might not hatch some mischief while we are gone?"

"He might make some fuss about the property," suggested Mark.

"Has he hinted anything of that kind to you?"

"Yes. Only yesterday he said that the property belonged by right to him."

Mr. Manning looked thoughtful, and after that watched Frank narrowly to see if from his manner he could divine the boy's intentions.

Later that same evening, Mark having retired early in consequence of a headache, Frank found himself alone with his stepfather, and took advantage of the opportunity to speak of the plan he had formed.

"Mr. Manning," he began, "if you are at leisure, I should like to speak with you a few minutes."

"Proceed," said his stepfather, waving his hand.

"But a week remains of the school-term. Did you propose that I should return there at the end of the vacation?"

"Humph! I had not thought much on the subject."

"It has all along been intended that I should go to college when prepared, but I really do not care much about it."

"In that case," said his stepfather, with alacrity, "you would only be throwing away time and money by going."

He was quite ready to agree to Frank's surrender of the college plan for two reasons.

A college course would be expensive. Again, should he turn his attention to the law, he might hereafter give him trouble about the estate.

"I don't think I should throw away my time, for, if I went to college, I should go there to work faithfully; but I have a fancy for a more stirring life."

"It might be a good plan for you to learn a trade," said Mr. Manning, reflectively.

"Learn a trade!" exclaimed Frank, in surprise.

"Yes; it would always enable you to earn a living."

"Do you intend Mark to learn a trade?" asked Frank quickly.

"No; his case is very different from yours."

"Why is it different?"

"It is not necessary for me to explain," answered his stepfather, stiffly.

"If there were any need of it, Mr. Manning, I would not object to learning a trade," said Frank. "I have no false pride on the subject. But my tastes are more for mercantile business."

"I may be able to find you a place somewhere. I have a friend in the dry goods business, who would receive you at my recommendation."

"Thank you!" said Frank, coldly. "But if you will allow me, I would prefer to look around for myself."

"What is it you want then?"

"Your permission to go out into the world, and try to make a living."

"And if you don't, I suppose you expect me to defray your expenses?"

"If I did have such an expectation, I think I should be justified, in view of the large property which my mother left at her death," said Frank, pointedly.

"She left it to me," reminded his stepfather.

"So it appears, at any rate. But I shall not call upon you to pay my board. Give me your permission to go where I please, with a small sum of money to start me, and I shall be satisfied."

"And what will the world say? That I, your stepfather, to whom you have a right to look for maintenance, had driven you out to earn your own living! It would be unjust, of course, but the world is ever unjust."

And Mr. Manning assumed a look of wronged innocence, which would have imposed on any one who knew him but slightly.

"I shall defend you from any such charge," assured Frank. "I shall say that you were only yielding to my request."

"I will think of it, my dear boy," said Mr. Manning, graciously. "I already feel inclined to grant it, because it is your request. I shall be sorry to be separated from you; but I am willing to sacrifice my own feelings, if it will give you pleasure."

This did not impose upon Frank, who had a correct idea of the degree of fondness which Mr. Manning had for his society, but he was too well satisfied with the prospect of obtaining the permission he desired to imply any doubts.

"Again," continued his stepfather, "whatever you may say to the contrary, I know that the world will censure me; but I shall have the approval of my own conscience, and with that I can defy the world."

Mr. Manning certainly did look like a righteous man when he said this, and he beamed upon his stepson with a glance that was actually affectionate.

"Go back to school," he concluded, "and when you return, I shall be able to give you a definite answer."

Indeed, nothing could have suited Mr. Manning's plans better. He would get rid of the care and nearly the whole expense of his obnoxious stepson, while with his son Mark he would be spending the revenues of the estate which belonged to Frank.

During the coming week he arranged his plans for a prolonged absence from the Cedars. He wrote to New York to engage passage on a steamer bound for Liverpool, and quietly waited for the end of Frank's school-term to release him from a care which had grown burdensome.

Frank returned to the Bridgeville Academy without Mark. As may be supposed, however, he did not feel the loss of his society.

He at once communicated to his chosen friend, Herbert Grant, his probable departure from school.

"I am sorry to hear it, Frank," said Herbert, soberly. "Do you think you are acting wisely?"

"I am not acting as I would have done had my mother lived," answered Frank; "but you must remember that my position in life has very much changed. I am a poor boy."

"Hardly that, when there is so much property in the family."

"I know Mr. Manning too well to believe that I shall derive much benefit from it. No, Herbert, I have my own living to make, and I want to make it in my own way."

"It is a sad change for you, Frank."

"No, I can't say that. I don't know how it is, Herbert, but I am rather glad to have all this thrown upon me. I enjoy feeling that I have got to work."

"I have a chance of enjoying the same feelings," said Herbert, with a smile.

"I wish we could start together, Herbert. Couldn't you go with me?"

Herbert shook his head.

"Father has a plan for me," he said. "I am to learn his trade, and shall commence next week. I don't particularly like it, but it is well to have a trade to fall back upon."

"Mr. Manning wanted me to learn a trade."

"There is no occasion for your doing so."

"I don't know about that. If I had a particular fancy for any, I wouldn't mind choosing it, but I am better suited for something else."

"What is your plan? What will you do first?"

"My father has a cousin in the city of Newark, New Jersey, only a few miles from New York. Four years ago, he and his family made us a visit, and he was urgent then that we should return the visit. I will, first of all, go to him, and ask his advice. He is a business man, and he may be able to put me in the way of obtaining a position."

"I think you will succeed, Frank, but it will be harder than you think for. You don't know what poverty is yet. I have never known anything else."

"If I do succeed, Herbert, I may be able to find something for you."

"I wish you might," Herbert replied; but he was not as sanguine as Frank.

He understood, better than his friend, that for a boy to set out alone into the great world to earn a living is a serious undertaking.

Chapter 16

GOOD-BYE

Frank had fixed upon the Tuesday morning succeeding the close of the academic term for his departure from home. Monday was devoted to a few necessary preparations and a few calls on old friends, among them Colonel Vincent, the owner of Ajax.

"My dear Frank," said the colonel, kindly, "I feel a strong interest in your welfare, more especially because of the wrong which I do not scruple to say has been done you. What does Mr. Manning say to your plan?"

"He makes no objection," replied Frank.

"Suppose he had done so?"

"I would not have run away. He is my stepfather and guardian, and I would have endured staying at home as well as I could."

"There you are right, Frank. Though I have a poor opinion of Mr. Manning, he is not likely to treat you in a manner to justify your going away without his permission. From what I have heard within the last week, I suspect that he feels relieved to have you go."

"What have you heard, sir?"

"That Mr. Manning will shortly sail for Europe, taking Mark with him."

Frank was surprised, having no suspicion of this.

"Now are you not sorry that you have decided to go out into the world to earn a living when you might have seen something of Europe?"

"Mr. Manning would never have taken me along," said Frank; "nor should I have enjoyed traveling with him and Mark."

"Of the two, who would interfere the more with your enjoyment?"

"Mark."

"Then you prefer the father to the son?"

"The father has much more agreeable manners. I don't think Mark could be agreeable if he tried."

Colonel Vincent smiled.

"Perhaps you are right, Frank," he said. "Now, as your father's old friend, I shall exact a promise from you."

"What is it, sir?"

"You are going out into the world to earn your own living. Boys of your age are apt to think it an easy thing. I have seen more of life, and I am sure you will find it more difficult than you suppose. You may find yourself in difficulty, possibly in want. In that case, promise to let me know, and I will come to your assistance."

"I will, sir," answered Frank.

Though he gave this promise, he was more than half inclined to question the truth of Colonel Vincent's remarks as to the difficulty of earning a living. He was full of confidence, as most boys are, the result of his inexperience.

To be sure, his scheme was not as Quixotic as that of some boys, who leave good homes, armed with revolvers, to hunt for Indians. If a real Indian, in his war paint, should suddenly make his appearance, he would put to flight a hundred of such boy hunters.

I wish it understood, therefore, that though Frank had the permission of his guardian to leave home, and though he was better fitted than the great majority of boys to make his way in the world, I agree with Colonel Vincent in considering his plan a doubtful one, requiring for success not only pluck and persistency, but good health and good luck. Not many boys can expect an uninterrupted course of prosperity when thrown upon their own exertions.

The time came for Frank to say good-bye to Mr. Manning and Mark, and the house which had been his home from infancy.

His stepfather handed him a small pocketbook.

"Frank," he said, "in this pocketbook you will find twenty-five dollars. It is not much, but—"

"I am satisfied, sir," said Frank. "It won't be long before I am earning something."

"I hope your anticipations may be realized, but it is possible that you may require help."

"I think not, sir."

"I will authorize my banker to pay you the same sum—twenty-five dollars—every three months. Of course, it is not enough to support you; but, as you say it is your intention to procure a place—"

"Yes, sir."

"It will probably be enough to make up any deficiency that may exist in your income. I am aware that you do not regard me as—as I would like to have you; but I am resigned to be misunderstood, and I merely call your attention to the fact that I have given you my free permission to carry out your own plans and have given you more assistance than you asked for."

"That's true, sir."

"Should any one in your hearing condemn me for what I have done, I depend upon you to defend me."

"I will state the facts, sir. I will take the entire responsibility for anything that may result from the step I have taken."

Mr. Manning looked well pleased. Things were taking the course he desired, and for the paltry sum of one hundred dollars a year, he was getting rid of an obnoxious stepson, while appearing to confer a favor upon him.

He was even enlisting the boy as his advocate and defender against any attacks or criticism from the world.

"I will give you the name of my banker in New York," Mr. Manning proceeded. "At the end of each quarter you may apply to him for the sum I have mentioned. I may—it is not quite decided—I may make a journey with Mark. I find that my health has been affected by the great trial I have met with in the loss of my lamented wife, and the anxiety I have naturally suffered on her account."

As Mr. Manning was looking unusually well, his attempt to appear weak and suffering was a failure, and Frank kept silence, being unable to express a sympathy he did not feel.

"If," said Mr. Manning, doubtfully, "you would like to give up your plan and travel with us, I think it can be arranged. You would be company for Mark."

Frank could not help glancing at Mark, to see how far his appearance bore out his father's statement.

He was not surprised to observe that his stepbrother's brow was overcast and that he looked angrily at his father, alarmed lest the offer should be accepted.

"Thank you, Mr. Manning," said Frank; "but at present I should prefer to go out in the world and see what I can do for myself. Some day I hope to travel; but I am young and can wait."

Mark looked very much relieved at this decision. Judging Frank by himself, he feared that it would be accepted, and he could not help deciding in his own mind that Frank was foolish to prefer work to a pleasant journey.

He was satisfied that his father never would have taken Frank, even had the latter decided to accept his proposal, but it would have occasioned delay, and Mark was impatient to get started on his journey.

The Cedars he regarded as a stupid place, and he was eager to visit the cities of Europe, where he could find plenty of amusement.

"Perhaps you are right, Frank," said his stepfather, disguising the satisfaction he felt. "If, however, you should find that you have made a mistake, you will do me the justice to remember that I gave you your choice."

Knowing, as he did, that the offer was not genuine, Frank remained silent. He could not make up his mind to express gratitude, and therefore said nothing.

Here the carriage drove up to the door to convey Frank to the railway station. Mindful of appearances, Mr. Manning accompanied him to the cars, and in presence of several neighbors bade him an effusively affectionate farewell.

So Frank was fairly started on his venture to earn a living for himself.

Chapter 17

ERASTUS TARBOX, OF NEWARK

Erastus Tarbox, Frank Courtney's cousin, kept a dry goods store in the city of Newark, in New Jersey. He was well to do, not so much because of his enterprise and skill as a merchant as because of his extreme economy. Some people call it parsimony. He only employed two clerks to assist him in his store, and they, as well as the boy who carried out parcels and ran the errands, were paid scarcely more than two-thirds the rates paid in neighboring stores.

To some it may seem strange that Mr. Tarbox was able to obtain assistants at such low rates, but those who know how many dry goods clerks there always are seeking employment will not need to wonder.

Neither will it be a matter of surprise that when Mr. Tarbox chanced to secure a superior clerk he was not able to keep him long, for, at the first hint of higher wages, the employer exhibited such dissatisfaction that the salesman was very apt to throw up his situation in disgust.

Mr. Tarbox prided himself upon his relationship to the Courtneys. They were rich, and riches, in his eyes, were a great merit. He often sighed to think that there was no chance for him to benefit by a share of the large property owned by his cousins. Without hope of personal advantage, however, he had always been obsequious to them, and often took occasion to mention them, by way of enhancing his own social credit somewhat.

Mr. Tarbox had heard of Mrs. Courtney's death, but had not heard the particulars of the will. He took it for granted that Frank was sole heir, and it did cross his mind more than once how very agreeable it would be if he could be selected as guardian of the young heir. Of course, he knew that there was no probability of it, since the stepfather would undoubtedly be appointed to that position.

Mr. Tarbox had just sold a calico dress pattern to a woman, when his attention was drawn to the entrance of Frank Courtney, who came into his store, valise in hand.

Mr. Tarbox was rather short-sighted, and did not immediately recognize the son of his rich cousin.

"What can I do for you, young man?" he asked, in his business tone.

"This is Mr. Tarbox, I believe?" said Frank, who did not know his relatives very well.

"Yes, that is my name."

"I am Frank Courtney."

"Bless my soul!" ejaculated Mr. Tarbox, surprised and delighted. "When did you arrive in Newark?"

"I have only just arrived."

"I do hope you are going to make us a visit," said Mr. Tarbox, cordially.

"Thank you!" replied Frank, cheered by this warm reception. "If you are sure it won't inconvenience you."

"Inconvenience me! We shall be delighted to have you with us."

"I wish," thought he, "that Frank would be contented to board with me. He can afford to pay a handsome price, and there would be a good deal of profit to be made. I must try to make it pleasant for him."

"You are very kind to think of us, my dear young relative," continued Mr. Tarbox, rubbing his hands in high good humor. "Accept my warmest sympathy in your great affliction. I was deeply grieved to hear of your dear mother's death."

Mr. Tarbox was a remarkably plain man. He had a mottled face, watery eyes, and a long, thin, tapering nose, and a low forehead, partially covered with iron-gray hair. Still he was a relation, and Frank's heart warmed to him when he spoke so feelingly of the mother whom he so much missed.

"You must come up and see Mrs. Tarbox. She will be glad to welcome you."

Mr. Tarbox lived over his store. There was a door from the street adjoining the shop front. Mr. Tarbox opened it with a pass-key, and conducted Frank up-stairs, ushering him into a gloomy parlor, with stiff, straight backed chairs, ranged at regular intervals along the sides of the room, and a marble-topped centre-table, with two or three books lying upon it. There was a framed engraving, representing Washington crossing the Delaware, over the mantel, and two plaster figures and similar ornaments on the mantelpiece. The whole aspect of the room chilled Frank.

"Wait here, and I will call my wife," said Mr. Tarbox.

Frank sat down on a hard sofa and awaited the entrance of Mrs. Tarbox.

She came in, a tall, thin woman, about as handsome for a woman as her husband was for a man. Indeed, they were very well matched. She was quite as mean as he, and between them they managed to make annually a decided addition to their wordly possessions.

Mr. Tarbox privately hinted his hopes respecting Frank to his wife, and she instantly agreed that it would be a most eligible arrangement.

"We must make him contented, my dear," said her husband. "Give him the best bedroom, and I think it might be well to have something a little extra for supper."

"I did intend to put on the rest of that cold mutton," said Mrs. Tarbox, doubtfully.

"It won't do, Martha. There is only a little of it, you know, and the boy has been traveling, and, of course, is hungry. What do you say now to some nice beefsteak?"

"Beefsteak is high now," reminded Mrs. Tarbox. "Still, if we buy round steak—that is cheaper than sirloin or tenderloin."

"And quite as good," said her economical partner. "We can tell Frank, however, that no sirloin was to be had so late in the day at the markets."

Mrs. Tarbox nodded her head, approving the suggestion.

This little matter being adjusted, the husband and wife entered the parlor where our hero was waiting patiently.

"This is our young cousin, Martha," said Mr. Tarbox, smiling pleasantly.

"Welcome to Newark," said Mrs. Tarbox, extending her hand. "And how did you leave your stepfather?"

"He is well," replied Frank, coldly.

The two exchanged glances. It was clear that Frank did not like his stepfather, and this was satisfactory to them. There was the more chance of his leaving him and boarding with them.

"The children will be so glad to see you," said Mr. Tarbox; "won't they, Martha?"

"Delighted!" assured the lady.

"Pliny must be about your age. How old are you, by-the-way?"

"Sixteen."

"Just Pliny's age. Do you remember him?"

Frank remembered a tall, thin stripling who had accompanied his parents to the Cedars, and who appeared to have an inexhaustible appetite.

"Yes, I remember him. Does he go to school?"

"No; Pliny is in a store," answered Mr. Tarbox.

"Your store?"

"Oh, no! I thought it would be better for him to enter the employ of a stranger. He is in a bookstore."

There was one great advantage in Pliny's entering the employ of a stranger. He was paid four dollars a week, whereas Mr. Tarbox paid his boy but two. Here, then, was a clear gain of two dollars a week.

"But you must be tired," said Mr. Tarbox. "You will see the children at supper. Martha, I think Frank would like to go to his room."

The best bedroom was over the parlor. It was rather more cheerful, because lighter.

"Here," said Mr. Tarbox, "you may make yourself at home. Martha, isn't one of the drawers in that bureau empty? I thought so. Take your clothes out of the valise and put them away. Now, is there anything you would like?"

"Only a little water to wash in," replied Frank. "You are both very kind."

"We hope to make you comfortable. You are our relative, you know."

The water was brought up by Mrs. Tarbox herself, and Frank was left alone, on the whole well pleased with his reception.

Chapter 18

AN UNPLEASANT DISCOVERY

It never occurred to Frank that his cordial reception was wholly due to his supposed wealth. Had he known the Tarbox family better, he would have had no uncertainty on this point. As it was, the discovery was soon made.

It was not long before the supper-bell rang, and Frank descended the stairs, guided by Mr. Tarbox himself. There our hero saw the younger branches of the family—Pliny, a thin, lanky youth, with pale-brown hair plastered to the sides of his head with bear's grease, and Julia, who was a smaller edition of her mother. There were two children still younger, who do not need describing.

"All my olive branches are before you, my dear young cousin," said Mr. Tarbox, waving his hand. "A peaceful, happy family. Children, this is our esteemed relative, Frank Courtney. You remember visiting his delightful home, the Cedars?"

"Yes, pa," said Julia.

Pliny said nothing, but stared at Frank, inwardly considering whether it would be possible to borrow some money of him.

Frank looked around him, and tried to believe that he should like his young cousins; but they did not look at all attractive. But he wished to be polite, and responded:

"I am glad to meet you all. I hope we shall become better acquainted."

"No doubt you will," said Mr. Tarbox. "They are rather bashful, but they long to know you."

"How are you?" said Pliny, in a sudden burst of sociability.

"Pretty well, thank you!" replied Frank, finding it rather difficult to preserve his gravity.

"I am in a store," said Pliny.

"In your father's store?"

"No. He wouldn't pay me as much as I get where I am."

Mr. Tarbox looked embarrassed.

"A smaller boy answered my purpose," he said, in an explanatory manner. "Pliny is suited for higher duties. But our supper is ready. It is frugal compared with yours at the Cedars, my dear Frank, but you are heartily welcome to it."

"It looks very nice, Mr. Tarbox," said Frank, "and I have not been accustomed to luxurious living."

This answer pleased Mr. and Mrs. Tarbox. Even if Frank should become a boarder on liberal terms, they didn't wish to spend too much on their table.

"We couldn't get sirloin steak," remarked Mr. Tarbox; "but I hope you will find this good."

"No doubt I shall," rejoined Frank, politely.

"You never do buy sirloin steak, ma," said one of the younger darlings.

Mrs. Tarbox frowned.

"Hush, Amelia!" she reproved. "Little girls should be seen and not heard."

"Do you have to go back to the store, Pliny?" asked Frank.

"Yes; I have to stay till eight o'clock."

"Do you like it?"

"Yes, pretty well; but I like the pay better," chuckled Pliny, who was under the impression that he had said something witty.

"Candid boy!" exclaimed his father, admiringly.

"They pay me four dollars a week," continued Pliny; "but I guess they'll raise me to five in a few months."

"Four dollars a week!" thought Frank. "That isn't much. I am afraid I couldn't live on it."

"Have you been in the place long?" he pursued.

"Three months."

"Is that the price usually paid to boys?"

"Pa only pays his boy two dollars a week," put in Amelia.

Here it was Mr. Tarbox's turn to frown.

"The duties of my boy are very simple," he felt obliged to explain.

Frank, knowing Mr. Tarbox to be in business before coming to Newark, had a vague idea of finding a place in his store, but this revelation convinced him that it would be necessary for him to look elsewhere. Even if there had been a vacancy, it was quite out of the question to accept two dollars a week.

"Won't you have another piece of steak?" asked Mrs. Tarbox.

Frank saw that there was but a small piece left, and, though his appetite was not wholly satisfied, he answered:

"No, thank you."

"I will!" said Pliny, quickly.

Mrs. Tarbox frowned at her son, but did not venture to refuse in the presence of her guest. She cut off a small portion of the steak and, with a severe look, put it on the extended plate of Pliny.

"You've got a good appetite, Pliny," said Julia.

"So would you have, if you had to work like me!" grumbled Pliny.

After the steak came an apple pie, which was cut into seven pieces. Mrs. Tarbox managed to make Frank's piece a little larger than the rest.

Her husband observed it with approval. He was very desirous that Frank should be satisfied with his fare.

When Pliny rose from the table, saying that he must be getting back to the store, Frank rose also.

"I will go with you," he said, "if you have no objection. I would like to take a walk."

"Come along," said Pliny. "I should like to have company."

"You will be a great deal of company for Pliny," observed Mr. Tarbox, rubbing his hands with satisfaction. "Just of an age and of congenial tastes."

Frank hardly expected to find Pliny very congenial, but he wished to obtain some information, which he thought the latter could give him, and he also wanted to see something of Newark.

"I say, your name is Frank, isn't it?" commenced Pliny.

"Yes."

"My father's awful glad to see you."

"I am glad of it. He has received me very kindly," said Frank.

"Got up an extra supper for you. We don't often get steak for supper."

This was rather an embarrassing revelation, and surprised Frank somewhat. The supper had not seemed to him at all extra. It would do, but was far from luxurious.

"I hope you'll stay with us a good while," continued Pliny.

"Thank you."

"You see we shall live better while you are with us, and the rest of us will be gainers."

"I don't want to put your father to any unusual expense."

"Oh, he can afford it! But he's stingy, father is. He doesn't spend any more than he can help."

"It is best to be economical, I suppose."

"When you don't carry it too far. I say, Frank," added Pliny, lowering his voice, "you can't lend me five dollars, can you?"

Frank regarded Pliny with astonishment. The proposal was very abrupt, especially when the shortness of their acquaintance was considered.

"Are you particularly in need of money?" asked Frank.

"Well, you see," said Pliny, "I want it for a particular purpose."

"Why not ask your father for it?"

"Oh, he'd never let me have it!"

Now, in Frank's present circumstances, five dollars represented a good deal of money. He was the more impressed with the necessity of economy since he had found out how small were the wages paid in stores to boys of his age.

He did not feel at all inclined to grant Pliny's request, especially as he had a strong suspicion that it would be a long time before the sum would be returned.

"Why do you apply to me, Pliny?" he questioned, seriously.

"Because you have plenty of money. Five dollars would be nothing to you."

"What makes you think I have plenty of money?"

"Didn't your mother die and leave you a big property? Father says you must be worth more than a hundred thousand dollars."

"Your father probably has not heard of the will," said Frank, quietly.

"What was there in the will?" asked Pliny.

"The whole property was left to Mr. Manning."

"Who is he?"

"My stepfather."

"And nothing to you?"

"Nothing to me."

"But he's got to take care of you, hasn't he?"

"It was expected, but I am going to earn my own living, if I can."

Pliny stopped short in blank amazement and whistled.

"Then you haven't got a lot of money?" he said.

"No."

"Won't your stepfather give you a part of the property?"

"I haven't asked him, but I don't think he will."

"And why did you come to Newark?"

"I thought your father might give me some help about getting a place."

"If this isn't the richest joke!" said Pliny, laughing uproariously.

"Where is the joke? I don't see it," replied Frank, inclined to be angry.

"The way you have taken in my father. He thinks you are rich, and has treated you accordingly—got up an extra supper and all that. Oh, it's too good!"

"I certainly didn't intend to take him in, as you call it," protested Frank. "The sooner you tell him the better."

"I'll tell him," assured Pliny. "I shall enjoy seeing how provoked he'll be."

"I think I will leave you," said Frank, shortly. "I will take a walk by myself."

"Well, don't lose your way. Oh, I wish the store was shut! I want to tell my father."

And Pliny laughed again, while Frank walked off in disgust.

Chapter 19

THE WAY OF THE WORLD

Frank felt like an impostor when he discovered that his cordial reception was wholly owing to the belief that he was his mother's heir.

The situation was unpleasant, and he was impatient to have Mr. Tarbox undeceived. He was sure that Pliny would lose no time in revealing his true position, and decided not to return to the house of Mr. Tarbox till nine o'clock, when the story would have been told.

He wandered about aimlessly till he heard the city clocks strike nine, and then rang the bell at his relation's house.

The family, with the exception of the two younger children, were assembled in the common sitting-room.

As Frank entered, instead of the cordial welcome he had previously received, he noticed a look of coldness and constraint on the faces of Mr. and Mrs. Tarbox, while Pliny looked as if some stupendous joke was being perpetrated.

"Good-evening!" greeted Frank, politely. "I have been taking a walk."

"My son Pliny tells me," said Mr. Tarbox, "that you have not inherited your mother's property."

Frank bowed.

"And that it has gone to your stepfather."

"It seems so."

"I am amazed."

"So was I, sir."

"Your mother has practically disinherited you?"

"It was not my mother," said Frank, hastily. "I can't explain it, but I'm sure she would not will away everything from me."

"Do you suspect your stepfather of anything irregular?" asked Mr. Tarbox, briskly.

"I would rather not answer your question, sir. I don't care to make any charges which I cannot prove."

"And so Mr. Manning has sent you out into the world to earn your own living, has he?"

"No, sir. He has consented that I may do so. It was my own plan."

Much as Frank was prejudiced against his stepfather, his natural sense of justice would not allow him to accuse him unjustly.

"Did he suggest that you should come to me?" went on Mr. Tarbox, in a tone which Frank did not like.

"No, sir."

"So that was your idea, too," continued Mr. Tarbox, with a palpable sneer.

"Yes, sir," replied Frank. "You are not a very near relative, but the nearest I know of, and I supposed you would be willing to give me some advice about the best means of earning my living. I remembered," he could not help adding, "that my mother received you all as guests for a considerable time, and I thought I might take the liberty."

"Oh, certainly!" rejoined Mr. Tarbox, rather abashed, "I am, of course, ready to give you advice, and my first advice is to seek a lawyer and let him institute a suit against your stepfather, on speculation. That is, he gets nothing if he fails, but obtains a commission if he succeeds. I could myself recommend a reliable man."

"Thank you, sir; but I have no present thought of contesting the will."

"I think you make a mistake. Do I understand that you expect to earn your own living?"

"I shall try to do so."

"You will find it very difficult. You may expect me to take you into my own store, but there is no vacancy, and—"

Frank hastily assured Mr. Tarbox that he had no such expectations. He had no wish to deprive the errand boy of the two dollars a week, which he probably richly earned.

"Situations in Newark are not easy to obtain," proceeded Mr. Tarbox. "I am willing that you should stay with us a day or two, but I don't think you will find it worth your while to remain here."

Mr. Tarbox feared that his young relative might expect to find a home free of charge in his house, and such an arrangement did not suit his economical ideas. There was no profit in it, but, on the contrary, a positive loss. Frank read clearly the thoughts of his host, with the help of what Pliny had told him, and, expressing his thanks very briefly, announced his intention of going to New York the next morning.

"It may be the best thing you can do!" said Mr. Tarbox, relieved. "New York opens a much wider field to a boy of enterprise than Newark, and probably you will pick up something to do."

"It won't be my fault, if I don't," said Frank.

"You have my best wishes," said Mr. Tarbox. "The demands of my family forbid my offering you any pecuniary assistance, but—"

"I don't stand in need of it, sir. I have money enough to keep me till I get started in something."

"Really, I am very glad to hear it!"

And there is no doubt that Mr. Tarbox was sincere.

"I wonder how much money he has got?" thought Pliny. "Perhaps he'd lend me two dollars. I'll ask him, if I have a chance."

Pliny proposed to borrow, not because he needed the money, but because he liked to levy contributions upon any available party, with a very faint idea of repaying the same. The money would go to swell his deposit at the savings bank. It was very commendable, of course, to save his money, but not at the expense of others, as Pliny too frequently did.

"I have moved you out of the spare room," said Mrs. Tarbox, when Frank asked permission to retire, "and put you in the same room with Pliny. I suppose you won't mind?"

"Just as you please, Mrs. Tarbox," replied Frank, though he would have prefered to have passed the night alone.

"Could you make it convenient to lend me two dollars?" asked Pliny, as they went up to bed together.

"Not just now," answered Frank. "When I get something to do I shall not need to be so careful of my money."

"One dollar would answer," persisted Pliny.

Without a word, Frank drew a dollar bill from his pocketbook and handed it to Pliny.

"Now," he thought, "I shall not feel under any obligations to the family."

"You're a good fellow, even if you are poor," said Pliny, in high good humor.

Frank was tired, and it was not long before all his anxieties for the future were lost sight of in a sound and refreshing slumber.

Chapter 20

FRANK ARRIVES IN NEW YORK

The breakfast the next morning was very meagre. It was no longer an object to gratify Frank's palate, now that he turned out to be a poor relation, and the family returned to their usual plain diet.

"So you are resolved to go to New York this morning," said Mr. Tarbox. "Of course it would gratify us to have you remain longer, but I appreciate your anxiety to get to work."

Frank was by no means deceived by this statement. He knew very well that Mr. Tarbox would be relieved by his departure, but of this knowledge he made no sign. He merely said that he thought it best to go.

He took leave of his hosts, and purchasing a ticket at the railway station, found himself within an hour in New York. He had been there before, but it was long ago, with his mother, and he had but a vague general idea of the city.

"Let me carry your valise," said a small boy, as he left the ferry-house.

"Do you think you are any better able to carry it than I am?" asked Frank, with a smile.

"I thought you might be tired," replied the street-boy.

"You may take it to Broadway for me," said Frank, to whom it occurred that he might obtain some needed information from his new acquaintance. "Is this the way you make your living?" he inquired.

"Sometimes I sell papers," said the boy.

"Do you get many bundles to carry?"

"Sometimes I do."

"Does it pay well?"

"Depends on the party. I carried a bird-cage for a lady about a mile once, and she didn't want to pay me more'n five cents."

"That wasn't very liberal," Frank said.

"If I had many such customers as her, I'd soon starve to death," declared the boy, in a tone of disgust.

"I've come to New York myself to earn a living," said Frank.

"Have you?" responded the boy, eyeing him in some surprise. "You look as if you had plenty of money."

"I have some, but I must try to earn my living. Do you know any cheap boarding house?"

"There's a place in Mott Street where some of us boys live, but I guess it wouldn't be good enough for you."

"Where is Mott Street?"

"It ain't a very nice neighborhood. The woman lets her rooms for a dollar a week, and the boys eat at the restaurants. How much do you expect to pay for board?"

"I should like to get board for five dollars a week."

"You can get a tiptop place for that up on Bleecker Street or Clinton Place."

"How far off are these streets?"

"About two miles."

"Then come with me and show me where they are. I'll pay you twenty cents an hour for your time."

"All right," assented the boy, cheerfully. "Shall we walk?"

"No; we will get into the street-cars."

"Then we'll take the University Place cars. There's one now."

And the boy signaled to the conductor to stop. The two boys got on board the car, and twenty minutes brought them to University Place.

As they left the car, Frank observed little slips of paper pasted on the outside of several houses with "Furnished Rooms," or "Furnished Rooms with Board," written upon them.

"I suppose I may as well inquire at some of these places," he said.

"I guess you'll get suited at some one of them," said his young guide. "Do you want me any more?"

"No, I believe not."

Frank paid the boy twenty cents and his return car-fare, with which the latter seemed to be well satisfied.

He then ascended the steps of a house which purported to furnish room and board, and rang the bell.

A slip-shod servant answered it.

"Have you got any small rooms?" asked Frank.

"Yes," replied the girl. "Missus is out, but I'll show you a hall bedroom, if you like."

"I should like to see it."

Frank followed the girl up-stairs.

He was not favorably impressed by the appearance of the interior. He did not so much mind its being shabby, but he was repelled by the evident lack of neatness.

The girl threw open the door of a small hall bedroom at the head of the stairs, but it looked so comfortless that he felt sure he should not like it. He thought it best, however, to inquire the price.

"Five dollars a week with board," answered the girl.

"I don't think it will suit me," replied Frank.

"There's a larger room for seven dollars," said the servant.

"No. I think I will look elsewhere."

The next house was not much better, but the third was much neater and more attractive, and Frank agreed to take a room at five dollars a week.

It was a small hall bedroom, but it looked clean, and the woman who showed him about the house seemed very neat in her dress.

"When will you come?" asked the woman.

"Now," replied Frank, promptly.

"Would you mind paying the first week in advance?"

"Not at all. Here is the money."

And Frank drew a five-dollar bill from his portemonnaie.

"Thank you!" said the boarding-house keeper. "I have lost so much by boarders going away owing me money that I am obliged to ask gentlemen to pay in advance till I am well acquainted with them."

"That is quite right," said Frank. "What is your dinner hour?"

"Six o'clock. We have lunch at half-past twelve for the ladies, but if any gentlemen happens to be at home at that time, he can go in."

Frank looked at his watch. It was only eleven o'clock, and as so much of the day remained, he decided, as soon as he had unpacked his valise, to go down town and look for a place without delay.

"I shall not be here at lunch to-day," he said. "You may expect me at dinner."

There was a small bureau in the room—a piece of furniture not often found in hall bedrooms.

Frank deposited the contents of the valise in the bureau drawers, and then went downstairs and out into the street.

Chapter 21

FRANK SEEKS EMPLOYMENT

It was a bright, pleasant day, and Broadway looked very lively. In spite of his being alone in a strange city, with uncertain prospects, Frank felt in good spirits.

Boys of his age usually like excitement and bustle, and Frank was quick to notice the shifting scenes of the great panorama.

"Here are thousands of people," he reflected, "all of whom make a living in some way. I don't see why I can't succeed as well as they."

Some of the objects he saw amused him.

In front of him walked an elderly man with a large placard strapped to his back, on which was the advertisement of a "Great Clothing Emporium."

"I don't think I should fancy that kind of employment," thought our hero.

As he was looking in at a shop-window, a boy about his own age hailed him.

"I say, Johnny, what's the price of turnips?"

"Do you want to buy any?" asked Frank, quietly.

"Well, I might. Have you got any with you?"

"I am sorry I can't supply you," replied Frank, coolly. "Up our way, we feed our cattle on turnips."

"You ain't so green, after all," said the boy, laughing good-naturedly.

"Thank you for the compliment!"

"I suppose I look country-like," thought Frank, "but it won't last long. I shall get used to city ways."

Close by he saw in a window the sign:

"CASH-BOYS WANTED."

Frank was not altogether certain about the duties of cash-boys nor their rate of compensation, but he made up his mind not to lose sight of any chances, and accordingly stepped into the store.

It proved to be a large dry goods store.

Near the entrance he met a tall man, with black whiskers.

"Do you want any cash-boys?" inquired Frank.

"Are you inquiring for yourself?"

"Yes, sir."

"You are too large. Besides, you would not be satisfied with the wages."

"How much do you pay, sir?"

"Two dollars a week."

"No; I don't think I should like to work for that," said Frank. "Are those cash-boys?" he asked, pointing out some boys of apparently ten to twelve years old, who were flitting about from desk to counter.

"Yes."

"I see they are much younger than I. Excuse the trouble I have given you!"

"None whatever," said the man, politely.

Frank left the store, and continued his walk down Broadway.

He began to feel a little serious. It was evident that the boys did not receive as large compensation for their services as he had supposed.

It was not likely to prove an easy task to earn his own living. His board and lodging would cost him five dollars weekly; more, in fact, because he had to buy his lunch outside. Then his washing would cost him something, and there were other necessary expenses, besides clothing.

This last item might be met by the quarterly sum with which his stepfather proposed to provide him.

The problem promised to be a perplexing one, but Frank was by no means discouraged. In fact, if he had been, he would hardly have deserved to be the hero of my story.

Though Clinton Place is not very far up town, it is a considerable walk from this point to the Astor House.

There was so much to see, however, that Frank did not become tired, nor was he sensible of the distance. He walked a little beyond the Astor House, and crossing Broadway turned down Fulton Street.

On the left side of the street his attention was drawn to a restaurant, and he was led by the prompting of appetite to enter.

The prices he found to be reasonable, and the tables were already pretty well filled with clerks and business men, who were partaking of their midday lunch.

Frank found that a plate of meat, with potato and a small supply of bread and butter, could be obtained for fifteen cents.

He afterwards found restaurants where the same could be gotten for ten cents, but generally there was a deficiency in quality or quantity, and there was less neatness in serving the articles.

Seated at the same table with Frank were two young men, neither probably much over twenty. One appeared to be filling a regular clerkship.

"What are you doing now, Jack?" he asked of the other.

"I am in the tea business."

"How is that?"

"You know the Great Pekin Tea Company, of course?"

"Yes."

"Well, until I can get a place, I am selling for them."

"How do you make out?"

"I can't tell you, for I have only just commenced," said his friend.

"How do they pay—salary or commission?"

"They are to pay me a commission—twenty per cent. on what I sell."

"That is a good commission."

"Yes; it is good enough, if I can make a fair amount of sales. There is a good deal of uncertainty about it, of course. I would much rather have a place like yours."

Frank listened with interest. He wondered whether the Great Pekin Tea Company would employ him. If so, he would have a field for his energy, and every inducement to work hard, since his pay would depend on the amount of his sales. Besides, as an agent, he would occupy a comparatively independent position, and Frank was ambitious enough to enjoy this.

When the two men at his table left the restaurant, Frank followed them. At the door the two parted, the clerk going toward Broadway, while the agent walked in the direction of Nassau Street.

"I beg your pardon," said Frank, overtaking him; "but may I ask you a question?"

"Half a dozen, if you like," was the kindly response.

"I overheard what you said about the Great Pekin Tea Company. Do you think I could get a chance to sell for them?"

"Oh, yes; there'll be no trouble about that!"

"I am looking out for something to do," continued Frank, "and I think I should like to try that."

"You'll find it up-hill work," said the agent; "hard work and poor pay. I shall leave it as soon as I can get a regular position. Can't you get a place?"

"Perhaps I can. I haven't tried very hard yet," answered Frank, "but I find boys are paid so little that I can't make enough to live on. If I were a man it would be different."

"I don't believe you can make more than a boy's wages at selling tea," said Frank's new acquaintance; "but you might try it."

"Would you mind giving me a note to the company?" asked Frank.

"I will write a line on one of my business cards," replied the agent. "That will be all you will need."

He drew out a card, and wrote a line commending Frank to the attention of the company.

Frank thanked him, and sought the direction given him.

Entering a large shop, not far from the Astor House, he looked about him inquiringly. Around him were chests of tea, inscribed with Chinese characters. A portly man addressed him.

"Well, my boy, what can I do for you?" he asked.

"Mr. Mason, one of your agents, has given me this card," said Frank. "He thinks you might be willing to employ me."

"We are ready to employ any competent person," said the gentleman; "but you seem very young."

"I am sixteen, sir."

"That is young. Have you had any experience as an agent?"

"No, sir."

"What kind of business have you been in?" continued the tea merchant.

"In none, sir."

"Do you live in New York?"

"I do now, but I only arrived this morning."

The merchant eyed Frank doubtfully.

"I suppose, then, that you don't know much about the city or the neighborhood?"

"No, sir," answered Frank, beginning to think that he had overestimated his qualifications for business.

"I am afraid, then, that you will find some difficulty."

"Let me try, sir. If I fail, or think I am likely to fail, I will give it up."

"Very well. I have no objection to your trying. Come with me."

Frank followed him to the rear of the store, where the merchant introduced him to one of his subordinates.

"Henry," said he, "this young man wants to act as our agent. Fit him out and give him such directions as may be necessary."

Frank was told that it would be well to take samples of different kinds of teas with their respective prices attached, and seek orders for them at private houses and groceries, noting down in a little book orders obtained. Small quantities he could himself deliver, and large quantities, should he be fortunate enough to obtain any, could be sent out from the store by their general delivery.

"What commission am I to get, sir?" inquired Frank.

"Twenty per cent. on parcels sold to private houses and ten per cent. when you sell to retail dealers. To the first you can charge a full price, but it is necessary to sell at lower rates to dealers."

"I understand, sir," said Frank.

"When do you want to begin?"

"To-morrow morning, sir. Where do you advise me to go?"

"New York has been pretty well canvassed, except perhaps the upper part, Harlem. It might be well to make a start in Brooklyn."

"Very well, sir. I will call to-morrow and get samples."

As Frank left the store, he reflected, with satisfaction:

"I have only been a few hours in New York, and I have gotten employment already."

This reflection raised his spirits, and disposed him to regard the future with a degree of confidence. He resolved to spend the rest of the afternoon in walking about in the lower part of the city, and acquiring a little familiarity with the streets, as this was a kind of knowledge he was likely to need.

Chapter 22

AN ADVENTURE IN WALL STREET

Frank strolled down Broadway, admiring the massive, stately structures that lined the street on either side. Very soon he came to Trinity Church, and, standing in front of it, looked down Wall Street. He had heard so much of this street that he felt inclined to turn from Broadway and walk down its entire length.

As he sauntered along a man whom he met scrutinized him sharply, as if considering some plan. Apparently making up his mind, he stepped up to Frank, and touching him on the shoulder, said:

"Boy, would you like a job?"

Now, Frank, though he had engaged to work for the Great Pekin Tea Company, was ready to accept any other proposal, and answered promptly:

"Yes, sir."

"That is right," said the man. "It is a mere trifle, but I am willing to pay you a dollar."

"What is it, sir?"

"Do you see that window?"

He pointed to a basement window, in which were exposed rolls of gold, currency and greenbacks of different denominations, and English sovereigns and French gold coins.

"I want you to do a little errand for me in there," he said.

Frank was rather surprised that the man did not do his own errand, when the broker's office was so near, but he had no objection to earning a dollar and signified his willingness.

"What I want you to do," went on his new acquaintance, "is to sell some government bonds for me."

"Very well, sir."

The man produced a large yellow envelope, already open.

"In this envelope," he said, "are two five-twenty governments for a hundred dollars each. Take them in and sell them, and bring the proceeds to me."

"All right, sir."

Frank took the envelope, and entered the office of Jones & Robinson, that being the name of the firm.

He advanced to the counter, and singling out a clerk, stated his business in six words:

"I want to sell these bonds."

The clerk took them and drew them out of the envelope. Then he figured a little on a slip of paper, and said:

"They are worth two hundred and twenty-two dollars and twenty-five cents."

"All right, sir."

"Will you take a check or currency?"

Frank hesitated.

"Perhaps I'd better ask the man I am getting them for."

"Very well. You can bring them here tomorrow."

"Oh, I will let you know in a minute! The man is just outside."

This answer immediately excited suspicion. Frank was too little versed in business ways to understand how singular it was for his principal not to transact his own business under the circumstances, but the brokers were necessarily keen, shrewd men.

"Wait a minute," said the clerk; "I will speak to Mr. Jones."

Mr. Jones came forward and addressed Frank.

"Are you acquainted with the man who gave you these bonds to sell?" he asked.

"No, sir. I met him in the street."

"Did he offer you any pay for selling them?"

"Yes, sir. He is going to give me a dollar."

"Will you go out and ask him to come in here a moment?"

Frank obeyed.

When his employer saw him coming, he asked, eagerly:

"Have you got the money?"

"No," replied Frank. "They asked me if I wanted a check or currency."

"Either currency or gold," said the man, hastily. "Go back at once, and don't keep me waiting."

"They want to see you, sir."

"What for?" inquired the man, looking disturbed.

"I don't know."

"There is no need of my going in," averred the man, angrily. "I paid you to sell the bonds. Now go back."

"He won't come," reported Frank. "He says I can attend to the business. He will take either gold or currency."

"No doubt," said Mr. Jones, significantly. "Thomas, go out with this boy, and tell the man that employed him that we do not purchase bonds unless we have a reasonable assurance that they belong to the person offering them. We will take the liberty of retaining them, giving him a receipt for them, and if we are satisfied, he can have his money to-morrow."

Robinson, who had been examining some newspaper slips, here came forward, and said:

"That is unnecessary. I find that these bonds are among those stolen from the house of Henry Percival, Madison Avenue, a week since. We must manage to delay the man while we notify the police."

Frank was very much surprised to learn that he was acting as agent for a bond robber, and was fearful that he might himself be regarded with suspicion; but he need not have troubled himself on this score. Wall Street men are good judges of human nature, and it was at once concluded in the office that Frank was the dupe of a designing knave.

A boy was despatched to the nearest police office, and Frank was directed to tell his principal that he would not long be delayed.

Naturally, however, the man outside had become suspicious.

"I can't wait," he said. "Meet me on the steps of the Astor House at five o'clock with the money. I am obliged to hurry away now to a business appointment."

Frank could think of no pretext for delaying him, and was forced to see him hurry away.

He hastened back to the office and gave the alarm.

"He has taken fright," said Robinson. "I fear we have lost him. Where did he go?"

Frank, however, was too ignorant of city streets to give any accurate information.

The consequence was that when the policeman appeared on the scene, there was no occasion for his services.

"At any rate," said the broker, "we have secured a little of the plunder. What is your name and address, my boy? We may wish to communicate with you."

Frank gave his name, and added the directions of his boarding-house.

"Shall I meet the man at the Astor House?" he inquired, as he was leaving the office.

"To be sure!" replied Mr. Jones. "I came near forgetting that. Officer, will you be on hand at the time?"

"Better employ a detective, sir; as my uniform would keep the thief at a distance. I don't think he'll appear, at any rate."

"I do," said the broker. "He won't give up the money while he thinks there is a chance of securing it."

Chapter 23
THE CAPTURE

At the hour named, Frank repaired to the Astor House, and took a position on the steps.

He looked about him for his street acquaintance, but could see no one who bore any resemblance to him.

Finally, a man dressed in a gray suit, with a pair of green glasses, walked carelessly up to him, and asked, in a low voice:

"Have you got the money?"

Frank looked at him in surprise.

This man had thick, black whiskers, while the man who had employed him had none at all, so far as he could remember. Besides, the green glasses altered him considerably.

To make sure that he was not deceived he inquired:

"What money?"

"You know very well," said the man impatiently. "You are the boy whom I employed to sell some bonds this morning."

"You don't look like the same man," said Frank.

"Because of my glasses. I have to wear them at times on account of the weakness of my eyes."

While he was speaking, a quiet-looking man approached and listened to the conversation.

"Then," said Frank, "you can tell me how many bonds you handed me."

"They were two five-twenty government bonds of a hundred dollars each."

"Correct, sir."

"Then hand me the money and be quick about it, for I have no time to waste! You shall have the dollar I promised you."

But here the quiet-looking man took a part in the conversation. Passing his arm through that of the man with the green glasses, he said:

"I will trouble you to come with me."

"How dare you touch me? Do you mean to insult me?" demanded the other, struggling with his captor.

"I will make all clear in due time. You must come with me and explain how you came in possession of the bonds you gave this boy."

"They were put in my hands by an acquaintance. If there is anything wrong I am not to blame,"

"In that case no harm will come to you; but now you must come along."

The other looked as if he meditated an escape, but the sight of a policeman near at hand convinced him that it would be impracticable.

"Do you want me any longer?" asked Frank.

"Not at present, but you may leave your address with me."

Frank did so; and then, feeling weary, he took a car, and, going up town, went to his boarding place, where he lay down for awhile.

At six o'clock the dinner-bell rang, and Frank went down and took his seat at the table.

Eight persons were already in their seats—two married couples, a young lady of twenty-five, who was the teacher in one of the public schools, as Frank afterward learned, a quiet-looking, elderly man, who was a bookkeeper for a Pearl Street house, and two young men, one employed as a salesman in a retail dry goods store, and the other in a gentlemen's furnishing store on Sixth Avenue. The last mentioned was Frank's next neighbor at the table.

He was rather a dashing-looking young fellow, with his hair elaborately oiled and brushed, an incipient moustache, and a large and showy necktie.

"Ladies and gentlemen," said Mrs. Fletcher, the landlady, "this is Mr. Courtney, who has just joined our pleasant circle."

Frank made a general bow, and received a similar greeting from his fellow-boarders.

"Have you just arrived in New York, Mr. Courtney?" asked the young man next him.

"Yes," answered Frank. "I only arrived this morning."

"Do you intend to remain in the city?"

"If I can find employment."

"Ah, to be sure! I hope you will. I am employed in a store on Sixth Avenue. I wish we had a vacancy. I should be glad to recommend you."

"You are very kind," said Frank.

He could not help wondering how his neighbor could feel justified in recommending him on so brief an acquaintance, but did not think it necessary to express this.

"I suppose you have never been employed in the city, Mr. Courtney?"

"I have never been employed anywhere," admitted Frank.

"This would be against you, of course. Still, you may find an opening. By-the-way, Mr. Courtney, allow me to introduce myself."

The young man drew from his pocket a highly-glazed card, bearing the name,

"P. PRESTON"

"I am glad to know you, Mr. Preston," said Frank, politely.

"You may wonder what the first letter stands for," said Mr. Preston, confidentially. "Now don't be shocked when I say Peter."

"No, I am not shocked," said Frank, smiling.

"Ugly name, isn't it? I really feel that I am very badly treated in having such a name fastened upon me; but I was named for my Uncle Peter."

"Where is your store?" asked Frank.

"Near Fourteenth Street. I shall be glad to see you there at any time. I suppose you are not doing anything at present."

"I have taken an agency to sell tea for the Great Pekin Company. I am to begin to-morrow."

"I am afraid you won't like it. A friend of mine tried it once and came near starving."

This was not encouraging, but Frank was not going to despair before he had fairly begun his work.

"I find that boys receive such small wages," Frank continued, "that I preferred to try an agency."

"Quite true," said Mr. Preston, condescendingly. "When I started I was paid a paltry sum; now I am not paid what I am worth. Still, twenty-five dollars a week is fair."

"Quite fair," responded Frank, who could not, of course, know that Mr. Preston did not receive one half of this sum, though he chose to give that impression.

After dinner, Preston was obliged to go back to the store where he was employed. By invitation, Frank walked with him.

Turning into Sixth Avenue, Preston said, as he pointed to a modest-looking shop on the west side of the avenue:

"This is my store. I wish I could keep you company longer, but business before pleasure, you know."

Before returning to his boarding-house, Frank sat down for a short time in Washington Park, and reviewed his plans and prospects. He could not tell how he would succeed in his tea agency; but if that failed, he was resolved to try something else.

He didn't feel homesick, for since his mother's death he had no longer any home-ties. Young as he was, he felt that one part of his life was at an end, and that a new life and a new career were before him.

Chapter 24

THE YOUNG TEA MERCHANT

The next morning, at breakfast, one of the gentlemen, who had been running his eyes over the morning paper, remarked, indifferently:

"Ah! I see they have caught one of the gang who robbed the house of Mr. Percival, on Madison Avenue a week ago."

"Read the paragraph, Mr. Smith," said one of the boarders.

Mr. Smith read as follows:

> "About noon yesterday a boy entered the banking house of Jones & Robinson in Wall Street, and offered for sale two one-hundred dollar 5-20 Government bonds. On inquiry, he said that the bonds belonged to a man in the street, whom he had never before met, and who had offered him a dollar to sell them. This naturally excited suspicion, and a policeman was sent for. Before he could arrive the man had hastily departed, requesting the boy to meet him at a specified hour in front of the Astor House and hand him the money. He came to the rendezvous, but in disguise, and, while talking to the boy, was arrested. It is understood that he has agreed to turn States evidence, and probably the entire sum stolen amounting to several thousand dollars, will be recovered."

Frank listened to this paragraph with interest. He was glad that his name was not mentioned in the account, as he didn't care for such publicity. He ventured to ask a question:

"Is Mr. Percival a rich man?" he said.

"Very rich," answered Mr. Smith. "He is not now in the city, but is expected home from Europe in three or four weeks. His house was left in the charge of an old servant—a coachman—and his wife; but the burglars proved too much for them."

"I am glad they are caught," observed Mrs. Fletcher. "It makes my blood run cold to think of having the houses entered at night by burglars."

"Preston, said Mr. Smith, jokingly, "I hope you have your bonds locked up securely."

"I don't believe the sharpest burglar can find them," laughed Preston. "I only wish I could get hold of them myself."

"The boy who helped to capture the burglar ought to be well rewarded," said one of the boarders.

"Don't you wish it had been you, Courtney?" asked Mr. Preston.

"It was," replied Frank, quietly.

There was a great sensation upon this announcement. All eyes were turned upon our hero—most, it must be admitted, with an expression of incredulity.

"Come, now, you are joking!" said Preston. "You don't really mean it?"

"I do mean it," assured Frank.

"Tell us all about it," said Mrs. Fletcher, who had her share of curiosity. "I didn't suppose we had such a hero in our house."

"It didn't require much heroism," said Frank, modestly.

"Tell us all about it, at any rate."

Frank told the story as simply as he could, much to the satisfaction of the company.

"You'll come in for a handsome reward, when Mr. Percival gets home," suggested Mr. Smith.

"I don't expect anything," said Frank. "I shall be satisfied if I get the dollar which was promised me. I haven't received that yet."

"I wish I were in your shoes—that's all I've got to say," said Preston, nodding vigorously. "Will you sell out for five dollars?"

"Cash down?" asked Frank, smiling.

"Well, I'll give you my note at thirty days," replied the Sixth Avenue salesman, who seldom kept five dollars in advance of his liabilities.

"I won't sell what I haven't got," said Frank. "Probably I shall hear nothing from Mr. Percival."

After breakfast Frank went down town and sought the store of the Great Pekin Company.

After half an hour's delay—for there were others in advance of him—he was fitted out with samples and started for Brooklyn.

It was his first visit to that city, but he had received some directions which made his expedition less difficult.

At the ferry he took a Flatbush Avenue car, and rode up Fulton Street, and past the City Hall, up Fulton Avenue, for nearly a mile.

Here were intersecting streets, lined with comfortable houses—for Frank had made up his mind to try private houses first. He had with him a few pound parcels of tea, which he thought he could perhaps succeed in disposing of at such places.

He selected a house at random, and rang the bell.

A servant answered the ring.

Frank felt rather embarrassed, but there was no time to hesitate.

"I have some samples of tea with me," he began, "of excellent quality and at reasonable prices."

"It's no use," said the girl, abruptly. "We never buy of peddlers," and she closed the door in his face.

"Not a very good beginning," thought Frank, rather mortified. "So I am a peddler," he said to himself, and he called to mind the agents and peddlers who in past years had called at the Cedars.

With some compunction, he remembered that he had regarded them with some contempt as traveling nuisances. Now he had entered the ranks of this despised class, and he began to see that they might be perfectly respectable, and were estimable persons, animated by a praise-worthy desire to make an honest living.

Thus thinking, he called at another door.

It was opened, not by a servant, but by an elderly lady, who had rather a weakness for bargains.

"I've got some nice tea," said Frank, "which I should like to sell you. It is put up by the Great Pekin Company."

"Are you sure it's nice?" asked the elderly lady. "We've been getting ours at the grocery store on the avenue, and the last wasn't very good."

"You'd better try a pound of ours," advised Frank.

"I don't know but I will," assented the lady. "How much do you charge?"

"I have some at fifty cents, some at sixty and some at seventy."

"I guess I'll take the sixty."

Frank had a pound parcel ready, which he delivered to her, and received his money.

"Seems to me you are pretty young for a peddler," said the lady, regarding Frank with curiosity.

"Yes, ma'am."

"How old are you?"

"Sixteen."

"Been long in the business?"

"No, ma'am; I've only just commenced."

"You don't say so! Do you make much money at it?"

"I haven't made much yet. I should be glad to supply you with some more tea when this is gone."

"Well, you can call if you are round this way. If I like it, I will try you again."

Frank's spirits rose.

His profits on the pound of tea were twelve cents. This was not much, certainly, but it was a beginning.

At the next three houses he sold nothing, being rather rudely rebuffed at one. At the fourth house, the servant called her mistress, a kind, motherly-looking woman, who seemed to regard Frank with more interest than his merchandise.

"I hope you are succeeding well," she said, kindly.

"This is my first day," replied Frank, "and I have made one sale."

"I have a son who is an agent like you, but he didn't begin so young. He is now traveling in the West."

"What is he selling?" asked Frank, with interest.

"Dry goods. He travels for a wholesale house in New York."

"I suppose he is a young man."

"Yes; he is twenty-five, but he began at nineteen in a small way. He sometimes got quite discouraged at first. That is why I feel interested in any who are passing through the same experience."

These pleasant words cheered Frank. Only at the nearest house he had been called a tramp, but here he found that he was regarded with consideration.

"It is rather up-hill work," he said.

"And you seem very young."

"I am sixteen."

"Are you entirely dependent on what you earn?" questioned the lady, sympathizingly.

"Not entirely," answered the young merchant, "but I hope to make a living in this or some other way. Can I sell you any?" he asked, hopefully.

"I believe we have some on hand. Still tea will always keep, and I would like to help you along."

The kind-hearted lady took three pounds—two at sixty cents and one at seventy. This gave Frank a profit of thirty-eight cents and put him in good spirits.

He worked his way back to the avenue on the other side of the street, and, coming to a grocery store, entered.

It occurred to him that he would try to sell some at wholesale.

Frank was so young that the dealer did not suppose him to be an agent, and asked what he would like to buy.

"I came to sell, not to buy," said Frank.

"What are you dealing in?" asked the grocer.

"I have several samples of tea. If you will give me an order, I will have it sent to you to-morrow."

The grocer found, upon examination, that his stock was getting low, and gave Frank an order, but he was obliged to sell below the regular price, and only cleared three cents a pound. Still, on a sale of twenty-five pounds, this gave him seventy-five cents, which was very encouraging.

Adding up his profits, thus far, Frank found that his commission amounted to a dollar and a quarter, which exceeded his anticipations.

He continued his calls, but sold only one pound besides, at fifty cents, netting him ten cents more.

By this time Frank was both tired and hungry. He boarded a passing car, and, returning to Fulton Ferry, crossed to New York, relieved of the greater part of his burden. On the New York side he stepped into a restaurant, and, for twenty-five cents, secured a hearty if not luxurious lunch.

Frank repaired to the headquarters of the tea company and reported his day's sales.

"You have done unusually well," said the proprietor. "Many of our agents do not succeed in making a single sale the first day. I should not have been surprised if your experience had been similar."

"It is hard work," said Frank, "and an agent is rudely treated. Sometimes I was called a tramp and a nuisance."

The proprietor laughed.

"Hard words break no bones," he reminded. "The business is perfectly honorable. Will you try it again to-morrow?"

"Yes, sir, as I have nothing else to do."

"Very well; we will fit you out."

Frank took a car and went home. He found that horse-cars were likely to cut largely into his profits. His expenses for the day were twenty cents for car fare and four cents for the ferry, or twenty-four cents in all. Besides this, he must count in twenty-five cents for lunch, which brought up the entire expense to forty-nine cents.

"But for the wholesale order," he reflected, "I should have cleared but eleven cents over and above expenses, while my board and washing will amount to nearly a dollar a day."

Thus Frank found that, though he had a fortunate day, he had not quite earned enough to pay his expenses.

This made him feel serious. Still, he reflected that it was only the beginning, and he might do better in the future.

Chapter 25

FRANK MEETS MR. MANNING
AND MARK

The next morning Frank resumed his tea agency. As on the day previous, he went to Brooklyn; but, though I should be glad to say that he was more successful than on the first day, truth compels me to state that the day was a comparative failure.

It might be that he was unfortunate in the persons whom he visited, but at all events, at the close of his labors he found that his commissions amounted to less than fifty cents. He contented himself, therefore, with a ten-cent lunch, and crossed Fulton Ferry between three and four o'clock.

"This will never do," thought Frank, seriously. "I shall have to be economical to make my earnings cover my incidental expenses, while my board and lodging must be defrayed out of the money I have with me."

Frank was disappointed. It is easy to think of earning one's living, but not quite so easy to accomplish it. A boy, besides being ignorant of the world, is inexperienced, and so disqualified for many avenues of employment which are open to men. It is generally foolish for a boy to leave a good home and start out for himself, unless the chances are unusually favorable for him. If he does it, however, he should not allow himself to be easily discouraged.

If Frank had given up the business in which he was engaged simply because he had met with one unsuccessful day, I should not have been willing to make him the hero of my story.

"This will never do," thought Frank. "I must make a greater effort to-morrow."

The next day his commission amounted to a dollar, and the fourth day to a dollar and twelve cents.

"You are doing well," said his employer. "You are doing better than the majority of our agents."

In one way this compliment was satisfactory. In another way it was not encouraging, for it limited his prospects. Frank began to think that he would never be able to make his entire expenses as a tea agent.

I do not propose to speak in detail of Frank's daily experiences, but only to make mention of any incidents that play an important part in his history.

He was returning from Jersey City on the tenth day of his agency, when in the gentlemen's cabin he saw, directly opposite, two persons whom he had reason to remember.

They were Mark Manning and his father.

Little reason as he had to like either, they reminded him of home, and he felt pleased to meet them.

He instantly crossed the cabin, and offered his hand to his stepfather, who had not yet seen him.

"When did you arrive, Mr. Manning?" he asked.

"Why, it is Frank!" exclaimed Mr. Manning, with an appearance of cordiality. "Mark, do you see Frank?"

"Yes, I see him," replied Mark, coldly.

"Haven't you anything to say to him?" said his father, who was much more of a gentleman than his son.

"How are you?" said Mark indifferently.

"Thank you for your kind inquiry," said Frank, more amused than vexed, for he cared very little for his stepbrother's friendship. "I am in very good health."

"And how are you getting along?" continued his stepfather, with an appearance of interest. "Are you in any business?"

"Yes," answered Frank.

"What are you doing?" asked Mark, inspired a little by curiosity.

"I am agent for a wholesale tea house in New York," Frank responded, briefly.

"You don't say so!" ejaculated Mark, rather impressed. "What is the name of the firm?"

"The Great Pekin Tea Company."

"Does it pay well?"

"I have met with very fair success."

"I congratulate you, Frank," said Mr. Manning. "Your energy and enterprise are creditable—extremely creditable. I always predicted that you would succeed—didn't I, Mark?"

"I don't remember hearing you say so," said Mark.

Mr. Manning shrugged his shoulders.

"Nevertheless," he said, "I have often made the remark."

"Where do you live?" pursued Mark.

"I board in Clinton Place."

"A very respectable street," remarked Mr. Manning.

Frank now thought it was his turn to become questioner.

"How long do you remain in the city, Mr. Manning?" he asked.

"Not long—only a day or two," said his stepfather.

"We sail for Europe on Saturday," interposed Mark, "on the Cunard steamer."

"Indeed! I wish you a pleasant voyage."

"I am sorry you won't go with us, Frank," said his stepfather, cautiously. "You remember I gave you the chance to do so, and you desired to devote yourself immediately to business."

"Yes, sir. I would rather remain in New York."

"It might possibly be arranged now, if you desire to go," said Mr. Manning, hesitatingly.

"No, thank you, sir."

"Well, perhaps you are right," replied his stepfather, considerably relieved.

"What parts of Europe do you expect to visit?" asked Frank.

"We shall visit England, France, the Rhine, Switzerland, and perhaps Italy."

"I hope you will enjoy it."

"Thank you; I think we shall."

Frank checked a sigh. It was certainly tantalizing. If he could travel with congenial friends, he felt that he would very much enjoy such a trip; but with Mark in the party there would be little pleasure for him.

"We are staying at the Grand Hotel," said Mr. Manning. "I would invite you to come and dine with us, but I have an engagement first, and don't know when we shall dine."

"I thank you, sir, all the same," said Frank.

They had reached the New York side, and were walking toward Broadway. It was necessary for Frank to go to the tea store, and he took leave of his stepfather and Mark, again wishing them a pleasant voyage.

"I hate that boy!" said Mark, as they walked away.

"You should not indulge in any such disagreeable feelings, Mark," reproved his father.

"Don't you hate him?"

"Certainly not."

"One would think by your soft manner that you loved him," sneered Mark, who was not noted for the respect with which he treated his father.

"Really, Mark, I am shocked by your strange words."

"What made you invite him to go to Europe with us?"

"I knew he would not go."

"He might have accepted, and then we should have been in a pretty pickle."

"Mark," said his father, rather irritated, "will you be kind enough to leave me to manage my own affairs? I believe I have succeeded pretty well so far."

"Yes, you have," Mark admitted. "All the same, we'd better keep clear of Frank till we get safely off on the steamer."

Chapter 26

A SERIOUS LOSS

Among the boarders at Mrs. Fletcher's, we have already named a bookkeeper. About a week after Frank's arrival, he left the house, and went further up town. His place was supplied by a thin, dark-complexioned young man, who gave his name as Herbert Montgomery. He said, indefinitely, that he was employed in the lower part of the city, but was not communicative as to details.

This young man's room was on the same floor as Frank's, and he soon manifested a desire to become intimate with our hero.

On the third day his intimacy went so far that he asked Frank to lend him five dollars.

Now Frank did not feel in a position to lend any one five dollars. Though he worked steadily every day, he found that his necessary expenses were making inroads upon his scanty reserve fund. Moreover, he was not attracted by Montgomery, and only responded to his advances to the extent required by politeness.

"I am sorry I cannot accommodate you, Mr. Montgomery," replied Frank.

"You don't mean to say you haven't got five dollars?" said Montgomery.

"I have got it, but I can't lend it."

"Why not?"

"It would not be convenient."

"You think you won't get it back, but you shall have it to-morrow night."

Frank could be firm when he chose to be, and he repeated his refusal.

"I don't see why you should be so disobliging," grumbled the young man, offended.

"In the first place, it would not be convenient, and in the second, you are almost a stranger to me. Three days since I had never met you."

"Oh, if you think I am dishonest," said Montgomery, in a tone of vexation, "I can only say that I thank you for the compliment!"

"I have not accused you of dishonesty," said Frank, calmly; "but still we are only acquaintances. What little money I have I am likely to need, for I am not yet earning enough to pay my expenses."

"Oh, well, drop the matter!" said Montgomery, checking himself suddenly. "Suppose we go out and have a game of billiards."

"Thank you, but I can't afford it."

"I'll go with you," said Preston, who overheard this proposal. "It is my evening off, and I'm in for a good time."

"Lend me five dollars, Preston—there's a good fellow," said Montgomery, transferring his attentions to the salesman.

"Do you take me for a millionaire, or do I look as if I had come in for a legacy?" replied Preston, jocularly.

Nevertheless, before the evening was over he had paid out a dollar for billiards and lent his companion two dollars besides.

"Preston, you're a good fellow," declared Montgomery. "You're not so mean as Courtney. I can't get a cent out of the cad, though I promised to pay him to-morrow evening. I suppose he's got money?"

"Oh, yes; he brought a supply of money with him to fall back upon, in case his business didn't pay!"

"I suppose he keeps it in a savings bank," said Montgomery, carelessly.

"Oh, no, I guess not! He probably keeps it in his trunk. That's where I would keep my money, if I had any to keep."

It may be mentioned here that, though Frank had not brought a trunk with him to the city, he had since sent for his trunk and some extra clothing, which had been forwarded from the Cedars by his stepfather.

I do not intend to keep my readers in doubt as to the true character of Herbert Montgomery. He had no real business, and made a precarious living by running up bills at boarding-houses, of which he paid as small a part as possible, and in levying tribute upon all his acquaintances by borrowing money, either with or without leave. Had Frank lent him the five dollars he asked for it would never have been returned.

He was interested in Preston's statement about Frank's reserve fund, and instantly began to consider how he could appropriate it to his own use.

The next morning he rose late, and did not breakfast till after Frank had gone down town. Then he went up leisurely to his own room, and, seeing the coast clear, entered the latter's bedroom.

Closing the door and bolting it, he kneeled down by Frank's trunk, and, drawing a bunch of keys from his pocket, tried one after another till he found one that would fit. With an exulting glance he lifted the lid and began to explore the contents.

At last he found a pocketbook, and, hastily thrusting it into his pocket, shut the trunk and relocked it. He had now accomplished what he intended, and, drawing the bolt, stepped out into the hall just as the chambermaid came up to put the room in order. The girl looked at him in surprise.

"I was looking for a book which Mr. Courtney promised to lend me," he said, rather embarrassed.

"What made him lock himself in, then?" thought the girl. "I think he was there for no good."

Montgomery was considerably annoyed by this encounter. Should Frank miss his money, it would cast suspicion upon him. He repaired to his own room, and, opening the pocketbook discovered to his satisfaction that it contained thirty-five dollars.

"Mrs. Fletcher," he said to the landlady, fifteen minutes later, as he descended the stairs with his valise in his hand, "I am obliged to go to Boston on business. I shall be back in a day or two. If any letters or parcels come for me, will you be obliging enough to keep them for me?"

"Certainly, Mr. Montgomery. No bad news, I hope?"

"Oh, no; only a little business trip. I am often called there."

He left the house, leaving the landlady quite unsuspicious of his reasons for going. It is hardly necessary to say that he did not go to Boston, nor did he again return to the boarding-house in Clinton Place.

Meanwhile, unlucky Frank, quite unconscious of his serious loss, was trying to sell tea in Harlem.

Chapter 27

A DISCOURAGING DAY

Seldom had Frank had a more discouraging day. Of course he knew nothing of the people who lived in the houses lining the streets through which he passed. He might hit a good customer, but it was very much a matter of chance. He was more likely to find himself regarded coldly and unfavorably.

There was another obstacle of which he soon heard.

At one house, a middle-aged lady came to the door, whose face indicated a temper very easily disturbed.

"Madam," said Frank, politely, "I should like to sell you some tea."

"I dare say you would," rejoined the lady, in no friendly tone. "So you are a tea peddler, are you?"

Frank did not exactly like the name of peddler, for in his mind it was connected with unpleasant associations. Still he could not refuse to be called so.

"I suppose I am," he answered.

"You suppose you are! Don't you know?" said the lady, sharply.

"I deal in tea," said Frank, rather offended.

"Who sends you out? Who do you work for?"

"The Great Pekin Tea Company."

"You do, hey? I thought so!"

"What made you think so?" Frank could not help asking.

"I'll tell you why," said the lady, aggressively. "You're the same one that came here and sold me one of your poorest kinds of tea at seventy-five cents a pound. It was an outrage and a swindle! I didn't know you at first, because I am near-sighted. And now what have you got to say for yourself, hey?"

Frank was taken aback by this unexpected accusation, and looked at the lady in surprise.

"What are you starting at? You thought I wouldn't know you, but you are mistaken."

"Madam," said Frank, recovering himself, "if you have been imposed upon, I am sorry, but you must not charge me with it. This is my first visit to Harlem, and I have never seen you before in my life."

"Do you expect me to believe that story, young man?"

"I am not in the habit of telling lies," answered Frank, with dignity.

"Do you mean to say you have never been in Harlem before?"

"Yes, I do!"

"Priscilla!" called the lady, raising her voice.

In answer, a girl about eighteen, her daughter, came down-stairs.

"What's wanted, mother?"

"You remember that tea-peddler that cheated me so a month ago?"

"Take a good look at this fellow, and tell me if it is the same one."

"Certainly not, mother. This is a boy, and that was a young man with a moustache."

"Are you sure of it?"

"Of course I am."

"I may be mistaken," said the lady, still glaring unpleasantly at Frank, "but I am not sure of it. Likely as not my daughter is mistaken and you are the same fellow after all. At any rate, you have probably played the same trick upon others."

"Oh, mother, how can you talk so?" expostulated Priscilla. "He looks like a very nice boy, I am sure."

"Thank you, miss, for your good opinion," said Frank, turning to the daughter. "I would not willingly play a trick on your mother or anyone else."

"You may believe him if you want to, Priscilla," said her obdurate mother, "But I've had more experience than you, and I wouldn't trust a peddler, however soft-spoken he was. You may go away, young man, and you needn't trouble yourself to call here again."

"I certainly won't madam," assured Frank, noticing the number of the house and mentally recording it.

Frank walked away, indignant and a little discouraged.

"Surely," he thought, "there are some disagreeable people in the world, and I have met a specimen. Her daughter looked ashamed of her, and I don't wonder at it. I don't believe all the people in Harlem are as unpleasant."

This was shown to be correct by the next lady he met.

She did not buy any tea, to be sure, but seemed sorry that she was already well supplied, and questioned Frank as to what success he was having.

Frank mentioned the reception he had met with from the lady next door.

"She is a very disagreeable woman," said her neighbor. "No one likes her. Agents stand a poor chance with her. One day last week I saw her chase one out with a broom."

"Then I suppose I am lucky to have gotten off so well," said Frank, smiling.

"Yes, you were. If you should be in Harlem two or three weeks from now, I may want some tea."

"Thank you!"

When twelve o'clock came, Frank had not sold a single pound. Even if he earned nothing, however, he had an appetite and must buy lunch.

He entered a small oyster house, and went to the proprietor.

"Can I sell you some tea?" he asked.

"No, I guess not. I get my tea in Harlem."

"Take a couple of pounds," said Frank, "and I will take part of the pay in lunch."

"That is business," replied the other. "Let me look at your tea."

Frank showed him his samples.

"Who employs you?"

"The Great Pekin Tea Company."

"They have a good name. Yes, I will try a couple of pounds at fifty cents."

This, of course, came to a dollar, and Frank's profit on the sale amounted to twenty cents. This was precisely the cost of the lunch which he ordered, so that he felt well satisfied with the arrangement.

He left in better spirits, and resumed his travels from house to house.

I am sorry to say, however, that though he certainly exerted himself to the utmost in the interests of the Great Pekin Tea Company and his own, he did not sell another pound of tea that day.

About three o'clock he got on board a Third Avenue horse-car, bound downtown, and sat quietly down in a corner.

"Harlem doesn't seem to be a very promising field for an agent," he said to himself. "Perhaps it isn't fair to judge it by the first day. Still, I don't think I shall have courage to come here to-morrow. I would rather go to Jersey City or Brooklyn."

"Frank got off the cars at the Bible House and walked to his boarding-house, where a disagreeable surprise was in store for him.

Chapter 28

FRANK DISCOVERS HIS LOSS

Frank rang the bell, finding that he had forgotten to take his pass-key with him.

The door was opened by the same girl who had detected Montgomery in Frank's room.

Frank always treated servants considerately, and Katy therefore felt well disposed toward him. She thought she ought to tell him of the morning's incident.

"Mr. Courtney," she said, as Frank was about to ascend the stairs, "did you offer to lend Mr. Montgomery a book?"

"No," replied Frank, in surprise. "What makes you ask?"

"I found him in your room this morning, with the door shut. He looked guilty like, but said he was after a book you promised to lend him."

"That is strange," said Frank, "I have no books with me—at any rate, none he would care to borrow. I must ask him what it means."

"You can't do that, Mr. Courtney," said Katy.

"Why not?"

"Because he took his valise and went to Boston. He started off just after he left your room. I hope he hasn't stole any thing."

Katy's education had been neglected, and her language, as I hope my young readers will perceive for themselves, was not strictly grammatical.

Frank did not think of that, however. He had something else to think about.

"All my money was in my trunk," flashed through his mind.

He hastily thanked Katy for her information, and went up-stairs two steps at a time. Reaching his room, he drew his key from his pocket, and unlocked his trunk. He could see that the contents had been disturbed, for he was neat and orderly in his arrangement, and now the contents seemed huddled up together. He thrust his hand into the corner where he had placed his pocketbook, but his worst fears were confirmed. The pocketbook was gone!

Frank sat back in a chair, and his heart beat rapidly, as he hastily reviewed the position in which he stood.

He was not quite penniless, but nearly so. He opened his purse and examined the contents. He found that his available resources amounted to about two dollars and a half. This would not have been so discouraging, had he been earning his expenses, but, as we know, he had not done this from the first. In four days a week's board would be due to Mrs. Fletcher, or, more properly, the advance payment for the next week.

"What shall I do?" poor Frank asked himself.

He had been trained to scrupulous honesty in money matters, and the thought that he might find himself unable to meet his obligations struck him with dismay.

"What will Mrs. Fletcher think?" ran his thoughts. "She may think that I am dishonest. Perhaps she may not believe that I have been robbed, but have only invented the story to impose upon her."

In this supposition, however, Frank did both himself and Mrs. Fletcher injustice, as he found when he communicated his loss to her, just before the evening meal. She exhibited great concern, and asked:

"Will this inconvenience you very much, Mr. Courtney?"

"I am afraid it will," Frank answered, soberly.

"It is a shame, I declare!" said the landlady. "I never did like that Montgomery, and I ought to have asked for references when he came here. If I had, it would have been better for you."

"Katy tells me that he has gone away."

"Yes; he told me that he was going to Boston, but a man that will steal will tell lies. I don't believe he has gone there. If he has gone anywhere, he has gone in a different direction."

In spite of his limited experience, Frank could see that this was probably the case.

"Well," he replied, "it is rather hard on me, but I must see what I can do."

"I want to say, Mr. Courtney," said the warm-hearted landlady, "that I will give you plenty of time. You can stay on, and pay me when you are able. I am sure I can trust you."

"Thank you, Mrs. Fletcher!" Frank said, brightening up at these words of trust and encouragement. "I am much obliged to you, whether I need the accommodation or not. I can assure you that you will run no risk, as I have friends that I can call upon in case of necessity."

He referred to the gentleman who had purchased Ajax, and who had authorized him to draw upon him in time of need.

The night brought perplexity to Frank, but not discouragement. He was naturally hopeful, and, in a large city like New York, he felt that there are always chances of obtaining employment, provided he could maintain his position, as he would have been able to do if he had not lost the thirty-five dollars which his fellow-boarder had stolen. Now, however, circumstances were materially changed.

One thing was tolerably clear to Frank, and this was, that he must give up his agency. He had tried it, and been unsuccessful. That is, he had failed to earn money enough to support himself, and this was necessary.

As to what he should take up next, Frank was quite in the dark. As a boy in a counting-room he would be paid not more than four dollars a week, if he could gain such a situation, which was by no means certain.

The more he thought about the matter the more perplexed he felt, and it was in an uncomfortable frame of mind that he came down to breakfast the next morning.

By this time Frank's loss was made known to his fellow-boarders.

"Have you heard anything of your friend Montgomery?" asked Preston.

"I don't think he has treated me as a friend," replied Frank. "I don't believe we shall see him again very soon."

"He owes me two dollars," said Preston. "I'll sell the debt cheap."

"You won't get any bidders, Mr. Preston," remarked Mrs. Fletcher. "You are lucky to get off so easily, in my opinion."

"I begin to think so myself. What are you going to do about it, Mr. Courtney?"

"I suppose I can do nothing. Montgomery has probably left the city."

Frank told no one how near he was to the bottom of his purse. He did not care to borrow money, even if he had been able to do so, noi was he inclined to admit how poor he really was.

Chapter 29

FRANK HEARS SOMETHING
TO HIS ADVANTAGE

Frank went out as usual after breakfast, and then walked leisurely down town. He proposed to go to the office of the Great Pekin Tea Company and resign his agency. He was on the watch during his walk for any opportunities to repair his unlucky loss.

At one place he saw a notice:

"BOY WANTED"

Though he felt sure the compensation would not be sufficient to allow of his accepting it, he thought it would do no harm to make inquiry, and accordingly entered.

It was an extensive retail store, where a large number of clerks were employed.

"Is a boy wanted here?" asked Frank of the nearest salesman.

"Yes. You may inquire at the desk."

He pointed to a desk some distance back, and Frank went up to it.

"You advertise for a boy," he said to a tall, stout man, who chanced to be the proprietor. "Is the place filled?"

"No," was the answer; "but I don't think it would suit you."

"Do you think I would not be competent, sir?"

"No, that is not the difficulty. It would not be worth your acceptance."

"May I inquire what are the duties, sir?"

"We want a boy to open the door to customers, and this would not be worth your accepting."

"No, sir. Thank you for explaining it to me."

The gentleman was favorably impressed by Frank's polite and gentlemanly manners.

"I wish I had a place for you," he said. "Have you ever had any experience in our line of business?"

"No, sir; I have had very little experience of any kind. I have acted for a short time as agent for a tea company."

"You may leave your name if you like, and I will communicate with you if I have a vacancy which you can fill."

Frank thanked the polite proprietor and walked out of the store.

Though this is a story written for boys, it may be read by some business men, who will allow me to suggest that a refusal kindly and considerately expressed loses half its bitterness, and often inspires hope, instead of discouragement.

Frank proceeded to the office of the tea company and formally resigned his agency. He was told that he could resume it whenever he pleased.

Leaving the store, he walked down Broadway in the direction of Wall Street.

He passed an elderly man, with stooping shoulders, and a gait which showed that he was accustomed to live in the country.

He was looking about him in rather an undecided way. His glance happened to rest on Frank, and, after a little hesitation, he addressed him.

"Boy," he said, "do you live round here?"

"I live in the city, sir."

"Then I guess you can tell me what I want to know."

"I will if I can, sir," said Frank, politely.

"Whereabouts is Wall Street?"

"Close by, sir. I am going that way, and will be happy to show you."

Frank had no idea his compliance with the stranger's request was likely to have an important effect upon his fortunes.

"My name," said the stranger, "is Peters—Jonathan Peters, of Craneville, Onondaga County, I am a farmer, and don't know much about New York. I've got a few hundred dollars that I want to put into government bonds."

"All right," said Frank. "There won't be any difficulty about it."

"I've heard there are a good many swindlers in New York," continued Mr. Peters. "The squire—Squire Jackson, of our village—perhaps you may have heard of him?"

"I don't think I have, Mr. Peters."

"Well, the squire told me I'd better take good care of my money, as there were plenty of rascals here who would try to cheat me out of it."

"That is true, Mr. Peters. Only yesterday I was robbed of thirty-five dollars by a man who boarded in the same house."

"You don't say so?"

"He opened my trunk and took out my pocketbook while I was absent on business."

"I wouldn't dare to live in New York!" declared the farmer, whose apprehensions were increased by Frank's story.

By this time they had reached the office of Jones & Robinson, with whom, it will be remembered, Frank had once before had dealings.

"If you will come in here, Mr. Peters," he said, "you will be sure of honorable treatment. I will introduce you if you like."

"I should be obliged if you would," replied the farmer. "Out in Craneville I am at home, but I ain't used to New York business men, and don't know how to talk to them."

It pleased Frank to find that, in spite of his inexperience, he was able to be of service to one more unaccustomed than himself to city scenes and city ways.

He walked up to the counter, followed by the farmer, and said:

"This gentleman wishes to buy some government bonds. I told him that he could transact his business here."

"Thank you! Mr. Benton, you may attend to this gentlemen."

Frank was about to leave the office, when Mr. Robinson called him back.

"You have been in the office before, have you not?" he asked.

"Yes, sir."

"Are you not the boy who assisted in the capture of the man who robbed Mr. Henry Percival of Madison Avenue?"

"Yes, sir."

"I thought so. I have been trying to find you for the last week."

"Naturally Frank look surprised.

"Mr. Henry Percival was at that time in Europe," said Mr. Robinson. "On his return, a week ago, he called on us, and expressed a desire to have you call upon him. We had mislaid or lost your address, and were unable to give him the information he desired."

Frank's heart beat high with hope as the broker spoke.

"Perhaps," he thought, "Mr. Percival may offer me a situation of some kind, and I certainly am greatly in need of one."

"Did Mr. Percival recover all his bonds?" he asked.

"Nearly all," answered Mr. Robinson. "He considered himself exceedingly fortunate, and he certainly was so."

"Do you know of how much he was robbed?"

"Rather more than five thousand dollars. Of this sum all has been recovered except three bonds of a hundred dollars each. Mr. Percival is a rich man, and he won't miss that small amount."

"I wish I were rich enough not to miss three hundred dollars," thought Frank. "If I had my rights, I could say the same."

Just now, in his extremity, the boy thought regretfully of the fortune he had lost. Had he been so situated as to be earning enough to defray all his expenses, he would scarcely have given a thought to it.

"You had better go up to see Mr. Percival this evening," advised the banker, "if you have no other engagement."

"Even if I had an engagement, I would put if off," rejoined Frank. "Will you give me Mr. Percival's address?"

"Number——," said Mr. Robinson.

Frank noted it down and left the office. By this time Mr. Peters had completed his business, and was ready to go out also.

"I'm much obliged to you," he said to Frank. "I was afraid I'd get into a place where they'd cheat me. I guess Mr. Jones and Robinson are pretty good folks."

"I think you can depend upon them," assured Frank.

"If ever you come to Craneville, I should like to have you stay a few days with me on my farm," said Mr. Peters, hospitably. "We are plain folks, but will treat you about right."

"Thank you, Mr. Peters. If I ever come to Craneville, I shall certainly call on you."

Though Frank was so near the end of his money, he had something to look forward to in his approaching interview with Mr. Percival. He had been able to to do this gentleman a service, and it was not unlikely that the capitalist would wish to make him some acknowledgment. Frank did not exaggerate his own merits in the matter. He felt that it was largely owing to a lucky chance that he had been the means of capturing the bond robber. However, it is to precisely such lucky chances that men are often indebted for the advancement of their fortunes.

While he was in a state of suspense, and uncertain what Mr. Percival might be disposed to do for him, he decided not to exert himself to obtain any employment. If he should be disappointed in his hopes, it would be time enough to look about him the following day.

What should he do in the meantime?

He determined to treat himself to an excursion. From the end of the Battery he had often looked across to Staten Island, lying six miles away, and thought it would prove a pleasant excursion. Now, having plenty of time on his hands, he decided to go on board one of the boats that start hourly from the piers adjoining the Battery. The expense was but trifling—ten cents each way—and low as Frank's purse was, he ventured to spend that amount for pleasure. He felt that he needed a little recreation after the weeks of patient labor he had spent in the service of the Great Pekin Tea Company.

Chapter 30

MR. MONTGOMERY TURNS
UP AGAIN

It was a pleasant day, and as Frank steamed out of the harbor, passed the fort, but a mile distant, and from the deck of the ferry-boat observed the vessels of every description darting here and there on their various courses, he felt quite cheerful.

"If I can only maintain myself here," he said to himself, "I shall be contented and happy. I would a great deal rather be usefully employed than travel in Europe with Mr. Manning and Mark."

The first landing, about six miles distant, was at New Brighton. The island looked very attractive, with its hilly shores dotted with handsome villas, standing in the midst of trees.

The boat made a brief stop, and proceeded successively to Castleton, Port Richmond and Elm Park. This Frank found to be the last stopping-place, and he landed, in company with many others.

A steep path led him to a hotel and adjoining park, in which were set tables for the accommodation of lunching parties. There were swings between tall trees and other arrangements for the pleasure of visitors. From the upper part of the inclosure there was a fine view of the water and places in the vicinity.

Frank sauntered about, enjoying himself in a quiet way. He assisted to swing some young children, with whom he became pleasantly acquainted.

When the next boat came in, Frank idly watched the faces of the passengers as they entered the park, not thinking it very likely, however, that he should see any familiar face. But he did.

Strolling along, in very complacent mood, came a young man whom he had good cause to remember.

It was Herbert Montgomery, who had robbed him of his little stock of money.

Frank's face lighted up with surprise and pleasure. He strongly doubted whether he should recover any of his money, but he would, at any rate, have the satisfaction of expressing to Mr. Montgomery his opinion of his conduct.

"Mr. Montgomery," he said, quietly, "I should like a little conversation with you."

Montgomery turned suddenly. When he saw Frank, he looked startled and even dismayed. But he quickly recovered his self-possession, and decided upon his course.

"I beg your pardon, my boy," he said. "Were you addressing me?"

Frank was a boy, but to be addressed in this patronizing way by the man who had injured him did not suit his ideas.

"I did address you, Mr. Montgomery," he said. "I will thank you to return me the thirty-five dollars you took from my trunk without leave. By so doing, you will save yourself trouble."

"Boy," replied Montgomery, loftily, "I don't know whether you are crazy or not, but I am quite sure that there is something wrong with you. What can induce you to address an utter stranger in such insulting terms I cannot guess. I decline to have anything further to say to you."

"An utter stranger!" exclaimed Frank, in the greatest amazement.

"I repeat that you are an utter stranger to me," said Montgomery, with unblushing effrontery. "I never, to my knowledge, set eyes on you before this morning."

"Do you mean to deny that your name is Herbert Montgomery?" asked Frank.

"I certainly do. I never heard the gentleman's name before."

"Do you mean to deny that you have been boarding at the house of Mrs. Fletcher, in Clinton Place?"

"I assuredly do."

"Perhaps," said Frank, not believing his statement, "you will tell me what your name is?"

"Certainly. My name is Ephraim Parker, at your service."

"How long has it been so?"

"Young fellow," said Montgomery, "I don't know who you are, but you are certainly very impertinent. If you have really lost any money, I am sorry for you, but it is nothing to me. This Herbert Montgomery, or whatever his name may be, may possibly look like me. I am not responsible for any accidental resemblance. Good-morning! and be careful next time before you insult a gentleman on an uncertainty."

It had never fallen within Frank's experience to meet a man so utterly reckless of truth, and he asked himself whether he might not be mistaken. He had heard of cases of resemblance so great that people were mistaken even by near friends for each other. Was it possible that the man before him was a case in point?

He scanned Montgomery's face carefully, and detected a lurking smile of exultation, accompanied by a characteristic lifting of the eyebrow. This satisfied him. It was Montgomery, and not Parker.

"Mr. Montgomery," he insisted, "I know you very well. You cannot impose upon me. I ask you again to return me my money, or as much as you have left."

"Leave me!" ordered Montgomery, angrily. "I have had enough of your impertinence. I am a gentleman from Chicago, temporarily in New York on business. I have wasted time enough on you already."

"Good-bye for the present, Mr. Montgomery," said Frank. "I think the time will come when I shall be able to unmask you."

Montgomery walked off in seeming indifference, but he was very glad to see Frank leave by the next boat.

"I don't want to meet that boy again," he muttered. "It was a close shave, and required all my impudence to get rid of him. I had better leave New York for a time."

He followed Frank back to the city by the next boat, and that afternoon embarked on the Fall River boat for Boston.

Chapter 31

AN ACCIDENT IN A STREET-CAR

When Frank returned to New York after his unsatisfactory interview with Montgomery, he felt annoyed and provoked. To have lost his money was bad enough, but to be treated with such cool impudence by the thief was quite as disagreeable. Had Montgomery admitted his guilt and showed penitence, or pleaded poverty, Frank would have been willing to overlook his offense, for he was of a generous nature; but to be openly denied made him angry.

Besides, he could not help reflecting seriously on the strait he was in. He was almost penniless, and knew not where to look for a fresh supply of money. At the end of the quarter he was authorized by his stepfather to call for twenty-five dollars, but this was still some weeks distant, and in the meantime he must either earn enough to defray his expenses or run into debt. There was, however, one hope—that Mr. Percival might give him employment—and this would probably be decided that same evening.

When Frank reached the city, he walked slowly up through the

Battery to the foot of Broadway. He passed the famous house, No. 1, which, a hundred years ago, was successively the headquarters of Washington and the British generals, who occupied New York with their forces, and soon reached the Astor House, then the most notable structure in the lower part of the city.

With his small means, Frank knew that it was extravagant to ride up town, when he might have walked, but he felt some confidence in the success of his visit to Mr. Percival, and entered a Fourth Avenue street-car. It so chanced that he seated himself beside a pleasant-looking lady, who had with her a boy about seven years old.

Soon after the car started the conductor came around to collect the fares.

Frank paid his, and the conductor held out his hand to the lady.

She put her hand into her pocket to draw out her purse, but her countenance changed as her hand failed to find it.

Probably no situation is more trying than to discover that you have lost or mislaid your purse, when you have an urgent use for it. The lady was evidently in that predicament. Once more she searched for the purse, but her search was unavailing.

"I am afraid I have lost my purse," she said, apologetically to the conductor.

This official was an ill-mannered person, and answered, rudely:

"In that case, ma'am, you will have to get off."

"I will give you my card," replied the lady, "and will send double the fare to the office."

"That won't do," said the man. "I am responsible for your fare, if you stay on the car, and I can't afford to lose the money."

"You shall not lose it, sir; but I cannot walk home."

"I think you will have to, madam."

Here Frank interposed. He had been trained to be polite and considerate to ladies, and he could not stand by and see a lady treated with rudeness.

"Take the lady's fare out of this," he said, handing the conductor some change.

"And the boy's, too?"

"Of course."

The lady smiled gratefully.

"I accept your kindness, my young friend," she said. "You have saved me much annoyance."

"I am very glad to have had the opportunity," said Frank, politely.

"Of course I shall insist upon reimbursing you. Will you oblige me with your address, that I may send you the amount when I return home?"

A boy of less tact than Frank would have expostulated against repayment, but he knew that this would only embarrass the lady, and
that he had no right, being a stranger, to force such a favor upon her.
He responded therefore:

"Certainly, I will do so, but it will be perfectly convenient for me to
call upon you."

"If it will give you no trouble, I shall be glad to have you call any
time. I live at Number——Madison Avenue."

Now it was Frank's turn to be surprised. The number mentioned by
the lady was that of the house in which Mr. Henry Percival lived.

"I thought Mr. Percival lived at that number?" said Frank.

"So he does. He is my father. Do you know him?"

"No; but I was about to call on him. This morning Mr. Robinson, a
broker in Wall Street, told me that he wished to see me."

"You are not the boy who caused the capture of the bond robber?"
asked the lady, quickly.

"Yes, I am the boy, but I am afraid I had less to do with it than has
been represented."

"What is your name?"

"Frank Courtney."

"My father is very desirous of meeting you, and wishes to thank
you for what you have done. Why have you not called before?"

"I did not know till to-day that your father had returned. Besides, I
did not like to go without an invitation."

"I will invite you," said the lady, with a pleasant smile, "and I, as
well as my father, will be glad to see you. And now let me introduce
you to my little son. Freddie, would you like to see the boy that
caught the robber?"

"Yes, mother."

"Here he is. His name is Frank."

The little boy immediately began to ask questions of Frank, and by
the time they reached the Cooper Institute, Frank and he were well
acquainted.

"Don't get out, Frank," begged Freddie.

"I am going home, Freddie."

"You must come and see me soon," said the little boy.

"Now you have three invitations," said the lady.

"I will accept them all," promised Frank.

And, with a bow, he left the car.

Chapter 32

FRANK MAKES AN EVENING CALL

After supper Frank walked up to Mr. Percival's residence. Now that he knew two members of the family, he looked forward with pleasure to the call he was about to make. His prospects seemed much brighter than when he woke up in the morning, and the annoyance of his meeting with Montgomery was nearly effaced by his pleasant encounter in the street-car.

On reaching the house of Mr. Percival, he saw at a glance that it was the residence of a wealthy man, and the hall, into which he was first admitted, was luxurious in its appearance. But Frank had been brought up to the enjoyment of wealth, and he felt more at home here than in the rather shabby boarding-house in Clinton Place.

A colored servant opened the door.

"Is Mr. Percival at home?" he asked.

"Yes, sah."

"I should like to see him."

"What name, sah?"

"Frank Courtney."

"Step in, sah, and I will 'form Mr. Percival," said the colored servant, in a consequential tone that amused the caller.

Frank stepped into the hall, but he was not left long without attention. Little Freddie ran down-stairs, eagerly calling out:

"Did you come to see me, Frank?"

"Yes," replied Frank; "but I came to see your grandfather, too."

"Come, and I will show you where he is," said the little boy, taking Frank's hand.

The two went up the staircase and into a handsomely furnished room, made attractive by pictures and books.

In a large armchair sat a pleasant-looking elderly man, of about sixty.

"Grandpa," said the little boy, "this is Frank. He wants to see you."

Mr. Percival smiled.

"I am glad to see Frank," he said. "It seems, my lad, that you are already acquainted with my daughter and grandson."

"Yes, sir. I was fortunate enough to meet them to-day."

"You relieved my daughter from some embarrassment."

"I am glad to have had the opportunity, sir."

Frank's manner was easy and self-possessed, and it was evident that Mr. Percival was favorably impressed by him.

"Take a seat," he said, "while I ask you a few questions."

Frank bowed and obeyed.

Mr. Percival now proceeded to interrogate Frank.

"Your name is Frank Courtney. Have you been long in the city?"

"No, sir; only a few weeks."

"What led you to come here?"

"I wished to earn my own living."

"Was that necessary? You do not look like a poor boy."

"I was brought up to consider myself rich."

"Indeed! Did you lose your property?"

"Perhaps I had better tell you how it happened, sir."

"If you don't object, I should be glad to hear."

Frank gave a brief statement of his position, and the circumstances that led him to leave his home and go out into the world.

Mr. Percival listened thoughtfully.

"It is a singular story," he said, after a pause. "Your stepfather's in Europe, then?"

"Yes, sir; at least he sailed for Europe."

"Have you heard from him?"

"No, sir."

"Do you expect to hear?"

"I think not."

"He can't feel much interest in you."

"I don't think he does," replied Frank. "Still, I can't say that he has treated me unkindly."

"Do you suspect that your stepfather has wronged you in the matter of the property?"

"I would rather not answer that question, sir. I might wrong Mr. Manning, and I have no proof to offer."

"I understand you, and I applaud your discretion. It does you credit. Some time or other the mystery may be cleared up, and the wrong, if there is one, may be righted. I can't understand, however, how this Mr. Manning should be willing to leave you dependent upon your own exertions with such a scanty provision as twenty-five dollars a quarter."

"I didn't ask for any more; and, besides, Mr. Manning offered to take me to Europe with his son Mark."

"Do you think that he was sincere in the offer?"

"I don't think he expected me to accept it, and I am sure that it would have been very disagreeable to Mark to have me in the party."

"Have you any objections to telling me how you have succeeded in your efforts to make a living?" asked the old gentleman, with a keen but kindly glance.

"I have been disappointed, sir," was the candid reply.

"I am not surprised to hear it. A boy brought up as you have been cannot rough it like a farmer's son or a street boy."

"I think I could, sir; but I should not like to."

"Precisely. Now, I am not sure that you acted wisely in undertaking a task so difficult, since it was not necessary, and your stepfather could hardly have refused to support you at home. However, as you have taken the decisive step, we must consider what is best to do under the circumstances. What work have you been doing?"

"I have been selling tea for the Great Pekin Tea Company."

"How have you succeeded?"

"I have not been able to make my expenses," Frank admitted.

"How have you made up the difference?"

"I brought fifty dollars with me from home."

"Is it all used up?"

"I had thirty-five dollars left, but a day or two ago one of my fellow-boarders opened my trunk and borrowed it without leave."

"Of course you won't recover it?"

"I don't think there is much chance of it."

"Then probably your money is nearly exhausted?"

Frank did not like to admit his poverty, but owned up that he had less than two dollars.

"And yet you paid the car fares of this little boy and his mother?"

"I hope, sir, I would not refuse to assist a lady when in trouble."

Mr. Percival nodded two or three times, smiling as he did so. He was becoming more and more favorably impressed with our young hero.

"Do you mean to continue this tea agency?" he asked.

"No, sir; I have already notified my employers that I do not care to continue it."

"Have you anything else in view?"

Frank felt that now was the time to speak.

"I came here this evening," he said, "intending to ask you if you knew of any situation I could fill, or could recommend me to employment of any kind by which I might make a living."

"I must consider that. Have you thought of any particular employment which you would like?"

"No, sir; I cannot afford to be particular. I will do anything that is honest, and at all suitable for me."

"What would you consider unsuitable?"

"I should not wish to black boots, for instance, sir. It is honest work, but I ought to be suited to something better."

"Of course! What education have you had? Good, I suppose?"

"I am nearly ready for college."

"Then you are already fairly well educated. I will put you to a test. Sit up to the table, and take paper and pen. I will dictate to you a paragraph from the evening paper, which I should like to have you write down."

Frank did as requested.

Mr. Percival selected a short letter, written by some public man, which chanced to have found a place in the evening papers.

Frank wrote rapidly, and when his copy was finished, submitted it to Mr. Percival.

The old gentleman took it, and, running his eye over it, noticed that it was plainly written, correctly spelled and properly punctuated. This discovery evidently gave him satisfaction.

"Very creditably written," he said. "I have known boys nearly ready for college who could not copy such a letter without blundering. I am glad that your English education has not been neglected while you have been studying the classics."

Frank was gratified by Mr. Percival's commendation, though he could not see in what manner his education was likely to bring him employment. It was desirable, however, to produce a favorable impression on Mr. Percival, and he could not help hoping something would result to his advantage.

At this moment Freddie's mother entered the room, and greeted Frank with a cordial smile.

"Freddie," she said, "it is time for you to go to bed."

"I don't want to leave Frank," objected Freddie.

"Frank will come and see you again."

"Will you, Frank?"

Frank made the promise, and Mrs. Gordon—for this was her name—left the room, promising to return before Frank went away.

He was now left alone with Mr. Percival.

Chapter 33

FRANK IS OFFERED A POSITION

Mr. Percival engaged Frank in conversation on general topics while Mrs. Gordon was out of the room. His young visitor had been an extensive reader, and displayed a good deal of general information. Moreover, he expressed himself intelligently and modestly, and deepened the favorable inpression which he had already succeeded in making.

When Mrs. Gordon returned, she placed in Frank's hands a small sum of money, saying:

"Allow me to repay my debt, with many thanks."

"You are quite welcome," answered our hero.

He had too much tact to refuse the money, but quietly put it into his pocket.

"Helen," said Mr. Percival, "I would like a word with you. We will leave our young friend here alone for five minutes."

"Certainly, father."

The two went into an adjoining room, and Mr. Percival commenced by asking:

"How do you like this boy, Helen?"

"Very much. He seems to have been brought up as a gentleman."

"He has. Till a short time since he supposed himself the heir to a fortune."

"Indeed!" said Mrs. Gordon, with curiosity.

Briefly, Mr. Percival rehearsed the story which Frank had told him.

"What a shame!" exclaimed Mrs. Gordon, indignantly. "His stepfather ought to be punished."

"That may come in time. Wickedness does not always prosper. But as regards our young friend, I have a plan in view."

"What is it, father?"

"I find he has an excellent education, having been nearly ready for college when the crisis in his fortunes came. I have been thinking whether we could not find a place for him in this house. My eyes, you know, are so weak that they are often strained by attention to my correspondence and reading. I have an idea of engaging Frank Courtney as a sort of private secretary, upon whom I can call at any time. Of course he would have his home in the house."

"There will be no difficulty about that. Our family is small, and we have plenty of vacant rooms. But, father, will he be qualified to undertake the duties you have designed for him? He is very young."

"That is true, my dear; but he is remarkably well educated. I have tested his capacity by dictating a letter for him to copy."

"Did he do the work satisfactorily?"

"Without a single mistake."

"Then, father, I would not hesitate to engage him. Freddie likes him, and will be delighted to have him in the house."

"Another idea, Helen. It is time Freddie began to study. Suppose we make him Freddie's private tutor—say for an hour daily?"

"That is really an excellent idea, father," said Mrs. Gordon, in a tone of satisfaction. "It will please and benefit Freddie, and be a relief to me. Do you think Frank will have patience enough?"

"I watched him with the little fellow, and I could see that he liked children. I am sure he will succeed in this as well as in the duties which he will undertake for me."

"I suppose he will have no objection to the plan?"

"I think he will accept gladly. He has had a hard struggle thus far in maintaining himself, and I can relieve him from all anxiety on that score. I am indebted to him for helping me to recover my bonds, and this will be an excuse for offering him a larger salary than the services of so young a secretary could be expected to command."

"Very well, father. Your plan pleases me very much, and I shall be glad to have Frank commence to-morrow, if he chooses. Now let us return to the library."

While father and daughter were absent Frank had taken from the table a volume of "Macaulay's History," and had become interested in it.

He laid it down upon their return.

Mr. Percival resumed his easy chair, and said, with a smile:

"My daughter and I have been consulting about you."

Frank bowed, and his hopes rose.

"I suppose you are open to an offer of employment?"

"I am not only open to it, Mr. Percival, but I shall be grateful for it."

He could not help wondering what sort of employment Mr. Percival was about to offer him. He concluded that it might be a place in some business house.

"The fact is," said the old gentleman, "I have a great mind to offer you a situation as my private secretary."

Frank was astonished. This was something he had not thought of.

"Do you think I am qualified to fill such a position, Mr. Percival?" he asked.

"The duties would not be difficult," was the reply. "Though not in active business, the care of my property, and looking after my scattered investments, involves me in considerable correspondence. My eyes are not as strong as they once were, and I find them at times taxed by letter-writing, not to mention reading. You can relieve me very materially."

"I shall be very glad to do so, sir. The duties would be very agreeable to me."

"But that is not all. My daughter proposes to employ you as private tutor for Freddie."

Frank smiled.

"I think my scholarship would be sufficient for that," he said.

"Freddie likes you," said Mrs. Gordon, "and if you think you would have patience enough—"

"I think I should," assured Frank. "I was always fond of children, and Freddie is a very attractive boy."

"I believe he has an equally favorable opinion of you," said Mrs. Gordon, smiling.

"We are very good friends, I think," said Frank.

"Then I am to understand that you will not object to this double positon?" asked Mr. Percival.

"I shall be very glad to accept," replied Frank, quickly.

"Of course you will need to make your home with us," continued the old gentleman. "My daughter will assign you a room, and you may move in as soon as you like."

"That will be to-morrow, sir."

"I like your promptness. There remains one thing to be considered. We have not settled about the amount of your salary."

Salary sounded well, and Frank began already to feel himself a young man.

"I will leave that entirely to you, sir," he said.

"Will fifty dollars a month satisfy you?" asked Mr. Percival, with a benevolent smile.

"Fifty dollars a month, besides my board?" ejaculated Frank.

"Yes."

"But I am sure I cannot earn so much," said Frank, candidly.

"It is, I am aware, more than would usually be offered to a boy of your age; but I owe you something for the service you rendered me, in helping me to recover my bonds. I have not offered you any pecuniary recompense, thinking you would prefer employment."

"You judged rightly, sir, and I feel very grateful to you."

"I did not think, this morning," said Mrs. Gordon, laughing, "that I should find a tutor for Freddie before night."

"It is rather a surprise to me," said Frank, "but a very agreeable one. I feel very much indebted to you both for the confidence you feel in me, and I will now bid you good-evening!"

"One minute, Frank," said Mr. Percival. "Would it be convenient for you to receive a month's salary in advance?"

"I shall not need the whole of it, sir; but if you will let me have twenty dollars, I can easily wait for the balance till the end of the month."

Mr. Percival drew from his pocketbook twenty dollars in bills and placed them in the hands of his young visitor. Frank thanked him earnestly.

"We shall expect to see you to-morrow," said Mr. Percival. "Goodnight!"

Frank left the house in high spirits. He had found strong friends, and secured a position and a salary beyond his highest expectations. He determined to do his best to satisfy his employer.

The next day Frank transferred his residence to Madison Avenue. He was assigned a pleasant room, decidedly superior, it need hardly be said, to his room at Clinton Place. It seemed agreeable to him once more to enjoy the comforts of a liberal home.

Frank had had some doubts as to how he would satisfy Mr. Percival in his capacity of private secretary.

He was determined to do his best, but thought it possible that the old gentleman might require more than he could do well. He looked forward, therefore, with some apprehension to his first morning's work.

Mr. Percival, though not engaged in active business, was a wealthy man, and his capital was invested in a great variety of enterprises. Naturally, therefore, he received a large number of business letters, which required to be answered.

The first day he dictated several replies, which Frank put upon paper. He wished, however, to put Frank's ability to a severe test.

"Here are two letters," he said, "which you may answer. I have noted on each instructions which you will follow. The wording of the letters I leave to you."

"I will try to satisfy you, sir," said Frank.

Our hero was a good writer for his age. Moreover he had been well trained at school, and did not shrink from the task assigned him.

He read carefully the instructions of his employer, and composed the letters in strict accordance with them.

Mr. Percival awaited with some interest the result of his experiment. If Frank proved competent to the task assigned him, his own daily labor would be considerably abridged.

"Here are the letters, sir," said Frank, passing the drafts to Mr. Percival.

The old gentleman examined them carefully. As he did so, his face expressed his satisfaction. "Upon my word, Frank," he said, familiarly, "you have done your work exceedingly well. They are brief, concise and yet comprehensive. I feared that you would use too many words."

"I am glad you are pleased, sir. Doctor Brush trained us to write letters, and he cut down our essays when they were too diffuse."

"Then I feel indebted to Doctor Brush for providing me with so competent a young secretary. You will be able to assist me even more than I anticipated. I shall, of course, read over your letters before they are sent, to make sure that you have fully comprehended and carried out my instructions, but I don't expect they will need much correction."

Frank was much gratified by these words. This was the only point on which he had felt at all doubtful as to his ability to please his employer.

Sometimes, when his eyes pained him more than usual, Mr. Percival also employed him to read to him from the daily papers, or from some book in which he was interested, but this did not occur regularly.

Every day, however, Frank was occupied with Freddie. The little boy knew the alphabet, but nothing more, so that his young teacher had to begin with him at the beginning of the primer.

He succeeded in interesting his little pupil, and did not protract his term of study so as to weary him.

Finding that the little fellow was fond of hearing stories, he read to him every day a story or two from Hans Christian Andersen, or from a collection of German fairy stories, and sometimes went out to walk with him.

Freddie was delighted with his teacher, and freely expressed his approval to his mother and grandfather.

"Really, Frank," said Mrs. Gordon, "I shall begin to be jealous of your hold upon Freddie. I am not sure but he likes your company better than mine."

"I don't think Freddie will prefer any one to his mother," said Frank "but I am glad he likes to be with me."

"You have certainly proved very successful as a private tutor, Frank," said Mrs. Gordon, "and my father tells me you succeed equally well as a secretary."

"It is partly because you both treat me so indulgently," answered Frank, gracefully.

This answer pleased Mr. Percival and Mrs. Gordon, who more than ever congratulated themselves upon the lucky chance that had thrown Frank in their way.

Assuredly he made himself very useful in the small household, contributing to the comfort and pleasure of Freddie, his mother and grandfather, in nearly equal measure.

While Frank's monthly salary was of great value and importance to him, it was nothing to Mr. Percival in comparison with the pleasure and relief afforded by his presence in the house.

It must not be supposed, however, that Frank's time was wholly occupied by the duties of his two positions. Usually he had several hours daily at his disposal, and these he was allowed to spend as he pleased.

Part of this he occupied in visiting different localities of the city and points of interest in the neighborhood, and part in reading and study.

Mr. Percival had a large and well-selected library, which, to a boy of Frank's studious tastes, was a great attraction.

He entered upon a course of solid reading, embracing some of the standard histories, and devoted some hours every week to keeping up his acquaintance with the Greek and Latin authors which he had read at school.

In this way his time was well and usefully employed, and the weeks slipped by till almost before he was aware six months had passed. The next chapter will record a meeting with some old acquaintances.

Chapter 34

PLINY TARBOX

One afternoon, Frank walked down Broadway, enjoying the bright sunshine and the animated spectacle which the leading New York thoroughfare always presents. He had completed his duties for the day, and felt at leisure to enjoy himself. He was no longer in any pecuniary embarrassment, having saved up one hundred and fifty dollars out of the salary paid him by Mr. Percival.

Besides this, he had two quarterly payments from his stepfather's banker. He had decided not to call for this money, but, on consulting his employer, he had changed his mind.

Mr. Percival represented that he need feel no scruples about taking what was, after all, but a small part of what he was entitled to, even admitting the will to be genuine, since Mr. Manning was expressly directed to provide for him.

Frank was wise enough to be guided by a man whose experience was so much greater than his own, and drew the money. He had, therefore, at present, two hundred dollars in all, which he had deposited in a savings bank recommended to him by Mr. Percival.

Now, two hundred dollars was but a very small sum compared with the fortune he had lost, but its possession gave Frank much satisfaction. Three-fourths of it he had himself earned, and this was a source of pleasure and comfort.

Frank had been obliged to make some purchases of clothing, since, as an inmate of such a house, he felt that he would be expected to dress well. Yet, over and above all expenses, he had saved, as I have said, two hundred dollars. Had such a sum been given him, he might have felt more disposed to spend it foolishly; but a boy who earns money knows better how to value it.

Then, as Frank walked down Broadway, he was able to resist without much effort the temptations that allured him from many a shop window.

Just in front of the St. Nicholas Hotel he heard his name called.

Looking up, he recognized, with some surprise, Pliny Tarbox, his cousin from Newark, whom he had not seen since his hurried departure from a house where his changed fortunes had made him unwelcome.

"Is it you, Pliny?" he asked.

"Yes."

"Are you in business here?"

"No. I am still in the book store. I came to New York to buy some clothes. I thought I could get them cheaper here than in Newark. Father makes me buy my own clothes out of my wages. Don't you think that mean?"

"I should not like to make such a charge against your father, Pliny."

"Oh, he is mean—awful mean! Everybody knows that," said Pliny, apparently not aware that it did him little credit to speak so of his father.

"Is it such a hardship to pay for your own clothes?" said Frank. "I do not only pay for my own clothes, but I pay all my expenses, with the help of only two dollars a week from my stepfather."

This drew Pliny's attention to his cousin.

"You're pretty nicely dressed," he said, scanning Frank's appearance critically. "I guess you must be prospering."

"I am doing very well, Pliny," answered Frank, smiling.

"And you pay your board, too—and washing?"

"I earn enough for all my expenses."

"Then you must get more'n four dollars a week."

"I don't think I could get along very well on four dollars a week."

"That's all I get. I ought to be raised, but my boss won't pay me a cent more. He's awful mean."

"It seems to me you are unlucky."

"So I am. I should like to come to New York to work. What are you doing?"

"I am a private secretary to a gentleman living on Madison Avenue."

Pliny opened his eyes in genuine surprise.

"Private secretary! What do you do?"

"I read to him, write his letters, and I also give lessons to his little grandson."

"You don't say!" ejaculated Pliny, in astonishment. "How much do you get?"

"Fifty dollars a month and my board," replied Frank, enjoying Pliny's surprise.

"You don't mean it!" exclaimed Pliny, opening wide his eyes in bewildered surprise.

"Certainly I mean it."

"Why, that's about twelve dollars a week, and board besides."

"Yes."

"Do you have to work hard?"

"Not very. I have three or four hours a day to myself."

"I never heard of such a thing!" averred Pliny. "You're awfully lucky. How did you get it?"

"It's too long a story to tell, Pliny."

"Do you think I could get a place like it?" questioned Pliny, anxiously. "I'd be willing to work cheaper than that."

"I don't think such chances are very common," said Frank, gravely.

"How old are you?" asked Pliny, abruptly.

"Sixteen."

"Just my age, and I'm working for four dollars a week," said Pliny, looking unhappy and discontented.

"I don't think you could get any higher wages in New York in the same kind of a store. I didn't try to get a place, because I couldn't support myself on a boy's wages."

"What did you do before you got to be private secretary?"

"I was for a few weeks agent for a large tea company."

"Did it pay well?"

"No. I couldn't make enough to pay expenses."

"How long have you been in this place?"

"Nearly six months."

"You must have saved up considerable money," suggested Pliny.

"I have saved up something."

Pliny became highly interested.

"How much?"

"I don't care to mention."

"Oh, I didn't suppose it was a secret. Will you lend me five dollars?"

"No!" declined Frank, decidedly.

"I should think you might," said Pliny, complainingly.

"I see no reason why I should. You have a good home, and enough to provide for all your wants."

"You are a good deal better off."

"I may lose my position, and then I must live on what I have saved till I can get something else to do. You ought not to stand in need of money."

Pliny had seventy-five dollars in a bank at Newark, but it struck him that it would be a good plan to borrow five dollars from Frank and add to his account. He would not have dreamed of repaying the money. He was essentially a mean boy, and considered all his friends and acquaintances who had money legitimate prey.

"I haven't had any lunch," he said to Frank, changing his form of attack.

"Shall I show you a restaurant?"

"No; I guess I will get along till I get home. I've had to pay out more for clothes than I expected, and then it's expensive paying railroad fares."

Frank understood very well what Pliny meant, and said, with a smile:

"Won't you come and lunch with me, Pliny? I can't invite you to the house, because that would be a liberty; but I will take you to a restaurant near by, and shall be glad to have you order what you like."

"I don't mind if I do," said Pliny, with alacrity. "You're a good fellow, Frank, and I'm glad you're getting on so well. Father said he didn't believe you'd make out in the city, but I thought different. He thought you wanted to stay in Newark, and live at our house, considering you had lost your property."

"I hope he has changed his mind about that," said Frank, feeling annoyed at the meanness of his relative.

"He will, when he hears what a good place you've got. You see father's been expecting you would get hard up, and write him for money."

"Would he have sent me any?"

"I guess not. It's as hard to get money out of father as—as anything. He ought not make me buy my clothes. I leave it to you if he should.

"I would rather not express any opinion about that," said Frank. "You may say to your father, when you get home, that he need not have been afraid of my applying to him for money. Once I got nearly out of money but I never even thought of him."

"Yes, I'll tell him. I guess he'll invite you to come out and spend Sunday, when he hears how well you are getting along."

Frank did not reply, but he privately decided that such a visit would offer no attractions to him. He would rather remain in New York.

"I hope I never shall think so much of money as Pliny and his father," thought Frank. "Money is a good thing to have, but there are some things that are better."

Pliny did justice to his cousin's hospitality. Accustomed to his father's meagre table, he enjoyed highly the restaurant dinner, and was by no means bashful in ordering. Frank was pleased to see how Pliny enjoyed the meal. In fact, he sympathized with him, knowing the plainness of his father's table.

Soon after they parted.

"I hope I'll see you when I come to New York again, Cousin Frank," said Pliny.

"Thank you! It will give me pleasure to have you lunch with me again, whenever we meet."

Chapter 35

A LETTER FROM MR. TARBOX

Frank did not speak to Mr. Percival's family of his meeting with Pliny. It was not pleasant to him to think that he was valued only for his good fortune. He had seen but little of the Tarbox family, but he understood very well what their professions of friendship amounted to, and that they were not to be relied upon in an emergency.

He was not much surprised on Monday afternoon to receive the following letter from Erastus Tarbox:

"My Dear Young Cousin: We have been wondering what has become of you, and Mrs. T. and myself have often wished

to invite you to pass a Sabbath at our humble home. Not knowing your address, I could not write to you, or I should have
done so. You can imagine, therefore, the pleasure we felt when
Pliny told us that he had met you, and gave us tidings of your
remarkable success, which I am sure does you great credit.

"He tells me that you fill a very responsible position, and receive a very liberal salary. I could wish that Pliny might be
equally fortunate, and shall esteem it a great favor if you will
mention him to your respected employer, and recommend him
for any lucrative position which he might bestow upon him.
Pliny is a very capable boy, and has been carefully trained to
habits of frugality and industry.

"Can you not soon come out and pass a Sabbath with us?
The esteem which we have for your late lamented mother alone
would secure you a cordial welcome, not to speak of our friendship for yourself. Pliny often says that you seem to him like a
brother, and he would truly enjoy your companionship.

"Your sincere friend and cousin,
"Erastus Tarbox."

The time was when Frank would have put confidence in the friendly expressions used by Mr. Tarbox, but his eyes had been opened, and
he understood that if misfortune should come to him, it would not do
to lean upon his cousins at Newark.

Frank wrote a civil reply to Mr. Tarbox, thanking him for his invitation, but saying that at present it would not be convenient for him
to accept it. He added that should an opportunity offer he would be
glad to assist Pliny to a better position than he now held.

In spite of his wish to be cordial, his letter was felt by the Tarbox
family to be cold, and they regretted that they had not treated him
better during his brief visit to them.

But then how could they suppose he would be so successful? If the
time should ever come when he recovered his property, they would be
prepared to make a determined effort to convince him that they had
always been his affectionate friends.

About this time Frank received another letter, which afforded him
greater satisfaction than the one from Newark.

This letter was from Colonel Vincent, who, it will be remembered,
had purchased Ajax when Mr. Manning persisted in selling him. It
was as follows:

"My Dear Frank: I learned incidentally from one of our
townsmen, who recently met you in New York, that you had
been very successful in obtaining employment, and that of an
honorable and responsible character. It relieved my mind, for,
knowing how hard it is for a boy to make his own way in a
large city, I feared that you might be suffering privation, or liv-

ing poorly. I hope, however, you would in that case have applied to me for such help as your father's old friend would have been glad to offer.

"Your stepfather has not been heard from directly. I learn, however, from some friends who have met him abroad that he is having trouble with Mark, who is proving difficult to manage, and has contracted some dangerous tastes. Mr. Manning was obliged to shorten his trip on account of these unfortunate tendencies, and is even thinking of returning to the Cedars, where his son will be removed from temptation. To this, however, Mark will be likely to make strenuous opposition. He would find it dull to settle down here after having tasted the gaiety of Europe."

Here followed a little local gossip, which the writer thought might prove interesting to Frank, and the letter concluded with a cordial invitation to our hero to spend a few days with him, or a longer time, if he could be spared from his duties.

Frank was disposed to accept the invitation but his acceptance was postponed by an unusual service which he was called upon to render to Mr. Percival.

Chapter 36

MR. PERCIVAL'S PROPOSAL

One morning, after writing several letters for his employer, the young secretary asked Mr. Percival if he had any further commands.

The old gentleman answered thoughtfully:

"I have been thinking of asking you to do me an unusual service."

"I shall be very glad to serve you in any way, Mr. Percival," said Frank, promptly.

"I have no doubt of it. I have observed your willingness to undertake any duty, and, still more, your disposition to perform it thoroughly. In this particular case, however, I have been considering whether a boy of your age would be competent to do what I desire."

Frank was not self-distrustful, neither was he over-confident. He was naturally energetic and ambitious to distinguish himself, and not afraid to undertake any difficult task.

"Will you try me, Mr. Percival?" he said. "I will do my best to succeed."

"I am quite inclined to try you, Frank," replied Mr. Percival; "the more so because I know of no one else in whom I could confide. But I must give you an idea of what I have in view. It would require you to make a journey."

Frank listened to this gladly. To a boy of his age, who had seen but little of the world, a journey offered attractions.

"I should like to travel," he made haste to say.

"I have no doubt about that," said Mr. Percival, smiling. "At your age I am sure I should have been equally willing to see something of the world, though traveling involved at that time far more hardships than at present. Now, however, I like best to stay by the fireside, and should dread very much a journey to Minnesota."

"To Minnesota!" exclaimed Frank, with sparkling eyes.

He had not thought of a journey so extended.

"Yes; it would be necessary for you to go out to Minnesota. Ordinarily, a man can best look after his own affairs; but in the present instance, I believe that you could do better than myself. I don't mean this as a compliment, but a boy like you would not be suspected, and so could discover more than I, from whom facts would be studiously concealed. But, of course, you don't understand my meaning. I will explain, and then you can comprehend me."

Frank was all attention.

"You must know that I own a good deal of property in a certain township in Southern Minnesota. When a young man, I bought three hundred and twenty acres of land in the township of Jackson, obtaining it at a slight advance on Government rates.

"Some improvements had been made, and I was induced to visit the place. I found but three families in residence, but I saw also that the place had large natural advantages, water-power especially, and presented an unusually favorable site for a village. I had considerable means, and started the village by erecting a dozen houses, a store, sawmill, grist mill, and so on.

"This formed a nucleus, and soon quite a village sprang up. The sawmill and gristmill proved profitable, all my houses were tenanted, and I erected more, securing also additional land. In course of time I was induced to sell some of my houses, but I still own two stores, a dozen houses, the saw and gristmills, besides two outlying farms.

"Living so far away, I could not attend personally to the business connected with my investment, and was compelled to appoint an agent. Up to four years ago, I was fortunate enough to possess the services of a capable and trustworthy man, named Sampson. He died

after a few weeks' illness, and I was compelled to look out for a successor.

"Now, I had a distant cousin, who had never succeeded very well
in life, and was at that time seeking for employment of some kind. He
heard of the vacancy, and importuned me to appoint him as my agent
in Jackson. I had no reason to doubt his honesty, though his repeated
failures might well have led me to suspect his capacity. I was weak
enough, as I now consider it, to yield to his importunities and give
him the post he sought.

"The result was that during the first year of his incumbency the
amount turned over to me was only three-fourths as much as in the last
year of his predecessor. The second year there was a further falling
off. The same happened the third year, until at the present time my
rents amount to less than half what they were during Mr. Sampson's
agency.

"Of course my suspicions that my cousin was at least inefficient
were aroused long ago. I have repeatedly asked an explanation of the
diminished revenues, and plenty of excuses have been made, but they
do not seem to me satisfactory.

"Moreover, I have heard a rumor that Mr. Fairfield is intemperate
in his habits, and I have reason to believe that the story is correct. I
have made up my mind that something must be done. A regard for
my own interests requires that if my agent is unfaithful he should be
displaced, and I wish to find out from some reliable source the true
state of the case.

"Now I will tell you what I have in view. I propose to send you out
to Jackson to investigate and report to me your impressions of the
manner in which Mr. Fairfield discharges his duties, and whether you
think a change should be made in the agency."

Frank listened to Mr. Percival with a flushed face, and a feeling of
gratification and pride that he should be thought of in connection with
such a responsible duty.

"I am very much obliged to you, Mr. Percival," he said, "for considering me in this connection. You may feel that I am presumptuous for
thinking I have any chance of successfully accomplishing what you
desire, but if you are willing to trust me, I am willing to undertake it,
and by following your instructions closely, and doing my best, I feel
convinced that I can succeed. "

"I am willing to trust you, Frank," said Mr. Percival. "You are a
boy, to be sure, but you have unusually good judgment, and I know
you will be faithful to my interests. I understand, then, that you are
willing to go out as my accredited representative?"

"Yes, sir. When do you want me to start?"

"As soon as you can get ready."

"I will start to-morrow, if you desire it, sir."

"Let it be to-morrow, then. We will now discuss some of the details connected with the mission."

After receiving certain instructions from Mr. Percival in regard to the manner of carrying on his inquiries, Frank said:

"There is one thing I have thought of, Mr. Percival, that may interfere with my success."

"What is it, Frank? I shall be glad to receive any suggestion from you."

"I have been thinking, sir, that it may excite surprise that I should come to Jackson, and remain there without any apparent motive. Perhaps Mr. Fairfield might suspect that I came from you."

"I hardly think so, Frank. He would not suppose that I would select so young a messenger. Still, it will be well to think of some pretext for your stay. Can you help me?"

"I might fit myself out as an agent, or peddler, or something of the kind. It would not only give me an excuse for my journey, but enable me to call from house to house and pick up information about Mr. Fairfield."

"A capital idea, Frank. I see that you are better fitted for the task than I supposed. I give you authority to fit yourself out in any way you choose. I shall have to leave a great deal to your own judgment."

"Then, sir, I think I might lay in a stock of stationery, pens and articles of that nature. Probably this is so common that I would be thought to be nothing more than I seemed."

"That strikes me rather favorably, Frank."

"I could fit myself out in the city, and take the articles on with me in an extra valise."

"Let me suggest an amendment to your plan," said Mr. Percival. "Wait till you get to Chicago, and lay in your stock there. The advantage of that arrangement will be that you will be saved the care of your merchandise up to that point, and, as you may be asked where you obtained your stock, it will create less surprise if you mention Chicago than New York. It would be considered hardly worth while for a New York boy to go so far on such a business trip."

This seemed to Frank an excellent suggestion, and he instantly adopted it.

He at once set about preparing for his Western trip.

He bought a ready-made suit of blue cloth, not unlike that worn by the district telegraph boys of to-day, which he judged would look more suitable than his ordinary attire for the character he was about to assume of a traveling peddler.

The next day Frank started on his long journey.

He carried with him a supply of money provided by Mr. Percival, and he was authorized to draw for more if he should require it.

He divided this money into two portions, keeping a small sum in his pocketbook, but the greater part in an inside vest pocket, where it would not be likely to be looked for by pickpockets.

He bought a through ticket to the railroad point nearest Jackson, and then, bidding good-bye to Mr. Percival and his family, started on his trip.

Chapter 37

FRANK REACHES JACKSON

It was four o'clock in the afternoon when Frank Courtney left the cars and set foot on the platform before the station at Prescott, five miles distant from the town of Jackson, in Southern Minnesota.

He looked about him, but could see no village.

Prescott was a stopping-place for the cars, but there was no settlement of any account there, as he afterward found.

He had supposed he would find a stage in waiting to convey him to Jackson, but it was clear that the business was not large enough to warrant such a conveyance.

Looking about him, Frank saw a farm-wagon, the driver of which had evidently come to receive some freight which had arrived by rail.

Approaching the driver, who seemed—though roughly dressed—to be an intelligent man, Frank inquired:

"How far is Jackson from here, sir?"

"Five miles," was the answer.

"Is there any stage running there from this station?"

"Oh, no! If there were, it wouldn't average two passengers a day."

"Then I suppose I must walk," said Frank, looking rather doubtfully at the heavy valises which constituted his baggage.

"Then you are going to Jackson?"

"Yes, sir."

"I come from Jackson myself, and in fifteen minutes shall start on my way back. You may ride with me and welcome."

"Thank you, sir!" replied our hero, quite relieved. "I hope you will allow me to pay you as much as I should have to pay in a stage."

"No, no, my lad," said the farmer, heartily. "The horse can draw you as well as not, and I shall be glad to have your company."

"Thank you, sir!"

"Just climb up here, then. I'll take your baggage and put it on the wagon behind."

When the farmer had loaded up, he started the team. Then, finding himself at leisure, he proceeded to satisfy his curiosity by cross-examining his young passenger.

"Do you come from the East?" he asked.

"I am last from Chicago," answered Frank, cautiously.

"I suppose you've got some friends in Jackson?" ventured the farmer, interrogatively.

Frank smiled.

"You are the only man living in Jackson that I ever met," he said.

"Indeed!" said the farmer, puzzled. "Are you calculating to make a long stay in our village?" he asked, again, after a minute's pause.

"That depends on business," responded the young traveler.

"Are you in business?"

"I have a stock of stationery which I shall offer for sale in Jackson."

"I am afraid you'll find it rather a poor market. If that's all you have to depend upon, I am very much afraid you'll get discouraged."

"I am also agent for an illustrated book," said Frank. "I may be able to dispose of a few."

"Perhaps so," answered the farmer, dubiously. "But our people haven't much money to spend on articles of luxury, and books are a luxury with us."

"I always heard that Jackson was a flourishing place," said Frank, who felt that now was his time to obtain a little information.

"It ought to be," replied the farmer; "but there's one thing prevents."

"What is that?"

"A good deal of our village is owned by a New York man, to whom we have to pay rent. He has a rascally agent—a Mr. Fairfield—who grinds us down by his exactions, and does what he can to keep us in debt."

"Has he always been agent?"

"No. Before he came there was an excellent man—a Mr. Sampson—who treated us fairly, contented himself with exacting rents which we could pay, and if a man were unlucky, would wait a reasonable time for him to pay. Then we got along comfortably. But he died, and this man was sent out in his place. Then commenced a new state of things. He immediately raised the rents, demanded that they should be paid on the day they were due, and made himself harsh and tyrannical."

"Do you think the man who employs him knows how he is conducting his agency?"

"No; there is no one to tell him. I suppose Mr. Fairfield sends him a smooth story, and he believes it. I am afraid we can hope for no relief."

"What would he say," thought Frank, "if he knew I were a messenger from Mr. Percival?"

"What sort of a man is this Mr. Fairfield in private life?" he asked.

"He lives very extravagantly," was the not unexpected reply. "Frequently he appears on the street under the influence of liquor. He spends a good deal of money, lives in a large house, and his wife dresses expensively. He must get a much larger salary than Mr. Sampson did, or he could not spend money as he does."

Though Frank had not much business experience, he could not help coming to the conclusion that Mr. Fairfield was acting dishonestly. He put together the two circumstances that this new agent had increased the rents, and yet that he returned to Mr. Percival only about half as much as his predecessor had done. Clearly, he must retain in his own hands much more than he had a right to do.

"I shall have to report unfavorably on this man," he thought.

One point must be considered—where he was to find a boarding-place on his arrival in Jackson.

"Is there a hotel in Jackson?" he asked.

"There is a small one, but it's an untidy place," answered the farmer. "And besides is used as a lounging place for many of the men of the neighborhood, and Mr. Fairfield, our agent, is one of the most constant patrons."

"I don't think I should like to stop there," said Frank. "Isn't there any private family where I can get board for a week or two?"

"If you don't object to plain fare," said the farmer, "I might agree to board you myself."

This was precisely what Frank wanted, and he replied that nothing would suit him better.

"We live humbly," continued Mr. Hamlin—for this, Frank learned, was his driver's name—"but we will try to make you comfortable."

"I feel sure of that, sir, and I am much obliged to you for receiving me."

"As to terms, you can pay whatever you can afford. My wife and children will be glad to see you. It's pretty quiet out here, and it breaks the monotony to meet any person from the East."

"How long have you lived in Jackson, Mr. Hamlin?"

"About eight years. I was not brought up as a farmer, but became one from necessity. I was a bookkeeper in Chicago for a good many years, until I found the confinement and close work were injuring my health. Then I came here and set up as a farmer. I got along pretty well, at first; at any rate, I made a living for my family; but when Mr. Fairfield became agent, he raised my rent, and, in other ways, made it hard for me. Now I have a hard struggle."

"I thought you were not always a farmer," said Frank.

"What made you think so?"

"You don't talk like a farmer. You have the appearance of a man who has lived in cities."

"Seems to me you are a close observer, for a boy of your years," said Mr. Hamlin, shrewdly.

Frank smiled.

"I should be glad if your compliment were deserved," he answered, and then added, pointedly, "it's a pity you were not agent, instead of Mr. Fairfield."

"I wish I were," said Hamlin. "I believe I should make a good one, though I might not turn over as much money to my employer. I should, first of all, lower the rents and make it as easy for the tenants as I could in justice to my New York principal."

"Do you know how much Mr. Fairfield receives—how large a salary, I mean?"

"I know what Mr. Sampson got—twelve hundred dollars a year; but Mr. Fairfield lives at the rate of more than twice that sum, if I can judge from appearances."

"I suppose you would be contented with the salary which Mr. Sampson received?"

"Contented! I should feel like a rich man. It would not interfere with my carrying on my farm, and I should be able to make something from that. Why, it is as much as I received as a bookkeeper, and here the expenses of living are small, compared with what there were in Chicago. I could save money and educate my children, as I cannot do now. I have a boy who wants a classical education, but of course there are no schools here which can offer such advantages and I am too poor to send him away from home. I suppose I shall have to bring him up as a farmer, though it is a great pity, for he is not fitted for it."

Mr. Hamlin sighed, but Frank felt in unusually good spirits. He saw his way clear already, not only to recommend Mr. Fairfield's displacement, but to urge Mr. Hamlin's appointment in his stead; that is, if his favorable impressions were confirmed on further acquaintance.

"It seems to me," said Mr. Hamlin, changing the subject, "you might find something better to do than to peddle stationery."

"I don't mean to follow the business long," replied Frank.

"It can't pay you much."

"I am not wholly dependent upon it. There is one advantage about it. It enables me to travel about and pay my expenses, and you know traveling is agreeable to a boy of my age."

"That is true. Well, your expenses won't amount to much while you are in Jackson. I shall only charge you just enough to cover expenses— say three dollars a week."

Frank was about to insist on paying a larger sum, but it occurred to him that he must keep up appearances, and he therefore only thanked his kind acquaintance.

By this time they had entered the village of Jackson.

"There's Mr. Fairfield now!" said Mr. Hamlin, pointing with his whip to a rather tall, stout man, with a red nose and inflamed countenance, who was sauntering along the sidewalk.

Frank carefully scrutinized the agent, and mentally decided that such a man was unfit for the responsible position he held.

Mr. Hamlin stopped his horse a quarter of a mile from the village in front of a plain farmhouse.

An intelligent-looking boy, of perhaps fifteen, approached and greeted his father, not without a glance of surprise and curiosity at Frank.

"You may unharness the horse, Dick," said Mr. Hamlin. "When you come back, I will introduce you to a boy friend who will stay with us awhile."

Dick obeyed, and Frank followed his host into the house.

Here he was introduced to Mrs. Hamlin, a motherly looking woman, and Annie and Grace, younger sisters of Dick.

"I am glad to see you," said Mrs. Hamlin, to our hero, after a brief explanation from her husband. "We will try to make you comfortable."

"Thank you!" said Frank. "I am sure I shall feel at home."

The house was better furnished than might have been anticipated. When Mr. Hamlin left Chicago, he had some money saved up, and he furnished his house in a comfortable manner.

It was not, however, the furniture that attracted Frank's attention so much as the books, papers and pictures that gave the rooms a homelike appearance.

"I shall be much better off here than I would have been at the hotel," he thought. "This seems like a home."

"I see," said Mr. Hamlin, "that you are surprised to see so many books and pictures. I admit that my house does not look like the house of a poor man, who has to struggle for the mere necessaries of life. But books and periodicals we have always classed among the necessities, and I am sure we would all rather limit ourselves to dry bread for two out of the three meals than to give up this food for the mind."

"I think you are a very sensible man, Mr. Hamlin," said Frank. "I couldn't get along without something to read."

"Not in this out-of-the-way place, at any rate," replied Mr. Hamlin. "Nothing can be more dismal than the homes of some of my neighbors, who spend as much, or more, than I do every year. Yet, they consider me extravagant because I buy books and subscribe for periodicals."

By this time, Dick came in from the barn.

"Dick," said his father, "this is Frank Courtney, who comes from Chicago on a business errand. He is a traveling merchant—"

"In other words, a peddler," said Frank with a smile, "ready to give the good people in Jackson a chance to buy stationery at reasonable prices."

"He will board with us while he is canvassing the neighborhood, and I expect you and he will become great friends."

"I think we shall," agreed Frank.

Dick was a little shy, but a few minutes set him quite at his ease with his new acquaintance.

After supper, Frank said:

"Dick, if you are at leisure, I wish you would take a walk about the village with me. I want to see how it looks."

"All right," assented Dick.

Chapter 38

MR. FAIRFIELD THE AGENT

When the two left the house, the country boy began to ask questions.

"How do you like your business?" he asked.

"Not very well," answered Frank. "I do not think I shall stay in it very long."

"Do you sell enough to make your expenses?"

"No; but I am not wholly dependent on my sales. I have a little income—a hundred dollars a year—paid me by my stepfather."

"I wish I had as much. It seems a good deal to me."

"It doesn't go very far. What are you intending to be, Dick?"

"I suppose I shall have to be a farmer, though I don't like it."

"What would you like to be?"

"I should like to get an education," said Dick, his eyes lighting up. "I should like to study Latin and Greek, and go to college. Then I could be a teacher or a lawyer. But there is no chance of that," he added, his voice falling.

"Don't be too sure of that, Dick," said Frank, hopefully. "Something may turn up in your favor."

"Nothing ever does turn up in Jackson," said the boy, in a tone of discouragement. "Father is a poor man, and has hard work to get along. He can give me no help."

"Isn't the farm productive?"

"There is no trouble about that, but he has to pay too high a rent. It's all the fault of Fairfield."

"The agent?"

"Yes."

"Your father was telling me about him. Now, if your father were in his place, I suppose he could give you the advantages you wish."

"Oh, yes! There would be no trouble then. I am sure he would make a better and more popular agent than Mr. Fairfield; but there is no use thinking about that."

"I myself expected to go to college," said Frank. "In fact, I have studied Latin and Greek, and in less than a year I could be ready to enter."

"Why don't you?" questioned Dick.

"You forget that I am a poor peddler."

"Then how were you able to get so good an education?" asked Dick, in surprise.

"Because I was once better off than I am now. The fact is, Dick," he added, "I have seen better days. But when I was reduced to poverty, I gave up hopes of a college education and became what I am."

"Wasn't it hard?"

"Not so much as you might suppose. My home was not happy. I have a stepfather and stepbrother, neither of whom I like. In fact, there is no love lost between us. I was not obliged to leave home, but under the circumstances I preferred to."

"Where are your stepfather and your stepbrother now?"

"They are traveling in Europe."

"While you are working hard for a living! That does not seem to be just."

"We must make the best of the circumstances, Dick. Whose is that large house on the left?"

"That belongs to Mr. Fairfield."

"He seems to live nicely."

"Yes, he has improved and enlarged the house a good deal since he moved into it—at Mr. Percival's expense, no doubt."

"He seems to have pretty much his own way here," said Frank.

"Yes. Mr. Percival never comes to Jackson, and I suppose he believes all that the agent tells him."

"He may be found out some time."

"I wish he might. It would be a great blessing to Jackson if he were removed and a good man were put in his place."

"That may happen some day."

"Not very likely, I am afraid."

At this moment Mr. Fairfield himself came out of his front gate.

"Hello, Hamlin!" he said, roughly, to Dick. "Is your father at home?"

"Yes, sir."

"I have something to say to him. I think I will call round."

"You will find him at home, sir."

"Dick," said Frank, when the agent had passed on, "do you mind going back? What you tell me makes me rather curious about Mr. Fairfield. At your house I may get a chance to see something of him."

"Let us go back, then," said Dick; "but I don't think, Frank, that you will care much about keeping up the acquaintance."

"Perhaps not; but I shall gratify my curiosity."

The two boys turned and followed the agent closely. They reached the house about five minutes after Mr. Fairfield.

They found Mr. Fairfield already seated in the most comfortable chair in the sitting-room.

He looked inquiringly at Frank when he entered with Dick.

"Who is that boy, Hamlin?" asked the agent. "Nephew of yours?"

"No, sir. It is a young man who has come to Jackson on business."

"What kind of business?"

"I sell stationery," Frank answered for himself.

"Oh, a peddler!" said the agent, contemptuously.

"Many of our most successful men began in that way," said Mr. Hamlin, fearing lest Frank's feelings might be hurt.

"I never encourage peddlers myself," said Mr. Fairfield, pompously.

"Then I suppose it will be of no use for me to call at your door," said Frank, who, in place of being mortified, was amused by the agent's arrogance.

"I should say not, unless your back is proof against a broomstick. I tell my servant to treat all who call in that way."

"I won't put her to the trouble of using it," said Frank, disgusted at the man's ill-manners.

"That's where you are wise—yes, wise and prudent—young man."

Mr. Fairfield was far from supposing that the boy whom he considered so insignificant was sitting in judgment upon him, and even held his fate in his hands. The idea would have seemed to him the wildest absurdity. Had he really believed it, however, he would have been as obsequious as he was insolent.

"And now, Hamlin," continued the agent, "I may as well come to business."

"To business!" repeated the farmer, rather surprised, for there was no rent due for a month to come.

"Yes, to business. I came to give you notice that after the next payment I shall feel obliged to raise your rent."

"Raise my rent!" exclaimed the farmer, in genuine dismay. "I am already paying a much higher rent than I paid to your predecessor."

"Can't help it. Old Sampson was a slow-going old fogy. He didn't do his duty by his employer. When I came in, I turned over a new leaf."

"You certainly did," the farmer could not help saying bitterly.

"What do you mean by that, eh?" asked the agent, suspiciously.

"I mean to agree with you, sir."

"I suppose you liked old Sampson better than you do me?"

"I got along better in his time."

"No doubt. He was a great deal too easy with you. Didn't do his duty, sir. Wasn't sharp enough. That's all."

"You cannot be in earnest in raising my rent, Mr. Fairfield," said the farmer, uneasily.

"I certainly am."

"I can hardly get along as it is. I find it hard to make both ends meet."

"Of course I expected to hear you say that, but it's all bosh," replied the agent. "Why, I need only to look around me to see signs of luxury—books, magazines, pictures, nice furniture. Come, Hamlin, that won't do. There's no one in Jackson, except myself, that can show such a sitting-room as this."

"If you allude to the pictures and furniture, I brought them with me. As to the papers and books, we economize in every other direction in order to afford these. Living out of the world, as we do, we can't get along very well without them."

"Just so; only you are not living like the poor man you pretend to be."

"I can't live at all if you increase my rent, which is already larger than I can afford to pay, Mr. Fairfield."

"Oh, I won't raise it much—say ten dollars a quarter."

"I can't pay it."

"Then I must find a tenant who can and will," said the agent, emphatically.

"In other words, you mean to turn me out, Mr. Fairfield?"

"Only if you won't pay your rent. That is fair, is it not?"

"The rent is very unfair. You are a very hard man, Mr. Fairfield."

"You forget, Hamlin, that I am only an agent. Mr. Percival writes me that he doesn't receive enough income from his property out here. Well, of course, I have to obey his orders. The only way to get a larger increase is to raise the rents."

"Is there to be a general raise, Mr. Fairfield?"

"Yes. You are the first one I've come to, but I shall see the rest."

"Then I am sorry for my neighbors. They are no better able to pay a larger rent than I am."

"Oh, they'll agree to it when they find they have to," said Fairfield, carelessly.

"I am sure Mr. Percival can't understand the true state of the case, or the circumstances of his tenants. If you give me his address, I will take the liberty of writing to him and respectfully remonstrate against any increase?"

Mr. Fairfield looked uneasy.

This appeal would not at all suit him. Yet how could he object without leading to the suspicion that he was acting in this matter wholly on his own responsibility, and not by the express orders of his principal? How could he refuse to furnish Mr. Percival's address?

A middle course occurred to him.

"You may write your appeal, if you like, Hamlin," he said, "and hand it to me. I will forward it; though I don't believe it will do any good. The fact is that Mr. Percival has made up his mind to have more income from his property in Jackson."

"He never troubled us when Mr. Sampson was agent, though we paid smaller rents than we do now."

"Very likely; but he was better off then. He has been losing money by bad investments lately, and this leads him to put on the screws here."

There was no truth in this story, as may readily be believed. It was the invention of the moment, and struck Mr. Fairfield as very clever. For truth he cared little or nothing, provided he could further his own designs.

The agent had said what he came to say, and took his leave.

Mr. Hamlin was depressed by his visit.

"I don't see what I am to do," he said to his wife. "It is only by the greatest effort that I can pay my present rent, and to pay forty dollars a year more is simply impossible."

"Won't Mr. Fairfield relent?" asked his wife.

"Not he. He will exact the last dollar of his demand."

"Mr. Hamlin," said Frank, "don't be discouraged. Better times may be nearer than you suppose."

"I wish I could think so."

"At any rate, hope for the best."

"I will, if I can."

That evening Frank wrote a long letter to Mr. Percival, communicating the information he had already obtained as to the character and methods of his agent.

He had been in Jackson only a few hours, but he felt that he had already discovered quite enough to condemn the unfaithful steward.

This letter he mailed the very first thing on the following morning, and then quietly awaited an answer. It might be a week before he could receive a reply to his letter.

Chapter 39

FRANK RECEIVES A LETTER FROM MR. PERCIVAL

While Frank was waiting for an answer to his letter, he devoted a part of his time daily to the business which was supposed to be his only reason for remaining in Jackson.

I am bound to say that as regards this business his trip might be pronounced a failure. There was little ready money in Jackson. Many of the people were tenants of Mr. Percival, and found it difficult to pay the excessive rents demanded by his agent. Of course, they had no money to spare for extras. Even if they had been better off, there was little demand for stationery in the village. The people were chiefly farmers, and did not indulge in much correspondence.

When Frank returned to his boarding-place on the afternoon of the first day, Mr. Hamlin asked him, not without solicitude, with what luck he had met.

"I have sold twenty-five cents' worth of note-paper," replied Frank, with a smile.

Mr. Hamlin looked troubled.

"At how many places did you call?" he inquired.

"About a dozen."

"I am afraid you will get discouraged."

"I am not easily discouraged, Mr. Hamlin."

"If you don't do better, you won't begin to pay expenses."

"That is true."

"But perhaps you may do better to-morrow."

"I hope so."

The next day Frank succeeded in making sales to the amount of thirty-two cents, and so reported to his host.

"I am afraid you won't care to remain long in Jackson," said the farmer, with whom, as well as his family, our hero had already become a favorite.

"I think I shall remain a fortnight," answered Frank, "whatever luck I have. I have done much better for some time past, and can afford to give myself a little rest."

"I am glad you don't feel troubled by your poor success, Frank."

"You make me feel so much at home," said Frank, "that I don't care much for a short time how my business prospers."

"I wish you could find something in Jackson that would induce you to remain here permanently, and make your home with us. I would charge you only the bare cost of board."

"Thank you very much, Mr. Hamlin. I should enjoy being with you, but I don't believe I shall find any opening here. Besides, I like a more stirring life."

"No doubt—no doubt! Boys like a lively place. Well, I am glad you feel independent of your business."

"For a short time. I am afraid it wouldn't do for me to earn so little for any length of time."

Frank enjoyed the society of Dick Hamlin. Together they went fishing and hunting, and a mutual liking sprang up between them.

"I wish you were going to stay longer, Frank," said Dick. "I shall feel very lonely when you are gone."

"We may meet again under different circumstances," said Frank. "While I am here, we will enjoy ourselves as well as we can."

So the days passed, and at length a letter came from Mr. Percival. I append the most important passages:

"Your report is clear, and I have perfect confidence in your statement. Mr. Fairfield has abused my confidence and oppressed my tenants, and I shall dismiss him. I am glad you have found in Jackson a man who is capable of succeeding him. Solely upon your recommendation, I shall appoint Mr. Hamlin my resident agent and representative for the term of six months. Should he acquit himself to my satisfaction, he will be continued in the position. I am prepared to offer him one hundred dollars a month, if that will content him.

"Upon receipt of this letter, and the accompanying legal authority, you may call upon Mr. Fairfield and require him to transfer his office, and the papers and accounts connected with it, to Mr. Hamlin. I inclose a check for three hundred dollars, payable to your order, which you may make payable to him, in lieu of three months' notice, provided he immediately surrenders his office. Should he not, I shall dismiss him summarily, and proceed against him for the moneys he has misappropriated to his own use, and you may so inform him."

With this letter was a letter to Mr. Fairfield, of the same purport, and a paper appointing Mr. Hamlin agent.

When this letter was received, Frank was overjoyed, knowing how much pleasure he was about to give his new friends.

With this appointment and salary, Mr. Hamlin would consider himself a rich man, and Dick's hope for a liberal education might be realized.

The letter came just before supper, and, at the close of the evening meal, Frank determined to inform his friends of their good fortune.

"Mr. Hamlin," said he, "I have some good news for you."

"Indeed!" said the farmer surprised.

"Your rent will not be increased."

"But how do you know this? Has Mr. Fairfield told you so?"

"No. I have a question to ask. Would you be willing to take Mr. Fairfield's place at a hundred dollars a month?"

"Willing? I should be delighted to do so. But why do you say this?"

"Because," said Frank, quietly, "I am authorized to offer it to you at that salary."

The whole family looked at Frank in bewildered surprise. It occurred to them that he might have become crazy.

"You!" exclaimed the farmer. "What can you have to do with the agency?"

"I came to Jackson," explained Frank, briefly, "at the request of Mr. Percival, and as his representative. You are surprised that he should select a young peddler, but I came here in that capacity only to avoid suspicion. I am Mr. Percival's private secretary when in New York, and he had sufficient confidence in me to send me here to make an examination and report. I have recommended your appointment as agent, and he authorized me to offer it to you."

"I can hardly believe my ears," said the farmer, amazement struggling with joy.

"Let me read you Mr. Percival's letter, just received," said Frank. "That will confirm my statements."

The whole family listened eagerly, while Frank read the letter already referred to. Of course this removed all doubt.

Mr. Hamlin was much moved.

He grasped Frank's hand, and said, fervently:

"I feel that I owe all this good fortune to you, my dear young friend. You will be able to feel that you have given me a new life, and made a whole family happy."

"I am glad on your account," said Frank; "but I must say, candidly, that if I had not believed you to be thoroughly competent, I would not have recommended you for this post."

"But would not Mr. Percival have given it to you? Have you not sacrificed your own interests to mine?"

Frank shook his head.

"I am but a boy," he said—"quite too young for such duties. Besides, I prefer to stay in New York. You are the man to discharge them to the satisfaction both of Mr. Percival and your townsmen."

Dick, who was an impulsive boy, put his arm affectionately around Frank's neck.

"Dear Frank," he said, "I liked you before; now you have won my everlasting gratitude."

"I accept your friendship, Dick, and I return it fully," said Frank, warmly. "And now, Mr. Hamlin, will you accompany me to the house of Mr. Fairfield? I wish to finish my mission, and go back to New York."

"I am sorry for the poor man," said the farmer. "I suppose he doesn't deserve it, but he has my sympathy."

The two set out for the house of the agent.

Chapter 40

THE AGENT IS NOTIFIED

It was still early in the evening when Frank and Mr. Hamlin reached the house of the agent. Had they come five minutes later, they would have found him absent. Usually, soon after supper, he made his way to the hotel, where he spent his time and money in a very unprofitable way.

The agent was surprised when his two visitors made their appearance.

"What brings you here, Hamlin?" he asked, with scant ceremony.

"I come on a little matter of business," replied Mr. Hamlin, gravely.

Mr. Fairfield concluded that the farmer had come to make an appeal to have his rent continued at the old rates, and answered, impatiently:

"I don't think it will be of much use. My mind is made up. Have you come on business, also?" he asked, turning to Frank, with a sneer.

"Yes, sir," was the quick response.

"That will be of no use, either," said the agent. "I am not in want of stationery, and, if I were, I should not buy of a peddler."

"I have not come here to sell stationery, Mr. Fairfield."

"Then, may I take the liberty of asking what is your business here?"

"I come on the same business as Mr. Hamlin," said Frank, who preferred that his companion should introduce the subject.

"I have no time for trifling," said Mr. Fairfield, angrily. "I am going out and can only spare you five minutes."

"Mr. Fairfield, I would advise you not to go out till you have heard what I have to say," interposed the farmer in a meaning tone.

"I certainly shall. You can call some other time."

"Another time will not do."

"Look here, sir! Do you know to whom you are talking? How dare you use such a tone to Mr. Percival's representative?"

"I suppose you don't always expect to be Mr. Percival's representative?"

"I suppose I shall die some time, if that's what you mean; but I am not dead yet, as you will find. To pay for your impertinence, I shall increase your rent more than I intended. I'll drive you out of town— that's what I'll do."

This was accompanied by an angry stamp of the foot, which, however, did not frighten Mr. Hamlin much.

"I shall not pay a dollar more rent, nor shall I leave the farm I occupy," declared Mr. Hamlin, whose patience was exhausted by the rough insolence of the man before him.

"So you defy me, do you?" demanded Fairfield, furiously.

"I shall resist your injustice, sir, or rather I would do so if you were able to carry out your threat. Luckily you have not the power."

"Have not the power? You will see if I have not the power!" roared the angry agent. "I give you notice that at the end of the quarter you must go, at any rate. After your insolence, I won't let you stay on any terms. I wouldn't let you stay if you would pay double the rent. Do you hear me, sir?"

"Yes, I hear you."

Mr. Fairfield looked at the farmer in surprise. The latter seemed perfectly calm and undisturbed by his threat, though it was of the most serious nature. He had expected to see him humbled, and to hear him entreat a reversal of the sentence; but his tenant was thoroughly self-possessed, and appeared to care nothing for the agent's threats.

"You need not expect that I will change my mind," he added. "Out of Jackson you must go. I know there is no other farm which you can rent, and while I am Mr. Percival's agent, you need expect no favors from me."

"I don't expect any while you are Mr. Percival's agent," said Mr. Hamlin.

There was something in the farmer's tone that arrested the agent's attention and excited his curiosity, though it did not awaken his alarm, and he could not help saying:

"Then what do you expect? Do you think I am going to die?"

"I don't expect that you will die or resign, Mr. Fairfield. You may be removed."

"Have you been writing to Mr. Percival?" asked Fairfield, in mingled anger and apprehension.

"No, sir; I have not communicated with him in any way. You would not give me his address."

"Of course I would not," said the agent, feeling relieved. "It would be mere impertinence for you to write to him."

"Fortunately there is no immediate occasion for me to do so, as he has sent a representative here to investigate your official conduct."

"A representative!" exclaimed Fairfield, now thoroughly startled. "Where is he? I have not seen him."

"He is present," said Mr. Hamlin, indicating Frank.

The agent broke into a scornful laugh.

"What! the peddler?" he ejaculated. "You are either crazy, or think I am!"

"Neither, sir" said Frank, thinking it was time to speak. "What Mr. Hamlin says is perfectly true."

"Do you mean to tell me," said the agent, incredulously, "that Mr. Percival would send out a boy—a mere baby—to look after his affairs, and sit in judgment upon me?"

"Perhaps Mr. Percival had too much confidence in me," replied Frank, "but it is so."

"You? Why, you are a peddler!"

"Only in appearance, Mr. Fairfield. I assumed that business in order not to attract attention or excite suspicion. I am really Mr. Percival's private secretary, as I can prove to your satisfaction."

The agent regarded our hero with amazement and alarm.

"Is this true?" he asked, in a changed voice.

"Yes, sir; quite true."

"Have you written to Mr. Percival?"

"Yes, sir; and this afternoon I received a letter from him."

"What did he write?" asked Fairfield, in a husky voice; for he was convinced now that Frank spoke the truth.

"He removes you, inclosing a check of three hundred dollars in place of notice, and appoints Mr. Hamlin in your place."

"This is a hoax! You are playing a joke upon me," said Fairfield, in dismay.

"Will you read this letter, sir?"

The agent took it mechanically and read it. Badly as he had mismanaged his office, Frank could not help pitying him.

"I should like a few words with you alone," he said.

Frank followed him into an adjoining room.

"Young man," began the agent, "I want you to use your influence with Mr. Percival to keep me in office. I may have made some mistakes, but I will reform. I won't raise Hamlin's rent. In fact, I will lower it to the figure he paid in old Sampson's time. As for you, I will make it worth your while."

Frank understood very well that a bribe was meant, and answered firmly:

"It is impossible, Mr. Fairfield."

"Then I will resist," said the agent, desperately. "What are you going to do about it?"

"You will forfeit the check I am authorized to offer you, and Mr. Percival will prosecute you for keeping back money that belongs to him."

It was enough. Fairfield knew that his management would not stand investigation, and he yielded with a bad grace.

Mr. Hamlin, the next day, to the great joy of the villagers, made known his appointment.

Fairfield left town and drifted to California, where he became an adventurer, living in a miserable and precarious manner. Mr. Hamlin moved into his fine house, and Dick was sent to a classical school to prepare for college.

The day following Mr. Hamlin's appointment Frank started on his return to New York.

Chapter 41

AN IMPORTANT DISCOVERY

On his return to New York, Frank had no reason to be dissatisfied with his reception. From Mr. Percival to Freddie, all the family seemed delighted to see him.

"We are all glad to see you back, Frank," said his employer. "But you have justified my opinion of you by your success. Some of my friends ridiculed me for sending a boy on such an important mission, but I don't believe any of them would have succeeded any better than you, if as well."

"I am glad you are satisfied with me, sir," said Frank, very much gratified by the commendation of his employer.

"I feel that you have done a great service, and indeed I don't know whom I could have sent in your place. However, as I said, I am glad to see you back again. I have missed you about my letters, and have postponed answering some till my young secretary returned."

Frank resumed his regular employment, and three months passed without anything that needs to be recorded.

At the end of that time, Frank received an important letter from Colonel Vincent, which gave him much food for thought.

The letter was as follows:

"DEAR FRANK: For some time past I have been intending to write to you, but have delayed for no good reason. Now, however, I am led to write by a surprising discovery which has just

been made in your old home, which may be of material importance to you.

"When your stepfather went away, he requested me to have
an eye to the estate, and order whatever I might think necessary
to be done. I am not, as you know, a very cordial friend of Mr.
Manning's, but I have always regarded the property as of right
belonging to you—that is, since your mother's death—and so accepted the commission.

"A few days ago I went over the house and found that it was
quite dusty and in need of cleaning. I engaged a woman to do
the work, so, if any of you should return unexpectedly, you
would find the house fit to receive you. This was a very simple
matter, you will think, and scarcely needs mentioning. But, my
dear Frank, events of importance often hinge on trifles, and so
it has proved in the present instance.

"On the evening of the second day I received a call from Mrs.
Noonan, whom I had employed to clean the house. She had in
her hand a folded paper, which she gave to me.

" 'Here is something I found, sir, while I was washing the
paint,' she said.

"I opened it indifferently, but conceive of my amazement
when I found it to be your mother's will, properly signed,
sealed and witnessed.

"Of course it was not the will which Mr. Manning presented
for probate. This will gave Mr. Manning ten thousand dollars,
and the residue of the property to you, except a small amount
bestowed upon Richard Green, the coachman, and Deborah—
sums larger, by the way, than those mentioned in the will which
was read after your mother's death.

" 'Where did you find this, Mrs. Noonan?' I asked.

" 'Sure, sir, I was washing the paint, when, all at once, there
was a little door opened in the wall, and, inside a cupboard like,
I saw this paper. I thought it might be something you ought to
see, and so I brought it to you, sir.'

" 'And you did quite right, too, my good woman—quite right,'
I replied.

"If you were here, you would probably ask me what infer-
ence I draw from this discovery. I will not wait till I see you,
but answer the question at once.

"I firmly believe, then, that the will which has just been discovered was the only will which your mother made—that Mr.
Manning knew of its existence, and, being dissatisfied with it,
suppressed it by hiding it where it was found. It would have
been safer for him to destroy it, but that requires courage and
boldness, and these are qualities which Mr. Manning does not
possess.

"As to the will which was substituted in its place, my theory is that it was prepared at the instance of your stepfather by some tool of his. We must now try to discover how, or by what means, or through whose agency, this was done.

"I think you had better come up here next Saturday, and remain two or three days. This will give us a chance to confer together upon the matter."

Thus ended Colonel Vincent's letter.

Frank showed it to Mr. Percival, and readily obtained permission to take a few days' vacation.

"I hope you will get back the estate, Frank," said Mr. Percival, "though I don't know what I shall do without my secretary."

"That need not separate us, Mr. Percival," said our hero. "I have no home but this."

Chapter 42

JONAS BARTON

Frank started for his old home on Saturday afternoon. He would arrive in time for supper, at the house of his father's friend. The train was well filled, and he was obliged to share his seat with a shabbily-dressed young man, with whom a single glance showed him that he was not likely to sympathize.

The shabby suit did not repel him at all—he was too sensible for that; but there was a furtive look in the man's face, which seemed to indicate that he was not frank and straightforward, but had something to conceal.

Half the journey passed without a word between the two. Then his companion, glancing at Frank, opened a conversation by remarking that it was a fine day.

"Very," answered Frank, laconically.

"A pleasant day to travel."

"Yes."

"Do you go far?"

Frank mentioned his destination. His companion seemed to have his interest awakened.

"Do you know a Mr. Manning, living in your town?" he asked.

"He is my stepfather," replied Frank.

"Then you are Frank Courtney?" said his new acquaintance, quickly.

"I am."

"Pardon me, but I think your mother died recently!"

"Yes."

"And the property was left chiefly to Mr. Manning?"

"Yes."

"Of course, you were surprised, and very probably disappointed?"

"Excuse me," said Frank, coldly; "but I am not in the habit of discussing my affairs with strangers."

"Quite right, but I think you will find it to your interest to discuss them with me. Not in a public car, of course; but I have something of importance to communicate. Where can I have a private interview with you?"

It at once occurred to Frank that here was an opportunity, perhaps, to solve the mystery concerning the will. This man might know nothing about it; but, on the other hand, he might know everything. It would be foolish to repulse him.

"If you have anything important to tell me, I shall be glad to hear it," he said. "I am going to the house of my friend, Colonel Vincent, to pass a few days. Do you know where he lives?"

"Yes, I know."

"If you will call this evening, after supper, I shall be glad to see you."

"I will do so. I will be there at eight o'clock, sharp."

On arriving at his destination, Frank found the colonel's carriage waiting for him at the station.

Colonel Vincent was inside.

"Welcome, Frank!" he said, heartily grasping the hand of our young hero. "I am delighted to see you. You are looking well, and, bless me, how you have grown!"

"Thank you, Colonel Vincent. Do you expect me to return the compliment?"

"About having grown? No, Frank, I hope not. I am six feet one, and don't care to grow any taller. Well, what do you think of the news?"

"I have some for you, colonel;" and Frank mentioned what his new acquaintance had told him.

"The missing link!" exclaimed the colonel, excited. "Do you know what I think?"

"What?"

"That this man either forged the will which gives the property to your stepfather, or is cognizant of it!"

"I thought of that."

"I shall be impatient to see him."

At eight o'clock the man called and gave his name as Jonas Barton. Whether it was the right name might be a question; but this did not matter.

"I understand," said Colonel Vincent, "that you have some information to give us."

"I have; and that of a very important nature."

"Is it of a nature to restore to my young friend here his property, now in the possession of Mr. Manning?"

"If it were," said Jonas Barton, with a cunning glance of his left eye, "how much would it be worth?"

"I supposed it was for sale," replied the colonel, quietly. "What is your own idea?"

"I will take two thousand dollars."

"Suppose we say one thousand?"

"It is not enough."

"Were you aware that the genuine will had been found?" asked the colonel, composedly.

Jonas Barton started.

"I thought Mr. Manning destroyed it," he said, hastily.

"No; he concealed it."

"Is this true?"

"Yes. You see that a part of your information has been forestalled."

"He was crazy, then, and still more crazy to refuse my last demand for money. I accept your offer of a thousand dollars, and will tell all."

"Go on."

"I wrote the will which Mr. Manning presented for probate. It was copied in part from the genuine will."

"Good! And you betray him because he will not pay what you consider the service worth?"

"Yes, sir."

Jonas Barton here gave a full account of Mr. Manning, whom he had formerly known in New York, how he had sought him out and proposed to him a job for which he was willing to pay five hundred dollars. Barton was not scrupulous, and readily agreed to do the work. He was very skilful with the pen, and did his work so well that all were deceived.

"You will be willing to swear to this in court?"

"Yes, sir, if you will guarantee the sum you proposed."

"I will. I shall wish you to find a boarding place in the village, and remain here for the present, so as to be ready whenever needed. I will be responsible for your board."

As Jonas Barton was leaving the house, one of the servants came in with important news, in which Frank was strongly interested.

Chapter 43

CONCLUSION

The news was that Mr. Manning and Mark had just arrived at the Cedars. They had come by the last evening train. Why they had come back so unexpectedly no one knew, but the servant had heard that Mark was in poor health. This was true.

Mark, in Europe, had proved uncontrollable. He had given way to his natural love of extravagance, had kept late hours, and had seriously injured his constitution. In consequence, he had contracted a fever, which alarmed his father and induced him to take the first steamer home.

"We won't call upon your stepfather this evening, Frank," said Colonel Vincent; "But early Monday morning we will bring matters to a crisis."

Mr. Manning did not hear of Frank's presence in the village. He was fatigued with his rapid travel and kept at home. Besides, Mark was prostrated by his journey and didn't wish to be left alone.

It was, therefore, a surprise to Mr. Manning when on Monday morning, Colonel Vincent was ushered into his presence, accompanied by Frank.

"Really, colonel," he said, recovering his composure, "you are very kind to call so soon. I hope you are well, Frank. Are you staying with the colonel? You must come back to your old home."

"Thank you, Mr. Manning, but I am living in New York. I am only passing a day or two with the colonel."

"It is very friendly in you to call, Colonel Vincent."

"Mr. Manning," said Colonel Vincent, gravely, "I am not willing to receive undeserved credit. Let me say, therefore, that this is a business, not a friendly call."

"Indeed," said Manning, uneasily.

"The business is connected with my young friend Frank."

"I am ready to listen," replied Mr. Manning. "If Frank wants a larger allowance, I am ready to give it."

"I venture to say for him that he will not be satisfied with that. Let me come to the point at once, Mr. Manning. Mrs. Manning's will has been found."

Mr. Manning started perceptibly, and his glance involuntarily wandered to that part of the wall behind which the will was discovered, for they were sitting in the very apartment where Mrs. Noonan had stumbled upon it.

"What do you mean, sir?"

"A will has been found, leaving the bulk of the property to Frank."

"Indeed! I am surprised. Is it a later will than the one which bequeathed the estate to me?" asked Mr. Manning, pointedly.

"It is Mrs. Manning's latest genuine will," answered Colonel Vincent, emphatically.

Mr. Manning started to his feet. He could not help understanding the colonel's meaning. It would have been idle to pretend it.

"What do you mean, Colonel Vincent?" he demanded, in a tone which he tried to make one of dignified resentment.

"I mean that Mrs. Manning made but one will, and that this bequeaths the property to Frank."

"How, then, do you account for the later will which was admitted to probate?"

"In this way. It was not what it purported to be."

Mr. Manning's sallow face flushed.

"What do you mean to insinuate?" he asked.

"That the last will was forged!" replied Colonel Vincent, bluntly.

"This is a very serious charge," said Mr. Manning, unable to repress his agitation. "You must allow me to say that I shall pay no attention to it. When you furnish proof of what you assert, it will be time enough to meet it. And now, gentlemen, if you have nothing further to say, I will bid you good-morning."

"I think you will find it best not to be in a hurry, Mr. Manning," said Colonel Vincent. "The charge must be met here and now. I charge you with instigating and being cognizant of the fraud that has been perpetrated!"

"On what grounds, sir? Do you know I can sue you for libel?"

"You are welcome to do so, Mr. Manning. I have a witness who will clear me."

"Who is he?"

"Jonas Barton!"

If a bombshell had exploded in the room, Mr. Manning could not have looked paler or more thoroughly dismayed. Yet he tried to keep up a little longer.

"I don't know any man of that name," he declared, faintly.

"Your looks show that you do. I may as well tell you, Mr. Manning, that resistance is useless. We can overwhelm you with proof if we take the matter before the courts. But we do not care to do so. We have something to propose."

"What is it?" said Mr. Manning, in a tremulous voice.

"The genuine will must be substituted for the fraudulent one. By it you will inherit ten thousand dollars, and Frank will consent that you shall receive it. He will not ask you to account for the sums you have wrongfully spent during the last year, and will promise not to prosecute you, provided you leave this neighborhood, and never return to it, or in any way interfere with him. To insure this, we shall have Jonas Barton's written confession, attested before a justice of the peace, ready for use, if needful. Do you accept?"

"I must, of course," said Mr. Manning, despondently. "But I shall be a poor man."

"No man who has health and the use of his faculties is poor with ten thousand dollars," answered the colonel.

"Mark alone will spend more than the interest of this sum."

"Then you must prevent him. He will be better off if he has to earn his living, as Frank has done for the last year."

In less than a week the transfer was made, and Frank recovered his patrimony.

Mr. Manning and Mark went to Chicago, and perhaps further West; but nothing has been heard from them for years.

Frank didn't return to the Cedars. The place was let until he should wish to return to it.

By the advice of Colonel Vincent, he resumed his preparation for college, and, graduating in due time, commenced the study of law.

Though rich enough to do without a profession, he felt that he should not be content to lead an aimless life.

He obtained for his school friend, Herbert Grant, the post of private secretary to Mr. Percival, and Herbert became nearly as great a favorite as himself.

Through Mr. Percival's kindness, Herbert was enabled, while still living at his house and attending to his duties as secretary, to enter Columbia College, and complete his course there, graduating with honor.

Herbert selected the medical profession, and, when he has completed his studies, will go abroad for a year with Frank, at the latter's expense, and, returning, open an office in New York.

While he is waiting for patients and Frank for clients, the two will live together, and their common expenses will be defrayed by Frank.

"If I didn't like you so well, Frank," said Herbert, "I would not accept this great favor at your hands—"

"But since we are dear friends," interrupts Frank, with a smile.

"I know that you enjoy giving even more than I do the receiving."

"Enough, Herbert. We understand each other. I have no brother, Herbert, and if I had, I could not care more for him than I do for you. Without you, I should feel alone in the world."

Frank does not regret the year in which he was thrown upon his own resources. It gave him strength and self-reliance; and however long he may live, he will not cease to remember with pleasure the year in which he had his own way to make in the world.